# Praise for the Bloody Jack Adventures

"No other series for YAs is like this one!" —*KLIATT*

★ "A rattling good read." —*Publishers Weekly,* starred review

"Meyer knows how to spin an exciting yarn, particularly
on the high seas." —*Booklist*

★ "A rousing adventure." —*Kirkus Reviews,* starred review

"Jacky's high-energy escapades will continue to thrill her fans."
—*Horn Book*

"This exciting tale barrels along with more adventures, romance,
[and] piracy . . . highly recommended." —*SLJ*

"[Delivers] the high adventure, good humor,
and bits of ballad that the Bloody Jack Adventures series
is known for." —*Booklist*

"Marvelous. . . . A first-rate read." —*Kirkus Reviews*

"[Jacky] uses her wit, beauty, charm, and numerous skills to
wiggle herself out of yet another fine mess. . . . Easy to read
and entertaining." —*VOYA*

"This exciting high seas adventure blows by at gale force." —*Horn Book*

"Crazy, inventive, and fun." —*KLIATT*

★ "This resilient and exuberant heroine deserves a stamp of approval."
—*Kirkus Reviews,* starred review

# L. A. MEYER

# Under *the* Jolly Roger

## Being an Account of the Further Nautical Adventures of Jacky Faber

Houghton Mifflin Harcourt

*Boston    New York*

All rights reserved. Originally published in hardcover in the United States by Harcourt Children's Books, an imprint of Houghton Mifflin Harcourt Publishing Company, 2005.

For information about permission to reproduce selections from this book, write to trade.permissions@hmhco.com or to Permissions, Houghton Mifflin Harcourt Publishing Company, 3 Park Avenue, 19th Floor, New York, New York 10016.

www.hmhco.com

The text of this book is set Minion.
Display set in Pabst.
Designed by Cathy Riggs.

The Library of Congress has cataloged the hardcover edition as follows:
Meyer, L. A. (Louis A.), 1942–
Under the Jolly Roger: being an account of the further nautical adventures of Jacky Faber/L. A. Meyer.—1st ed.
p. cm.
Sequel to: Curse of the blue tattoo.
Summary: In 1804, fifteen-year-old Jacky Faber heads back to sea where she gains control of a British warship and eventually becomes a privateer.
[1. Orphans—Fiction. 2. Sex role—Fiction. 3. Pirates—Fiction. 4. Seafaring life—Fiction. 5. Sea stories.] I. Title.
PZ7.M57172Un 2005
[Fic]—dc22 2004022463

ISBN: 978-0-15-205345-1 hardcover
ISBN: 978-0-15-205873-9 paperback

Manufactured in the United States of America
DOC 10 9 8 7 6
4500607218

*Again for Annetje . . .*
*. . . and for*
*Martha Marie Meyer*
*and Nancy W. B. Lawrence*

# Under the Jolly Roger

# PART I

# Chapter 1

"Ishmael!" I call out as I skip down the gangplank of the *Pequod*, my seabag on my shoulder. "Good sailing to you!"

"And to thee, Jacky," he says. The boy stands by the rail watching me leave the whaler for good and ever. "Thee are sure thee will not marry me?"

I swear, these Quaker lads are so cute with their *thee*s and *thy*s.

"Go find yourself a nice girl, Ishmael," I say by way of answer to his proposal. "Not one that stinks of whale oil!"

"I thinks thee smells just fine, Jacky Faber." I know he is genuinely sad to see me go, just as I am sad to see the last of him. I blow him a kiss and give him a final wave and go down the gangplank and step onto the wharf and hence onto the land that is England.

I was brought on board the whaler three months ago after I had run away from the Lawson Peabody School for Young Girls in Boston, which is where my mates on HMS *Dolphin* had dumped me after finding out that I was a girl, which was against the rules. Their rules, not mine.

Aye, they put me off the *Dolphin* even though I was a perfectly good sailor and was just made Midshipman, even. Before I was found out, the only person aboard the warship who knew that I was a girl was my own dear Jaimy, to whose home I am now going to travel to find out what's up with him. I ain't heard anything from him since he left on the *Dolphin*, leaving me behind, alone and friendless, and in a strange land.

Things didn't go at all smooth for me at the Lawson Peabody School, where they tried to make a lady out of me and I gotta say they didn't have much luck in the attempt. In fact, there wasn't that much left of the Lawson Peabody, itself, after I got done and lit out, the school being up in flames behind me, with a good bit of Boston burning merrily as well. And it wasn't *all* my fault, either, no matter what anyone tells you.

After I got clear out of the city, I had run on down to New Bedford, a port well to the south of Boston, and 'twas there I found a whaling ship, the *Pequod*, lying alongside a busy wharf. Bold as brass, I walked up to the table on the pier where they was signing up sailors for the voyage and applied for a berth, presenting myself as a seasoned sailor, which I was. This got a good, hearty rouse of laughter from all assembled, but against all odds, I was signed on as companion to the Captain's wife, who was great with child, and as teacher for her little boy, as well as being cook's helper. The Captain was taking his family along, which whalers often do, until such time as his wife had her baby, and then wife and children would be debarked in England to stay with relatives for a time. So, not only would I get passage back to London and maybe to Jaimy, but I would also get a quarter of a share of the ship's profits as pay. *And,* I would surely pick up more knowledge of seamanship, which I know will come in handy someday. Although I've had my ups and downs, I've always been pretty lucky, by and large.

After provisioning and signing up the rest of the crew, we finally set sail and left the land behind us. I soon found that bein' on a whaler wasn't like bein' on a Royal Navy Ship, no, not at all. The Captain is still the Lord and Master of everything and everybody, but the day-to-day hard discipline and rigid regulations just ain't there. Everyone is bent toward the Almighty Profit and anyone who can add to that profit is held in high esteem, and anyone who slacks off ain't treated all that kindly. So, when they found that I could steer a course, trim a sail, and stand a watch, I was added to the watch list. Daytime watches only, for a while, and then, after they knew they could trust me, nighttimes, too.

The crew was a rough bunch, of course, but I was used to that, and I quickly made friends with them all—especially with Ishmael, and, of course, with Patience, she bein' the Captain's wife and a perfect joy. Heavy with child though she was, she was always jolly and brave right up to and through the birth of her fine, fat daughter. In addition to my other duties, it was understood that I was brought on board to help Patience during the birthing, but when her time did come in the middle of the night in the midst of a living gale, I was no help at all. *She* had to comfort *me* when it was all going on, which was probably *not* what the Captain had in mind when he signed me on board. But I did hold her hand, and when the baby finally slid out all slippery and bloody, I picked it up by its feet as I was told and I saw that it was a girl. I slapped her tiny bum and she coughed and started wailing, and I laid her down and cut and tied the cord as I was told, and then I cleaned up mother and child as best I could in the tiny cabin that was pitchin' up and down and back and forth with the wind howlin' like a demented banshee outside. I got a clean cloth wrapped around the baby and put her on Patience's breast and kept sayin' *I'm sorry, I'm sorry* over and over, but Patience said I did just fine and she wanted no other midwife in attendance for future babies, none other than Jacky Faber. As for Jacky Faber, her own self, she's more than a bit glad that her own adventures in birthin' babies are at least a few years off in the future.

So I'm bouncing merrily on down the pier, gratefully suckin' in the air of my own country once again, and there I see the Captain and Patience, who's got our lovely little Prudence cradled in her arm and my star pupil, Increase, by her side. I embrace Patience in farewell and we babble our good-byes and I give Increase a kiss, him being the son of the Captain and his missus. Part of my job was teachin' him his numbers and letters, and though he was a willing and bright student, he really wanted to be out and off in the riggin' and I could hardly blame him, bein' of a like mind myself. I give him the farewell kiss and he says, "Yuck," and rubs the kiss from his cheek, but I don't hold it against him, and just ruffle his curly head fondly. He is a good boy.

The family is leaving this morning to stay with relatives in Maidstone until this voyage of the *Pequod* is over, and so my time on the ship is also over—no good reason to have a lone female on board, so off I am booted.

As the Captain handed his family up into the coach, he

turned to me and said, "Farewell, Faber, and Godspeed. Know thee that I hate to lose a good sailor," which for him was a long speech. 'Cept when he was goin' on about that whale. Then he never seemed to stop. I nodded and thanked him for taking me on board and he turned and left, his peg leg tappin' on the pier as he went 'round the coach to the other door to mount up. When he is in, the coachman gives a chuck to the horses and they are gone.

On the wharf, too, is the First Mate, Mr. Starbuck. He is overseein' the off-loadin' of the barrels of the whale oil, it already being sold and paid for. My own quarter share is snug in my money belt, the gold coins being warmed by my belly, next to the coins I had earned playin' and dancin' in the Pig and Whistle in Boston and actin' in the theater with Mr. Fennel and Mr. Bean.

We had excellent luck in baggin' the poor whales, which nobody can ever again tell me is just cold fishes—I learned that to be true the first time I jumped onto the back of a whale brought alongside and felt the heat of its dying body comin' up at me. The men were there with flensing tools, blades with long handles for strippin' off the blubber that would be passed up on hooks to the deck where the great cauldrons were fired up for boiling down the blubber into oil for the lamps of Britain and America. I had a different job and a disgustin' job it was: Along with the big barrels of oil there on the deck, there are smaller casks of spermaceti, an oily, waxy goo that's taken out of a pit in the sperm whale's head—and *that* was my job, to shovel out the stuff into a pail while the rest of the crew stripped the remainder of the creature of its parts. It is hard to believe that spermaceti is used for makin' ladies' perfume, as it sure didn't smell very perfumy to me, sittin' there on the whale's head, scoop-in' out the stuff.

I don't think I'll be signing on a whaler again, as it's a nasty business.

I turn the corner and the *Pequod* goes out of my life forever. It is September in the year of 1804, and I am fifteen years old. I think.

I go on down the street, lookin' for a coach to bear me away for London, 'cause right now the *Pequod* is docked in the port of Gravesend, which is about twenty-five miles east of the big city. I'm hopin' to get in a coach and get some dis-tance on my way and then stop for the night at a nice clean inn and have a bit of a bath and have my clothes cleaned of the whaler's smell before I head into London proper.

I know that I'm holdin' back from just divin' straight into London, 'cause I don't know what's waitin' for me there, in regards to Jaimy. I didn't get any letters at all from him when I was in Boston, not even one, the whole time we've been apart. I don't know if any of my letters got to him, either. I don't know if he thinks of me at all or if he's gone off with some other—someone prettier or grander, or more of a lady than me, which wouldn't be hard to find. Lord knows I didn't do too well at that lady school—I'd have been run off for sure by now if I hadn't caused the place to be burned to the ground.

I don't know anything about anything, so I will have to just wait to find out and then get on with things, with Jaimy or without, and...

There! A coach is loading and is pointed in the right di-rection. I go up and find that the coach is going to Greenwich and will only cost me one and four if I ride up top, which is fine with me 'cause that's where I'd want to be, anyway, out in the air instead of bein' buffeted back and forth in the stuffy coach with the swells. *And,* I can get another coach for London early the following day. Perfect!

My seabag is thrown up top and I sling the Lady Lenore in her fiddle case over my shoulder. The Lady is a fine, *fine* fiddle that I got sort of legal-like, which is a little uncommon for me, I know, and I've been practicing on her like crazy the past five months and I'm almost getting good. I settle myself into the seat next to the driver and we are off, rattlin' through the port town, which quickly thins out into small shops and farmsteads. The driver and me starts sharin' a few tunes together, it bein' a beautiful day and him havin' a fair baritone and me pullin' out my fiddle and pennywhistle and holdin' forth in my usual loud and brazen fashion. It ain't too long 'fore a couple of the swells in the coach below climb out and join us up top and soon we've got a real party goin', laughin' and singin' and makin' the miles fly by.

Finally we pull up to a respectable lookin' house and I hop down and get my gear and I go up to the landlord and ask for a room for the night. He looks at me all suspicious, like I'm goin' to be up to no good, and what with one of the swells still singin' out loud behind me, I can't say I blame him. But I tell him that I'm strictly an entertainer with a nice clean act, and, "Speakin' of clean, I'll be needin' a bath, too, so if you could arrange for one, Sir, I'd be most pleased. And, speakin' of acts, maybe we could set up somethin' for tonight in your main hall, hmmmm?"

We settle on two one-hour sets for half the room rent and whatever tips I can pick up. I haul my stuff off to my room, after telling one of the fancy young men with whom I had shared a song or two on the way here that I would *not* be sharing my room or my bed with him, thank you, no matter how pretty he is or how sweet his words of love. I get ready for my bath, my wonderful bath, my first bath in three months, which is what I'm wantin' right now over any young man. Almost any. I'd take Jaimy right now, I would, dirty as I am, as he's seen me filthier than this, that's for sure, and yet he still said then that he loved me.

I take a deep breath and think on that. That, and the fact that I might see him tomorrow. That, and I'm afraid of what will happen when I do.

There's a tap on the door and a young girl's voice says, "Miss? Your bath is ready."

I am sunk up to my nose in the lovely hot water, with great gobs of suds drifting about me like ships on the ocean sea. My knees stick up out of the water and I name my left one there to be Gibraltar and the right one to be the coast of North Africa and now the mighty ships of suds sail majestically through the Strait. With a puff of my breath, I speed the great galleons of suds through the channel like a fair and following wind. That one shall be the *Raleigh* on which Davy sails—whoops, a little rough weather there, Davy? Did you run aground on mighty Gibraltar? *Tsk!* Sorry, Mate. And that one is the *Endeavor,* which holds Tink, and that one's the *Temeraire* with Willy on board, and there, that fine shapely one there, that is the *Essex,* whereon my true love Jaimy lies—Midshipman James Emerson Fletcher, that is. That one sails all pretty right between my knees and on toward my toes. I slide a little bit up against the high back of the tin tub to let my chest come halfway out of the water. Let's see if we can get the boys to come sailing back to me. I wriggle my toes to send the ships back upstream.

There's a rap on the door and once again I sink beneath the waves, but it is only the girl, this time lugging a large steaming pitcher. "More hot water, Miss?" she pipes. She must be all of ten, the daughter of the house, dressed plain but clean.

"Bless you, child, yes," I sigh, relaxing back into the water. She pours it in over the edge. The new hot water swirls about me, making what I thought was hot before seem now to be merely warm. "And there'll be an extra penny in it for you if you bring me another in a little while."

The girl leaves and it's time for me to stop daydreaming about ships and shores and start getting down to the business of washing the stink of the whaler off me.

I'm soaping my armpits and wondering—I had heard that fine French ladies had the hair under their arms shaved and the hair on their legs, too, but I never got a chance to ask Amy whether that was true or not. She, being very proper, wouldn't have thought it a decent question, is why I never asked. Amy Trevelyne was my best friend back at the school, but she sure ain't now, that's for sure—not after I shamed myself at the big party at her house last spring by getting stupid drunk and bringing disgrace to her family. Besides making a complete fool of myself, I got Randall hurt and almost killed and it's no wonder she betrayed me to the Preacher's men and I don't blame her a bit for doing that.... *Stop thinkin' about that now. What's done is done and thinkin' about it ain't gonna do you any good at all...*

11

Looking at my toes sticking up at the other end, I reflect that my toenails could use a bit of a trim so I haul the right foot up and start gnawing 'em off all neat and trim with my teeth. It's easy to do since they've got all soft with the hot water. Thinkin' back on Amy and hairy armpits puts me back to thinking about Mistress Pimm. She was the head-mistress and tried her best to make a lady out of me. Well, some things stuck, Mistress, and some things didn't. I pull up my other foot and fix up its toenails in the same way. I know I learned enough to *act* like a lady, if I'm dressed for the part, but I know, too, that I'll never actually *be* one. Not down to the bone.

I've found that boys seem to like me, though, and that has been a constant surprise to me, since I consider myself quite plain and even a little bit worked over—I've got a scar under my left eyebrow, which makes the hair of it come in white, and I've got sort of a welt on my neck from when the pirate LeFievre strung me up that time—usually you can't see it, but if I get excited, it flares up red. There are other scars, too, but mostly in places what can't be seen. No, I am not beautiful—that Clarissa Worthington Howe back at the school sure showed me what was a beautiful and cultured lady, that being her, and what was not, that being me. So, I don't know....Maybe Jaimy's found some-one more pretty than me and that's why....*Just stop think-ing that way. You just go round and round and that's not going to help...*

I spit out the last toenail clipping and turn to my hair. I dunk down face-first in the water to get it good and wet, then come up like a dolphin and start in to soaping it up.

After it's good and soaped and rubbed all in with my fingers, it's back down under to rinse. My hair has gotten really long, in spite of the singeing it took on that last day when the Lawson Peabody burned to the ground along with the church that was next to it and the stables, and maybe other stuff, too....I don't know. I didn't stick around long enough to find out. *Poor Mistress. I hope they build you another school, this time one of brick that I can't burn down. You were fierce, but you tried to do your best for me, in your way.*

I bring my face back out of the water and let my hair come down in streaming rivulets over my face and shoulders and back. It's probably not gonna dry in time for tonight's show, but I'll just put it up in a braid and it'll be fine.

*That Ishmael was a fine lad, though,* think I, musing back on the voyage again. He certainly made the trip a pleasant one, to have one such as him as your mate. I toss a thought out to Jaimy, somewhere out there in the world, but, at least, a lot nearer now. *Don't worry, Jaimy, I was a good girl, mostly*...I mean, what's a little kiss here and there. Here. And there. Between friends.

The girl comes back in with another pitcher and pours it in and I groan and writhe in absolute sinful pleasure and think about nothing except how good it feels. Then I start to think on the songs I'll do in tonight's show. This being England I'd probably better stay away from the Irish and Scottish stuff and stick to the British. Hmmm. Just coming off a whaler as I am, maybe I'll start with "The Bonny Ship the *Diamond.*" It's got that good, rousing chorus. That'll get 'em started.

*"Cheer up me lads,*
*Let your hearts never fail,*
*For the Bonny Ship the* Diamond
*Goes fishing for the whale!"*

I sing a bit more of it:

*"Well, it'll be light both day and night*
*When the whaler lads come home,*
*With a ship that's full of oil, me boys,*
*And money to their names.*

*"They'll make the beds all for to rock,*
*And the blankets for to tear,*
*And every lass in Peter's Head*
*Will sing hush-a-by my dear."*

Boys and men, I swear, they always get back to that. Having their pleasures and then going off having adventures and stuff and leaving the girls behind to rock the cradle. Not this girl, though, by God.

After I had hauled myself out of the bath and dried and dressed, I went out of the inn and found the town crier, who for a few pence would go about the neighboring streets ringing a bell and crying out, "Hear ye! Hear ye! Hear ye! To-night for one night only the re-nowned Miss Jacky Faber will be in per-for-mance at the Rose and Crown Pub-lic House! New-ly re-turned from a tri-um-phant tour of the Am-er-i-cas, Miss Faber will en-ter-tain with songs and bal-lads both joy-ful and sad, se-ri-ous and com-ic, and will ac-com-pany

14

herself with the fid-dle, con-cer-tina, and flage-o-lay! All are wel-come and are sure to be pleased! Eight o'clock at the Rose and Crown! Hear ye! Hear ye..."

I was glad I had hired the crier, for the tavern was full to overflowing come night with a jolly, good-natured crowd. The show went over right well with the cheering audience demanding three encores before they finally let me bow off for good. I left flushed with pleasure, for I so very much love both the joy of the performance that I give, and the applause that I receive in return.

So now, having gotten some more coin for my money belt, I'm lying in bed thinking of tomorrow and what it might bring. *Not one letter, Jaimy, not one, except for the one you pressed into my hand on the day you left me in Boston.*

I take a deep breath and let it out slowly. Ah, well, tomorrow I will know. Even if he is out at sea, which he very probably is, then I will find out from his family and friends just how he feels about me. I just hope he's all right. A lot could have happened since....No, don't think about that.

I turn on my side and pull my knees to my chin.

*Yes, my girl, tomorrow you will know, but right now you will go to sleep.*

# Chapter 2

I take the coachman's offered hand and step down from the carriage. Again my new friends and I had sat on top of the coach and laughed and sang our way into London on this glorious, sparkling day. It is late morning as I bid farewell to my companions, pick up my seabag, and enter the coach house. Five minutes later I have hired a one-horse carriage.

On this day, this special day, I have put on my glorious riding habit, the one Amy gave me for Christmas last year, the coat all maroon and the skirt all dark, dark green and the trim all gray and beautiful—with a gathering of white lace at my throat and the stiff lapels turned back just so. I put some powder in my hair and comb it so that it sweeps up under my jaunty Scot's bonnet. My hat's got a gold pin on one side and feathers hangin' down all elegant. Why us young women put white powder in our hair to make it look gray, I don't know, but it's the *ton*, the style, so I do it. And I must admit it looks grand.

I really like the way the jacket clutches my chest and makes me feel all trim and taut. Also, I can tuck my shiv in its usual spot next to my ribs and I can't do that in a dress.

Plus, I think I look smashing in it. I really think I could charm my way into Buckingham Palace in this rig. I know I could. Yes, Little Mary Faber, late of the Rooster Charlie Gang, formerly residing under Blackfriars Bridge, Cheapside, returns to London in fine style.

"Nine Brattle Lane, Driver," I say grandly, and climb aboard. "If you please."

As we clatter through London, I get more and more nervous about what's going to happen today. Jaimy and I *had* exchanged promises to marry, promises that I *know* were heartfelt and true, and we had even exchanged rings, sort of rings, anyway—they were the rings of the Dread Brotherhood of Ship's Boys of HMS *Dolphin* that we had put through our ears and welded shut that wonderful day in Kingston on the island of Jamaica. I have mine on a chain about my neck so that it hangs close to my heart, since Mistress Pimm had it snipped out of my ear the first day I was at her school. Sometimes I put it back in my ear to remind me of the old days, but today I had thought I'd better look as ladylike as possible, so I didn't. I take a deep breath and try to calm the butterflies kicking up a fuss in my belly.

Not only did I get no letters from Jaimy when I was back in the States, there's a good chance he didn't get any of mine, either. I saw our old mate Davy last fall when his ship came into Boston, and he told me Jaimy hadn't got any letters from me and I had sent a whole bunch of them. I figured out that someone in Jaimy's household must have been intercepting the letters and I have a good idea who. I hated the idea that Jaimy might think I was faithless because of this, so before Davy left, I dashed off a letter and made

Davy swear on his Brotherhood tattoo to put the letter in Jaimy's hand and his hand only if they should meet. I do hope their paths did cross, I do hope....Ah, we're here.

It is a nice-looking brick house with stone steps and curtained windows and it has two stories with a chimney at each end and appears to have a yard in back. There are some small boys playing with a hoop in the street and it gives me pleasure to think of Jaimy as a boy playing in this same street and in that yard.

I ask the driver to wait a moment, as I do not know what will happen inside. I walk up the stairs, brush my hands over my skirt, adjust my gay bonnet, take a deep breath, and lift the knocker and rap three times. The old Brotherhood secret number.

*You calm down now, you. Jaimy's probably not even here, he's surely at sea, he's...*

The door opens and a young woman in serving gear peeks out.

"Yes, Miss?" she says. She is ginger haired, round faced, and appears cheerful and good-natured.

"Good day, Miss. My name is Jacky Faber and..."

Her smile broadens and she says, "Oh, yes, Miss! Please come in."

*Well, that's a good sign,* I'm thinking, as I step into the foyer and look about.

"I'll go get me mistress," says the girl as she spins and leaves the room.

I look about at the pictures on the wall, thinking that Jaimy must have known this room very well. *Is that a portrait of him and his brother? I think the one on the left is...*

I hear a rustle behind me and I spin around to find a woman of medium height with dark hair going gray. She is well dressed in what I know to be the latest fashion and in what appears to be the finest of fabrics. She holds herself rigidly upright, and she is glaring at me most severely.

*Uh, oh...*

I gulp and drop down in my best curtsy. "Good day, Missus," I quavers, coming up from the curtsy and meeting her eyes, eyes that look to have very little love for me in them. "If it please you, my name is Jacky Faber and I'm a friend of..."

"It does *not* please me in the slightest. I know *who* you are and I know *what* you are," she says, coldly, indignation plain upon her face. "You will not step any further into this house."

*What?*

"I cannot believe you would be so brazen as to come here," she continues, biting off every word. "Even one such as you."

"I...I don't understand, Missus," says I, stunned. "I was only..."

"You have come here only to bring more disgrace upon my family. I know your history, and I must say I find it appalling. And now, with this latest outrage, the whole world knows of your illicit liaison with my son."

*This latest outrage? What is she talking about? What latest outrage? What...I ain't believin' this, but she ain't done yet, oh no, she ain't.*

"You are obviously a cunning and opportunistic adventuress. As such, you forced your attentions on a young and impressionable boy under very questionable circumstances, and now you come here to seek to better yourself by marrying into my family." She takes a deep breath, looking down her long nose at me. "I can assure you that will not happen, not as long as I live. He is not a match for you and you are *certainly* not a match for him."

She has worked herself up into a fine lather of hatred for my poor self, me standin' there shakin' in front of her, my belly churnin' in dismay. I am unable to speak.

"I am gratified to inform you that James has, at last, seen the folly of his ways and wishes no more to see you nor to have any sort of communication with you."

*Oh, Jaimy, please, no, it can't be, it can't...*

"Be gone, girl, and do not come back. You will receive no welcome from anyone in this house, as we do not welcome tramps!"

*Tramp? She called me a tramp?* That's enough to shake me out of my confusion, and I throw my chin in the air and put on the Look and rear back and say, "What you say may be true, Mrs. Fletcher, but I'll believe it when I hear it from Jaimy's own dear lips! Lips with which, I might add, I am *very* familiar!"

"His name is James, you *dirty* thing, you! Pah!" spits Mrs. Fletcher. "Hattie, put her out!"

The girl rushes to the door and opens it.

Shattered, I stumble through the door and it slams behind me. I grab the railing and stand there stunned and disbelieving. *My worst fears...*My chest is heaving and my heart is pounding and I think I'm going to be sick. I think I'm going to throw up. I think...

I hear the sound of a window opening behind me, and in a daze I turn to see that it is Hattie, the serving girl, who has opened it. She leans out and whispers loudly to me, "Don't you believe everything the old dragon says, Miss. Mr. James is home on leave and is out in the country with friends today, but he'll be at the races at Epsom Downs tomorrow. And, Miss, he always speaks most highly...Ow! Oh! Mistress, please!"

The girl disappears back into the house and there are more cries of pain.

I stand there and bite my knuckles, thinking...*I am sorry, girl, that you got a beating because of me, but I bless you for it, I do, for you have given me back some hope. I will see Jaimy and I will hear it from him.*

I climb back into the carriage and take several deep, very deep, breaths to calm myself down. *Well, that couldn't have gone any worse,* I reflect, after I've collected my mind somewhat, and settle back in the seat.

"Cheapside, Coachman," I say to the driver. "The Admiral Benbow Inn, near Blackfriars Bridge."

We rattle off.

The coachman gets me to the Benbow, but he doesn't want to leave me off.

"It's a dangerous place, Miss, are you sure..."

"I am sure, and I thank you for your concern," I say as I pay him his fare. "Don't wait for me as I will be taking lodgings here." He drives off, shaking his head.

I pick up my seabag and look at the Admiral Benbow, sitting there on the corner of Water Street and Union. Was it only a little over two years ago that I stood right here on this spot, a beggar in rags, listening to sailors singing of Bombay Rats and Cathay Cats and Kangaroos? Then, ragged Little

Mary Faber couldn't even go in the back door of this place. Now, with the Look—eyes hooded, head up, lips together, teeth apart—she sails right in through the front door.

"Ah yes, my good woman," I say to the astounded landlady behind the bar, frosting her with my Look, "I am Lady Faber and I have business hereabouts and I will have a room." With that, I snap one of my silver coins down on the counter. Then I brush off my fingers as if I am not used to handling money directly, because of my high station, don'cha know?

She eyes the coin greedily, with nary a thought in her mind to deny me entry.

"Yes, Milady," she says, scooping up the coin. "Jim, take up the Lady's bag, for Chris'sakes; don'cha know quality when you sees it?" Jim shambles out of the shadows and picks up my seabag. "The good room, Jim. I'm sure it will be to milady's likin'," she says, grinning a gap-toothed smile.

"I am sure it will be...adequate," says I, growing not the least bit less haughty. "I will go up and refresh myself and when I come down in an hour, will you see that I have a basket of food prepared—breads, meats, cheeses, puddings? Some cider, perhaps? A large basket, if you would? Thank you so very much."

I follow this Jim up to my room, give him a penny for his troubles, and, after the door closes behind him, Lady Faber flops back on the bed and reflects that all the world's a fake.

A tousled head pops up from under the pile of rags and straw that is the old Blackfriars Bridge kip. It belongs to a boy of about eight years of age, and it is plain that he is the sentry posted to stay behind and watch and make sure that

22

no one tries to take over the kip while the rest of the gang was out and up to the day's mischief. His eyes go wide at seeing me ducking my head under the edge of the bridge and entering the hideout. Scurrying outside, he puts two fingers in his mouth and lets out three piercing whistles.

Three blasts—that was our old signal, too—*trouble at the kip! Everybody get back!* Guess it got handed down from gang to gang. Ah, tradition...

It all comes rushing back at me—the memories of this place....The kip itself, the place where we slept all in a pile of urchin, rag, and hay, sits up on a sort of stone ledge. I dust off a spot on it and sit myself down, placing the basket next to me. I don't remember the kip smelling quite this bad, but back then I was part of the smell and so wouldn't notice. The rest of it is the same, too—the river slipping by below, the heavy stones looming overhead, interlocking together to form the underside of the bridge, arching away in the distance. Those stones always scared me a bit, thinkin' that some day or night they would let loose and come down and crush us all like bugs. But they never did, and I guess they never will.

The boy comes back and sits down on the pile of old rags and smelly hay and stares at me, saying nothing. I don't say anything, either—I'll wait for the others to get here.

While I wait, I look about and think back to that first terrible night I spent in this place—the gang had picked me up in some dark alley where I had run to in grief and horror after my family had died and I had been put out in the streets in order to conveniently follow them in death—put out and placed in the streets by Muck, the Corpse Seller himself, may he rot in everlasting Hell for his crimes. But I didn't die, and Charlie and the bunch picked me up and brought me here, and the next day I was set to the begging and, after a while, this dank and forbidding place began to look like home. I shiver a bit, thinking of all that.

Soon there's the sound of pounding feet outside coming from several directions, and then a boy and a girl, both about twelve, come in. Then from the other side, two girls about nine and then another boy of the same age. The boys are all dressed in ragged shirts and trousers, most barely reaching their knees before turning into tatters, and the girls in formless shifts that come down to midthigh in some, midcalf in others. The shifts, once white, are now gray. One of the younger girls has tied up her hair with a piece of old blue ribbon that she undoubtedly had picked out of the trash. Her face is dirty, her hair is a tangled mess, and the ribbon itself is wrinkled and stained. Still, the sight of it touches me.

The oldest girl looks at me with deep suspicion plain on her face. I do not blame her—what's somebody like me, dressed as I am, doing in their kip? I look at her with special interest 'cause I know she's the me of a couple of years ago, and it is she who says, "Ain't nobody here wants to be 'dopted, Mum, so you best be on your way."

My, my. It's a great day for putting Jacky Faber out, I'll own.

"That's right, Mum. Now...," begins the older boy. I notice that all of them are carrying rocks.

"Now, now, mates," I say, turnin' back to the old talk to put them at their ease, "I ain't here to adopt none of yiz. I'm just here to visit me old kip and maybe find out what happened to me old mates what used to live 'ere with me."

There are snorts of disbelief all around.

"Nay, it's true, and I'll prove it to you," says I, and I point to a place between two of the overhead stones. "There's a leak there, and there, and there, but the biggest one is right there, which we called Old Guzzler, from the sound it made when it was really rippin'."

"That's what we call it, too," says one of the younger girls, shyly.

"There. You see? I lived here when I was with Rooster Charlie's gang, two years back. I was called Little Mary then, but you can call me Jacky now."

"I remembers you," says the older girl, coming closer to me now and looking in my face. "I was with Toby's bunch when you came that night to where we was livin' under the gratin' on West Street and said we should all come here 'cause Rooster Charlie was killed and we should put the two gangs together."

"That's right. And now you shall tell me what happened to my mates," says I, pulling my shiv out of my sleeve and opening my hamper of food. "But first, let's eat."

I open the hamper and their eyes grow wide and they all put down their rocks. First I take out a loaf of bread and slice it in eight pieces and put each portion in front of me and then I do the same with the cheese and the meat. When all is set out, I ask the boy to do the honors, to see if it's still done in the old way. It is.

He turns away and faces outward. I point at a portion and say, "Now," and he says, "Jennie," and one of the girls comes up and takes that portion.

"Again," I say, pointing at another portion. "Billy," and Billy comes up and takes his.

"Again."

"Mary." *Ah. Yet another Mary.*

"Again."

"Me." That portion is put aside for the head boy.

"Again."

"Susanna."

"Again."

"Joannie." The older girl, the leader, takes hers.

"Again."

"Ben."

And that's the last of it and all fall to in the eating of it, me included. When we are done, I pass around small cakes and the jug of cider, which we all take slugs out of.

"Well, then," I say, wiping off my mouth with my handkerchief, which I have stored up my sleeve. Putting them at their ease is one thing, but nothing is gonna make me wipe my greasy mouth on the sleeve of my riding habit. "What can you tell me of my mates? Polly Von? Judy Miller? Hugh the Grand? Nan Baxter?"

Joannie takes a mighty swig of the cider. "A press-gang got our Hughie one day," she says, chuckling at the memory. "It were a true Battle Royal. You should have seen it, Miss. It took twenty of the bastards to haul him down, with all of us about throwin' rocks and curses, him bellowin' and layin' about with his fists, but it didn't do no good at the end. They bound him up good and proper and hauled him off, and that's the last we seen of him."

*Poor Hughie. I hope you found good quarters, wherever you are.*

"And Polly and Toby both disappeared one other day. They went off together and never come back. We think Toby was got by a press-gang, too, them gangs bein' right numerous and fierce around here. Polly, we don't know, she bein' so pretty and all..." Joannie lets this trail off.

*Our pretty, pretty Polly, the one that looked like an angel even under all the dirt. I so hope you're all right. But I do fear the worst.*

"Nan went off with a country bloke, what come in for the big fair, who said he was gonna set her up as a barmaid in his tavern out in the country. I guess he did, 'cause she never come back," Joannie continues. It's plain she does the talking for this bunch.

"Now Judy, she was taken into service a while back by a man who hired her to take care of his old mum. We had a little party for her when she left. She must be awful busy with the old lady, 'cause she ain't been back to see us, she hain't."

I catch the slight edge of hurt in her voice. You're supposed to come back and take care of your mates if you had a bit of good fortune. *What happened, Judy, that you didn't?*

"Is she near here?" I ask.

"Up on Bride Street, she said it was," says Joannie. "We don't go there as that's the Shanky Boys turf."

"I see. And what about Muck? Is he still around?"

"Aye, he is, the miserable bugger," growls Joannie, "but we ain't seen him in some months now. The constables is after him on charges of grave robbin' and he's layin' low. The word is out that sometimes he don't wait for people to die natural-like, but speeds things up a bit on his own." She sighs and goes on. "But he'll be back, and what's the difference, anyway—there's plenty more of his kind about, ready to sell our bodies should we die."

"Well, you must be careful and I must be off," I say, getting up. I pull my small purse from my jacket. "So what did you say your name is?" I ask the head boy.

"Zeke," says he.

"Do you share equal, Zeke?" I ask.

"We do," says the head boy, and heads nod all around.

"Good. Here's half a crown." Eyes widen at the sight of the coin. I put it in the boy's fist—I want to put it in Joannie's hand but that would shame him and cause discord in the gang, him being the oldest boy and all.

"Make it last, Zeke. See if you can get them some warm clothes for the winter, and here..." I count out seven pennies. "Here's a penny for each of you to buy a treat tomorrow all for yourself that you don't have to share."

I put a penny in each outstretched hand.

"Good-bye, then. I'll try to get back to visit, but I don't know what my situation will be."

"Good-bye, Jacky," says Joannie. "We're glad you came," is all she says in way of thanks 'cause you don't thank a fellow gang member for sharing what they got.

I'm heading up toward Bride Street, thinking about how Judy always said she wanted to go into service for a fine lady, so maybe it worked out for her. We shall see.

As I cross Fleet Street, I see again the printer's shop where I used to sit on Hugh the Grand's shoulders and read the broadsides out loud, hopin' to get a penny or two from the crowd that would gather to listen, me being the only street kid that I knew of who could read, having been taught that by me mum and dad before they died. There's a crowd here now, too, but they ain't here to hear some half-naked urchin spout off, no, they're lined up to buy something, and I'm curious enough to go look to see what it is.

The owner, whom I recall as a decent sort, in that he didn't shoo away my filthy, ragged young self from in front of his business back then, is outside the shop hawking copies of something. A book, it looks like. I get closer.

"Yes, Ladies and Gentlemen, we have it again!" he crows, holding up and waving a book above the heads of the crowd. "Sold out on its first printing and the sensation of London and all the English-speaking world, it is back in its second printing and available right here. Only one shilling a copy and guaranteed to please—I know you will not be able to put it down! And to think the plucky heroine of this grand story is a local girl, our own Mary Faber, whom…"

*What?*

"…I well remember standing right here where you stand today, the plucky little tyke who read the broadsides to the illiterate masses…"

*What?*

"…and then went off to glorious adventure on the high seas! Hurry, they won't last!"

In a not-very-ladylike fashion, I elbow my way to the front of the shop, where pinned to the wall is the cover of…

***Bloody Jack,***
***Being an Account of the Curious Adventures***
***of Mary "Jacky" Faber, Ship's Boy,***
as told to her dear friend and companion
Miss Amy Wemple Trevelyne

*Oh, Lord.*

In shock, I get in line to buy one. After all, I do have to know what is being said of me. *Hmmm…* so this is what Mother Fletcher was talking about when she said the "latest outrage." What she must have thought when she read about this. What did Jaimy think when he read it?

*Oh, Amy. What have you done to me?*

On the cover of the book, the printer has added a woodcut of a woman standing on the deck of a ship with crossed belts on her ample chest, firing a pistol out of each hand. The woodcut is crude and doesn't look at all like me— much too buxom, for one thing, and for another, I never smoked a pipe. Oh, well…

As I stand and wait my turn, I put it all together: Amy, who had been scribbling on this thing all winter, asking me questions about my life and all, gets it done after we have our falling-out. She then takes it to a printer in Boston, partly, I guess, because she's resentful and wants to pay me back and partly because she wanted people to read her words. It is sold in the bookstores and then some passenger bound for England must have seen it, found it interesting, and took a copy back to a friend who's a printer in London, and here it is.

When I give the man a shilling for the book, he looks concerned and says, "Now, Miss, there's some rough stuff in this book. Maybe you'd best let your father read it first to see if it's all right for you, it being plain that you are a person of breeding and all."

"I thank you, Sir, for your consideration of my tender sensibilities," I say, trying not to snort out loud. "I will take your advice to heart and I shall give it to my pastor for his review to see if it is appropriate for one such as I." I lower my eyes demurely and clasp the book to my chest and retreat.

I'll think about this later, I decide, as I continue on my way up to Bride Street.

I ask on Bride Street for a serving girl named Judy Miller, but all I get is *Sorry, Miss,* and *Never 'eard of 'er,* till an old woman working at a churn in her doorway gives a loud *tsk!* and says, "Ye will find the poor soul four houses down thataway."

I look in the doorway and see that it is a wash house, and there, bent over a tub, is Judy Miller, my good and true mate from the Rooster Charlie Gang. Steam fills the place as does wood smoke from the fires to heat the tubs, and there are piles of dirty laundry everywhere. Judy is dressed in a formless gray dress, not much more than a shift, really, and her arms, what I can see of 'em, are red and raw and chafed from the harsh soap. And though I am overjoyed to see her again, this doesn't look much like being a maid to a fine lady to me.

I step into the laundry and she looks up, and I see that she does not recognize me. She has become a rawboned, large girl, a good foot and more taller than me. In the gang she was not among the most clever, but she was solid and fiercely loyal to the pack. She was generally cheerful and quick to laugh in spite of our troubles. No more, though. Her eyes are listless and dead, and her shoulders slump in fatigue and defeat. Her arms are in the water up to her elbows, and when she brings them out, I can see that they are red and sore and split from the work.

"Yes, Milady" is all she says upon seeing me standing there in my fancy rig. She waits there as if expecting someone to hit her.

"Judy. It's me. Little Mary from Charlie's Gang. Remember?"

Her eyes go over me without interest. "Little Mary?" she says in confusion. "But you're a fine lady, Miss, not the Little Mary that I knew."

"Nay, I ain't a fine lady," I say, and laugh to put her more at ease. "I'm just dressed like one." Which is the truth, but she doesn't know that yet. "But I *am* the girl you knew as Little Mary."

She doesn't know what to say, just stands there stunned, but finally she hangs her head and says, hardly above a whisper, "So you done good, Mary, and I done bad."

"The kids down at the kip told me you had gone into service. Is that right?" I ask, not feeling good about this at all.

She turns back to her tub. "No, it ain't right, Miss. A man come to see me one time when I was beggin' up on Ludgate and 'e asks would I like to be maid to 'is mum and 'e seems such a decent sort so I says yes, I would, and so I goes to the gang and tells 'em I'm leavin'. And they give me a little party with cakes and all; and I don't know where Toby come up with them, but 'e did and we was all right merry. I said I wouldn't forget 'em as soon as I got set up, and they cheered me off. But it didn't happen that way at all. Not at all."

She reaches in the steaming tub and pulls up a shirt and begins scrubbing it against the washboard that she hauls out and leans against her chest.

"What happened, then?" I ask.

She waits for a while, as if it's hard for her to speak, but then she does. "There weren't no 'Mum.' There was only him, and he used me most cruel, he did. He used me in shameful ways that I ain't gonna tell you about and I don't want to even think about ever again, and then when he was tired of using me that way, he put me out here. I couldn't go back to the gang as I'm grown up now and shamed. It was either here or the whorehouse, so here I am."

I try to keep my voice level and calm. "Did you sign any paper when you came here? Did you put your X on anything?"

She shakes her head.

"Does he pay you anything? Give you anything?"

Again she shakes her head. "Only thing he ever give me was this dress, which somebody left here and didn't bother to pick up." There are tears in her eyes now and she has stopped scrubbing.

"Would you like to be maid to me, Judy?" I say, looking at her all steady, so she'll know I ain't foolin'.

She looks at me, her mouth open in amazement.

"Good," I say. "Let's go. I don't have much money, but I have enough to keep us both for a while."

We got out of there quick, though I was ready if the sod should appear. Judy had nothing to take—just a little rag doll that she had got somewhere and which probably gave her a little comfort at night when she slept on a pile of rags in the corner of the wash house.

"Come on," I say. "We've got to get you into some proper

clothes. Then we will get something to eat." I ain't hungry, but I know she is and has been for a long, long time.

We find a dressmaker's shop and are able to fit Judy off a rack of maid's clothing all ready made. It's a blessing that she's clean, having worked at the laundry, so she ain't shamed by that, at least.

There's a different style of maid's clothing here in England from the ones in the States. Softer and more loose-like, so fitting Judy out ain't a problem. There's a pink dress with pleats that gather below the chest and then a white collar thing and puffy sleeves, then a white apron. And a cap. Judy is in a daze and can only run her hands down the soft new cloth in wonder. A nightshirt, some new drawers, stockings, and petticoats, and we're done at the dressmaker's shop.

To the shoemaker's for a pair of slippers and then back to my digs at the Admiral Benbow.

I think about taking our dinner in the main room, but I know that will be too much for Judy right yet, so when I sweep back through the Benbow with Judy in tow, I say to the landlady, "We'll take our dinner in our room. Send it up. Tea, and some wine, too, if you please."

A table is set up and the food and drink is placed upon it. The food is good and the wine even better. Judy eats carefully, watching me to see what I do with the tools. She still casts her eyes about, as if not believing any of this.

"Well, that was good," I say, dabbing my lips with the napkin. "What do you think, Judy?"

She bends her face forward and starts crying into her hands. "I'm sorry, Mistress, I'm sorry, I..."

I put my hand on her shoulder and draw her to me. "I know, I know, it's a shock. There, there. I know you've had a rough time, but things will be different now, I promise, I do."

She will not call me Mary or Jacky or anything but Mistress and I let her do it. I certainly understand the comfort of knowing one's place.

I pat her back and say, "You settle in, now. I've got one more thing I've got to do this day."

I go back to Bride Street with Judy's old dress in my hand and my riding crop under my arm. When I get to the house where Judy was so cruelly deceived, I rap on the door.

The door opens and a man stands there, his pants not buttoned, his vest hanging open, his face unshaved, his hair uncombed. A musty smell comes off of him.

"Wot?" he says, his eyes blinking at the light. "Wot the devil do you want?" He is not pleased at the intrusion. He idly scratches his belly and looks out over my head.

I fling the shift in his face and say, "Here. I've taken poor Judy Miller off your dirty hands. May you roast in Hell for what you did to her, you piece of filth!"

I'm about to leave it at that and I turn to go, leaving the scum with the rag of a dress wrapped around his face.

*Then I see her.*

She is cowering back in the shadows behind him, and she is clad in rags, and she can't be more than twelve. I see how things are and I lose control of myself and I rear back with my crop and whip him across the face as hard as I can.

"You miserable bastard!" I yell, and I hit him again and

35

he screams and stumbles out into the street. The girl behind him puts her hands to her mouth in terror.

"Get back to your gang, girl! This man means you no good!" I yell to the girl. She jumps out and runs past me and off down the street like a startled rabbit, the soles of her bare feet flashing in the dimming light of the day.

I'm little but I'm strong, and I'm quick and I'm mad, and he's fat and slow and he stumbles to the ground crying out, *Stop, please, for the love of God, stop!* But I don't stop. I bring the crop down and down again and he squeals like the pig he is when he feels it bite into his legs and his fat buttocks, down and down and down again with all the strength and rage I've got in me. And while I'm doing that, I'm cursin' him straight to Hell and back again, and I get him across the shoulders and then twice across the face, back and forth, and he howls and curls up in a ball. Then I stop and stand over him, my chest heaving, and I tell all the people standin' around watchin' just what he's been up to, and then I work up a wad of spit and I spit it on him and then I get out of there before the peelers come.

I slip around the corner of Trumbull Lane, tryin' to get back to the Benbow without being seen. I don't know what kind of friends that slime bag has with the local constables, and my experience with constables, both here and in the States, not bein' all that cordial, I lay low.

I peek around the corner and find myself lookin' square into the eyes of Joannie, the girl from the Blackfriars Bridge Gang. We both start back.

"Wot? Miss? Jacky? You?" she says. "What's going on?"

I see that she's got the younger ones spread out around the square, hands out in begging, with eyes out for any chance for something better. Zeke leans against the Benbow, keepin' an eye out for any trouble.

Joannie seems to have trouble speaking. She flushes and stammers, "I...I'm sorry, Jacky, it ain't easy for me to talk like this wi' someone lookin' like you."

I see, and I put my hand on her bare arm. "It's all a game, Joannie," I says, "and it would be good for you to remember that. Now listen," and I tell her what happened to Judy and about the girl I saw there and what's likely to happen to anyone who that man gets behind his door.

She sags against the wall and lets her face become a mask of cold indifference like she's seen all this before, time and again. Then she says, "We'll tell all the other gangs. We'll work up a truce concerning Bride Street. We'll get there." Then her face gets hard as stone and she turns to me face on and hisses, "Depend upon it, Jacky. That dirty bugger'll never pass a peaceful day or night again. We'll take care of that!"

I pop back into our room to Judy's great relief. "Mistress, I was so worried."

"Just takin' care of some business" is all I'll say. "Now, let's get ready for bed. I plan a big day for tomorrow." With that I start undressing and she comes over and helps me get my clothes off and hung up proper.

Later, when we've both got our nightdresses on and are under the covers, I say, "Now, Judy, would you like to hear a story?"

"Coo, yes, Mistress, I would." She is easier with me now, now that I'm not in the lady clothes anymore.

"Very well, get over here next to me and I will read you a

story," and, as I feel her head on my shoulder, I pick up Amy's book and begin.

*"My name is Jacky Faber and in London I was born…"*

When I'm done with the first part, I ask her what she thinks and she says that this Amy's got it just about right, but didn't we do as much stealin' and scammin' as we done beggin'? And warn't there a whole lot of drunkards who regretted passin' out on our turf, with us swarmin' over 'em as soon as they hit the cobblestones? And I have to say aye, but Miss Amy, bein' a Puritan, felt she had to clean us up a bit—and I didn't tell her all of it.

Judy giggles. "Remember the time you stole the famous Darby Ram right from under the noses of his keepers at the Great Fair and brought 'im back to the kip and…"

Yes, I say, but that's another story.

I read on far into the night, till she falls asleep, and then I read on silently till I am done. When I finish, I turn back to the cover and read once again *as told to her dear friend and companion Miss Amy Wemple Trevelyne.* Hmmm. Strange, that. I thought she hated me, betraying me to the kidnappers and all.

Well, maybe someday we'll see. I snuff out the candle, draw Judy to me, and I go to sleep.

# Chapter 3

"Mistress, I wish you wouldn't do this," wails Judy. "I really wish that, I do."

I've stripped off the clothes I had worn down to breakfast—dress, drawers, and stockings—and I rummage in my seabag and pull out my jockey silks, the outfit I had gotten back in the States as a reward for riding the Sheik of Araby to victory in the Great Race.

I stick one foot in the tight white pants, then the other, then pull them up to my waist and do the buttons. Judy, like any dutiful maid, is standing by with the green-and-white striped top over one arm and the white stockings over the other, fretting all the while.

"But, Mistress, you're gonna have nothin' on under these flimsy things! You can't go out like that!"

"Yes, I can," I say. "I've done it before." I pull the blouse on over my head and Judy does the side tab buttons. White stockings next, and then we do the little cinch-belt things on the pants below the knees. *What a strange thing to have someone help you dress. Sinful, I know, but I can't say I find it unpleasant. I've tried to get her to call me Jacky, but she* won't do it. "Mistress Mary" is as close as she'll get to calling me by my name.

Now the soft leather boots. "Now braid up my hair, Judy, if you would, so's I can stuff it up into my cap." I sit in the room's only chair and she comes around in back and takes my hair and begins to do it. I can sense her dismay at all this from the heavy sniffing and sighing coming from behind me.

"Look, Judy, it's the only way I can get into the track as a single female," I say. "They won't let me in without a male escort 'cause they'll think I'm just a girl of easy virtue trying to get in to do some business with the swells. It'll be all right, you'll see. I'll wear my cloak with its hood pulled up till I get there, and then I'll pop out in this gear and fit right in and I'll be able to find my young man and see what's up with him. See?"

"No, I don't, Mistress."

I'm thinking the disguise will both get me into the place *and* remind Jaimy of my wild and adventurous ways, which he said he liked. I hope he still feels that way.

She gets done braiding and ties up the end with a bit of ribbon and I get up and look at myself in the mirror with satisfaction. *Tight and trim and back in harness again, my girl.* My blouse is loose enough to hide what I got in the way of chest, and my cap hides my hair and, if pulled down far enough, part of my face, too.

I complete the outfit by putting my ring, the ring Jaimy put on my finger back in the goldsmith's shop in Kingston, back in my ear and squeezing it shut so it doesn't fall out.

Then I lift up the front of my blouse and reach two fingers inside the money belt that's wrapped around my belly and pull out several coins. "Here's some money. If I don't come back, pay the landlady for our lodgings and take a carriage to number nine Brattle Lane."

"What do you mean, if you don't come back?" she gasps. "Please come back, Mistress, please..."

"If I don't come back, it'll just mean I'm with Jaimy and that's where he lives and you'll come join me there," I say, and present my back. "Here, give me my cloak."

She gets it and puts it around my shoulders and fastens the bonnet ties.

"It'll be all right, you'll see," and I plant a kiss on her frowning forehead and I'm out the door.

It doesn't take me long to get to the track. I know from my begging days in this area that the jockeys have an entrance around back so I go back there to see about gaining entry. I'm in luck—they've got the big doors open to let in some horses, so I stride through the gates and whip off the cloak and blend right in with the crowd of jockeys and handlers and stableboys milling about.

The stands are filling with people and, on the track, horses are being exercised and there's a feeling of great excitement in the air. The day is bright and clear and there are flags snapping and jockeys strutting about in their colorful silks and...

"Jacky!"

My heart leaps in my chest. *Jaimy? Is it...*

No, it isn't. I turn around and see Peter Jarvis standing there in his silks grinning at me.

"Petey!" I shout and go to throw my arms around the little man, but remember in time and instead grab his hand and give it a manly handshake. "So good to see you, Petey, oh, it is!"

"Back in Old Blighty, eh, Jacky?"

"Oh yes," I exclaim, "and you, too?"

"Well, yes, now that I'm a man of great renown since I rode the Sheik of Araby to victory at Dovecote Downs, I'm much in demand. So I decided to come back to the old sod and go right famous here, too." He winks and says, "But why are you back in male rig?"

"It's like this, Petey," I says, and blush in spite of myself, "I'm...I'm looking for a certain young man who's gonna be here today, and I figured this was the best way for me to get in here to look for him."

"Aw, our little Jacky in love. Ain't that sweet?"

"Well, we'll see about that," I simper. "But, Petey, if you could get me a mount, so's I could get about a little easier..."

"Sure thing, Jacky," he says and leads me over to a stall. "Here, take out Gwendolyne's Fancy for a little warm-up." He gestures to a stableboy, who quickly puts a saddle on the mare and then hands over the reins.

"Just take her around a few times slow, none of that crazy stuff like you used to pull with the Sheik. She's got to race today."

"I was wild then, Petey. I've calmed down a lot since then."

Petey looks me up and down and grins. "Right-o, Jack-o."

I take the reins and mount up and kick her up to a brisk trot. It feels good to be up in a saddle again and it calms my worried heart a bit. I scan the crowds as I go, trying to spot Jaimy. Would he be at the rail, or up in the grandstand? So many people, all dressed in their best, the men in tight jackets, the women in long, flowing dresses and wide, beribboned hats. Where is he?

I make one circuit of the track and see nothing of him. I begin to despair—maybe the girl was wrong—maybe he's not coming here today after all? Maybe his mother was right and he really doesn't want me anymore? Maybe he...

*Wait, now...* I pull up on the reins and slow to a walk, my eye on a figure sitting in a box. Is it? I get closer. I can't see the face, but the set of the shoulders, the way the head is held...closer...closer.

*Yes, it's him. Oh, dear God, it is. It's Jaimy.*

He's sitting in a box close to the rail, and I give the horse my heels and head straight for Jaimy, my eyes fixed on his face, my heart pounding in my chest and *Oh, Jaimy, it's been so long, so long* and I get to the rail and jump off the horse and spring up on the rail and look down into the box where Jaimy is sitting and...

And then my heart sinks. And dies.

Next to Jaimy is a girl, a beautiful girl, a finely dressed girl, all pink and frothy and fine, and she is holding Jaimy's hand and their fingers are entwined. They are facing each other and then the girl leans over and whispers something in Jaimy's ear and he smiles as her lips brush his cheek as she turns and sees me. And what she sees is a jockey with one leg over the rail, with mouth wide open, and with, unaccountably, tears running down his face.

The girl looks at me in wonder and Jaimy follows her gaze and his eyes meet mine.

*Oh, Jaimy, you are so beautiful and I loved you so, but you have proved false!*

43

He looks at me, astounded, as I pull his ring from my ear and fling it at his feet. It hits the deck with a *ding!* and flies off. And then I fly off the rail and run away.

"Jacky, stop!" I hear him shout behind me. "Wait!"

*But I ain't stoppin', I ain't waitin' no more, no I ain't, Jaimy, no more being stupid faithful Jacky, no more being the stupid fool...* my mind is churning as I'm running for the door—my chest racked with sobs and tears pourin' out of my eyes. *Oh, Jaimy, you have proved false and all my dreams are dust...*

"Jacky, come back, you don't under—"

*I understand all right, Jaimy, you don't want me anymore! Or you just want me to be your miss, your girl on the side who you come to visit when you can get away from your wife and children, but I ain't gonna be your miss, Jaimy, I ain't never gonna be nobody's miss!*

But then I'm through the door and out into the street and then I cut right and head down a side street so he can't find me and catch me. *I'm gonna leave this town I'm gonna go back to Boston and I'm gonna let that Randall—*

But I ain't gonna do anything like that at all, 'cause when I run around the corner of Duke Street, I run smack into the midst of a gang of men armed with clubs and ropes and sacks, who are pounding some poor bloke down to his knees, and one of them takes one look at me and yells, "A jockey, by God! Take him!"

Through my tear-bleared eyes I see a cart all loaded with bound men with hoods over their heads, some sittin' up, some lying down with their feet sticking out the back, and everybody's hollerin' and cryin' and all of a sudden I ain't so worried about my broken heart. *A press-gang!*

Two of the gang rush at me standin' there all open-mouthed and stupid and one grabs my arm and twists it way up behind me and I gasp in the shock and pain of it.

"Oh, won't this little fellow skip merrily through the riggin'!" says one of the brutes, while his pal brings up the rope to bind me.

"Wait!" I shout, "I'm a—" but my shout turns into a scream of pain as my arm is twisted ever higher.

"What you is, Jock, is a loyal servant of good King George, and yer gonna get a chance to prove it!"

"But I'm a girlummmmphh!" I tries to say, as the other cove grabs my head and puts his hand across my mouth.

"This one's a talker, he is," he growls, as he lifts his one hand off my mouth and with the other shoves in a dirty rag. "That'll shut 'im up proper!"

With that, my arms are brought down and my wrists are tied behind my back and the sack is put over my head and I'm lifted and thrown in the cart with the rest of the poor sods. I keen and struggle and twist, but then a club or rod or something hard and cruel comes down twice on my rump and I don't do that anymore, no, I don't.

After a while, the cart starts up and we rumble off to God-knows-where.

*I am pressed.*

I'm lyin' here fuming, looking at the inside of the hood. It's a rough open weave so us pressed ones can breathe through it, but we can't see out and nobody can see who we are, which is why I figure they got the hoods on us—a bloke's friends or family might see him bein' hauled off and cause some trouble for the press-gang. Since I don't hear nothin' but moans from my fellow prisoners, I guess they've got gags, too.

I figure they'll take us down to some ship in the harbor and we'll all be stood up and then they'll have to let me go when I inform them of my female nature. *And I'm gonna give you thugs a real piece of my mind then, too, by God, just you wait.*

I got lots of time to think on things as we rattle along, and what I'm tryin' not to think about is Jaimy, as I'm done with him and all that. *Lies, all lies, is all it was, and now you've got to put it out of your mind, girl, and put it out right now.*

I had told Judy that if I didn't come back to our room, she was to go to Jaimy's address 'cause that would have meant that Jaimy had joyously swept me off my feet and carried me back to his home for us to live happily ever after. Thinking of that stupid girl dream, my tears start up again, rolling across the bridge of my nose and down my cheek and into the rough cloth of the hood. I've been down before, but never have I felt so worthless and so unloved.

I will now harden my heart against Mr. James Fletcher and I will neither speak of him nor think of him ever again, as of this moment.

I have learned and I have decided that I will live single all of my life.

# Chapter 4

If I thought this was gonna be over quick, I was wrong. We rode in that damned cart for over an hour, and I felt every rock or cobblestone it bounced over. If I didn't have that slimy rag stuffed in my mouth, I swear my teeth would've been shaken loose long before now. I've about put a cramp in my tongue tryin' to work out the damned gag, but it just ain't no use.

Finally the rig stops and my feet are untied and a hand is put on my neck and I'm shoved up a gangway and pushed down on some sort of bench, as far as I can make out. I can smell the sea and hear the lapping of waves and it gives me cheer. Soon this will be over and I'll go back to collect Judy and we'll...

But it doesn't happen. My feet are tied again and I hear some bloke say, "Cast off," and I feel us heel over as a sail is set and takes the wind. *Uh-oh.* This ain't any big ship, this is a small boat, by the feel of it, no more than twenty feet long. It's plain that they're taking us out to a ship lying off the coast.

———

Trouble is, it's been hours and hours. Where are they taking us? The waves have been making up higher and higher, and some of the pressed landsmen are moaning with seasickness. And I don't feel so good myself. Lord, what would happen if you threw up with a gag in your mouth? Why, you'd choke and die for sure, and for sure this is a cruel press-gang as they don't have to keep us hooded and gagged by now, but still they do, and I curse them to the deepest pit of Hell for it.

More hours go by and I've got to go real bad now and I doubt if I can hold it much longer. From the smell of things in this boat, some of the men have already given up. I don't want to mess my silk britches, but I might have to soon and maybe it would be best to do it so I'll be less appetizing to whatever male I'm presented to. I'm speculating on this when I hear a hail and then a bump as we come up alongside something. Something big.

More shouts and a net is lowered and someone picks me up and throws me in it and a few others are tossed in on top of me and we are lifted up all tangled together and then dumped on a hard deck.

The net is jerked from one side and I am tumbled out of the net and rolled over the deck. I feel my feet being untied and then the hood is whipped off and the sudden light blinds me for a moment. I'm blinkin' away and after my sight clears, I find I'm looking into the face of the man lyin' next to me, not six inches away, and I gasp in recognition. To me, it is the very face of Horror, itself—the horror of my younger life, the face of Muck, Cornelius Muck, Muck the Corpse Seller, right here, right now, lying beside me, tied and gagged and eyes rollin' around, just like me! I'm taken back, back to when I was a little girl and Muck was slingin' my dead baby sister over his shoulder right after my mum had died on That Dark Day when my whole world fell apart. It's Muck, all right, bearded now, with longer hair, but still the accursed Muck and that little girl in me is kickin' and screamin' in terror. *Don't let him get me! Don't let him take me!*

I twist away from Muck and look up to see a seedy-lookin' cove dealin' out coins to what my reeling mind sees to be the head of the press-gang, who then bows to this cove and ties the purse around his waist and turns to leave. He goes down to his boat, the boat that brought us here, and casts off.

*Wait! You can't leave yet! Wait for me—*

"MMMMMmmmmmmpffff!" I try to yell through the gag. Desperate, I hunch over and manage to pinch twixt my knees a piece of the gag stickin' out of my mouth. I jerk back my head and the spit-soaked rag comes out of my mouth and I get to my knees and I shout, "Stop that boat, you fool, and let me go! I'm a girl!"

There is a sudden dead silence. I look about and see that I am on some sort of ship, and I look over the starboard side and see land about a half mile off. I try to struggle to my feet, despairing to see the boat pull farther and farther away, but I can't with my hands tied behind me. I can only remain on my knees.

The seedy-lookin' man peers down at me and smiles. His shirttail is out and his trousers are stained and dirty. He is unshaven and his hair is unruly and uncut. He opens his mouth and says, "Girl, eh? We'll see." He comes up to me and he grabs me by the arm and yanks me to my feet. With his other hand he pulls off my cap and my hair spills out onto my shoulders, but that ain't proof enough for this cove, no it ain't. He grunts and puts that same grubby hand on my chest. I recoil but think, *Better this than having to drop my pants in front of the whole ship's company for proof.*

The man smiles and makes a mock bow. "Welcome to His Majesty's Ship *Wolverine,* girl. I *know* you're going to enjoy your stay," he says, looking me up and down. His teeth are worn gray stubs and his puffy face bristles with several days' growth of beard. "But if you ever again call your Captain a fool, I will hang you from that yardarm there. Do you understand, girl?"

*Captain? This man is the Captain?*

He is a large man and he has a prominent hooked nose and full, almost womanish lips. There is a whitish residue on the lower of those lips and I'm amazed to see a tic tighten in a neck muscle and suddenly pull down the left side of his mouth. Then, incredibly, his left eye takes off on its own, independent of the right one, and appears to be looking up into the rigging while the right eye stays on me. *What kind of creature is this?*

An officer, a lieutenant, has come up next to the Captain. He, at least, is dressed as a naval officer and he says, very respectfully, and very cautiously, "Begging your pardon, Sir, but might it not be best to call back the…"

The tic relaxes its grip on the Captain's face and he turns to look at the officer. "Mr. Pinkham," he says with undisguised contempt, "shut up. If I wanted your opinion, I'd ask for it." He turns again to me. "I paid for eight bodies, Mr.

Pinkham, and I shall have eight bodies. And hers will do just fine."

The Captain looms over me, legs wide, hands on hips. "How came you to be dressed like this?" he demands.

"It was for sport," I says. "Now..."

"For sport, eh? Well, you shall certainly find some sport here, my girl. Yes, you shall, and very quickly, too," he says, winkin' at me so I can't mistake his meaning. "This is turning into a really fine day. Yes, it is." He turns and faces up into the sky. "I got up this morning thinking all I had to look forward to was bad whisky and the worst crew ever assembled on a British warship. And now this. Thank you, Lord." He comes face-to-face with me and I can smell the whisky on him. Whisky and something else, I can't tell what. "Untie her hands and take her to my cabin."

*Oh, Lord, this doesn't look good at all.*

As my hands are being untied, I look about me and see that I am on a Brig-of-War—two masts, probably eighteen guns. There is land over the horizon and from the position of the sun, I figure it to be the coast of France and this ship is on the blockade. There are men looking on from the rigging and on deck, but they are strangely quiet, as if they are afraid to do or say anything about my arrival, which one would think would be cause for great uproar and hilarity. I'm thinkin' they're deathly afraid of the Captain. I am, too.

The press-gang boat is too far gone to be called back, I see with a sinking heart. Looking toward the land, I see that we are quite close, not more than a quarter mile from a rocky peninsula jutting out into the Channel.

I pretend to be resigned to my fate, and I stand there with my head down and shoulders slumped, but as my bonds are being loosened, I toe off my boots and the instant my hands are free, I bolt across the deck and dive over the side. *I ain't stayin' here, that's for sure.*

There are shouts as I fly over the rail. *Better France than this,* I'm thinkin' as the water comes up to meet me.

I hit clean and come up pullin' for the shore. I gasp, but the water has kept some of its warmth from the summer and the seas are calm, with gentle swells and no chop, so I'm hopin' I'll be all right.

As I'm strokin' away, I'm figurin' I'll tell the Froggies that I'm American and ask would they please direct me to the nearest port where I can book passage back there. I have my money belt on and my French is good enough to get along.

*Whew! That was a close one,* I reflect. *Lord, that crazy Captain was gonna keep me as his miss, he was. Yes, and Muck on board as well! Keep pullin' away, girl, keep strokin'. Sorry to lose those boots, though.*

I strike out for the shore, getting into a nice even rhythm. I swim for a while and then pause to let the sea take care of that still nagging call of nature. I gratefully relax and feel a warm gush around my loins for a bit, and then the cool ocean sweeps it away. *Ahhh.*

I learned, back when I was marooned on that beach in South America and practicing my swimming, that when I got tired swimming frontwards, I could turn over on my back and take a little rest, like, floating and just paddling along. I do that now to pace myself and relax a bit—at least I don't have to worry about sharks here and...

*Uh-oh.*

I look back at the ship and see that they have put in a boat to chase me down. *Damn!* And they've got an alongshore breeze so they'll be on a beam reach and able to come at me right quick! I turn back over and stretch out, really digging into the water for all the speed I can get, my eyes on the shore.

*That lunatic Captain don't know me, he don't know that all I do is spread discord and havoc and destruction wherever I go and he'd be better off without me. But it looks like he ain't gonna listen. No, he ain't!*

The shore doesn't look like it's any closer, but I know it is, and if I can just keep going—*Pull! Pull! Pull! Dig deep! Faster! Faster!*

But I can hear the lap of the bow wave on the boat and I can hear the shouts of the crew as they draw near. "There she is! Get her! Get her!"

I jerk my head back and see they are a scant twenty feet behind me.

"You there!" calls out a man in the bow of the boat. He's got a coil of rope in his hand and he flings it toward me. "Give it up and grab that line!"

But I don't give it up and I don't take the rope. What I do is dive down deep and look up at the bottom of the boat as it surges over me. I kick with my legs and shoot back up and come to the surface oh-so-quiet at the stern of the boat, right next to the rudder.

I see that they are all looking forward to the last place they saw me. Close to the boat and with just my eyes out of the water, I keep an eye on the coxswain's back, and when I see him lean forward and loosen his grip on the tiller, I grab the rudder and give it a quick jerk straight up. The pintles slip out of the gudgeons and the rudder comes off in my hands and I let it sink down into the depths.

"Let's see you sail without a rudder, mates!" I shout and then go under again and get out in front of them and come up and start strokin' for the shore again, and it looks closer! I can hear the waves beatin' on the shore!

"Like tryin' to catch a bleedin' mermaid!" I hear behind me, but then I hear oars being shoved in oarlocks so I know they're still after me, and I pull and I pull, making my aching arms and legs push on and on. Their oars dip into the water and start their rhythm, and I know they'll be up on me again real soon. That Captain must have threatened them with some awful punishment to get them to chase me like this.

They're gettin' close again, I know, 'cause I can hear 'em puffin' and gruntin', and I figure this time they'll try to whack me with an oar to stun me and get me that way, so I try to keep low down in the water so's the water'll take the impact instead of my poor back.

But when they come up on me again, what I feel instead is something hard against the small of my back, which then runs down the crack of my bum and I feel a tug on my britches as they are pulled down to my knees. *A boat hook's got my pants!* I reach back and slip the hook off and yank the pants back up. *Christ! I can't go into France without pants!* I get it done, but I'm losin' ground, too. Back up for another breath.

"I've a harpoon here, and I'll use it!" I hear the shout, and I look up and sure enough this hard-eyed bloke in the bow of the boat has got a real sharp-looking harpoon in his fist and I quick dive back down. I don't believe him, but I ain't takin' no chances. For sure, I know now how those poor whales felt.

Looking up at the bottom of the boat, I see the paddles dipping down into the water, and then, as they don't know where I am, they lie still, their blades just sitting there, barely cutting the surface. Desperate, I kick up and grab an oar and pull down as hard as I can.

Sure enough, the boat rocks violently, her balance upset, and then, wonder of wonders, a sailor plunges into the water next to me. He must have been on that oar I pulled. Well, that oughta keep 'em busy, rescuing their mate while I push on to freedom.

But it doesn't happen that way. I pop up on the other side of the boat, and they're all lookin' off the other side and sayin' things like *Poor Billy, drownding over a stupid girl,* and *Woe, oh woe, he was such a friend to me!*

Christ! None of the lubbers can swim! Typical bleedin' British sailors! I dive down once again, and, sure enough, there's Billy down there, slippin' down into the murk, bubbles comin' out of his nose and mouth. I dart down and grab him by the hair that floats out about his head and kick and dart back to the surface. I lift his head out of the water and he coughs, water pouring out of his mouth and nose, and hands reach out and grab him. I twist away, but not fast enough 'cause another rascally hand reaches out and gets a fistful of my own hair, and I am hauled to the side of the boat and held fast there while they get soggy Billy aboard.

*Damn!* If I had my shiv I could cut the hair by which I am held and escape, but I don't have my shiv! I remember, only this morning, thinkin' about whether or not to take it with me. *Stupid!*

Then I am pulled aboard and I kick and twist and fight my way to the side and look out toward France and *there's the shore right there! I am so close! I can hear the breakers! I can smell the spray! Damn!*

"Hold her, dammit! Goddamn slippery eel, she is! Hold her, for Chris'sakes! Look out! Hold her! Watch out, she'll bite! *Ow! Damn!*"

I put a heel in one bloke's crotch and my elbows wherever I can and I get *Oooofs!* and *Arrrgghhhs!* but I don't get loose. Eventually there're three sets of arms around me and a pair of hands gripping my ankles and one hand still entangled in my hair so I give it up and lie there panting.

The grizzled old seaman who has me around the neck puts his rough lips against my ear and whispers, "Ye would've gotten clean away from this Hell Ship, girl, if'n you hadn't stopped to save poor Billy, and me mates and me ain't gonna be forgettin' that."

Well, at the very least I shall have a few friends aboard.

"Do you know that desertion is a hanging offense, girl?" roars the Captain when I am taken back aboard.

The unfortunate Billy is stretched out over a barrel and his mates are rolling him back and forth to pump out the water. It looks like he will live, if only just.

"How can I desert from something that I don't belong to?" says I to the Captain. I stick my chin in the air and put on the Look, which probably looks right stupid on me standing there dripping in my clinging wet silks, which have gone all transparent, leaving no doubt in anyone's mind as to what exactly I am in the way of gender, but I do it, anyway. I know that Mistress Pimm would have wanted me to,

56

so I stick my nose high in the air, eyes hooded, lips together, teeth apart. Though that last bit is gettin' kinda hard to do as I'm beginning to shiver and my teeth are chattering.

"Belong? Ah, well, then let's have you belong for sure," says the Captain, and he turns to the officer I had seen before. "Mr. Pinkham, have her read into the ship's company log as an Ordinary Seaman. Then take the ship another half mile offshore so she doesn't get the notion to try to swim for it again."

"But, begging your pardon, Sir," says the obviously distressed Mr. Pinkham, "you can't—"

"Where does it say that I can't? I'm Captain of this goddamned ship and I can do whatever I goddamn well want! Now do what I goddamn tell you."

Pinkham doesn't answer. While this is going on, I'm shivering and forcing myself to think, *Girl, you are in a lot of trouble here! What's best to do?* and then I decide.

"If you are going to do that, Captain," I pipe up and say, "then you must enter me as a Midshipman, as that is my true rank. My name is Jacky Faber, and I was commissioned by Captain Locke of HMS *Dolphin* on July the twentieth, eighteen hundred and three."

Now *that* finally gets a murmur out of the crew.

The Captain barks out, "Do any of you here know that to be true?" He looks around at the men silent in the rigging.

Finally a voice says, "Aye, Sir, that's Jacky Faber, all right. I was on the *Dolphin* with her."

I look around for the owner of the voice, but I can single no one out. I shall have to find out. Perhaps it will be another friend, and I know I will need all the friends I can muster.

"A Midshipman, hey?" He looks amused. "Then let's see

what you know, Midshipman. What is the procedure for getting under way and standing before the wind?"

Well, ain't I seen that done a hundred times, standing on the quarterdeck with my drum? Ain't I heard the *Dolphin*'s middies recite this a hundred times for Captain Locke, the sweat pouring out from under their caps as they squirmed under his gaze? I put my hands behind me in Parade Rest and I start:

"Sir. Make all preparations for getting under way, heave in, and make sail as before. Lay the main and mizzen topsails square aback; the fore one sharp aback, according to the side it is intended to cast—heave in, cant her the right way with the helm before tripping, and as soon as the velocity of the stern board is greater than that of the tide, shift the helm, grapple the buoy, run up the jib as soon as it will take, and haul aft the weather sheet. While falling off, cat and fish the anchor, as she gathers headway, shift the helm: When before the wind, right it, square the head yards, and brail up the jib—set topgallant sails, royals, and foresail— haul taut the lifts, trusses, and backstay falls, and, if necessary, set the scudding sails."

Then I pause. Then, in conclusion, I say, "Sir."

The Captain sneers off in the direction of four boys of various ages standing off to the side dressed as midshipmen and looking confused and abashed.

"Hear that, my fine midshipmen?" They don't say anything, they just look at their feet or straight ahead, depending on how old they are. The Captain turns his attention back to me.

"So you are that one, then, that one who is the talk of the fleet?" asks the Captain, beaming. "Yes, Midshipman would definitely be better. No problem with fraternization with the lower decks then. Good, good," he says, nodding. "Mr. Pinkham! Write her in as Midshipman Jack Faber. If Locke could do it, so can I, by God!"

Then, suddenly, as if all this shouting had broken something inside him, he groans and grabs his side. "Send for Earweg," he wheezes, doubling over. "I need my medicine! Now!"

He staggers to the hatchway, which must lead to his cabin, but before he goes down, he turns and gasps, "Take her below, fit her out, and mark me, every last one of you dogs—nobody lays a hand on her, d'ye hear? Captain Abraham Scroggs will not have soiled goods!" The silence on this ship is such that all hear his words very plain.

In a few moments, I'm taken down a ladder and into the midshipmen's berth and the four of them stand there lookin' at me standing there shivering in my silks.

"Date of rank," I say, lookin' about the dim interior for something to cover myself with.

They are confused. "What? We..."

"When were you made midshipmen is what I mean." I'm losing patience. I'm cold and getting very cranky.

The oldest of the lot, a likely looking boy of about sixteen, clears his throat and nervously says, "We were all brought aboard about a month ago and—"

"So that makes me Senior Midshipman, then," I says, cutting him off cruelly. "So get me a blanket and be quick about it, boy. And where's my bunk?" *Sorry, lad, but I've got to establish myself right off.*

He is startled by my rudeness, but he stifles his anger and

says, "Here." He goes over and opens a door to a closet-sized room, and he stands back and I go in and look about. A bed, with drawers underneath. A dry sink and basin. Some hooks on the wall. That's it, but I've seen worse, and tired as I am, it looks like home to me.

A knock on the side of the cabin and a hand holds out a blanket to me. I take it, close the door behind me, and strip off my poor silks. I hang them on the hooks in hopes they'll dry in some sort of shape. I towel off with the blanket and rub myself briskly to take out some of the cold. After a little while my skin starts to pink up and I stop shivering so violently.

Then I wrap the blanket about me and step back out into the midshipmen's berth. There is a table and some chairs and an open hatch overhead letting in the air. At least we shan't suffocate on days when it ain't raining.

"What have you got for me to wear?" I say, sitting down at the table. I know I must present a comely sight, my hair plastered to my head, made thick with the salt water, and my nose red and running, my feet all veiny and blue. "Is there any hot tea?" Then I sneeze a fine spray of mist all over the table.

The older boy jerks his head at the littlest boy, who ducks his head and scurries out. The rest of them stare at me. Aside from the older boy, there are two who seem to be of the same age, that being about twelve.

"I'll need drawers, a shirt, trousers, and a jacket. And stockings. My boots will serve me for shoes. A cap, if one can be found," I say. "And the loan of a comb and some ribbon to tie back my hair."

The younger ones scurry into their cubbyholes and come out with the drawers, shirt, pants, stockings, and other items. The older boy goes into his room and comes out with a black midshipman's jacket. "I have grown out of it, and I will take great pleasure if you will accept it. We will have to share the comb."

*Hmmm. Courtly. Has manners. Here's a likely one, maybe.*

"And what is your name, Sir?" I ask.

He bows and says, "Robin. Robin Raeburne, at your service, Miss, and I am sorry for your recent troubles." He has dark, curly, reddish brown hair, and a fine straight nose, good chin, with a high, clear, and intelligent forehead. He's probably a Scot with that name and that hair.

I give a slight dip by way of an answer to his bow and say, "Don't be. I brought it on myself, as usual."

The small boy comes back in, bearing a mug of steaming tea. He seems to be all of eight years old, his black midshipman's jacket hanging rather loosely on him. Comically loose. He hands the cup to me with both hands, slightly shaking so that some of the tea sloshes out over his hands.

I take the cup and gratefully bring it to my lips. "Ahhh." I breathe as the hot liquid goes down my throat, warming me. "And you, young sir. What is your name?" He is short, round in the face, and blond. His ice blue eyes are open in unabashed wonder.

"Georgie Piggott, Miss," he pipes. "And are you really the girl in the book?"

*Oh, Lord.*

I sigh and say that I suppose I am, but you shouldn't believe everything you read. The other two squeakers are looking at me in wonder, too. I raise my eyebrows in question at them and one says, "Ned Barrows, Mum," and the other says, "Tom Wheeler."

Ned is a dark-haired boy, with thick curls close to his head, and an open face—cheerful, honest, and slightly pug-nosed. Tom is blondish, with his hair hanging to his shoulders, and he has blue eyes, and a foxy, inquisitive face. Ned is sturdy, while Tom is slight. Again, I place them both at the age of twelve and it is plain that they are close friends.

"Fine. What's for dinner?"

Dinner turns out to be simple seamen's rations—salt pork, biscuit, and pease porridge—brought on a tray by a sullen sailor who dumps the stuff on the table without a word. As he leaves, I give the sailor a look that says, *We'll be taking care of that attitude in the future, mark me, man.*

We turn to and I tap my biscuit and sure enough several weevils fall out. I brush them off the table and take a bite of the biscuit, taking care to see what the bite exposed in the way of further bugs. Not too bad, I notice. Then I tuck into the salt pork, using my fingers, as I have no knife. Not yet I don't. The three younger ones regard me with unwavering stares. Robin, however, just looks quiet and withdrawn. Sullen, even. You'd think he'd be delighted by being presented with the close company of what has already proved to be a frolicsome young dame, but he ain't. Maybe he's just shy, or maybe I just look too ratty.

"Best tuck in, Mates," I say, "never can tell when next you'll eat again." That bowl of pease porridge—I ain't shy about putting that away, either. Nothing like a brisk swim for the appetite. "So who's got what watch? Are we One-in-Three, then?"

Robin shakes his head. "We don't stand watches. We don't know enough yet. And we haven't been taught anything." His face flames in humiliation. And now, in addition to his previous unhappiness, he is being replaced as Senior Midshipman by a girl.

"Aye, Miss, it's horrible here!" blurts out Georgie. "The Captain..."

But Robin flashes him a warning look and puts his finger to his lips and looks up to the open hatch, where I almost hear the ears flapping. There are no secrets on a ship, and Robin, at least, knows that.

"Good advice, young George," I say, and remove my hand from beneath my blanket and place my hand on his sleeve. "Don't worry, Georgie, I'll find the way of things around here right quick." A bare female shoulder and arm probably ain't the best thing to be presenting to these boys and this young man right now, so I pull my arm back and clutch the blanket around my neck once more.

I signal for a rag to wipe my hands and Ned and Tom trip over each other in finding me one. "Well, we shall see about the watches and the education, too," I say, and rise. "Where's the Watch, Quarter, and Station Bill?"

"I believe Mr. Pelham keeps it, Miss," says Robin. "He's the Second Mate."

"Then we'll have a look at it come morning, Mr. Raeburne," I say. He nods. I look up through the hatch and see that it has gotten quite dark. That bed in there calls me.

"Well, I thank you gentlemen for the use of your clothes. If you'll excuse me..." With that I scoop up the pile of clothing and pad back to my room. "Oh, and I'll need several pitchers of water. Hot water."

———

I've wiped the salt off me as best I can with a cloth dipped in the hot water and I've stuck my head down into the basin and rinsed my hair. It's still a tangled mess, but at least it's clean. I work at it with Robin's comb, after I wash it off—it's tough, but I get it done.

Robin had also given me one of his old shirts to use as a nightdress and I put it on and lace it up. It will serve, though it only comes down to just above my knees.

Sticking my head out the door, I call out, "Mr. Barrows. Mr. Wheeler. Go back up on deck and see if you can find my boots." I hear them scurrying out, eager to please. It's nice being senior, and it's well that I assert my authority right off, no matter what else is going to happen to me.

I'm considering curling up in bed and allowing myself a few tears of self-pity as I sit back down and think about things....What's going to happen to me? I mean, it sure doesn't look good for my future as a maiden, that's for certain. What will I do if the Captain has me taken into his cabin and just orders me to strip down and climb in his bed? He's the Captain—no one would stop him. What if the order comes right now? What could I do? The ship's too far out now for me to swim to shore—and it's dark, too, and getting cold.

Plus, there's something in me, and I know it's stupid, but there's something in me that doesn't want to desert after bein' signed on official-like.

I know I'm in deep trouble here, but maybe, just maybe, as I am now read in as a member of the ship's company, that fact will accord me some rights. Especially if I act like I really *am* a member of the crew, instead of the way they expect me to act, which is like a whining, scared girl. Scared I am, and certainly given to whining, cajoling, wailing, begging, pleading, *anything* to get out of a fix. But somehow I don't think all that's gonna work here. All I can do is start acting like I belong here, like it's natural. I must start acting like the ranking Midshipman. Starting first thing in the morning. I resolve to get up early to embark on this plan. Very early.

They expect me to hide, so I shall not hide. I shall make myself *very* visible. It is not much of a plan, but it is a plan, and, as usual, I feel a little better for having one. I turn on my side and, bringing my knees to my chin and hugging my legs to my chest, I go to sleep.

# Chapter 5

James Emerson Fletcher
9 Brattle Lane
London, England
September 6, 1804

Miss Jacky Faber
Somewhere in the World

Dear Wild and Stupid Girl,

I am going to continue to write you, Jacky, even though I have not the foggiest idea where you are or where to send these letters or whether you shall ever read them. I am doing it in this manner for several reasons: One, it preserves some sort of communication between us, a spiritual one if you will; and two, it helps calm my raging mind. The third reason is that I hope that we might be reunited soon to enjoy a good laugh over these words.

The girl at the track? Lovely, wasn't she? She is my cousin Emily, my uncle Jemmy's girl. We grew up together, not four doors apart on Brattle Lane. We played together as children *and now she is a delightful girl of sixteen who enjoys pretending that I am her amorous escort when we are out and about. I suppose she does this to drive the other young men viewing us crazy with envy. I believe she is using me for practice and it is to my discredit that I rather enjoyed the game. I had thought it a harmless diversion, but I was wrong. You really would have enjoyed her company if you weren't so damned impulsive. But, then, that's not your way, is it, Jacky? Oh no—look but never think; oh no, never to think but only to plunge. Have you ever considered how much more pleasant your life would be if you just stayed in a damned dress once in a while and didn't... oh, to hell with it!*

*I am sure you have just gone off to sulk and I will find you soon and all will be explained and all will be well.*

*I am in port to study for my lieutenancy exams. How I will be able to face a board of post captains and admirals with your foolish self on my mind, I do not know, but I will try.*

*Still your humble and etc....*
*Jaimy*

# Chapter 6

The next morning, when I hear the bell ring Five Bells in the Four-to-Eight watch, I throw back the covers and make myself get out of bed and go splash the cold water from the pitcher on my face, take care of the necessaries, comb my hair, and begin to dress. It is six thirty in the morning.

I balance myself against the roll of the ship and stick my foot in the right leg of the drawers, and then the left, and yank them up to my waist, right over my money belt. I sit on the edge of the bunk and pull on the stockings and then I pick up the shirt and give the armpits a bit of a sniff—pretty clean, I reflect, but then just how stinky can little boys make things? I pull it over my head and down to my waist. It fits fairly well and has ruffles at the cuffs and neck and lacings that go halfway down the front. I lace it up and pull on the britches. Tight, but serviceable.

The last thing I do is put on the black jacket with its two up-and-down rows of gold buttons. Nice and trim and tight it feels. Hat on, with hair tucked up under, and wishing for a mirror, I'm strapped back in harness again, ready for whatever else happens.

I step back into the midshipmen's berth and almost trip over two of the boys, as Ned and Tom had pulled their mattresses to the floor and are sound asleep outside my door, one to each side—I imagine they are there as protection for my own frail self. *My two Knights Errant.* Three, actually, as Georgie is curled up over there at the foot of the ladder. *Did you all swear mighty oaths on your knightly armor and intend to keep a watchful vigil over yon fair maiden? I am touched. How sweet.*

Robin Raeburne is asleep at the table, his head on his arms. There is a cup in front of him and I pick it up and sniff it and it smells strongly of rum. *Does it help you sleep, young Robin? Does it help make you forget where you are? If it does, then I shan't blame you for it.*

I quietly put the cup back down next to his hand and tiptoe past the sleeping boys and go out of the room, up the hatchway, and into the light.

All on board expect me to hide. Therefore, I shall *not* hide.

It looks to be a bright clear day with the sun coming up over France out there to port. I grab a ratline off the foremast and climb up into the rigging. I go up past the foretop and gain the fore royal yard and straddle it, looking out toward France.

France seems to be a pleasant place, in spite of all the awful tales I have heard of it ever since I got old enough to listen. I had half-expected there to be ogres and trolls and other of Napoleon's minions hanging about, but instead there are gently rolling hills going off into the distance, marked with neat pastures and farmsteads. There are some inlets set into the coast with a few fishing boats coming out of them to set their nets. But they do not come out too far,

I notice, as they know we are lurking out here. Back there, behind us and out of sight below the horizon, is England... England and Ja— Judy. Back there is Judy, and I hope she managed to make do on the money I left her. *Hang on, Judy, till I get out of this mess and can get back to you.*

I look down at the *Wolverine* lying down there below. It is, as I suspected when first I caught a glimpse of it, a Brig-of-War, about a hundred feet long and twenty-five feet wide at the beam—which is half the size of the dear old *Dolphin*. Two masts instead of three. It probably carries about a hundred men and officers—one-quarter the number on the *Dolphin*. Looks to be eighteen cannon and they seem to be eighteen-pounders, and they are all right there on the top deck itself, not down on the second deck like on a frigate. I'll bet there's a Long Tom nine-pounder up front as a chaser and another in the stern.

It's plain that the *Wolverine* is on blockade duty—helping to keep the French warship fleet bottled up in their harbors and disrupting the enemy's seagoing commerce by stopping smugglers. All for the good and glory of Britannia, she who rules the waves, at least for now. And forever, it is hoped.

I look up at the sails and see that she is trim and the decks down below are scrubbed clean, so it is not a sloppy ship. My fear is that she is all spit and polish and not in fighting trim because that's a dangerous situation. I already feel, deep in my bones, that there are some things very, *very* wrong on this unhappy ship.

Today is Sunday, so I expect there will be a muster of the crew and church, but I don't know. I will wait and see. I know from the smoke curling up from the cooking fires that the next watch is getting their breakfast, and so I slip back down to the deck to get me some. I duck down into the fore hatch and stride into the teeming mess deck. All heads lift up upon my entry and the hum of conversation stops dead. There is a low whistle from some cheeky cove, but that's it. I get a cup of tea and some johnnycake and I sit down across from a seaman seated at the long table. I am used to being the center of attention. Most times I like it. Sometimes I do not.

"Well met, John Harper," I say, sitting myself down next to a man I now recognize. The johnnycake is good and the tea is hot, at least.

"Well met, Jacky," says Harper, smiling slightly. "Or I should say, *Miss* Faber." He is the man who fingered me as the one and only Jacky Faber the day before. The last I saw of him, he and I were both lookouts on the *Dolphin* on the day the ship was blasted and sinking and without hope. He is young but balding cleanly back from the forehead, and he affects a goatee, which makes him look like a devilish Spanish pirate, but I know him for a good man.

"So, Johnny, what kind of berth have we found here? Are there any more Dolphins aboard?" I ask. I finish off the cake and sip at the tea.

"As for Dolphins, alas, nay. As for the other question, I go on watch as lookout on the mainmast when the watch changes." He looks around at his fellow crew members and casts me a significant look.

I understand. We swap harmless tales of former shipmates and then I knock off the rest of my tea and stand. "Till later then, John Harper."

I know every eye in the place is on me, so I lift my chin and loudly say, "Good morning, mates. Thank you for sharing your breakfast with me. Is it not a glorious thing to be serving His Majesty the King on this fine day!"

With that, I turn and stride out of there, bootheels rapping on the deck, leaving a roomful of gaping mouths behind me.

I go back up the foremast and get to the topgallant brace and wait till I see Harper take over from the lookout, and then I take the foregallant brace, a line that goes between the two masts for support of both and is under such tension that it's like the wire a circus performer would walk, and I go over, hand over hand, till I reach the mainmast and the grinning Harper.

"Still at home in the riggin', eh, Jacky?"

We are on a very small platform, high, high on the mainmast. Back on the whaler this would be called the "crow's nest." It is where sharp-eyed men looked out constantly across the waves for the spume of a blowing whale.

"May it ever be so, John, as I am never happier than when I am up here," I say and settle myself against a brace. "So what's the story on this bark?"

His face darkens. "'Tis a Hell Ship, for sure, and I've never been on a worse one and it's all on the Captain's head."

"Careful, John," I say, looking about to make sure we are not heard, "you're getting close to mutiny."

"Mutiny!" he snorts. "The crew has been at the edge of mutiny for months. The officers should have done it long ago, but they are frozen in fear of him, just like anyone on board. He has flogged men half to death for sport and he keelhauled a man last month for merely lifting his hand in protection from a beatin' by the Bo'sun. Poor Spooner was alive after he was hauled back aboard, but he was cut up so bad by bein' scraped against the barnacles on the bottom that he died soon after from the infection."

That sends a shiver up my spine. Keelhauling is a cruel punishment wherein a poor seaman is taken up to the bow and a long rope is tied to each of his legs and he's thrown overboard and the ropes are walked back, one on the port side and one on the starboard side, drawing the man underwater all along the encrusted keel and back to the stern of the ship, where he's hauled back up, half drowned and bloody. I have never seen it done, Captain Locke of the *Dolphin* being a good and fair man, but I have heard accounts of it.

Harper's normally cheerful face is full of anger as he continues. "...And he gave Teddy Smallwood a hundred lashes, a *hundred!*—just for havin' a bad shave, for Christ's sake, and Teddy still can't stand up straight or put on his shirt in any comfort. I tell you, Jacky, the only times when this ship breathes easy is those times when the Captain is sick and stays in his cabin." Harper pauses and calms himself and sighs, "But he is sick a lot, and we thank God for it."

"Can nothing be done?" I ask.

"No. It would be up to the officers and they ain't done nothin'."

"And the crew?"

He thinks for a moment, then says, "The crew is split up in different gangs with different loyalties, which ain't surprisin' on a ship like this. A man's gotta know who his friends are."

"Who can be trusted?"

"Drake, the Master-at-Arms. Harkness, a gunner, and Jared, the Captain of the Top, are all good men. They command the loyalty of most of the crew."

"Most?" I ask.

"Aye. That gang of lubbers brought on with you looks to be a real bad lot. They've been put with the Waisters, which wasn't a good bunch to begin with."

*Ah, Muck is at it again, sowing suspicion and hatred and discord even in the short time he has been aboard. It ain't surprising that he would end up with the Waisters, them being the worst sailors on board any ship, good only for the most simple and brutish of tasks.*

"...and watch out for Bo'sun Morgan—he's the Captain's man, all the way. He's a cruel bastard who enjoys carrying out the Captain's punishments."

"I will, John," I say, glad of the information.

"I'm sorry, Jacky, that you ended up here on this Hell Ship. I knew you for a good kid back on the *Dolphin,* and as I see it, you're more in danger than anyone else here."

I put my hand on his arm. "Don't worry about me, John. I'll be all right."

He nods and shakes his head like he doesn't believe it. Like he doesn't believe *anybody* on this ship's gonna be all right. "You do have friends here, though. The men that saw you save Billy Barnes at the expense of your own freedom, well, they ain't forgot, and they have spread the story throughout the ship."

I think on this. "Thanks, John. That is good to know," I say, and swing out to go back down. "Oh, and one other thing. I need a shiv. Can you get me one?"

I start back down toward the deck, but I cock my head as I hear voices raised down on the quarterdeck below me. It is the Captain and the First Mate, Mr. Pinkham. I quietly drop down to the maintop and sit down to listen.

"Complications? What complications? A girl shows up on my ship and I bed her. What's complicated about that? I'm the Captain of this bloody ship, and I do what I bloody well want. And I remind you, Pinkham, this is a warship, with rough men on it, not some bloody Asylum for the Protection of Some Poor Bloody Orphans."

"Well, Sir, if you will pardon me, there are several complications here. First, there is that *book:* Because of it this girl is well known throughout the fleet, throughout all of London, for that matter—and who knows what foolish wife of a commodore or sister of an admiral or even First Lord has read this book and sees this foolish girl as a heroine or at least a poor victim? And for you to be the one that takes this girl under these circumstances, it would not be seemly, Sir. Your reputation, your career, your future promotions..."

"To hell with all of that and all of them, too." I sense, though I can't see it, that the Captain's tic is pulling his face into another grimace and his eye has gone a-wandering again.

"Secondly, Sir, there is the question of fraternization."

"What? What do you mean?" demands the Captain, his irritation plain.

"If I may be blunt, Sir, a Captain cannot mount a Midshipman. Captain Douglas, you may recall, was executed by firing squad on his own quarterdeck for just that indiscretion."

"Yes, but that Midshipman was a boy."

"I don't think the Court-Martial would make that distinction, Sir. You have entered her on the books as a Midshipman."

"Hmmm. So if she was a Lieutenant…"

"But that's impossible, Sir!"

"Oh, bugger all that! I don't give a good goddamn for any of it! If I didn't have an attack of that cursed gout last night, I'd have strapped her on right then, by God, and to Hell with all of them! And to Hell with you, too! Damn! Accursed gout! Why does God hate me so? Delivers a tooth-some wench into my very grasp and then unmans me. *Pah!*"

"The very fact that she's on board, Sir, is—"

"There's nothing in Regulations about it, Pinkham. A good many of the Captains on this godforsaken blockade have got their wives put up in their cabins and the whole fleet knows it. There's thirty women on the *Orion* at last report and every-one knows there were three hundred women that had to be taken off the *Royal George* when she sank in Portsmouth Harbor back in eighty-two! Admiral Durrette's got his god-damn mistress down in his bed right now, for Chris'sakes!"

"The Admiral's mistress is a grown woman, Sir. This girl is scarce fifteen," says the good Mr. Pinkham. "Perhaps…"

"Perhaps, Mr. Pinkham, if you would go to Hell," says the Captain, and I hear his unsteady tread as he takes him-self off the quarterdeck. "Send the loblolly boy to my cabin with my medicine and then muster the bloody crew for my inspection!"

The Bo'sun's pipe shrills out and the men are called. I slide down the shroud after the Captain has left the quarter-deck and gone down to his cabin to get his medicine and tend his misery. May he well enjoy his pain.

It seems the Captain never misses an opportunity to shame his men…or his officers—half the ship must have heard him dress down poor Mr. Pinkham like he was a common seaman. I can imagine what this inspection is gonna be like.

As the men assemble in their divisions, all cleaned up and in their best uniforms, I seek out and find Mr. Pelham, the Second Mate, and present myself in front of him.

"Good morning to you, Sir," I pipes, bringing my hand to the brim of my hat and snapping off a brisk salute. "Would you be so good as to tell me my division?"

Mr. Pelham looks down at me, astounded. "Don't make this any more of a travesty than it already is, girl," he growls, after he has recovered from the shock of my appearance. "Why don't you just take yourself down below and stay out of the way?"

I puff up a bit and say, "While I am here, Sir, I expect to do my duty. And for me to go below and hide till...You know that it would be the worst thing for me to do, don't you, Sir."

"*Hmmph!*" he says, and looks me over. I hit a brace under his inspection, thinking that I'm looking right trim and well decked out and that he should notice. I suspect that he's thinking that if the Captain could do something as outrageous as commissioning a girl, then he himself could go along with it and maybe compound the Captain's folly. I guess this is what he figures because he says, "Very well. Gun crew, Division One. The port bow guns. Right over here."

He leads me over to my division and leaves me there. I look them over and a motley bunch they are, from a little boy, who is undoubtedly my powder monkey, to young men who look like they're right off the farm and have yet to shake the manure from their feet, to grizzled old veteran man-of-war men. They are sloppily lined up in front of the guns.

I plant my feet on the deck and I address them. "Good morning, men. I am Midshipman Faber and I am your new division officer." This is met with snorts and grunts of disbelief. I put on the Look and say, "Excuse me, did one of you wish to say something?" I put on my best hooded-eye, haughty upper-class Look. They don't say anything. "I thought not. Now, let's straighten up that line, shall we? Are you in the positions you would be around the guns? Swabbers there, Second Captain there? What? You don't know? Well, we'll have to fix that later, won't we? As for now, line up by height so you look more presentable. No, you here. That's right. Now make sure your toes line up. Good. A little more space between you two. All right."

I go back to the head of the line and say, "I will now inspect you before the Captain gets here. Stand at Attention."

They manage a sorry version of Attention and I take one step, bring my heels together, and execute a smart Left Face and am facing the first man in line. I look him up and down. "Name and rating?"

"Simmons, Miss, Able Seaman."

"You will address me in the future as Miss Faber, or, if it is easier for you, as Midshipman Faber. Is that clear?"

"Yes, Miss Faber," says the miserable Simmons.

"Is that clear to all of you?" I say to my division. They mumble assent.

"Good," I say and resume my inspection of Simmons. I reach up and flick a piece of lint off his jacket. "All right, Seaman Simmons. A better shave next time, if you please."

With that, I do a Right Face, take one more step, bring the heels together, and a Left Face.

"Name and rating," I say.

"Shaughnessy, Able Seaman."

"Able Seaman, what, Shaughnessy?"

"Shaughnessy, Able Seaman, Miss Faber."

"Good." I give him the once-over. Reasonably present-able. On to the next.

"Name and rating." As I turn to face this one, I see he is shaking with fury at being subjected to this indignity, this scrutiny by a woman, a woman not halfway out of her teens, to boot. Finally he gets out through clenched teeth, "Harkness. Gunner. Rated Able."

*Ah.* This is one of the men Harper mentioned as being a leader belowdecks. He is a solidly built man, broken nose, scar on left cheek, muscles working in his strong jaw. His eyes are cased and look out over the top of my head. *Hmmm.*

"Perhaps, Seaman Harkness," I say, "it would be well for you to give your deference and your obedience to my uniform and position and not to the person in it. I think it might be easier for you to think of it that way."

"Yes, Midshipman Faber," he says, taking my advice.

I turn to the next man, and so on down the line.

I know, of course, that the entire crew is watching this ritual with the keenest of interest, and that is good. I have never been shy about being onstage, being the center of attention, and, in fact, I have often craved it, but that is not why I'm doing this now. I'm doing it because I want every man aboard to come to know me very, very well.

I come to the end of the line, to the boy. He is the only one shorter than me, and not by much.

"Name and rating."

"Tam Tucker, Ship's Boy," he says, with a bit of cheekiness in his voice. He is a curly headed, good-looking boy with an air of good humor about him.

"Very good, Tucker. I was once a ship's boy and I enjoyed it very much. How many of you are there?"

"There's three, Mum...er...Miss Faber. It's me, Eli, and—"

"Attention on Deck!"

I turn and go back to the other end of the line and take my position in front and wait for the Captain to get to us. It doesn't take long.

He stumps up in front of me, leaning on a cane. His ship is immaculate, but he, for certain, is not. His eyes are bleary and his chin unshaven. His clothes are dirty and I swear he smells of old, dried piss. And, again, the white stain on the lips. I whip my hand up to the brim of my hat and say, "Division One, ready for Inspection, Sir."

He looks me over and grunts. It is to be hoped that the pain of his gouty leg and whatever is happening in his vile guts has overpowered any amorous thoughts he might have had of me. *May it be so,* I wish with all my heart. He turns and walks down the line, with me following behind. He stops in front of a young seaman whose name is Langley and who is plainly terrified by all this.

The Captain looks back at me and, with a sly look on his face, says, "This is what I think of your division." He lifts his cane and whips it across Langley's cheek, cutting him most cruelly. The boy cries out at the suddenness of the blow, but thank God does not lift his hands in protection, as it probably would have been the end of him if he had raised his hand to his Captain. The blood pours out of the wound and down his face and into the neck of his shirt.

"Your men are a disgrace and your guns are a mess," the Captain snaps to me. I look in his face and see again the horrid tic and evil eye heading off on its own.

"Yes, Sir," I say, knowing full well he did not even glance at the guns, which I had already seen were in good order. "I will attend to it."

The Captain lurches on. I see him go on to cause the same sort of havoc in each of the other divisions until finally he goes to the podium set up on the main hatch. He faces his crew.

"Today's sermon will be the Articles of War." And he proceeds to read the offenses that a poor seaman might commit in the line of duty, most of which are punishable by death. The Captain roars out the word *death* each time it is called for.

"Death! Do you hear me, you miserable whoreson bastards! Death for Insubordination! Death for Mutiny! Death for Anything I Goddamn Well Say! Death!"

He pauses for breath. It is no wonder every man aboard lives in mortal fear of him. Hell if a man abides all this, death if he resorts to mutiny.

"This ship is a pigsty and everyone aboard, officer or man, is a pig, wallowing in his own filth! There shall be no holiday routine today! Back to work, all of you!"

With that, he turns and goes down to his cabin, no doubt to put his leg on a pillow and curse the fates that afflict him so.

Mr. Pinkham, his face red with shame, calls out, "Division officers, you may dismiss your sections. Turn them to and commence ship's work."

I turn to mine. "Harkness. See that the men get something to eat and then muster them here at the guns at Three

Bells. Make sure a plate is kept for Langley. Langley, you come with me. Division One, dismissed!"

With that, I lead the bleeding Langley forward to find the orlop and what passes for a surgeon on this bark.

My cheeks are burning with my own shame at my conduct in not speaking up after the Captain hit Langley. The correct procedure for a captain who finds a minor fault in an inspection is to inform the division officer, who would then dish out the proper punishment to the wrongdoer, and I should have spoken up and said that, but I didn't, and shame on me.

We go down two decks and find what passes for a surgeon sitting in his dark hole of a surgery surrounded by evil-looking saws and knives, which I know are for the cutting off of arms and legs after a battle. He's called a loblolly boy, which is the Navy's word for a surgeon's assistant. This particular loblolly boy is about sixty years old and half blind, peering up at me through dirty spectacles. *Quite a specimen,* I'm thinking, hoping I'm never quite so unlucky as to *ever* come under this man's care.

"Is this part of the Inspection, then?" he says. No, on a normal ship a decent captain would have gotten down this far, but not on this one.

"No," I say, looking around at the dim light and sniffing the fetid air. "We need this man stitched up."

I had examined Langley's wound and I could see the whiteness of tendons beneath the gore, and so knew it needed to be sewn up, otherwise it would maybe fester and would certainly leave a ghastly scar. And on such a pretty lad, too.

"I don't know, Miss Whatever-you-are," he shakily says. "I don't know…"

And then I see his hands shaking with palsy. *Christ!*

"Do you even know your own name, man?" I demand, furious as Langley stands bleeding helplessly beside me.

"Why, yes, Miss, it's Earweg, Miss," he stammers, "Edwin Earweg, loblolly boy."

"All right, then, Earweg," I say, "where's the thread? And I'll need a hooked needle."

"Here, Miss," he says, obviously relieved of not having to do his job. He opens a drawer and hands me the needle and thread.

"Spirits of wine. I'll need some of that, too. And bandages. And healing salve."

"Spirits of wine? Oh, I don't know, Miss, I can't..."

"Yes, you can, unless you want to be brought before your Captain."

"Oh, yes, right now, Miss, right now," he says as he fumbles for a key that hangs on a cord about his scrawny neck. After he manages to grasp the elusive key, he inserts it into the lock of a large chest. "I just now saw the Captain and I gave him his medicines, I did—those on the shelf right there—Salts of White Mercury and Tincture of Lead Antimony, and Arsenic Powder, too. I'll bleed him again tomorrow, I will. He's coming along just fine, he is. Soon be good as new."

He pulls out a quart bottle of spirits that's half full—probably been at it himself, the sod—and I spot another bottle in there with cloudy contents that look familiar.

"Is that paregoric? Tincture of Opium?"

"Yes, Miss. Oh, my, yes. Oh, my."

"Good. Give him a shot of it."

He takes a small glass and, for all his shaking hand, the loblolly boy does not spill a drop.

Langley takes it and tilts his head back and swallows it.

"Like candy," he says.

"A lot have said that," I say, refilling the glass with the clear spirits of wine. "Let's go find some light."

We go forward and find ourselves in the tiny midshipmen's berth with its open hatch above letting in plenty of light. Ned, Tom, and Georgie are there, looking wide-eyed at me and the bloody-faced sailor.

"Here. Langley, get up on the table. Boys, get me some clean rags and some clean water. Georgie, go get Robin." They leave to do it.

Langley climbs on the table and lies down faceup, not looking all too happy. I look up, sensing that there are some above the hatch keeping an eye, or at least an ear, on the proceedings.

"What is your first name, Langley, and what is your age?"

"Joshua, Miss Faber, and I'll be seventeen come Friday, and I...didn't do nothin' wrong, I..." Tears course out of his eyes and down his temples.

"I know, I know," I say. *You were just the youngest and most handsome in the line, which is why he did it.* "Just relax now."

He ain't relaxing, watching me thread the hooked needle and dipping it and the thread into the spirits. I see Robin come into the room.

"We've got to do this, Joshua, otherwise your face might not heal proper, and at the very least you'll have a big nasty scar there and you want the girls to still blink their eyes at you, don't you?" I say in a singsong soothing way. "I know you've got a girl back home, and I bet she's proud of her salty sea sailor, ain't she, Joshua? What's her name? I'm sure she's pretty."

The Midshipmen have come back with the cloth and water.

"Yes, Miss, her name is Rose and she is very, very pretty, and I want to see her so bad."

"Hold Joshua's hands now, Ned and Tom. Robin, if you will hold his head steady." And I lean over. "Time to be brave for Rose now, Joshua Langley."

He is brave.

"We are done now, lad," I say, when I'm mopping the blood from his face and neck. I dab the stitched wound with the last of the spirits and then carefully apply the salve and then wind the white bandage about his head and fasten it with the metal frogs.

I compliment myself on a neat and fast bit of stitching—try doing *this* kind of embroidery, Amy, Dolley, Clarissa, and the rest of you fine ladies back at the Lawson Peabody School for Young Girls, just you try it.

"And you could not have been more stoic, Joshua. You know, I had that done to me once—see, under my white eyebrow here?—and what I remember most about it now is how I cried and howled all the way through it. Here. Sit up."

He sits up, looking slightly woozy.

"Mr. Piggott. Lend your arm to Seaman Langley and take him back to his berth and see that his hammock is slung. He will be on the Sick List for the remainder of this day, at least. Oh, and get his plate of food from the mess deck." They go out, Georgie maybe a bit more shaky than Langley.

I take a pitcher of water and a basin and go into my room to wash up. I leave the door open so I can see Ned and

Tom out there looking greenish—and I don't blame them, as that's probably the first real blood they've seen, close up like that. Robin seems all right, though. He just stands there looking in at me, without expression, as I wash my hands and splash water on my face.

After I'm done, I poke my head out my door and ask, "So what's to eat then, mates?"

What's to eat is burgoo. Burgoo can be a lot of things, from simple oatmeal and molasses, to ground-up hardtack and molasses, to a stew with any number of things in it. Thankfully, this burgoo is the latter and comes with a biscuit. I pack it in with gusto. The others have less appetite after their time in our makeshift surgery. Georgie comes back in and sits down and pokes at his food.

I had done some of that kind of work on the *Pequod*. Being that I was hired on as companion and midwife to Missus Captain, it was assumed that I could bind up the minor wounds that would naturally occur on a whaler— rope burns, cuts that sometimes needed to be sewn up, bashed shins, crushed toes, that sort of thing. They were wrong in that assumption, but I did grow into the role. After all, thanks to the *Dolphin* and the Lawson Peabody, I did know how to sew. What I found to be most effective, however, was the simple laying on of sympathetic female hands, and soft, soothing words.

"Um. This is good," I say with my nose in the burgoo. Someone has gotten me a spoon. I tap the biscuit to deal with the bugs and I put that down my neck, too.

Georgie and the other two boys continue to regard me with some kind of awe. Robin looks like he wants to talk, but I don't let him. I hear the ringing of Three Bells in the Afternoon Watch from the quarterdeck above and aft of us. I stand and go to the small barrel of water lashed to the bulkhead, lift the ladle, and take a long drink.

"I must go and drill my division. Mr. Raeburne, I'll meet you by the foremast at the beginning of the First Dog Watch."

Then I turn and go out to my men.

They are there standing about the guns, looking watchful, as I approach.

"At ease," I say, as I go into their midst, even though not one of them has snapped to attention. At least the ones sitting on the cannons manage to stand up. "Do we have everyone here?"

"Everyone 'cept Joshua," says Harkness, looking straight at me without deference. *Just 'cause you sewed him up don't make you one of us,* I see in his eyes. He's not giving me an inch.

"Yes. Well, I have placed him on the Sick List for the time being, at least. I am sorry for what happened to him today. I am sorry I was unable to prevent it, but that is the way of it here, and well you know that," I say, chin up, and looking at each of them in turn. I see resistance in some, indifference in others, but in others I see a glimmer of hope. And in Tam Tucker's eyes I see boyish glee. *Ah, God save ship's boys.*

"Very well. Take your stations. We shall exercise the guns."

Someone finds his voice. "Pardon, Miss?"

"'Pardon, Miss Faber.' Yes, what?"

"We have never exercised the guns," says the man I recognize as one named Hodge, a seasoned seaman. "We've never been given the powder."

"Then how can you be ready if there's an action?" I say, incredulously. "Have you not even done dry runs?"

"No, Midshipman Faber," says Harkness, rising up before me. "We have not."

*This is amazing, and on a British Man-o'-War, yet. The Captain must, indeed, be mad as a hatter.*

"Well then, now we shall," I say. "Let's everyone go to what they think is their station."

It is a mess. The men mill about, looking confused and shamefaced. They want to do well and they can't. And no wonder, for they have never been shown.

"All right," I say, wearily. "Line up."

They do so and I address them. "Men, we have four eighteen-pound guns under our care. I am, of course, First Captain, and I will aim and fire the guns. Harkness, you shall be Second Captain. You shall second me and act in my place should I fall. You will stand here, between Gun Two and Gun Three."

They are all looking at me, not knowing that, once again, sweat is trickling out of my armpits and down over my ribs. I had seen the guns on the *Dolphin* readied, primed, and shot a hundred times from my perch up on the quarterdeck, standing with my drum next to Captain Locke as he bellowed out *Fire!* and beating on that drum when the occasion called for it, so I know the routine. I know how to do it.

It's just that I never have actually *done* it.

"Shaughnessy, Roberts, Gibbons, and Dalton on pikes. Stand here, here, here, and here. You'll use your pikes to ratchet the guns back and forth, up and down on my command." They move and stand in the right places.

"Now swabbers and rammers: Ropp, Mill, Rusby, Kelly,

Pye, Nichols, and O'Grady, you stand here and here and there and there. You will ram the powder charges in, then the ball, and then the wad. After firing, you will wet the swabs there on the bulkhead to clean and cool the barrels to make them ready for the next charge. If you don't do it thoroughly, the next bag of powder in it may misfire and the gun may explode, which will cause us all great harm. Do you understand?"

Dubious heads nod. But I see some curt nods, too. Some of these men have fired guns and that gives me hope.

"On the ropes we will have Yonkers, Taylor, Clark, O'Leary...er...Hutchinson, Davies"—I'm desperately trying to remember their names from the muster—"Myrick... Batson..." and so on.

Everyone seems to be in place. I look down at the willing face of Tam Tucker, my powder monkey. "Master Tucker. We will need more than one monkey for the bringing up of the powder. Go fetch Mr. Piggott."

He races off and is back in a moment with a perplexed-looking Georgie.

"Shed your jacket, Mr. Piggott. Tucker here will show you the way to the magazine. Since these will be dry runs, you will each take a ball from the pile there down to the powder room. It will take the place of the bag of real powder you will be hauling in a real fight. Tucker, you will take your pretend powder to Gun Number One. Mr. Piggott, you will take yours to Gun Number Three, right there. Do you understand?" They both nod. "Very well, then. We will start the drill when you reappear. Go!"

The boys scurry out, the cannonballs clutched to their bellies.

"Open the ports," I say, "and drop the barrels from the lintels. Rope men, haul 'em back! Now, back out the ports!"

I check the flintlock firing device on Gun Number One. It seems to be in order. I then take the long spike that is hanging next to the powder horn on the bulkhead and ram it down into the touchhole to pierce the bag of powder lying in the breech below so it will be open to receive the priming powder, which I will now pour in. I reach over and take the powder horn from its hook on the bulkhead and throw its lanyard around my neck. I open its top and pour a priming directly in the hole. We now have a column of powder leading down from the top directly into the bag of powder, waiting only for the spark from the flintlock to ignite it.

Harkness has taken up his post of Second Captain between Two and Three. "I assume, Harkness, the reason we did not fire out last night's charge is because it's Sunday? I shall have to go ask permission to fire." It's common practice on ships on a wartime footing to leave the guns loaded overnight and then fire out the damp powder in the morning.

Harkness takes a deep breath and clasps his hands behind his back. "Don't bother, Midshipman Faber. The guns are not loaded."

"What! Why the hell not?" I cry. "What if a French patrol boat snuck up on us in the night?"

Harkness shrugs. "The guns are never loaded. We have never fired them."

"*Never?*" I am astounded. Even though I now knew that the men were not practiced in the firing and rapid reloading of the guns, I expected the guns to be loaded, at least. "Why not? You may speak plain."

"I can't speak plain. You might ask the officers, Midshipman Faber. Common seamen can't question orders from above," he says, his tone implying, *as well you should know, Midshipman Whatever-you-are...*

"Well, we shall see about that," I say. "Meanwhile, we shall have dry runs. Here comes the powder. Prepare to fire Number One!"

I squint over the barrel and see France lying out there beyond the portal. Pretending to be aiming at an enemy ship, I say, "Pikes! Ratchet up Two! Pull around One Point!"

One of these things happens, the other doesn't. Exasperated, I say, "Fire!" anyway, and pull the lanyard on the firing mechanism and there is a snap and a puff of smoke. Had there been a charge in the barrel, there would have been a roar, and the gun would have slammed back on its carriage.

"Pull it back! Swabbers! Up now!" The boys come back with their cannonballs, but no swabbers swab, and the guns stay where they were. Several men grab tools that they obviously have no notion of what they are for and trip over one another and fall to the deck. Everyone looks at me blankly.

"All right. Everybody stop. Stand where you are," I say, glaring out from under my hat. I look at a man standing behind the cannon I had just mock fired. "Do you know you would be dead now from the recoil of this gun? Your legs crushed and your back broken?"

He mumbles, "No, Mum," and moves belatedly out of the way.

"Have any of you ever been swabbers?" A few hands are raised. "How about ratchet men?" A few others raise their hands. "Rope and carriage men?" Even fewer hands are seen.

"Very well," I say, "let us start with just this one gun, with the experienced men at their positions." They move to their proper places.

"All right, we will begin. Fire!" and I click the firing lanyard. "The gun recoils and the swabber shoves his swab down the barrel. Do it!"

It is Shaughnessy who pushes the wet swab down the barrel.

"Now the charge! Tucker!" The boy hands his ball to Shaughnessy and Seaman Yonkers rams it down with his tool.

"The ball, Mr. Piggott!" and Georgie hands his ball to Shaughnessy, who drops it into the barrel. It rolls down to touch the mock powder.

"The wad!" Seaman Yonkers looks about for the wad, but they are not stacked in the slot on the bulkhead where they belong. "Pretend, then!" I shout. I pour more priming powder in the fire hole.

He does and I squint over the barrel again and say, "Pike up Three! Swing her tail two points forward. Fire!" Again I snap the lanyard, and the bit of powder ignites and *pops* and I look at my crew and say, "Let's do it again."

And again, and again, and again.

At last I call a halt. We've been at it for two hours and men are beginning to be placed in positions where they might be of use.

"Men," I say, trying to keep the weariness out of my voice, "we've got to be able to fire each gun and reload in under ninety seconds. Right now it's taking us over four minutes. That is unacceptable. We would be destroyed by even the meanest of French vessels."

I tread back and forth in front of them, thinking. At last I say, "Harkness, you shall drill the men for another hour, bending all your efforts to getting the right man in the right position. I shall see about us getting some powder so that we might have a proper exercise of our guns. Carry on."

With that, I spin on my heel and leave. It is possible that I hear the word *bitch* whispered under someone's breath as I go, but so be it.

It is just before the First Dog Watch and Mr. Pelham is on the quarterdeck as Officer of the Deck. I go up to him and salute.

"Begging your pardon, Sir, but I have several concerns."

His eyes roll heavenward, asking, I assume, for deliverance from this pesky female. "What is it, Miss Faber?"

"Number one. Why do we not have powder to exercise the great guns? We are woefully unready."

He stiffens and says, "The Captain has not authorized the powder. It is not for you to question that."

*Umm.* I decide to hold my tongue on that. "Number two. As ranking Midshipman, I must insist that the midshipmen be put on the quarterdeck watch schedule. They are not learning anything just sitting around their berth." I gulp it all out. I still am not easy at speaking plain to regular officers.

Mr. Pelham eyes me coldly. "Are you implying by all this that the officers on this ship have been derelict in their duties?"

"No, Sir. I know how things lie on this ship and I have nothing but the utmost respect for both you and Mr. Pinkham, and I admire your fortitude in enduring it all. It is because of my special condition that I might have a little more latitude in the correction of some things."

Mr. Pelham looks down at me, a half smile playing about his mouth. "I'll be damned," he says. He looks off over my head. I know he has very little use for me. I know, too, he was certainly looking for a better post than this when he gained his lieutenancy—a fine ship, a fair and noble captain, a chance for glory. Instead he got this—standing on the deck of a Hell Ship commanded by a vile and sick fiend, talking to a girl. "Very well, Miss Faber, you shall draw up a Watch list for your midshipmen and it shall be added to the Quarter Bill. You, yourself, will start it off by standing the Midwatch with Gunner's Mate Smythe tonight."

I hit a brace. "Very good, Sir. While I am here, I expect to do my duty. I assume the Messenger of the Watch will be sent to waken me?"

"Oh, you may count on that, Miss Faber," he says, and turns away. I salute and turn away and go to meet Robin Raeburne at the foremast.

On the way there, Harper comes up next to me and says, *"Psst! Jacky!"* and pushes something into my hand. I look at it and see that it is a fine knife in a smooth leather scabbard and has a tooled leather belt with a shiny brass buckle.

"Thanks, John, but this is much too fine..."

"Don't thank me," says Harper, "it's from Billy Barnes. He was too shy to come up and give it to you himself, to thank you for saving his life."

"Ah," I say, strapping it around my waist. It feels good there. I draw out the blade and test its edge. It is sharp as a razor. "Then thank him for me. And one more favor, John, and then I'll bother you no more: I'll be needing sea dads for the four midshipmen. Older men, well seasoned. All right?"

"Sure, Jacky, anything for an old shipmate."

"Let us go up to the top, Mr. Raeburne," I say when I meet him at the appointed time. Without waiting for an answer, I swing into the ratlines and head up, and he follows.

When we get up under the top, he heads for the lubber's hole and I say, "Wait. Don't do it that way. The men will think less of you for it. Do it like this." And I turn and slip under the back of the ratlines so that I am hanging sort of upside down, but so I can gain the outside edge of the fore-top platform and so slide on that way, which is considered the seamanly way to do it. Me and the other ship's boys on the *Dolphin* would rather be stripped bare, whipped, and keelhauled than be seen going up through the lubber's hole.

He doesn't like it, but he does it. I can see that he's a bit scared, hanging up there all precarious like that, but he gets it done. We go and sit down, him with his back to the mast, and me sitting cross-legged before him.

"There is so much I don't know," he says, miserably.

"You will learn. I will teach you what I know and we together will teach the other lads. To begin with, I have set it up so that we will be standing watches as Junior Officers of the Deck, starting with me on the Midwatch and you relieving me for the Four to Eight. We'll put the boys on a regular schedule, but I think it would be well that they split the long night watches into two-hour sessions. What do you think?"

He regards me. That wounded male hurt comes into his eyes. "You know," he says, "I was well on my way to becoming a man before I was brought here. And now a girl..."

I get up on my knees in front of him. "Robin, I know I'm just a stupid girl, but I know some things, a lot of things, Robin, and I will teach them to you, and then you will be better than me 'cause you're a man and you're stronger and brighter and braver. But right now it's a question of circumstance and experience, and I've got lots of experience in things that I know you want to know about, and I will see that you learn them."

I see that the laying on of hands is necessary now, and I do it. I put my hands on his forearms and lift my eyes to his. "So you see, Robin, that this is the way it has to be. I *must* have you with me on this, else all is lost. Else I am lost, and that's the truth."

*I know, I know, it is a blow to your male pride, but it will be all right, you'll see...*

At the beginning of the Second Dog, Robin and I slide back down to the deck. We have some things resolved and we go into the berth for dinner. The others are there, playing at cards. They look up as we enter.

"Stand up," I say, and when they do, I continue. "Tomorrow, lads, your education as naval officers begins. Mr. Raeburne and I have the two night watches tonight, but in the morn you, Mr. Wheeler, will be the Junior Officer of the Watch for the Morning Watch, and you, Mr. Barrows, shall have the Afternoon Watch. Mr. Piggott, the First Dog. And back again to me for the Second. And so on, in never-ending rotation. Is that clear?"

They gulp and say yes, but Georgie pipes up with, "But what will we *do*, Miss?"

"You will do what the Officer of the Watch tells you to do. If he tells you nothing, then you will stand there at Parade Rest until he does tell you to do something."

They look uneasy and I continue. "You might tell the Officer of the Watch that I expect you to know the name of every single sail that is drawing wind tomorrow, and if you do not know that when I come on watch at six in the evening, you two will each receive two demerits and no dinner. Do you understand?"

They nod.

"Good. And at noon we will join Mr. Barrows on the quarterdeck, and I will show you how to take a sun line to determine our longitude. And then all will join me on the Second Dog to shoot Polaris for our latitude, weather permitting. In the morning Mr. Raeburne shall conduct math class for those not on watch, and I shall drill you in writing, reading, and spelling. All right?"

More nods.

"Good. One other thing. When we are here in the berth, we are Robin, Jacky, Tom, Ned, and Georgie, as we are all fellow midshipmen. But when we are on deck, we are Mister and Miss, for that is how we want the men to address us. Clear? All right then, lads, let's eat."

Just then the door is kicked open and our food arrives, borne by the same surly cook's helper who had delivered our rations before. He is a miserable looking creature, slump shouldered and chinless and not very clean. He drops the tray upon the table and goes to leave.

As he does so, I stick out my boot between his feet and trip him, such that he pitches forth, facedown on the deck.

"Wot? Wot, the hell!" he says, scrambling to his feet, full of indignation.

"Belay that," I say. He looks at me in openmouthed wonder. I put on the Lawson Peabody Look and gaze down my nose at him. "Pick up the tray and go back out and ask permission to enter." He now looks confused. "Do it, or you shall feel the Nine-Tailed Cat scratch your worthless back!" I hiss, and he jumps to his feet, takes the tray, and scurries back out.

Soon there is a scratching at the hatchway door.

"Yes," I say, as icily as I can.

"Dinner, Miss."

"You may enter."

He comes back in.

"What is your name?" I demand.

"Weisling, Miss."

"Very well, Weisling, you may serve us our dinner."

The now thoroughly cowed man enters and goes to put the tray on the table.

"No," I say. "Serve each of us our plates. From the right, if you please. Thank you."

He does it and puts a pitcher of hot tea on the table and a pint of rum in front of Robin and another in front of me. *Hmmm.* At least I'm to get a full ration. I pick it up and hand it back to him.

"I do not drink spirits. Take it back, please. If there is wine, I will have some. If not, I will content myself with tea. *And,*" I say, "make sure that pint finds its way back to the Bo'sun. I *will* check, count on it."

He leaves, and we fall to, talking easily among ourselves of the day's events. Presently, our reluctant servant comes back in bearing a bottle of red wine. He uncorks it and pours me a glass. It is not a great vintage, but it is drinkable.

"Thank you," I say. He leaves the bottle on the table and goes out, no doubt to spread tales of my vicious nature.

"A glass of wine with you, Robin," I say, tipping the bottle over his still empty glass. "It would be better for you to help me with this, rather than to drink that, for you will have to get up for the Four to Eight."

Later, the gentle roll of the ship lulls me as I lie curled in my bed. I think: *It has been two days since I got here and at least half the crew knows my name and who I am. I think I can count some as my friends, and that is good. Tomorrow I shall acquit myself in the same way. If enough are on my side, then maybe I will be all right.*

Little mutinies it will have to be, if I am to be saved.

I wish I had my pennywhistle and was allowed to play it. I wish I had Amy here by my side. Or Judy. I wish I had my seabag and my paints and brushes and disks of ivory—I would do a portrait of Joshua Langley for his Rose. I would like to do that.

I know I have one portrait I will erase so I can use the ivory disk again...no, no...I won't do that at all. What I'll do is wrap that one in a cloth and put it away and maybe someday I'll be able to take it out and look at it again.

A line from a song comes unbidden into my mind. *I wish that my love were in my arms and I lie in my bed once again.*

*It doesn't matter what you wish, girl. Just go to sleep. The Midwatch is a scant three hours away.*

# Chapter 7

James Emerson Fletcher
9 Brattle Lane
London, England
September 9, 1804

My Dear Lost Girl,

My hopes that you were merely off pouting somewhere and soon would turn up all dewy eyed and sorrowful were cruelly dashed this morning when what proved to be your servant, a Judy Miller, appeared in tears on our doorstep with your seabag under her arm.

Poor, red-nosed thing, snuffling about her mistress and how she warned her not to go off dressed like that and how she was supposed to wait till her mistress got back:

"But she never come back, Sir, no, she didn't and I fears that somethin' awful has happened to Mistress Mary, I do, Sir. And she told me to come here if she didn't come back; and she didn't come back, so here I am, Sir. Is she here, Sir?"

My heart sank for I knew that you would never leave your precious seabag, much less leave this poor girl to her own de-

*vices if you were not in some serious trouble. I told your Judy that you were, alas, not here, but I assured her we would find you and she would stay with us until we did. I eagerly questioned her about you and was thunderstruck to be told that you, yourself, had been here at my house the day before yesterday and had been turned away by my mother. Most cruelly turned away, it seems. I will give you an account of what passed that day, as scratching away with my quill keeps my mind off what you might be going through right now.*

"Surely your mistress was mistaken," I said, standing there astounded.

"Oh no, Sir, yer mum throwed her right out in the street! It was your girl Hattie what told me mistress you'd be at the races the next day, which was why she dressed up that way 'cause she thought that would be the only way into the track and I said, 'No, Mistress, don't do it. We'll get in—ain't we the last of the Rooster Charlie Gang what can get into any place in Cheapside,' but she wouldn't listen. No, Sir, she wouldn't. She thought it'd be such a lark and that you'd like to see her in that old carefree way. But it didn't work out like I knowed it wouldn't work out, and now what have we got?"

We have got nothing. Nothing but a growing, seething anger born of a sudden parting of the clouds of doubt and suspicion in my mind, that and a low, animal growl of rage working its way out of my throat…*Motherrrrrr*…

I took Judy by the wrist and we went upstairs to my mother's room.

"What is this, James?" asked Mother. "We do not knock outside a lady's chamber?" Hattie was standing next to her, combing out her hair. She looked up but continued to comb the hair.

101

"Listen to this, Mother, then you will speak to me," said I, pulling poor Judy forward. Judy blubbered out her tale again.

A look of coldness came over my mother's face. Affecting calmness, she took the hairbrush from unsuspecting Hattie's hand and quick as a snake, whipped it across the astounded girl's face. "Get out! You are no longer in my service, Hattie!" Mother hissed, no longer calm.

Hattie, shocked by the pain of the blow, put her hand to her reddening face and tears came from her eyes. Then anger overtook her urge to cry and her voice hardened and she said, "I have served you for eight years, Mistress, ever since I was a girl of twelve. I considered your family to be my family, and this is the thanks I get for my years of faithful service—a kick out into the streets."

She paused and seemed to come to a decision. "All right," she said, "I'll go. But first…"

Hattie turned and looked at me. "Third drawer, right side," she then said, pointing down at my mother's desk. "I should have done that long ago and for that, Master James, I am heartily sorry. I thought I owed my loyalty to your mother. I was wrong."

With that she covered her face with her hands and ran from the room. I went for the drawer, got there before my mother's staying hand, and I pulled it open. There lay a pile of letters that I could plainly see had both your name and your handwriting upon them. I picked them up and looked at my mother in shock and disbelief.

"How could you do such a thing?" I asked, hardly above a whisper.

Mother rose to her full height, her eyes furious. "That

girl is as common as dirt! I have seen her and I know! She is not for one such as you!"

"Mother, I love that girl to the depths of my being and I know she loves me the same and yet you felt compelled to turn her out? How could you do that when you knew how I felt about her?" I was breathing hard, consumed with hurt and outrage. "Or loved me, that is. She could well be dead now, lying in some gutter, because of your unkindness. How could you have watched my face every time I asked about letters, the crushing disappointment writ there each time, when all the while you had those precious letters hidden in that drawer? How could you do that to me?" I was close to tears of rage over such treachery. "I am your son. I thought you loved me."

"I do love you, James, I love you with all my heart and every fiber of my being. I was merely protecting you, my beloved son!"

"Protecting me? From her? From that girl who bestowed her affections upon me wholeheartedly and without reservation and without guile, with open eyes and open heart? From the trusting and brave girl who saved my very life at least twice?"

"Just because thy mare gives thee good service does not mean that thee will dine with her," hissed my mother.

That was the end of it. I knew I could stay no longer in that place. I stood and looked at my mother for what I believe will be the last time.

"Good-bye, Mother. I will send for my things. Judy, come along."

And so I left my beloved childhood home.

James Fletcher
Bartleby Inn
September 28, 1804

Dear Jacky,

The only possible clue to your whereabouts that we have found so far is the fact that, on that day, there was a press-gang roaming the neighborhood where you disappeared. It is possible that they scooped you up, thinking you to be male because of your clothing. If that was the case, you would have been taken to a ship, discovered, and then released; and you shall turn up shortly. That is what is to be hoped for. Until then, I have the bittersweet joy of reading your letters, over and over.

I hope you will not consider it a violation, but I went through your seabag for a possible clue to your whereabouts, an address where you might have gone or somesuch, but it yielded nothing, nothing but the scent of you on your clothing that I confess I pressed to my face and kept there for a long time. I also found the miniature painting of me that you had done and that you reported in your letters that you kept next to your heart. To think that you had kept up your affection for me during all that time with no letters, no word of mutual affection from my unworthy self. That your mistress Pimm and my mother could have caused such a thing makes my very blood boil, and I cannot bear to think of it.

I have left my mother's house, of course, and have taken rooms at the Bartleby, which I can ill afford, having taken both Hattie and your Judy with me. My mother sacked Hattie on the spot, and she certainly was not going to fill her position with your Judy. I am going to try to find good places for the two of them before I return to sea, and I will be glad when I do it as they fuss over me and drive me to distraction.

All this would not have happened if you hadn't been so foolish as to dress up as a jockey. What did you hope to gain? And then running off like that—Jacky, we were so close, so close to being reunited....If you had not run away, we would be planning a wedding right now, not desperately searching for you. Why do you act the way you do? Why can't you ever think? Why, oh why can't you...There. I have kicked over a chair and broken a glass. Judy and Hattie are looking worried.

Jacky, where the hell are you?

I hope for the best but fear the worst.

Jaimy

# Chapter 8

It seems like I had just put my head down on my pillow and gone off to sleep when someone is outside my cabin tapping on the door and saying, *Miss! Miss! You must get up!* And I do, flinging back my wonderfully warm and comforting blanket and planting my bare feet on the cold deck. "All right," I say, all groggy, "I am up."

I sit there and shiver a moment. I can see by the sliver of light under my door that the Messenger of the Watch has left the small lantern outside my door, so I get up and reach out and bring it in.

I splash water on my face and visit the chamber pot, knowing I ain't gonna see it for another four hours. I dress and then douse the lantern and, in the pitch darkness, head up on deck to assume the midnight-to-four watch as Junior Officer of the Deck.

When I get there, my eyes have adjusted enough to the darkness for me to see that Mr. Harvey, the Sailing Master, is passing the watch to Mr. Smythe, the gunnery officer.

"Sailing on the port tack, course zero-zero-nine, main, royals, and gallants set, Mr. Smythe," says Mr. Harvey.

"No sign of enemy activity, Mr. Harvey?"

"None, Mr. Smythe," replies Mr. Harvey, I think a bit drily, as if there has *never* been any enemy activity on this post. "Due to turn to course one hundred eighty-seven degrees Two Bells in the Morning Watch."

I have the feeling the exact same thing is said every night.

"Very well, Mr. Harvey, I have the con."

"This is Mr. Harvey," the Sailing Master calls out to no one in particular, "Mr. Smythe has the con."

"This is Mr. Smythe. I have the con," says the gunnery officer in a similar voice, and so the watch is officially passed. Mr. Harvey leaves the deck.

I go up and present myself. I salute and say, "Midshipman Faber, Junior Officer of the Watch, reporting for duty, Sir."

He looks down at me incredulously. He does not return the salute. "What the hell is this then?" he asks. It seems that Mr. Pelham has not seen fit to tell his fellow officers that this was going to happen. Probably his idea of a good joke on them. Well, this ship could use a few jokes, so I don't mind.

"The midshipmen have been added to the Watch list, Sir. As part of our training."

"And who ordered this?"

"Mr. Pelham, Sir." It's sort of true.

"Christ," he says, without emphasis. "Well, stand over there out of the way."

I go over and stand behind the helmsman at the great wheel so I can keep an eye on the course and the set of the sails. I assume the Parade Rest posture, feet about a foot apart, hands clasped behind back, and wait.

And wait. And wait.

There is a Bo'sun's Mate of the Watch in front of the quarterdeck, as well as a Messenger of the Watch, both of them trying not to snicker at me. *Just you wait. We'll see about that.*

I'm standing next to a brass tube, which I know to be the speaking tube that runs down into the Captain's cabin, which is right under us. The tube ends just above the Captain's bed, and through this device he can both send orders and receive messages from his watch. Through it, I can hear him down there wheezing and grunting, and I move a little bit away.

It is a clear, starlit night, with the moon just coming up, and I can see the loom of the land faintly off to starboard. There are no lights there, and there are no lights shining on us, either. There's only the sound of the water rushing by our side and the creaking of the rigging, that sound that never ceases on a ship under way.

Mr. Smythe lets me stand there a full half hour, I assume to show me my place, till the First Bell is gently rung and then he says with acid contempt, "Very well, Junior Officer of the Watch, let us throw the log."

Gratefully, I leave my spot, reflecting on just how long a half hour can be, and go to the Bo'sun's Mate of the Watch and say, "Give me the log."

With a smirk, he leans down and opens a cabinet built into the edge of the quarterdeck and hands me the log with its knotted line wrapped around it. It is actually *not* a log but a piece of board cut in the shape of a triangle with a hole drilled in each point and a knotted rope run through each of the holes and then braided up and attached to the main line—so that when it is thrown out, it will catch the water and act as a sea anchor and not just skip about on the surface. I take it back on the deck and go up next to Mr. Smythe and unravel it. When I have the log in my right hand and the coiled-up line in my left, I say, "Ready, Sir."

"All right," he says, and I know he's surprised I got this far. "Give me the glass." The Bo'sun's Mate hands him a small sandglass and he squints at it in the moonlight. "Let it go."

I lean out over the rail and I toss the log a little bit forward. I hear it hit the water and the line starts to play out through my fingers. There's fifty feet of clear line and then there's a knot tied every seven fathoms—every forty-two feet, a fathom being six feet—and when the first knot hits my hand I call out, "Turn!" and start counting the knots that slip through my fingers, knowing that Mr. Smythe has turned the glass, which will measure out thirty seconds.... One, two, three...and so on till I hit five and then Mr. Smythe says, "Mark," and I clench my fist around the line and bring it up. I see that my hand is halfway between two of the knots and I sing out, "Five and a half knots, Sir!" Not bad, for light winds, I'll own. The *Wolverine* is not a bad sailor.

I rewrap the rope around the log and hand it back to the Bo'sun, who hands it to the Messenger, who puts it away. I think all are disappointed that I didn't mess up and run away crying.

I reassume my position and resume looking up the sails, to make sure all are drawing well. *Could take a bit of a tuck on the main royal and...there's a light on the shore.*

"Sir!" I say. "There's a light! One point on our port quarter! On the beach, and it's blinking!"

Mr. Smythe slowly turns to look at the light. He seems unimpresssed. "Yes," he says, "it occurs every week or so.

Seems to have no connection with anything. It makes no sense, spells out nothing in either English or French. If it is a code, then we do not know what it is, and we do not know for whom it is meant. I think they do it just to make us wonder. That is so very much like them," he sighs. "We must, however, report them to the Captain in the morning. He insists upon it."

I notice the lookout did not report the light, so it must be a common occurrence, not worthy of mention. But I wonder about it, and my suspicious nature is aroused. Nobody gets up at one in the morning to flash bothersome nonsensical messages. More study is indicated, of that I am sure.

I go back into my usual posture, but after a short while, Mr. Smythe takes mercy on me. Perhaps he thought I did well at casting the log. I don't know. All I know is that he says to me, "Take an inspection tour about the deck. Check the fastenings on the hatches. Make sure the lookout on the bow is attentive. And if, on your way back, you pass through the mess and happen to find a cup of coffee, then you may bring it to me."

"Yes, Sir!" Joyously, I skip forward, delighted to be freed from standing there all motionless and bored. I head down the port rail toward the bow. I put my hand on various lines, but all is taut, as I knew it would be. I come upon the lookout standing in the bow, his foot up on the rail, looking out forward.

"All clear?" I ask as I come up so as not to startle him. It is a seaman I haven't yet met and he turns and regards me with amazement. "I am Midshipman Faber, the Junior Officer of the Watch, and I am making an inspection tour. What is your name, and what is the bottom like here and where are the nearest rocks?"

He stammers out that his name is Gates and that the bottom is sand and mud, which is what the anchor has pulled up so far every time they've dropped it, and the rocks of a jetty are about a half mile off to starboard. "We generally pulls out to sea a bit at night, Miss, especially if we've got an onshore wind, 'cause—"

"I know. Because we don't want to have to try to claw off a lee shore, is why," I say, not to show off but just to let him know. The wind tonight is alongshore, which is good for us—we go up wind, close-hauled on the northern leg of our patrol and run with the wind on our quarter on the southern one.

"Even so, Miss."

"Well, very good, Gates." I say in leaving, "Carry on."

Going back aft, I reach the foremast and look up into the gloom and figure I'll go check on the lookout there and then go down to see about the coffee. I put my hands on the ratlines and up I go.

He either saw or heard me coming for he is standing, leaning back against the mast, arms crossed and looking at me as I step onto the platform. He does not move but continues to regard me in a most self-assured way. The moon is well up in the night sky now and I can see that he is a man of some height, well proportioned about the shoulders and hips. His waist is slender, and his belly is flat, and, I am sure, well-muscled. His hair is curly and light brown and his face has a straight nose and firm chin and good cheekbones. He is most pleasant to look upon, I must say, the very picture of the bold British Tar. He has a merry glint in his eye, and I see his teeth gleam as he smiles at me in an almost insolent way.

I react to this show of disrespect by slapping the Look on my face and saying, "I am Midshipman Faber, the Junior Officer of the Watch, and I am making an inspection tour." I say this in my haughtiest tone, but it doesn't have much effect.

"And I am Joseph Jared, Captain of the Top," he says, and then with the slightest of pauses, "Miss Faber."

This takes me a little aback. This is the other man that Harper said was one of the leaders of the belowdecks men. What's he doing here?

"And why is the Captain of the Top standing a watch that would ordinarily be stood by a common able-bodied seaman?" I demand.

"One of my mates was sick, and so I took his watch."

"That was commendable of you," I say, realizing I'm coming out the worse for this conversation. This man is not going to be an easy one to be won over by my dubious charms. I turn away from him and look out over the sea toward France. "Do you have anything to report?"

"It is a beautiful night, Miss Faber." *Is the man mocking me?*

"Is that all? What about those flashing lights? Why did you not report them down to the quarterdeck?"

"I have been told not to bother with them, and so I don't."

"Do you think they could be smugglers' signals?"

He gives a low chuckle. "Smugglers ain't got no trouble from us. They get right through every time."

"What? Why don't we take them?"

"We always seem to be in just the wrong place to do that, Miss. At the end of our patrol leg, they slip through at the other end. They are quite good at it. They don't even bother to go at night."

"In broad daylight they do it?"

"Even so." He pauses, as if choosing his words very carefully. "It's said that the Captain has ordered that we are on patrol to blockade warships and not common smugglers. 'Course I don't know, just bein' a common seaman and all." Again the merry smile.

*Hmmm.*

"You know, Miss, I was in charge of the boat that brought you back the other day, when you made a run for it. I was the one with the boat hook. You put up quite a fight."

He is perhaps being a little over familiar, but somehow I don't mind. I feel my face reddening in remembrance of that boat hook dragging down my pants. This man must have gotten a real good look at my bare tail.

"But not quite enough of a fight," I say.

"Thanks for saving Billy. He's one of my mates and I would have been sorry to lose his company."

"Well, all right," I say, completely flustered now.

"You won't try another run? None would blame you if you did. You do know what kind of ship you are on, do you not?"

I nod and say, "I am listed on the ship's company now. To run again would be desertion and I will do my duty. I will take what comes."

I go to the edge to go back down.

"I am glad to have met you, Jared," I say in leaving.

"You be careful, Miss," I hear him say. "Do you know what the men call the *Wolverine* when no officers can hear?"

"No. What?"

"The *Werewolf*. You watch your back, Miss."

*That's not all I'll watch, Jared, but thanks,* I think, descending.


There is a cook's helper there in the galley tending the banked cooking fires so they don't have to be relit in the morning, and soon the coffee is brewing. I have a bit of a chat with the man and learn how to make coffee. It is good to know things and I find that people like sharing with you what they know. Makes them feel good and closer to you, like.

I see Muck and his cronies off in a dark corner, muttering amongst themselves. They see me and mutter some more, but I pay them no mind. Gives me the creeps, though—every time I see him, my flesh crawls.

I quickly down a cup and take one up to Mr. Smythe, and as I do, I hear the ringing of Four Bells.

Ah, halfway through, and that bed will feel good, I'll own.


"Robin. Psst! Robin," I say outside his cabin, lantern in hand. He doesn't stir, so I go in his room and hold the lamp up over him. He is on his back and his face is turned to the side and his breath stirs a lock of hair that has fallen over his cheek. He really is a lovely boy, so innocent and boyish looking all asleep like that.

*Seems to be your night for encountering beautiful males, Miss Intending-to-Live-Single-All-of-Your-Life,* I think, ruefully. I put my hand on his shoulder and give him a shake.

"Robin. Come on. It's your watch. You must get up."

His eyes fly open and he looks at me, confused, and he plainly hasn't yet come to his senses because he lifts his hand toward my face and says a word and that word is *Angel.*

"Angel?" I snort. "Hardly an angel, mate. Up with you, now. If you think for one moment, Mr. Raeburne, that I'm standing one minute of your watch so that you can slumber blissfully on, you are mistaken." It's probably the lantern light on my face that made him think that angel stuff.

Then his mind clears and he puts his hands to his face and rubs his eyes. "All right," he says.

A short time later, after we have passed the watch, me telling Robin our course and condition, and him saying he has the watch and Mr. Pinkham watching astounded, I crawl gratefully back into my bed for another three hours of sleep.

My last thoughts are of those lights on the shore.

# Chapter 9

Morning comes early. Very early.

I roll out in my nightshirt to make sure my watch schedule is observed, and sure enough, there's Robin waking Tom for the Morning Watch. He glances over at me, but I just yawn and wave him away, as if I am not yet fit for viewing, as, indeed, I am not. Still, he is slow in leaving the berth until I go back into my room to get ready for the day.

When I come out, Robin is back and Georgie and Ned are at the table and our steward, Weisling, is serving breakfast, keeping himself just this side of surly. *This is much more like it,* I think. Hot tea and oatmeal porridge with maple syrup. I dive in, without ceremony.

When I am done, I pat my mouth and rise. "I'm off to see my division. While I am at it, I will try to see that all of you are assigned to divisions as well. Be back here at ten o'clock for academics. We will all meet at quarter till noon in front of the quarterdeck to take a sun line." And I am off.

When I come on deck, I first check on Tom, to see how he's doing on watch. He's standing there sweating bullets at Parade Rest, and Mr. Pelham, the Officer of the Deck, is pointing out the sails to him. Apparently, Tom had the courage to tell Mr. Pelham what would happen to him at the merciless hands of Senior Midshipman Faber if he did not have the names of all the sails by sundown, as I had ordered.

"And if that is the Foremast, what do you think that sail might be called, Mr. Wheeler?" asks Mr. Pelham, his hands clasped behind him and looking up at the Foresail.

"The Foresail?" quavers Tom.

"Very good, Mr. Wheeler, and the next one up would be called..."

"The Next Sail, Sir?"

"Alas, no, Mr. Wheeler," sighs the Second Mate, "it is the Fore Topsail. And the one over that is the Fore Topgallant, and the one way up there is the Fore Royal. Do you have that?"

"Yes, Sir," says Tom.

"Good. Repeat them back to me."

"Foresail, Fore Topsail, Fore Topgallant, and Royal," says Tom.

"*Fore* Royal, Mr. Wheeler. There are several Royals on this ship," says Mr. Pelham, severely.

"Sorry, Sir. Fore Royal it is, Sir," says Tom, miserably. I can see his knees shaking. This is probably the first time he has spoken directly to the second officer.

"Good," says Mr. Pelham. He turns to the Bo'sun's Mate of the Watch and says, "Acquaint Mr. Wheeler here with the rest of the square sails and make sure he knows them. Then on to the fore-and-aft sails. We must ensure that Senior Midshipman Faber will not have our young Mr. Wheeler lashed to the grating and whipped for not having yet mastered the principal sails and all the attendant lineage by nightfall, as she has promised would befall him."

I step up on the quarterdeck, salute, and say, "Good morning, Sir. I hope you are well."

"Yes, Miss Faber, I am quite well," he says drily. "What do you want now?"

"Sir, I would like the other midshipmen to have assignments for Quarters, Special Sea Detail, in fact all the Special Conditions on the Watch, Quarter, and Station Bill."

"And that has not yet been done?"

"No, Sir. The midshipmen have not been aboard that long," I say, to cover up any officer's negligence in not making those assignments. I know how things go here. If there is no direction from the top, then there is no direction.

"Why is it, Miss Faber," he says with a heavy, theatrical sigh, "that I am sure that you have some suggestions concerning this?"

"Well, Sir, I think it would be well if Mr. Raeburne was made head of Division Two, the after four port guns, just aft of my Division One, so that I might be able to pass on to him any small knowledge of gunnery that I might have, such that we might get to such a level of competence that Mr. Smythe could give us some real instruction in the art of gunnery, Sir." There, I've covered Smythe's tail, too. He really should have been doing that all along. But then, if he's not given the powder, how can I blame him?

"And just where did you learn this rudimentary gunnery?"

"On the deck of HMS *Dolphin*, Sir. The quarterdeck was my station in all the Special Conditions, and I was able to observe much."

"Ah, yes. I forgot. 'Bloody Jack,' and all that. So that book is true?"

"Some of it, Sir."

"All right. What of the others?"

"Mr. Wheeler and Mr. Barrows would serve well as Fire Snuffers. It is a common midshipman billet. As for Mr. Piggott, I would like to keep him close to me, as he is young and has much to learn."

I see Tom's chest rise in a bit of pride at being given a real job and not lumped in with little Georgie. Males are *so* transparent, whatever their age.

"Consider it done, Miss Faber. Join me below in the gun room after my watch and we will pen them in."

"Thank you, Sir," and with that I salute, do an About-face, and head for my division.


"Harkness, I was much pleased with yesterday's drill. We will carry on in the same way today. Stations, everyone! On my signal...Now!" Tucker and Georgie dash off for the powder and the drill is on.


After an hour, we have got the turnaround time down to two minutes. Not quite good enough, but better than yesterday's mess. I leave Harkness in charge and go to help Robin set up his crew. They have been observing my crew and it goes well. So well, in fact, that Robin is able to assign a good man, one Seaman Merrill, to conduct the drills and follows me to the berth to start on the boys' academic education. Robin will do the math, and I will do the reading and writing.

I believe Robin is standing up somewhat straighter today.

The boys are certainly not lacking in some education, being nobs and all, compared to the Dread Brotherhood of

119

the *Dolphin,* us bein' street scum and all. Except for Jai—
Never you mind.

At the ringing of Seven Bells in the Morning Watch, which means eleven thirty, I get up and say, "That's it for today. Take up your slates, lads, and I'll meet you on deck and we'll do a sun line for longitude. Briskly, now. I must go see Mr. Harvey for some equipment."

I knock on the door to the gun room, the place where the officers hang out and take their meals.

"Enter."

I go in and look about. I see the doors leading to the officers' rooms. I see a long table, no doubt where they dine. I see books and charts. I see Mr. Harvey seated at the table, engrossed in writing in what appears to be a journal. He has a glass containing some brown liquid in front of him. He looks up and sees me. He doesn't groan out loud, but I know he wants to.

"What is it, girl?"

"Midshipman Faber," I say, correcting him. "I would like to borrow a quadrant and a local chart to take a sun line with the other midshipmen."

He barks out a short, bitter laugh. "Of course. A Child Shall Show Us the Way. Right over there in that cabinet."

I follow his gaze and go to the oak box and begin to bend over and then think better of it. I kneel down in front of it instead. The less I wave my tail around in the air, the better, I figure, no matter which male is in attendance.

The quadrant is lying on a velvet cushion and I gently take it up. As I rise, Mr. Harvey hands me a rolled-up chart.

"And a parallel rule, too, if you would, Sir, and then I will bother you no more."

He reaches back on the shelf behind him and slides it over to me, smiling in a strange sort of way. "Oh, but you have bothered me, you have, Miss. But think nothing of it," he says.

As I leave, I'm thinking it's a little bit early for him to start in to drinking.

"Mr. Pelham, may I borrow Mr. Wheeler for this exercise?" I ask.

"What? And give up the indispensable Mr. Wheeler? Oh, very well. I imagine we shall survive his absence." There are some snickers from his watch. Mr. Pelham is a man who hugely enjoys his own wit, I have seen, but I like him anyway.

"Thank you, Sir," I say as Tom joins Robin, Georgie, and Ned by the starboard rail. "And, Sir, if you will tell us the time when we say, 'Mark,' I will thank you for it." He nods and pulls out his watch.

"Now, lads, here's the way of it. Robin will take the quadrant here and find the sun in this little smoked mirror here on the bottom. No, you idiots! Don't look directly at the sun. You'll go blind! You three just look at the scale here while Robin rocks the quadrant back and forth, making the mirror image of the sun swing back and forth, this image of the sun's lower edge just touching the horizon, and read out the degrees on that scale right there. They will get bigger and bigger until the sun reaches its apogee and that will be the Local Apparent Noon, and then the degrees will get less, and you'll say, 'Mark!' when that change happens and

Mr. Pelham will mark the time on his watch and then we'll be able to figure out our degree of longitude by comparing the time here with Greenwich time to which Mr. Pelham surely has set his watch. Simple but elegant, don't you think?"

"I can't see the horizon, Miss Faber," says Robin, squinting through the eyepiece. "France seems to be in the way."

I look out and see the truth of that. *Damn! Every time I get full of myself I get slapped down!*

There are guffaws from the quarterdeck.

"Come up here, all of you," says Mr. Pelham, laughing. "Try shooting it off the fantail where you have a horizon to the south. You ought to know, Miss Faber, that, unless you have willed it otherwise, the sun does rise in the east and sets in the west, so the south would be the place to take its apogee."

My cheeks are burning. The whole ship has seen my stupid mistake. I meekly take my place with the other boys as Mr. Pelham explains the procedure much more clearly than I did, and soon they are reading the numbers as Robin swings the quadrant back and forth, now making the sun's image just touch the knife-edge horizon.

"Sixty-eight degrees, two minutes, seven seconds... eight seconds... nine seconds... eight seconds. Mark!"

Mr. Pelham looks at his watch. "Twelve o'clock, two minutes, thirty-five seconds. Get out your slates and figure it out, lads!"

The boys whip out their chalks and cipher away. To make up for my mistake on the horizon, I disdain the slate and do the figuring in my head and I do it fast.

"Three hundred and forty-nine degrees, twelve minutes, thirty-five seconds, Sir!" I bark out.

A smirk crawls across Mr. Pelham's face. He spreads out

the chart on a table that is there for just that purpose. "Let's see here. Hmmm. What have you got, Mr. Raeburne?"

"Three hundred and fifty-nine degrees, twelve minutes, thirty-five seconds, Sir." Robin looks at me sheepishly, like he knows something.

*Fifty*-nine degrees? Oh, Lord, another mistake! I forgot to carry the nine!

"Wait, Sir...," I stammer, but I am not to get out of it.

"Now, now, Miss Faber. Let's just see where you have us now." He affects a look of amazement. "Why, my word! You have placed us right here in the very middle of Paris, itself!"

There is laughter, not only from the deck, but also from the rigging.

I bow my head and get ready for more abuse. Mr. Pelham strides over to the rail and looks down. "Why, our bow is cleaving the very cobblestones of le Boulevard de la Madeleine right now! See how they part and fall to the side."

There is more laughter...and then there is not.

There is a dead silence and a chill. I turn around. The Captain has come on deck. He looks around at us and says to Mr. Pelham, "Playing with the brats, are you, Pelham?"

I quietly say, "Attention on deck," and get my boys in a line.

"No, Sir, begging your pardon, I was merely instructing the midshipmen in taking a sun line," says Mr. Pelham. The Second Mate keeps his head up, showing some spine, it seems to me.

The Captain looks down the line of my midshipmen. "Why are they here?"

I save Mr. Pelham from more woe by stepping out and saying, "As Senior Midshipman, I have instituted an education program for the middies, as well as adding them to the

Watch, Quarter, and Station Bill." I pause. "If it please you, Sir."

Well, it doesn't please him. He turns on me and says, "You are a cheeky one, ain't you?" he says, looking around my back all plain at my bottom. "In any number of ways."

*Maybe it would be well if these britches weren't quite so tight.*

"Well. We shall see about your cheekiness soon, shan't we?" says the Captain.

Mr. Pinkham is by his side and the Captain turns to him and says, "The same sailing orders as yesterday. Do not diverge from them in the slightest degree. Do you understand?"

"Yes, Sir," says Mr. Pinkham.

"Good, now, now call..." and a spasm of pain crosses the Captain's face and he doubles over and almost falls to his knees.

"Sir!" says Mr. Pinkham, putting his arm under his Captain's and trying to hold him up.

"Damn!" says the Captain, sinking to his knees.

It is plain that he is very sick. Mr. Pelham goes over to him and takes his other arm and helps him to his feet.

"My cabin! Get Earweg! Tell him medicine... and I need to be bled!" gasps the Captain, and the two officers take him down. Before Mr. Pelham leaves the quarterdeck, he says, "Mr. Wheeler has the con. I will be right back."

Tom looks up at the sails, astounded. Well, after all, he was the Junior Officer of the Deck at the time and it is his right. I am jealous, of course, as I feel that I should have been the first middie to have the con, but so be it.

———

At the noon meal, served by the still sullen Weisling, whom I have nicknamed the Weasel, to the delight of the lads, the dinner really *is* meal with some bits of meat in it. I tuck it in and head back out to see about things.

My division is securing from drill. I shall drill with them each day, but I feel that they have come as far as they can without live fire. We shall have to live with it.

Leaving Harkness to dismiss them and put them to useful labor, I cross the deck, heading for the other rail to have a look about and I pass through a group of Waisters pretending to work on some chafing gear. Muck is among them, smirking away as I pass, then I hear low mumbles and then low and insinuating laughter. I have been trying to avoid him as much as possible, but I know I can't let this go, so I turn around with my haughty Look and say to Muck, "Is there something you wish to say to me, man?"

He ducks his head and puts his knuckle to his brow. "No, Miss," he says, "it warn't me what spoke." I have noticed that Muck has grown in confidence as he has found no one on board who recognizes him as a corpse seller. No one but me, that is, and I shall keep my own counsel on that, at least for the time being.

Muck seems to have become the leader of this surly bunch, and I know how he did it, too. He did it by stirring up and feeding their discontent with his lies and whispered insinuations. I look around at the other Waisters, and a worthless bunch they are, sitting there smirking and fiddling with pieces of line and canvas.

"If there is any among you who would doubt for one moment that I would not have you lashed to that grating and given a dozen for insubordination and lack of respect, let him stand up now," I say.

The grins disappear. I notice Harkness has come up next to me, with a belaying pin in his hand. I have the feeling he has as much use for this bunch as I have.

"Very well," I say. "This deck is in need of cleaning. Holystone and sand. Now! I will inspect in two hours and this deck had better be gleaming whiter than snow, or, by God, your backs will pay!"

I've got the First Dog Watch and I'm looking out toward the land. We are at the southernmost point in our patrol and there, there, way to the north is a ship heading out from the coast.

I leap into the rigging and gain the foretop. Shielding my eyes, I see that it is a two-masted schooner, probably 120 feet long, and very probably laden with rich contraband.

I feel my larcenous Cheapside self rising to the surface, elbowin' my fine upright Lawson Peabody lady self rudely to the side, and I realize I ain't come so far from Little Mary, that small thief who ran the streets of London not so long ago. It is she who now shouts in my ear, *Prize Money! Prize Money!*

Every Man Jack—and one Jill—on this ship knows these would be lawful prizes. *Why ain't we takin' 'em?*

I notice a movement at my side and I see that Jared, the Captain of the Top, has joined me.

"That is a legal prize, Seaman Jared," I hiss and grab his forearm. I can feel the corded muscles tighten under my grip.

He looks down at my hand and then in my eye. "Aye" is all he says, but he gives me a significant look.

I watch the smuggler heave out of reach. She seems to show us her tail with impudence. *Damn! Something is going on here that ain't right. We ain't doin' our job!*

"All hands aloft to make sail!" comes the cry from below. The ship is going to turn to the northern leg of her patrol. *A little late now,* I think.

I can see, far off to the south, another ship making a turn. That would be the British patrol just below us, linking the northern limit of his patrol with our southern one.

I climb on down to the deck.

And so the day is done. For me there were setbacks, humiliations, and such. But then, every man on board now knows my name and who I am, for better or for worse. I think I have done what I can, for now. The rest is up to Providence, or to luck. And so to sleep. I've got the Four-to-Eight.

# Chapter 10

The Captain is sick. He's bad sick. We can hear him thrashing about in his cabin, groaning and cursing everything about him. Every soul on this ship hopes with all his heart that he dies of this affliction, and soon.

The ship hums right along in the Captain's absence. It's been a good two weeks now and we all rejoice in it. We *generally* rejoice, for he did appear once—about a week into the Captain's illness, he staggered out onto the open deck, cursing and clutching his belly, when he tripped over a sailor named Micah James who was bent over scrubbing the deck where some tar had spilled. When the officers had pulled the furious Captain back to his feet, he ordered the man bound up, hands and feet, and set upon a barrel. A noose was knotted and put around his neck and drawn up tight to the main yardarm. We all had to watch in horror and pity as young Micah messed his trousers as he stood there crying and shaking on his tiptoes, sure in the knowledge that he was going to die.

The Captain then crept back down to his cabin, ordering that Micah be kept teetering there till the ringing of the noon bell and then taken down and given twelve. That is, if he had not fallen off the barrel and choked to death before then.

Mr. Pinkham, upon seeing that the Captain was in his cabin and not likely to come out, allowed several of Micah's mates to stand about him to catch him should he fall. He was, however, given the twelve lashes when he was taken down. Though he was not in my division, I went down to the orlop, where he was taken afterwards, to put on the salve myself and to say soothing words.

Down there in the orlop, Earweg, the loblolly boy, said it was the Captain's recurring ill humors and bad phlegm, picked up when he was on a slaver on the west coast of Africa, that's causin' all this. *Serves him right then,* I thought, as I put the greasy balm on the welts of the crying boy's bloody back, tears comin' to my own eyes, *for him bein' a slaver and all.*

I reflected that, once again, Captain Scroggs had managed to strike fear and terror into his crew, while staying just this side of a chargeable offense under Naval Regulations.

*Oh, may you truly rot in Hell forever, Captain, for the things you have done!*

Several days later, as Robin was relieving me of the watch, I saw Earweg go down into the cabin with a scalpel and a bowl still crusty with dried blood to bleed the Captain again. I clutched Robin's arm and made him promise me that if ever I am sick or wounded, that man is *not* to be let anywhere near me. Not even for amputations, which are what the surgeons and loblolly boys are mainly here for. I'll take my chances without them...and without their so-called medicines.

———

I had the Midwatch last night and it is now morning and I'm at the table with Ned and Tom and Georgie going over some geography. I've found some books lying about and gotten others from the officers, and I'm pointing out places on the charts that are in the books and telling them that they may very well visit those places of wonder. Their eyes grow big as their fingers trace over the lines of latitude and longitude and the trade winds and the trade routes and names like Singapore and Madagascar and Cancún, names of places that do not sit easy on their British tongues but do excite their young minds.

There are pieces of rope and metal strewn about the berth, evidence of the boys studying their marlinspike seamanship with their sea dads.

"All right, lads, that's enough for today. Do your penmanship exercises later and put them...Oh, never mind," I say as Tom and Ned skip out with their whipcords in their hands. I know they're heading for the rigging to sit at the feet of Morrison and Brady, their sea dads, and learn their knots and splices and such, but really, mostly to sit there and listen to their sea stories.... *"And then, lad, we doubled the Cape with half the men dead and the other half drunk and we come upon the Dutchman himself, glimmerin' all ghostly and white out there on the horizon, the moans of the damned souls within comin' at us from across the water, their dead and rotting arms reaching out of the gun ports, the putrid flesh hangin' like rags off 'em, and I swear on me sainted mother's grave that it's true and..."*

Georgie, though, doesn't run out with the others, even though I know he's been getting along famously with Amos

Gooch, a disreputable and bewhiskered old reprobate who is, of course, a perfect sea dad for young George.

"What's the matter, Georgie?" I ask, when I see him hanging his head and running his finger aimlessly through some spilled tea on the tabletop.

He doesn't say anything. "Come, Mr. Piggott," I say. "Let's have it out."

He reddens and stammers, "I...I don't think I'll be able to stand up...in battle, like...when it comes time for me to do that, I don't, Jacky, I don't think I'll be brave enough to do it. Not like you were."

"Like I was what?" I ask.

"Brave. In the book. You were brave. You stood up."

*Oh.*

"Has everybody read that damned book?"

"Everyone who can read, I guess. There's two copies on board. There are some who can read who've read it to those who can't. I've read it twice."

*Sweet Jesus, what next?*

"Hmmm." I think it over. "Well, for one thing, I wasn't brave at all. I was terrified, and anyone who isn't terrified at a time like that is a fool. You just concentrate on doing your job and try not to think about it. Think about your duties, not the fight. Pretend it's an exercise. Anything to get through it. Like they say about the life aboard a Man-o'-War—a year of sheer boredom and five minutes of sheer terror."

I pat his hand. "Put it out of your mind, Georgie, we might be here on this patrol forever, growing old together."

He nods, but I don't think I made him feel any better about it.

I reach out and put my arm around his waist and pull him to me and say, "Georgie, I don't know why the world is the way it is. I don't know why we can't all, French and English alike, throw the cannons over the side and sail off as merchant ships, or ships of discovery, and see the wondrous world in all its splendor—see the Bombay Rat and the Cathay Cat and see the kangaroos and wombats and Hottentots and all of it. I've met some French people and they ain't all that bad. Some are downright good, even."

I do know why, of course—it's 'cause if Bonaparte destroys the British fleet, then all he will have to do is put a line of frigates at the top of the Channel and a line at the bottom and then he could ferry his army across in barges and England would lie there helpless to stop him.

"I know it's all stupid, Georgie, but it comes down to this: If Boney kills us all and sinks our ships, then he'd be in the homeland, Georgie, he would. And I've read what he said he'd do—conquer and pillage and I don't know what all. He ain't gonna be nice if he wins, Georgie, no, he ain't, and so it comes down to that. And all I can say is keep your head down, your backside covered, and hope you don't disgrace yourself when the time comes. That's all I ever did."

I think back to my days up on Hugh the Grand's shoulders, reading the newspapers pinned outside the printer's shops and seeing cartoons of Boney getting his troops over the Channel by balloon, by kite, by barge, any way he can. In a land war we would probably prevail, eventually, but it would be bloody. Blood would run in the gutters of the streets of our cities, as it now runs from the scuppers of our ships during battles.

I know the why of it, but I don't have to like it.

"So, Georgie," I say, running my hand over his curly head, "put it all out of your mind and go see Amos Gooch and listen to some more of his lies. Learn how to put an eye splice on a line. All right? Good." I give him an affectionate pat on his tail as he goes out.

I get up and stretch and head out. I cross the deck, checking the rigging and gear and find nothing out of order. I do notice, however, some thick clouds building up on the western horizon. We'll have to keep an eye on that.

I ain't got a sea dad, none assigned, anyway, but Joseph Jared always seems to be around when I might be needing some instruction in seamanship. Like now, when I sit down on the capstan, with my own bit of line, he sits down beside me.

"The Turk's head knot, Jared, I swear I'll never get it," I say, helplessly.

He chuckles and takes the line from my hand and says, "Here now, Miss Faber, you just take the bitter end and put it over the lay of the line and bring it around here..."

There are days when the ocean is a serene wonder, delighting the heart and mind of all who observe her with its infinite variety—beautiful greens and blues, mirroring the soaring sky and puffy white clouds above. Seabirds play above the swells and gentle waves, and God lays His hand upon the waters and all is calm.

This ain't one of those days.

The sea has been working up all this day—first the freshening breeze that had a sense of foreboding in it, then the quickening whitecaps whose tops were quickly sheared off by the wind and sent scudding over the darkening seas, then the skies turned to dark gray. There is a deepening of the wave troughs and then a howling gale comes right down upon us. It is a dangerous storm for it comes at us from the sea and not the land, which means if anything goes wrong, and things go wrong at sea all the time, then we will be driven ashore, wrecked, and if any of us live, we shall be captured and stuffed down in some French prison.

It is what the sailors call a living gale, a storm so powerful and treacherous that it seems to be actually *alive*, driven by some evil force that has it in for you, personal-like. I have the Evening Watch and throughout the watch we have trimmed back sail to almost nothing—there is only the forestaysail up to keep us pointed right, so we can take the heavy seas on our bow. Mr. Pinkham has the watch.

Three hours into the watch and I'm wet and bone tired and looking up at that lonely sail quivering up there, stiff and taut under the tremendous pressure of the wind, the only thing keeping us from disaster. *I don't know if it looks quite right*, I'm thinking, *but maybe it's just my nervous imagination.* I wipe the rain out of my eyes and peer more closely at each part of the sail and the lines that hold it. *What's that flutterin' there at the foot of the sail? Is it... Yes, it is! The chafing gear has torn away!*

"Mr. Pinkham!" I shout over the wind. "The forestaysail! It's chafing at the clew! Look! The line might part!"

He looks up through the rain and says, "Damn! You are right. Messenger, call for Seaman Jared and—"

But I'm already gone. I jump off the quarterdeck and go hand over hand along the rail against the wind and spray, already drenched and wishing for my old oilskins from the *Pequod*. There are coils of rope every few yards along the side, and I take one and throw it over my shoulder. I find Jared and his topmen together in the fo'c'sle, looking worried.

"Jared! The forestaysail sheet is chafing at the clew!" I shout over the howling of the gale as I mount the ratlines. "We've got to double up that line in case it fails!"

And with that I'm on the ratlines heading up the foremast to the foot of the forestaysail. I think I hear Jared shout something, but I can't hear what it is. When I reach the sail, I put my hand on the clew where the line is attached and sure enough I can see it is almost worn through where it has rubbed against a bare yard. The line has three thick strands in it and two are already gone. The canvas chafing gear that was supposed to protect the line had slipped and come loose. I think of Muck and his slackers who are supposed to take care of chafing gear. *Damn! I've got to hurry! If that last strand parts, the sail will let go and we will be lost! We'll fall off the wind and be caught broadside to the waves and swamped! Hurry!*

The sail is quivering like a live thing under my hand, but I manage to get the whipped end of my rope through the eye of the clew and throw several half hitches on it and when I get it done I find Jared by my side and I think he's snarling at me for being up here.

"I got it!" I shout in his ear. "Get this line down to the men on deck and have them haul it in and secure it!" He takes it and flings the coil below. In a moment I let my breath out in relief at seeing the line jerk, then grow straight and hard as it takes the strain of the sail.

"I'm going up to check the head halyard to see if that's chafing as well!" I yell to Jared.

"Wait, you fool! You—," I hear Jared say, but I'm already climbing farther up the mast, up to where the forestaysail halyard at the head of the sail secures it to the fore-topmast.

I get there, check it out, and it seems all right—under a lot of strain but holding, with no signs of wear. The mast is whipping great arcs in the sky with me clinging to it—I must be traveling twenty to thirty feet through the air on each swing.

I hang on and look out into the gale at the mighty waves heaving and roiling and coming at us is…*Oh, my God*…I am not quite believing what I am seeing off the port bow. There are waves, yes, and they are many and huge but there, there about fifty yards out, is a monster comber, a wave twice, three times bigger than any of the others. *Oh, Lord…*

"Green water comin' over the bow!" I shriek. "Look out! Clear the fo'c'sle!"

All below dive for the hatch or else grab onto tackle and wedge themselves in and try to tie themselves down with whatever they can find, for what they know is coming.

I hang on without a shred of hope. I have no line with which to tie myself down, I have nothing to shield me from the inevitable. In desperation I wrap both arms and legs around the mast and helplessly watch the approach of the rogue wave. Then the ship dips down, way down, impossibly down into the trough of the wave and the *Wolverine's* bow is swallowed up. The whole front end of the ship disappears under water that is not white foam but pure green water. Then that green wall comes rushing up at me and hits me hard, so hard, and I ain't in no wave, I'm in the body of the sea itself, and I redouble my grip of both arms and legs but I know it ain't gonna do any good as the wave slams up into my nose and claws at me and proceeds to rip me off the mast to take me into its belly for good and ever.

*I commend my body to the sea and my soul to God* is what I think is gonna be my last thought, as my hooked fingers are pulled off the mast and my legs let go but then, oh then, an arm of iron goes around my chest and tightens and I am held fast as the wave tears through us and past.

The first thing I see as the water leaves my face is the furious eyes of Joseph Jared a few scant inches in front of my nose.

"You are a *stupid* girl, no matter what else you believe yourself to be!" he shouts over the roar of the retreating wave. He takes his arm from around my chest and puts his free hand around my neck and brings us face-to-face, nose to nose. "Now get down below and let us do our damned job!"

I look at him through the strands of my hair and nod weakly. He lets me go and I slink back down to the deck, considerably chastened. I could write him up for that. Touching me like that, I mean.

But I won't.


"You are useless to me in that condition," snarls Mr. Pinkham upon seeing me stagger back on the quarterdeck, knees shaking, teeth chattering. "Go below and go to bed. You may consider yourself on report for leaving the quarterdeck without permission. We will deal with that in the morning. Mr. Raeburne may assume the Midwatch, but I do not want the squeakers up during this as I do not want to have to watch out for them. Do you understand?"

"Yes, Sir." *And bless you, Sir . . .*

———

I stumble down to the berth and stand dripping, my body shaking with cold and I say, "Give me something hot to drink," and a cup of something is put in my hand and I think it's tea with maybe a dollop of rum in it *and I'm sorry, Millie,* but I gulp it down anyway and there's some hot stew and biscuit and I get that down, too. I look at them standing about staring at me as the *Wolverine* pitches back and forth. The overhead hatch has already been secured. It is very dark in the berth.

"Robin, Mr. Pinkham says you may assume the Mid-watch, but you younger ones are to stay below tonight..."

To their credit, both Tom and Ned protest, but I know their hearts are not in it. Georgie doesn't say anything. He just crouches, curled up in the corner, white with fear as the *Wolverine* pitches and yaws and creaks and groans and slams back and forth as it is flung about by the storm. The lantern is hung above and it swings, casting crazy patterns on the faces below it. I don't blame Georgie—what sane person could think that such a fragile thing as the *Wolverine,* with its hundred or so scared souls, could possibly survive something like this?

"It is almost time for the Mid, anyway," says Robin, putting on his oilskins. "I'm sorry. I should have offered these to you before you went on watch. I forgot that you had none."

"You are good, Robin, and think nothing of it. I have found that my pride needed a good soaking down anyway, for all of that."

I get up and stand dripping before him, and I reach out and take his hand and hold it in mine. "Take care out there, Robin Raeburne. It is a hellish night."

He sucks in his breath. Abruptly, he takes my hand and

raises it to his lips. He looks at me over our clasped hands but says nothing. He turns on his heel and leaves, closing the hatch behind him.

"Go to bed, boys, and be thankful for Mr. Pinkham's kindness," I say, and gather myself up and head to my room. I go in and strip off my soaked garments and wring them out in my basin and hang them as best I can to dry. Tomorrow I'll hang the clothes close to the cooking fires to help them along, but I know I'll be back in my jockey garb in the morning.

I towel off, throw on my nightshirt, whip back the cover, and crawl gratefully into bed, and never was bed so soft and never was bed so sweet. The storm is abating in the way of wind and high waves and only presses my face against my pillow in a gentle way now. It's funny, but when I'm in my bunk, I feel the motion of the ship, of course, but the closest and most personal thing I feel is my face being pressed into the pillow as the ship comes up from a roll, and then not being pressed as the ship falls back down, and then pressed again, so it's like there's a hand on the side of my head mashing me down and then not and then...

And then there's this tremendous *Crrraaaacccckkkkkkk!* as a thunderclap explodes overhead, and then the long, low rumble of the thunder as it washes over the ship and fades away. The winds and waves are dying, but here come the rainstorm and lightning and now the rumbling thunder and...

*Crrrraaaackkkkkkk!* There's another, and it sure sounds close. Sure hope it doesn't hit the mainmast. Sure hope they've got Doctor Franklin's lightning rod, sure hope...

*Christ! Somebody has just crawled into my bed!*

I feel the body slip in next to me, and I grab the knife that I keep at my bedside, but...

*Georgie?*

"Georgie? What are you doing here?" I ask, astounded.

"Please, Jacky, I'm so scared..."

"But, Georgie, you can't stay here, I'm not..." I'm not dressed is what I'm not. Oh, well...

I lift the edge of the covers and the puff of hot and moist air that comes up to my face tells me that he has been crying. *Oh, Georgie, no...*

*Crrraaaaaccccckkkkkkk!* Another salvo from the heavens hits the ship and he shudders and burrows into my side.

"I'm scared, Jacky, please let me stay with you!" That's backed up with another *Crikkklecrikklecaraaaaakkk* from the sky and his trembling redoubles.

"It's just lightning and thunder now, Georgie, and I can tell it's moving away. Come, let's try it on the next one. Here."

There is a flash of lightning—I can see the faint light flicker through the seams in the wall to my left, which is also the side of the ship. The boards do not fit all that tightly together and there is a coating of droplets on the inside tonight—they will collect and form rivulets and course down my wall and then down into the bilges. It will be damp in here for a few days after this storm, I know, but still, better in here than out there.

Upon seeing the flash of lightning, I put my arm around his shuddering form and count, "One, one hundred, two, one hundred, three, one hundred, four..." and then the roll of thunder comes. *Rumblerumblecrrraaaaaaaackkkkkkk!*

"See, Georgie, it's four miles away now."

"Don't care, don't care. I'm scared and I want…"

"What, Georgie, what do you want?"

He gasps at the next thunderclap and says something that I know is from the very bottom of his little soul.

"I want my mother…"

The breath goes out of me. There it is.

*Ah. Georgie, we all want our mothers, don't we…*

I gather him to me and say, "All right, Georgie, but this has to be the last time you do this."

He burrows his face in my chest. His breath is hot for a while and then it is not. Soon his breathing becomes regular and I know he is asleep.

I smooth back his hair from his damp brow with my fingers and I look off in the darkness and think:

*I know all of the reasons why we are here and why we fight, but still I do not know why little boys have to stand up in front of cannons. I do not understand it and I do not have to like it.*

# Chapter 11

Comes the morning, I give Georgie a nudge, and rubbing his eyes, he slips out of my bed and stumbles out the door of my room.

*Little sod!* I hear from outside, and then the sound of a solid punch, then...*Ow! In with our Jacky, are you? Take this!* Again I hear *Oooff!* as another fist is put in his belly. *Little bastard!*

I poke my head out my door. "Let him alone. He promises never to do it again." Wrapping my blanket around myself, I stumble out and plop down at the table. I know my hair is tangled and my nose is bright red and dripping. "Got any tea, Mates? Me mouth tastes like I been cleanin' out the head wi' me tongue."

*That* oughta take the bloom off the Jacky Faber rose for 'em, I'll wager. They recoil, but their eyes still show resentment and many a barbed glance is directed Georgie's way.

"I'm probably on report for my conduct last night. I may be busted down to Seaman. So be it. But right now I am Senior Midshipman and I want some tea or some coffee, and I do not care who gets it for me."

Several sets of feet scurry out. Robin does not. He sits down across from me. "So you think you are in trouble, then?"

The coffee appears with Georgie's hands around the mug, and I take it and sink my nose in it and I drink. "I'm always in trouble," I say, and then gulp down some more. "I don't know. I only know that Mr. Pinkham was mad. And I did get above myself, as I am sometimes wont to do."

"What a surprise," says Robin, drily, sipping at the coffee that was slid in front of him by Ned.

"We will see. Tom, will you go get my wet uniform and give it to the Weasel to dry up next to the cook fires? Thanks."

Georgie nurses his wounds but does not seem sorry for his transgression. In fact, he comes over and sits next to me, enduring the barbed looks from his fellows.

"Well," I say, rising. "I must get dressed and we must get the watch rotation going again or we will be seen as less than scrubs. Tom, you take the Morning Watch. Go out now and assume it. I'll be out in a minute to see how things lie. As soon as I dress." Tom and Ned give Georgie some final nasty looks and go out together.

I get up and go back into my room and throw off the blanket, making sure the door is closed behind me. Jockey pants, jockey top, stockings, and boots is all I got so I put 'em on and stride back out.

"Are you sure you're going to go out like that, Jacky?" says Robin, rising.

Before I can reply, Ned comes back into the berth. "Mr. Pinkham wants to see you," he says ominously.

*Uh-oh.*

"What else shall I wear while my other clothes are drying?" I look at my face in the communal mirror, which is placed there for the midshipmen to shave. Robin is the only one who could use it and him just barely. They shan't see me looking worried. I take inventory of my appearance. Clean enough, I think. I take my hair and twist it and pile it up under my hat. There. I'm presentable.

"Ned, lend her your jacket," orders Robin.

Ned strips off his midshipman jacket and goes to hand it to me, but Robin takes it instead and holds it open for me to put on. Well, it won't hurt to be a little more modest when I go out to face Mr. Pinkham, I'm thinking.

"Ned, Georgie, go find out where the Weasel is with our breakfast," says Robin.

They leave, a little resentfully, but, after all, Robin is second in command of midshipmen.

I grab the cuff of my jockey top with my right fingers and shove my right arm through the proffered jacket. Then the same thing with the left. Not a bad fit, I think, as I bring the front together and start to button up. I face Robin. "I wish Ned and Tom weren't being so mean to Georgie over last night. I mean, he is just a boy."

"They are just jealous," he says, getting a bit red in the cheeks. "As I was jealous, as well."

*Hmmmm…*

"I can button my own buttons, Robin," I say, as he begins to button the jacket. He steps away, shamefaced and confused. I finish the buttons and go to him and put my hands on his shoulders. "But it's nice of you, Robin. Most males I have met so far have tried to unbutton my clothes, rather than the opposite."

He blushes all the more.

I pause for a bit and then say, "I'll wager you have no sisters, Robin."

"What...?" he says, confused. "No...no, just two brothers. How did you know?"

"Because you are not easy with me, Robin, and you are probably not easy with any girl. If you had sisters, especially older sisters, then you would know that girls are not mystical beings but people just like you, and then you would be easy with them. But you will never know that ease, and that is all right, because you are a shy, sweet boy and you will do all right with the girls because of it. We like shyness in a boy...sometimes. Now, brush me off and I will go see Mr. Pinkham."

He flicks some pieces of lint off the jacket with the back of his fingertips, careful not to touch my front.

"You must know, Robin, that I have decided to live single all of my life," I say, putting my hand on his chest and looking in his eye.

"If that proves to be true, then it will be a shame, Jacky," he says. "Just because he was not good enough for you does not mean that another might not be more true."

*What?*

"That James Fletcher. He was not good enough for you. He should never have left you alone in Boston."

*What?*

"I would never have left you there in Boston. I would have run away with you."

*That damned book!*

"Robin. I don't want to hear that name mentioned again. And I don't want to hear about that book anymore, either!"

With that I wheel and stalk out of the berth.


I go to the quarterdeck and present myself to Mr. Pinkham who lets me cool my heels off to the side for a long time before addressing me. Finally, he does.

"You left the quarterdeck without being ordered to do so last night. Do you admit that?"

"Yes, Sir," say I. It would do no good to protest that I was doing it for the good of the ship.

"You endangered the men in the top who were trying to do their duty while you were showing off and who had to rescue you instead of doing that duty. Is that true?"

I grit my teeth. "Yes, Sir."

"And what do you have to say about that?"

"No excuse, Sir."

"Very well. Into the foretop till noon."

I salute and head up into the top. I have always wondered at the mildness of this traditional punishment for wayward midshipmen, it being so mild in comparison with that dealt out to the common seamen. I guess it's supposed to have a certain amount of humiliation in it, but it doesn't bother me any. I just settle in at the top and look at the clouds drifting by and wish I had my pennywhistle and was allowed to play it. Or the Lady Lenore. Or my concertina. But that all seems so long ago, so I put it out of my mind.

The other lads ain't allowed to visit during this punishment time, so when I see Ned down below, I just take his jacket off and float it back down to him so he can wear it when he relieves Tom on watch. He catches it and waves. Then I settle back and watch the coast of France drift by on the starboard beam, the *Wolverine* being on the northern leg, and think about things.

I think about how lucky I've been so far on this voyage, and I'm hoping that my luck holds. If the Captain stays sick, or even dies, then I should be all right. I'm sure to be put off if the Captain is replaced, and then I'll be able to get back to poor Judy. I hope she's all right. I imagine she went to...his place, but what happened there, I can't guess. Probably got booted out, and then headed back to Cheapside. Hope I gave her enough money to get by for a while. I had some scrimshaw in my seabag that I told her I was going to sell when I got a chance. Maybe she'll sell those to get enough money to keep herself till I get back. Hope she gets a good price, 'cause that is some prime scrimshaw, some of which I had done myself, some of which was done by others to pass the time on the whaler. We would take a piece of white whalebone, scratch a drawing on it with a needle, rub ink on it, and then wipe it off quick. The ink would stay down in the scratches and there we'd have a nice black drawing against the white bone. Mostly I'd do whaling scenes with harpoons and boats and lines and whales, of course, but the men would sometimes do mermaids and such, so you knew where their thoughts were. Men, I swear...

"On deck there! Boat heading out from the land!"

That jerks me out of my reverie right quick and I jump to my feet and look at the coast. What, another smuggler that's going to get away? No...strange...it is a large boat that has no sails, but instead has great long oars sticking out either side. But what's that big thing in the middle? It looks like...

"It's a gun shallop!" roars the lookout. "And it's headed right for us!"

"Beat to Quarters! All hands clear for action!" shouts Mr. Pinkham on the quarterdeck and the sounds of whistles and shouts and pounding feet are heard as all hands head for their battle stations. I slide down the port ratlines right into mine.

"Mr. Piggott! Tucker!" I shout as I see the boys running up to our gun. "Powder! Now!" They hie off in the direction of the magazine as the rest of the men get into position.

"Haul 'em back! Open the gun ports! Harkness, we'll load One and Three first, then the other two!" I say. "Swabbers! Make sure your buckets are full! Carriage men! Pull now!" Guns One and Three rumble back on their little wheels. On any decent ship, they would be loaded already, us being close to the enemy as we always are. I will keep my mouth shut about that as I think the folly of the Captain's ways are about to be forcefully shown.

The boys come back bearing the bags of powder and Harkness takes the one from Georgie and drops it down the barrel of Number One.

"Ram!" I say, from my position to the left of the gun. Shaughnessy rams the charge home. "Ball! Wad! Ram!"

I take the spike and the horn of priming powder from their hooks on the bulkhead and ram the spike down the fire hole to pierce the bag of powder, pour in the priming charge, and set the flint firing mechanism. "Out!" I yell and the rope and carriage men haul the gun forward so the muzzle goes back out through the port. "Set the blocks!"

Number One is ready to fire. And now Number Three. They are hauling back Two and Four. I take a few strides across the deck to scope out the enemy. It is indeed a gun shallop—a big thirty-two-pound cannon mounted on a sturdy boat that is rowed into position to do its murderous work. The boat has to be built extra strong to withstand the repeated shocks of the recoil and, therefore, is not fast, but it does not have to be—it has the advantage of maneuverability of oars over the speed of sail and it is maneuvering right at us. I can see the blue-striped tops of the sailors as they bend their oars or stand by their gun. The French flag, the Tricolor, waves from the rear, and all aboard are singing the French national anthem, the "Marseillaise," at the tops of their lungs.

*"Allons enfants de la patrie,*
*Le jour de gloire est arrivé!"*

Even as they arrive, they fire, and the boom of the cannon rolls out toward us, as does a cannonball. I can see the ball and I know it will be short. It is. It splashes into the water about thirty yards off our beam.

All is in disarray on the starboard side of the *Wolverine*. The men who are not cowering under the rail are dashing about in confusion, trying to get the guns loaded. I look to my right and see that Robin's not having much luck with his guns, either.

The Captain has been hauled to the quarterdeck and he leans on Mr. Pinkham and bawls out orders that nobody is able to carry out. He is white in the face with the ravages of his sickness and his clothes are stained and filthy. And he seems incredulous that this is going on. I swear he even tries to wave the attacker off, like this is all a mistake. He has Mr.

Smythe, the Gunnery Officer, on the quarterdeck. *The mistake, Captain Scroggs, was in not training your crew.*

The French gunboat fires again. They had reloaded in under two minutes. Probably more like ninety seconds. They are well trained.

I cannot see the ball this time, but it makes itself apparent soon enough. A man is crossing the deck in front of me and there is a *whap!* His head explodes in a red mist. The headless body stands for a second and then flops down, the remaining blood oozing out of the stump of his neck and spreading across the deck. I look down and see that I am splattered with it and again my knees turn to jelly and my bowels threaten to shame me, same as it ever was when I am in battle and people are doing their level best to kill me. *Stop that. Just think about what you have to do.*

> *"Aux armes citoyens!*
> *Formez vos bataillons!*
> *Marchons! Marchons!*
> *Qu'un sang impur*
> *Abreuve nos sillons!"*

I go back to my guns and to my men and stand there ready. We can do nothing for we are pointed the wrong way.

"What are they singing? What are they saying, Miss?" Tucker asks, as he brings up another bag of powder and hands it over.

"Oh, never you mind, Tucker. It's only something about them calling other Froggies to arms so's they can march through rivers of our blood."

Tucker allows that we'll see about *that* and then goes down for more powder.

"Fire, fire! Oh, why will you not fire?" I look up on the quarterdeck and hear the Captain shouting, but it is to no avail. No gun on the starboard side can answer the fire from the gunboat. He is reduced to crying, "Will no man do his duty? Will no man do his duty?"

I fill my lungs with air and shout out to him, "Turn the ship about and we will do ours!"

The Captain turns, as if in a dream, and looks at me standing there speckled with that poor seaman's blood and he says, "What? What are you saying?"

"Guns One through Four are ready for firing! Bring the ship about so we can bring them to bear! Or else sit here and be beaten to death by a one-gun boat!" I bellow with absolutely no respect in my voice.

The Captain jerkily gestures to Mr. Pinkham to do it, and Mr. Pinkham roars out "Hard alee! All topmen aloft to make sail!" and the helm is put over and slowly, ponderously, the *Wolverine* turns into the wind. And as we do, we hear the strains of the "Marseillaise" yet again, and yet again the gunboat fires. This time the ball whistles over the Captain's head but does no damage to the ship. The Captain ducks when the ball whizzes by. *A little lower next time, Froggies.*

And we turn and turn and turn, but we are not there yet and I'd be damned if I'll have my men sing "God Save the King," in reply to the Frenchies and I think back to something that Jared told me one time and I stick out my chest and start chanting, *Were-wolves! Were-wolves! Were-wolves!*

over and over till my men pick up the chant, too. Finally we are pointed south and the French gunboat is about to come within our sights. *Now, Frenchmen, we shall see.*

*Another verse? Don't they ever tire of their bloody song?*

I lean over Gun Number One and wait for the gunboat to appear in my sights. I hold my breath, for while I know how to load and fire a gun, I've never actually *done* it. *Please, gun, please, go off.* I pull the lanyard.

*Crack!*

There is a thunderclap and the gun whips back under my cheek. I look out through the port—my shot was wide, but it got their notice. I leap over to Number Two and aim. Behind me I hear "Swab! Powder! Ram! Wad! Ram!" as Number One is reloaded. *Good boys!*

"Harkness! Fire Number Four when she bears!" He leaps over to take the Gun Captain's spot.

"Fire!" I yell and pull the lanyard. The gun *cracks* and bucks back. Just then Harkness fires Four and a shout and a cheer goes up from our ship. I look out and see that one of our shots has ripped into the oars on the starboard side of the gunboat and its crew is furiously trying to ship new oars over on that side. They ain't singin' no more, that's for sure.

"*Were-wolves! Were-wolves! Were-wolves!*" I continue to chant as they reload, and soon all aboard pick up the chant. "*Were-wolves! Were-wolves! Were-wolves!*"

I leap to Gun Number Three and sight along it. "Ratchet over two! Pike up one! Fire!" and I pull the lanyard and the gun barks out its charge. A near miss, but they're getting worried. I'm sure the gunboat only came out to stir up a little trouble and its commanding officer and crew probably were astounded by how close they were able to get to a King's ship. The miss is all right with me, as I sure as hell don't want to kill anybody, even though they got one of ours. The Frenchies looked so merry, coming at us, flying their colors and singing. It would be a shame to kill them, but that is the way of it, ain't it?

"Harkness. You may aim and fire at will," I say, and look over to Robin's crew. He is furious, mostly with himself, I think, for his failure so far to fire a gun. It looks like he's about ready, though. *Good lad.*

Harkness fires again and his aim is deadly. It hits the oarsmen on the port side and again they scramble to reship oars. They are in full retreat. *Let them go,* I say to myself, but Harkness is not in such a forgiving mood. The gun barks again and it hits the boat amidships and men go over the side.

Then Gun Number Five fires, and I look over at Robin, who has fired it. He is leaning over the gun and looking out through the port. The ball arcs through the air and, incredibly, hits the boat square on, and the boat, weighed down by the massive gun, points its bow in the air and then goes straight to the bottom. Maybe some of the Frenchmen are able to reach the shore, but I doubt it. It was a lucky, or an unlucky shot, depending on how you look at it. I look at Robin and he is ashen. He staggers to the rail as if he needs to throw up over the side. *That, Robin, is what killing men feels like.*

Had I not been sent to the top this morning without breakfast, I might have joined him there at the rail. But I don't. Instead I stand on the deck and address my men.

"Good shooting, Harkness. Good job, Werewolves, all of you. You should take pride in your actions today. You saved the ship. Let us clean up the guns and make them ready."

I'm putting the matchlocks away when I hear the Captain call.

"You. Faber. Get over here."

*Uh-oh...*

I go over to the foot of the quarterdeck and wait.

The Captain weaves unsteadily on his feet, leaning on a cane. Now that the danger is past, his sneer is back in its place on his white-stained lips. His officers stand behind him in a state of mortal humiliation, as if it were their fault that the ship was so woefully unprepared for such an attack. I am sure he has told them just that.

"I should hang the lot of you," snarls the Captain to his crew, "and I just might do that, one at a time, starting tomorrow." His tic comes on him, pulling his mouth down into that horrid grimace. "It would be no loss to the Navy, for you are the most pathetic bunch of pansies that *ever* tried to pass for men!"

The tic relaxes, but the eye wanders off. The crew is dead silent.

"That being the case, I now direct that the sailmakers shall fashion skirts of light cloth and every member of the starboard gun crews, every one of you loutish dolts who could not get a single shot off to save your sorry asses, shall wear them! And you will wear them, ladies, till such time as I say you may take them off!"

There is a collective intake of breath from the crew at this incredible insult. I reflect that the Captain, though a cruel and despicable tyrant, is not completely mad—had he made the entire crew wear dresses, there would have been an outright mutiny, no question, but with only twenty-four or so singled out, well...

"Now, as for you," he says, turning and fixing his mad stare upon me, "you are now Acting Lieutenant Faber, Assistant Gunnery Officer."

My gasp is echoed by a hundred others.

The Captain looks sideways at Mr. Smythe, who looks like he's been punched in the belly. "Perhaps you can teach Mr. Gunnery Officer Smythe here something about gunnery."

I think back with horror on the conversation I had overheard between the Captain and Pinkham about fraternization and about him making me a lieutenant so's he could get on me. And now he's done it. My horror is nothing compared to that of the ship's officers, who recoil from the Captain's statement.

"Sir! You cannot!" says Mr. Pinkham.

"Sir, I just did," says the Captain. "Now get out of my way. I'm going below. Mr. Smythe, I'll decide later whether or not you will wear the skirt, too. On yours, of course, we'll have a bit of gold lace put around the hem as befits your rank." He staggers down the ladder, his steward holding his arm.

In shock I turn and go back to my division. All, of course, have heard. They are all still there, even though we have secured from Quarters. All except for Georgie. I look around and spy him standing stock-still a little bit away.

He is watching some men take up the headless corpse of the killed man to bear him below to strip him and clean him and sew him up in his hammock and so prepare him for burial. Those men would be the dead man's mates. Other men come with mops and buckets and start swabbing at the blood. It has already started to clot and turn brown, but it goes all pinkish when the water hits it.

I go over and put my arm around Georgie's shoulder. He quivers and he looks up at me, and a look of horror comes over his face and he tears out of my grip and plunges below.

I had forgotten that I was splattered with the dead seaman's blood and must present an awful spectacle. I move the muscles of my face about and can feel the dried blood caked there. Do I hear it said, or is it only in my own mind? *Bloody Jack* yet again. *Sorry, Georgie.*

Before I follow Georgie down into the berth, I go into the gun room, the officers' quarters.

They stiffen as I enter, the hatred and humiliation plain on their faces.

"I know you do not want me here, gentlemen, and I will not stay long."

I go up to the gunnery officer and stand before him. "The shame here is not yours, Mr. Smythe. I hope you know that, and do not do anything rash to yourself. This will right itself soon."

He looks at me with eyes burning in rage and shame. He says nothing, but he nods.

I turn to Mr. Pinkham and ask right out, "There is nothing that can be done? Like a complaint made to his superior officers?" If this be mutiny, then so be it.

Mr. Pinkham shakes his head sadly, totally defeated and caring not that this is being discussed in the open. It occurs to me that these four would have talked about this among themselves many times before. Now there are five officers in on it.

"No, the Captain is always able to pull himself together when he is under scrutiny from above. I have seen him do it. The Flag would agree that, though he is a harsh commander, he is not insane. They would side with him and nothing would be accomplished."

*Hmmm.* I think on this for a moment and then I say, "Thank you, gentlemen, for receiving me so kindly. We all know what happened today was a sham and a mockery. I will continue to stay in my quarters in the midshipmen's berth, and I will take my meals there as well. I think that would be best. Good day, gentlemen."

With that I turn and leave.

I go down into the berth and find Ned and Tom already there.

"You two all right?" I ask. They are subdued, but they nod. "Good. Go find the Weasel and tell him to get us something to eat and drink. Tell him I want a half ration of rum drawn for the two of you. You look like you could use it. Oh, and find out if my uniform is ready yet."

I go in my cabin and strip off my silks and wrap them in a bundle and wash the blood off my face and hands and hair and then put on my nightshirt till such time as my uniform arrives. Then I go in to see Georgie.

He is lying facedown on his bunk. He is crying, and he shudders when I put my hand on his shoulders.

"You saw something horrible today, Georgie, but you will get over it."

"No, I won't! I won't never forget him lying there without his head. I'll never forget that!"

"Come. Turn around." He does, and I put my arms around him and he puts his head on my chest.

"You look just like my sister Theresa when you're dressed like that," he says, his voice shaking.

*Ah.*

"There, there," I say, as I rock him back and forth. The crush of the day does its work on him and soon he falls asleep. I lay him back on his bunk and pull up the covers.

Why did they send you off, Georgie? Did they think it would be like it was in the books? With bright fancy uniforms and flags snapping and all that? Well, maybe it would have been like that if you'd been sent to a grand flagship where you'd be some admiral's pet and set up as a side boy with nothing else to concern you except etiquette and naval rituals and traditions, instead of being sent here to this Hell Ship. But then, the flagships have to fight sometimes, too, so you never know.

I leave his cabin and sit at the table and think about food. And maybe a drop of wine.

Then the hatch door opens and the Weasel falls in, but not with food. No, he is kicked into the berth by Robin, who is red with rage, and who, obviously, has had some of his rum ration already. The Weasel is howling piteously and covering his head with his arms to ward off further kicks from Robin.

"What's this, then?" I say, mystified. I see that Ned has come in bearing my uniform jacket and my trousers. But not my...

"Ask him," says Robin, delivering another kick.

"I warn't doing nothin'," wails the unfortunate Weasel, "just spreading a little joy is all."

"What?" I say.

"The wretch was exhibiting your drawers and charging one penny to...handle them," says Robin. "Here's his bag of pennies. And there was a line of men clutching other pennies."

I am aghast.

"Kick him again," I say. Robin does. The Weasel howls. "Again," I say. "Penny a sniff, hey?" I pick up my bundle and throw it at him.

"Here are my silks," I say. "You will wash them and you will dry them and you will carefully iron them. You will *not* put them on and prance around. You will *not* wear the pants over your face or anything like that or I will have you lashed to the grating and given twenty. Remember that I have friends in the crew and they will be keeping an eye on you. I know several who would cheerfully slip a knife twixt your ribs. Do you understand? Good. Now, get out and get us some food and drink or I will get us another steward and put you in with the Waisters and the rest of the trash."

The Weasel slinks out, limping.

*Men,* I swear.

Soon he is back, seeming all contrite, bearing steaming plates of food, and we fall to. I give Ned and Tom some watered rum to make them sleep better. I send them off to bed, saying Tom will have the Four-to-Eight. I will take the Mid and Robin will shortly go up and take the Evening Watch. He is very quiet.

"Robin," I say, "it is rough, but it is war. They were trying to kill us." I put my hand on his arm.

He doesn't say anything for a while. Then he takes another sip of wine and sighs and puts his hand on mine. "I know, but still. All those young men. Singing and all..."

"That was a lucky shot, your first time aiming a gun."

He snorts. "Aiming? I didn't aim. I just pulled the cord."

"So you see, it was just Providence. God called those Froggies to Him."

He smiles in spite of his gloom. "I suppose…"

"I suppose you should go up on watch, now. I'll see you when I relieve you for the Mid."

We rise and face each other…*closely* face each other. He is dressed for his watch and I am still in my nightshirt since I'm going right to bed anyway.

"Jacky. I…I…" he stammers.

"I know, Robin, I know," I say and take his hand and squeeze it in both of mine. I go on my tiptoes and give him a light kiss on the cheek. "I know, too, that you did very well out there today. Now go on watch, knowing that I am very, very proud of you."

# Chapter 12

We have the funeral for the fallen sailor the next morning. I was hoping he would turn out to be one of the worthless Waisters, one of Muck's bunch, but no such luck. He was Simon Baldwin, a good man and a good seaman. All, except for the Captain, who is either too sick or too uncaring to come up, turn out for the words to be said over poor Baldwin, and then the plank is lifted and the canvas-covered body slips off into the sea.

After the ceremony, Baldwin's things are auctioned off at the foremast, the money taken in to be kept for any family he might have. I bought his oilskins.

The sailmakers do make the skirts for the unfortunate starboard gun crews, and they put them on. The rest of their friends look about—daring anyone to make a comment. After some snickers and guffaws from Muck and his crew, when it looks like it might come to blows, Mr. Pinkham lets out the word, very quietly, that those men should take off the skirts but keep them tucked in their belts, should the Captain come back on deck and they have to get them back on right quick. I'm coming to have more and more regard for Mr. Pinkham every day—how he could have put up with the

Captain's cruelty for so long, and still kept on, I don't know....

The ship returns to its ordinary routine, day after day, watch after watch. I continue to drill the gun crews, being Assistant Gunnery Officer now, *all* of the gun crews, not just the now overly proud Division One. I have put Robin in charge of the four forward starboard guns and he is bringing them, and himself, along nicely. He drills his crew relentlessly and his men are coming to respect him. He really is growing into a man before my very eyes.

We are discovering that there are experienced gunners amongst the crew. I have put Harkness in charge of the four port quarter guns and Shaughnessy, the starboard four. We all drill over and over, every day, but it is back to dry runs—no powder to be used. I am left to do what I want—Mr. Smythe, the Gunnery Officer, has turned to the bottle.

The entire ship's company now calls themselves the Werewolves.

I continue the boys' schooling—it is good for them, as it gets their minds off the past battle. Ned and Tom have bounced back all right, but Georgie still mopes about. If he just had someone his own age to help him through this time in his life.

The boys' schooling is sometimes not exactly what I had laid out for them in the way of worthy study. One day, I came silently into the midshipmen's berth where Tom and Ned were bent over what I assumed was their navigation book when I heard both of them stifle giggles.

*What? Navigation is good, useful, and interesting, but it is seldom funny,* I'm thinking.

"So what are you two buggers going on about?" I ask

and march up to them. I look down, and there, nestled in the book of navigation, is a copy of The Book. I feel my face turning red.

Ned, his pug-nosed face suffused in glee, squeals out, *"You and Jaaaaaaaymmeeee in the haaaaaaammock!"*

Tom, his head down and keening, rocking back and forth in joy, has both his arms thrust down hard between his thighs. *"Jacky and Jaaaymeee sittin' in a tree, K-I-S-S-I-N-G...."* he squeals in delight.

I grab The Book and fling it into my cabin. "You little rotters! You are supposed to be studying! Where's my switch? You'll get it now, by God!"

But they flee the room in time to escape my wrath. "And don't believe everything you read!"

*Christ! That book will be the end of me!*

I have found that the Master-at-Arms, Peter Drake, is a skilled swordsman, so I have arranged for him to give the lads lessons in swordsmanship, a skill no young gentleman can do without. Me, too.

So, each day all the middies and I line up on Three Hatch, which is right in front of the quarterdeck and is open and free of gear, and we are taught. I have told Drake that he is allowed to yell at us during instruction.

We are all equipped with fencing foils—sort of practice swords made only for poking at your opponent, no slashing. That's for sabers, later.

Drake barks out the commands.

*En garde!* We get down in a crouching position, with our foils held in our right hands about breast level. Our left hands are in fists and on our hips.

*Advance!* We whip out our front foot to take a step and bring up the back one to maintain the crouch. *Advance!* We do it again. The foil begins to feel heavy in the hand. *Retreat!* We reverse the steps and go back. *Advance! Advance! Lunge!* On the last command, we extend our back legs and lunge forward and we extend our sword arms as if we were plunging our weapons into the belly of our opponent. *Recover!* We pull back to the original en garde position just in case we didn't finish him off and he's about to plunge his sword into our own dear bellies.

*Lunge! Recover forward! Lunge!* That is the one that finally gets us. We have to extend, lunge, and then bring our back leg up and lunge again.

We are pathetic. Robin manages to complete the thing without falling over. The younger boys don't. I have ridden spars in storms and I have ridden Thoroughbred horses to victory in hotly contested races, but my legs just ain't up to this. I barely manage to pull up after the final lunge.

Drake says, with great contempt in his voice, "You know those moves. Practice them. I will be back tomorrow at the same time." With that, he leaves the deck.

We are up there again the next day. And the next. We practice constantly, on deck or in the berth. We get better at it.

Sometimes, when neither Robin nor I have the Evening Watch, we go up into the maintop to just... well, just sit and talk.

*Will you sit with me here, Robin? Can I put my head on your shoulder for a bit? Could you put your arm around me and hold my hand and give me some comfort, without expect-*

*ing too much from me? I don't know what I want or what I'm going to do or what's going to happen to me, but I do get so scared sometimes, Robin, oh yes, so scared, even though I may never show it, but yes, I do. You know, Robin, even though I have decided to live single all of my life, you could still learn a lot from me about girls and how to love them if you will be my friend. You could...*

He puts his arm around my shoulder and I put my head against his neck and we look up and watch the stars.

Then, one day, I meet the rest of the ship's boys. I am on the Morning Watch and Tucker comes up to me, prodding two young boys along with him.

"Good day, Miss Faber," says the grinning Tucker, putting his knuckle to his brow by way of salute. "I thought that, since you was once a ship's boy yourself, you might like to make the acquaintance of the other boys. This 'ere's Eli Chase..."

Eli Chase is a curly headed blond boy with a shy smile who looks most anxious to get away from my awful majesty. I am dressed like a dreaded officer, after all.

"Good day to you, Eli," I say, nodding. "I hope you are a good boy and are attending to your duties?"

"Yes, Mum," he says, and he retreats gratefully to the safety of the fo'c'sle.

"...and this 'ere," says Tucker, proudly, as if he's introducing King George, himself, "is our own Tremendous McKenzie, Hero of the Glorious First, and a true Son-of-a-Gun!"

There steps forward a very small and very skinny boy who is wearing the remains of ragged trousers that do not quite reach his knees and a tattered shirt. On that shirt, right in the middle of his thin chest, hangs a once-bright ribbon and from that a brass medal. He salutes and says, "McKenzie, here."

"Well, McKenzie," I say, "that is a most impressive medal. Would you like to tell me how you got it?" smirks I, thinking he had found it in a gutter somewhere.

"Yes, Ma'am, I would," says Tremendous, not at all cowed by my high station. "I was born on His Majesty's Ship *Tremendous* during the Great and Glorious Battle of the First of June in seventeen hundred and ninety-four wherein we kicked the crap out of Boney's Navy, we did."

He says this in a sonorous tone, which shows me that he has delivered this speech many times before.

"That was indeed a glorious victory," I say, doing the math. "That makes you all of...ten years old now, right, McKenzie?"

"Right, Miss," says McKenzie, and, not to be interrupted in his speech, goes on. "Me mum, havin' gone on board secretlike with me dad, was havin' trouble birthin' me, so they picked her up and spread her out between two of the great guns and they fired 'em off and out I popped, clean as a whistle, and a true Son-of-a-Gun!"

I had heard of that practice and that term before, and here, standing right in front of me, is the issue of such a birth.

"That is quite a story, Tremendous," I say, duly impressed. "Now, how came you by the medal?"

He puffs out his chest and says, "Them in power decided to give the Naval General Service Medal, which this is, to all the men aboard the ships on that great day, and as I was aboard, I got one. Here it is."

"Indeed it is. Tell me, what was your rating on that ship? What was your job...was it shipfitter, sailmaker, able seaman, carpenter?"

"I was entered in as 'Baby,' Miss, that was me rating, and that was the job I did," says the boy, with great pride.

*Ah, just like the Royal Navy, to be ever so precise, even when it makes itself look ridiculous.*

"And your mother, Tremendous...Did she get a medal, too?" I ask, knowing full well the answer.

"No, Miss," he says, "she didn't. For one thing she wasn't supposed to be there, and for another the Admiralty said the country would run out of brass if they give a medal to every woman aboard those ships on that day."

*And I used to think I was the only female what had ever snuck aboard a Man-o'-War...*

There was another incident about the skirts. Seaman Elias Hart, a slight young man of about seventeen and a member of Gun Crew Number Ten, had his shameful skirt tucked in his belt and was coming back from the mess deck when several of Muck's bunch paraded in front of him with their hands held up but with their wrists limp, prancing and mincing with their eyelids flapping. The young man, slight as he was, flew at them with curses and fists flailing, but they were ready for him and clubbed him down to the deck and were about to do some real damage when Jared and Harper and some others floated down from the rigging and put a stop to it right quick. Jared had one Waister by the throat and was about to pound him into the deck when I came up and got myself between them all and yelled, "Stop it! You know the penalty for fighting! Back off! Now! Get back to your quarters!"

They do it, but looks are exchanged that say, *Things ain't over yet, you rotten bastard....*

They disperse, sullenly, and I catch Jared's furious eye and pointedly look up to the foretop. After a few moments, I go up there, and a few minutes later, he joins me.

"So what is the way of things, Jared?" I lean against the mast so I can't be seen from below. Jared comes up and stands beside me.

"That Horner has been trouble since the day he got here, him and his gang of worthless sods!" says Jared with uncharacteristic venom. Horner, Asa Horner, is the name that Muck has been using since the day he got here. Each day he grows ever more bold.

"I had heard, Jared, that you command the loyalty of a certain part of the crew, and Harkness, some of the others."

He looks at me, amused now in the way a parent might look at a child who had unexpectedly discovered something that the parent felt was beyond the child's reach.

"Yes," he says. "Harkness has his mates and I have mine. Peter Drake has a following, too. Considering the state of this ship, a man's got to know who his friends are and who ain't in order to survive if worse comes to worse."

*If it comes to mutiny, you mean, and chaos rules?*

I nod in agreement. "And this Horner. What has he got?"

Jared snorts. "He's got nothing but meanness and guile, but that he has in great store. He tries constantly to stir up trouble between the men…diggin' a little here, insinuatin' a little there, you know…"

Well I know. "Well, Jared, we must keep an eye on him then, mustn't we? Good order is important on a ship. Even on a Hell Ship like this."

"Aye, Miss, that we must."

There is silence between us for a bit and then he moves in such a way that our shoulders touch as we stand against the mast. When he speaks again, I can hear the cockiness back in his voice.

"You do know what the men call you, don't you? Behind your back, I mean, when you can't hear?"

*What? I had thought that they called me Miss Faber, but…*

"What do they call me then?" I say, suddenly wary and resentful.

"You won't take offense, Lieutenant?" he says, his eyes sparring with mine.

"No. Out with it."

He crosses his arms and looks steadily at me. "They call you 'Puss-in-Boots.'"

"Oh…," I say, and sag against the mast. "So I have gained no respect at all since I have been here. None at all."

"I wouldn't say that, Miss," says Jared, serious now, without his usual bantering tone. "I think they mean it kindly, and with great affection. Which could be a good thing for you."

I think about that for a while, and then I cut my eyes over to him. "It is not too much of a stretch, Joseph Jared, to figure out who came up with such a name."

He lifts his hands, palms up in a gesture of innocence, but the cocky grin is back and does not leave his face.

*Puss-in-Boots, indeed,* I think with indignation as I slide back down to the deck.

The smugglers continue to get through our blockade, as the Captain's orders remain in effect as long as he is alive, and he does hang on. Though he has not come back on deck since that day when we fought the gunboat, he makes his presence felt—we can hear him groaning and beating the wall of his cabin with his fist, and, when on the quarterdeck, we can hear his mutterings and curses and labored breathing come up through the speaking tube.

We see the flashing lights at night, again, and yet again.

# Chapter 13

We are at swordsmanship when the Captain comes back on the quarterdeck. It appears he has gotten over his sickness and looks to be making up for lost time in the way of vileness.

He looks at us standing there. We're suddenly feeling foolish in our fencing poses. I say, "Attention on deck," and we straighten up and our swords are put to our sides.

"Such nonsense," he mutters. His skin is a dead white, except for a band of red that stretches across his cheekbones and nose. His hand still shakes, but his eyes glitter with the old malice. Behind him, I see some of the men hurriedly putting on skirts.

"Looks like things have got right soft around here in my absence. Right soft. What is this, then?" He looks at us, and his gaze lingers on me.

Mr. Pelham has the watch, along with Georgie. The rest of us put our foils aside and stand there waiting. Mr. Pelham, to his credit, says, "Your young gentlemen are being exercised in swordsmanship."

"My young gentlemen, eh?" sneers Captain Scroggs, still looking at me. "But this is stupid stuff. Let's have some *real* exercise." I glance at Mr. Pelham and see dread in his eyes. Mr. Pinkham has come on deck, too.

"Good day, Captain. It is good to see that you are feeling better, Sir," says Mr. Pinkham.

"It is good to see that you are still an ass-kissing syco-phant, Mr. Pinkham," says the Captain. Poor Mr. Pinkham bows his head and steps back.

"Yes," says the Captain. "Let's see some real exercise." He looks up into the sails. "You men aloft! Last one to reach the deck gets ten for sloth! Go!"

Men pour out of the top, their feet thudding on the deck as they reach it, each one relieved that he will not be the one suffering under the lash. The last several risk broken bones by letting go of the rigging and dropping down from risky heights.

The last man hits the deck hard and limps off to the side, terror writ large on his face. It is Yonkers, of my Division One. It is plain that he has sprained his ankle.

"Lash him up!" roars the Captain. Muck and a few of his crew take up the hatch grating and lash it upright to the mast. Then they seize Yonkers and drag him to the grating. They rip off his shirt and haul him up and tie his wrists and stand back, letting him hang there, spread-eagled. Muck looks to the Captain for approval. He gets an approving nod and looks most satisfied.

"Bo'sun! Ten of your best!" The Bo'sun takes the Cat from its hook on the mast and stands to the side, ready to deliver.

I step forward.

"Sir, I must protest. This man is a member of my divi-sion. I have always found his work and his seamanship to be above reproach."

The Captain peers at me. "Is that so? Then give him twelve because of your mouth! Now!"

The Bo'sun swings and swings hard. He can do no less. Should it be seen that he is holding back, he, himself, would be lashed to the grating and one more willing to swing the Cat would do the job.

Yonkers stiffens. That's *one*. Then *two*. *Three*. He sags in his bonds. *Four*. *Five*. His back is red, now. *Six*. *Seven*. The welts on his back are now bleeding down into his trousers. *Eight*. *Nine*. *Ten*. Then my two added on. *Eleven*. I believe he is unconscious. *Twelve*.

It is over. I hear Georgie being sick beside me. No one moves.

"Take the slacker down," says the Captain. Two of Yonkers's mates go to him and cut him down and drag him off toward the fo'c'sle. They will take him down to the orlop and to the loblolly boy, and once again salve will be put on yet another bleeding and scarred back. *This poor, unhappy crew...*

The Captain seems extremely pleased with himself. "Getting back in fighting trim! Nothing like it for banishing softness and idleness." He may be feeling better this day, but I notice his tic still works.

He looks at me and the midshipmen standing there in a line and puts his finger by his brow and pretends that he has just had a great idea.

"But why should the common seamen have all the fun?" he asks. "Midshipmen! Line up at the foot of the mainmast! You, too, Lieutenant Faber, being only an *acting* lieutenant, and so late a midshipman yourself."

*Uh-oh*.

We assemble in a line on the quarterdeck. The Captain paces back and forth in front of us, looking us over. I can sense Georgie quivering by my side. The Captain stops in front of me. He smirks as he looks me up and down. I keep my eyes cased, my face without expression.

"Time to toughen up these soft *lads*," he says, poking me in the belly with his thumb. He turns and points up. "You will all race up to the main royal yard, touch it, and race back down. The last of you to reach the deck shall be bent over that cannon and get ten from the rod! Now advance to the mast!"

We break ranks and go and put our hands on the ratlines. I look at the others. Robin's eyes are full of fury. The others' eyes are full of fear, especially Georgie's, for he knows he's sure to be the loser, sure to be beaten, sure to cry like a baby in front of the crew. Robin looks at poor Georgie and then he looks at the Captain and he takes his hands off the ratlines and I just know he's going to do something rash.

I grab his arm and whisper, "Don't, Robin. I'll take care of this."

But he ain't listenin', I can tell. I feel him move toward the Captain and I tighten my grip. "Robin. If you catch the Captain's eye, you will be in trouble. I need you, Robin, I do, and I need you alive. You will do me no good in the ranks of the Heroic Dead!"

Robin looks at me and I push him back to the ratlines. "I have a plan. Let me handle this."

Before Robin can ask me what I mean to do, the Captain shouts, "Go!" and we leap up the lines.

I really put on the speed 'cause I want to make sure I am

the first one back down and that everyone sees it. Up to the maintop, past the main, my hands and feet quick and sure on the ropes. There's the t'gallant yard and now the highest sail of all, the royal. I touch its yard and head back down.

I meet the boys coming up on my way down, and sure enough it's Georgie at the rear, looking ashen. I continue down to the maintop, swing out on the ratlines and slowly climb down till I am on the last rung and there I stay. Within a moment Robin hurtles past me to the deck. He stands there and looks up at me, his eyes hot, for he has suddenly realized what I intend to do. Then Tom goes past and is down, then Ned, and finally, huffing and puffing, comes little Georgie. An instant after Georgie's feet hit the deck, I drop lightly down.

I look my defiance in Captain Scroggs's furious face.

"You would mock me, bitch? Then get over that gun!"

"You would beat a little boy? And now a girl?" I say, my chin quivering in fear but up in the air.

"Sir," begins Mr. Pinkham, "please..."

The Captain ignores his first officer and swings his arm and catches me behind my neck and I go down. I get on my hands and knees and crawl toward the gun. I stagger to my feet and see that the Captain himself has taken the rod from the Bo'sun. I turn toward the gun.

As I lay myself across it, I hear a hum. *Hmmmmmm.* It grows louder and I realize that it is the men, or most of them anyway, giving the time-honored warning to a captain that mutiny is imminent if he doesn't change his ways. The sound is made deep in the throat, the lips not moving, so the object of the mutinous sound cannot tell who is doing it. When the Captain moves close to a man, that man stops doing it, only to pick it up again when the Captain moves away.

*Hmmmmmmmmmmmmmm...*

Captain Scroggs looks up at the men in the rigging and around at those standing about. "So, you mutinous dogs, you would warn me then? Well, let me warn you—you will stop that or I will pick four of you at random and hang you right now!"

The humming dies away. *Thanks, anyway, mates.*

The Captain looks about at his crew, and he smiles. "I thank you, men, for pointing out to me that there are *much* better uses for something like this," and he lays the rod lightly on my backside. "*Much* better uses."

He flings down the rod and steps over me and grabs my hair, pulling my face up to his. "Your punishment is going to have to be more private, I see. Report to my cabin at the beginning of the Evening Watch and we'll see about you then."

"Captain..." The good Mr. Pinkham tries again.

"Mr. Pinkham!" roars the Captain. "You will pen a letter to the squadron commander telling him of the lamentable state of the masts on this ship. Upon completion of that, you will have the port lifeboat put down and you and Mr. Pelham and Mr. Harvey and Mr. Smythe will personally deliver that letter to Commodore Shawcross and attend upon him until he gives a reply. Do you understand me, Sir?"

Mr. Pinkham looks at me with sorrow in his eyes. He knows the Captain is sending all the regular officers off the ship so they cannot interfere with his plans for me.

"No dinner or rum ration for the crew tonight, and no

breakfast, either!" snarls Captain Scroggs, and he lurches down to his cabin.

I go to the officers' quarters down on the gun deck, and I do not bother to knock as I go in. The time for politeness and manners is over. I find Mr. Pinkham seated at a table, writing. Mr. Pelham is at the same table and he is loading a gun. Mr. Smythe and Mr. Harvey are making themselves ready in a similar way. I go up to Mr. Pelham and lay my hand upon the gun and push its muzzle down.

"Nay, Sir, you cannot," I say. "Should you mutiny because of me, he would only have to deny that he had any such intentions to disprove your claim, and then you would be court-martialed and hanged and he would still be the Captain and he would dance on your graves, count on it. If you try this, and I'm sure the men will be with you, all of you will have trouble to the end of your days because of it. No, Sirs, I will not have that. Being taken against one's will in a shameful way is one thing—to be hanged and choked and killed is quite another. Believe me, I know. Now, go. I can take care of myself. Please, Mr. Pinkham, write the letter, and then go."

Mr. Pinkham looks up from his writing and gazes significantly at Mr. Pelham and the others. Mr. Pelham nods and then so do the other two officers and they all look at me. Mr. Pinkham is silent for a moment and then, in a firm and even voice he says, "I am not writing the letter the Captain wants me to write. I am writing an account of today's events. We have been keeping a log of the Captain's depredations, day by day, cruel event by cruel and heartless event.

We have described the events in extreme detail and cited names and witnesses."

Mr. Pinkham's demeanor is no longer the deferential one he showed the Captain—his look is now one of steely resolve, as he goes on.

"We will leave in the boat, aye, but what we will be carrying to the Commodore is not the Captain's stupid complaint but this very log, the evidence that will put an end to his tyranny. We know"—and here he stumbles—"we know this thing today...with you...and what is going to happen tonight...will be the final straw and he will be broken and dismissed. I hope that gives you...some comfort."

Instantly, I see the wisdom of the plot. All of them, *sent by the Captain, himself,* to present the case against him.

Mr. Pelham rises. "All four of us are agreed. But"—he struggles with the words—"but we cannot just leave you to..."

"All *five* of us are agreed," I say, firmly. "If you rise up in arms against him now, all will suffer. No, it shall not be. Ridding this ship and the Service of that man is worth...whatever it costs. Go, gentlemen, and Godspeed to you and your mission."

All of them rise to their feet as I turn and leave the gun room.

Later, the boat is put down and readied for the officers. I go to see them off.

Before getting in, Mr. Pinkham looks me full in the face and says, "Are you sure?"

"Yes, I am," I say. "I know you to be a man of honor,

Mr. Pinkham, and I thank you, Sir, for all you tried to do for me. It will be all right, you'll see."

He nods grimly and goes over the side. The other officers follow him down into the waiting boat and it pushes off. The sail is raised and soon they are out of sight.

I stand there watching them go. *The Captain has surely cooked his own goose this time,* I'm thinking, *but a lot of good it's gonna do me. If I could just hold out for another day or two...* but I know I ain't gonna be able to—not the way he's been up and roaring around today.

I think about things and I come to a decision. I take a deep breath, hold it, and then let it out and go looking for Robin Raeburne.

I find Robin and the other boys in the midshipmen's berth. Robin sits at the table with his fists clenched, his face red with helpless, impotent rage. Ned and Tom look worried. They know something is up, but they don't know quite what. They just know that something is going to happen to me.

Georgie says, "What's the matter, Jacky? You're just going to get a good dinner, is all, right?"

"Right, Georgie," I say, ruffling his hair and smiling at him. "Now you and Tom run along. Ned, haven't you got the watch? I've got to talk to Robin."

They leave, mystified and somehow wretched.

"I'm going to kill him," says Robin, after they are gone. He continues clenching and unclenching his fists and staring straight forward.

"No, you won't, Robin. You won't do any such thing. What you are going to do is come into my cabin." I reach out and take his hand and lead him into my little room. There is barely enough room for the two of us to stand. I close the door and turn around and say, "Kiss me, Robin, if it will please you."

Astounded, he does it and we hold the kiss for a long, long time. When our lips finally part, I say, "Undress yourself, Robin."

"What? Why...," says Robin, confused.

"Because I am going to give myself to you, Robin Raeburne, for we both know what is going to happen when I leave here. And because I want the loss of my maidenhood to be, well...a good and loving thing and not a thing of tears and shame. I want it to be with someone for whom I have great admiration and affection. I want it to be with you." *And if I am got with child this day, I will be able to tell myself that it is your child, Robin, and then I will be able to love it.*

I unbutton my jacket and take it off. I pull off my shirt and I drop my trousers and then pull down the drawers and step out of them and stand naked on the deck. I hold my hands out to my sides with my palms up and I say, "But only if it pleases you."

He is speechless, amazed.

"So hold me and kiss me again and then undress yourself, if it please you, Robin, and then I will lie with you and we will be as one."

We come together again and I can feel his heart pounding against my own racing heart. When we part, our breathing has greatly quickened. I turn from his embrace and put my knee on my bed and then lie down upon it. "Be gentle with me, Robin. Treat me like a lady," I say, as I reach up for him.

He rips off his jacket and fumbles with the lacings of his shirt and...

...and then there is a furious pounding on the door.

"Lieutenant Faber! The Captain wants you in his cabin right now!" I recognize the voice as belonging to Private Rodgers, one of the ship's two Marines.

"But I am not expected till the Evening Watch," I say, getting up on one elbow. Robin looks stricken to the core.

"The Captain says right now, Miss, please! It will go hard for me if you don't hurry!"

"Very well," I sigh. "I'll be right out."

I rise from the bed and put my hands on Robin's sagging shoulders. "I'm sorry, Robin, I really am," I whisper so the Marine outside can't hear. "Kiss me one more time and then I must dress and go."

"No," he says, standing, his eyes feverish. "No. Come, Jacky, and we will rush outside right now and throw ourselves over the side and sink down and die in each other's arms!"

I kiss him on the lips and then put one on his forehead and smile my bravest smile and say, "Nay, Robin, I know myself and I know I am not a 'Death Before Dishonor' type. I have seen Death too many times up close to surrender myself willingly to his embrace. I do have great affection for you and I *will not* sacrifice you on the altar of my maidenhead. I will survive this."

With that, I get dressed and, leaving Robin despairing and miserable behind me, I go out to meet my fate.

On our way aft to the Captain's cabin, me between the two Marines, I notice no one is on watch. It's just the helmsman at his wheel, steering the course. It's a calm night, with scarcely a breeze and just a little roll to the ship, so I guess the Captain felt the helmsman could handle things by himself. This leaves him to the business at hand, that business being me.

Halfway there, one of the Marines reaches around me and takes my knife from my side.

"Sorry, Miss. Orders."

I enter the cabin.

Captain Scroggs is seated at his table with a bottle and two glasses in front of him. It is plain he has already been into the bottle as his face is even more puffed and florid than it was before. His steward is putting plates of food on the table in front of him.

The Captain swats him away, catching him across the face with the back of his hand. "There's man's work to be done here, pansy. Get out." The poor man seems to be used to such treatment. He bows and leaves.

That shows me what I can expect here, too.

"Come in, girl," he says, "and sit down." I am not even to have the honor of my rank, it seems. *Just girl*, I think sadly. *After all is said and done, just girl, and nothing more.*

"You there!" he says to the Marine guards who were about to take up their stations next to his door. "Go away!" The Marines look at me with sympathy in their eyes, but they go away. The Captain closes the door himself and turns back to me.

"Sit down, I said," says the Captain. I pull out a chair, the farthest one from where he is sitting, and sit down. The Captain does not have his jacket on and his shirt is not laced up and it shows the grizzled hair thick on his chest. I look away from him so as not to be sick. I see that the windows are open. People will be listening.

"Sir, I really don't...," I say in a small voice.

"Here. Have a drink." He grabs the bottle and pours a brown liquid into a glass and hands it to me.

"I don't drink spirits, Sir. I took a vow."

"A vow?" He laughs. "What nonsense. Do what I tell you and have a drink. That is the finest of whisky." There is menace in his voice.

I lift the glass to my lips and pretend to drink, and then set it back down again. My hand trembles and he notices.

"Have another drink. It will calm you. You may take off your jacket."

"That's all right, Sir, I am quite comfortable..."

"Take off your jacket!" he orders, and puts out his hand and undoes my top button.

I put my fingers to my jacket, undo the rest of the buttons, and I take it off. Then I start crying. I did not think this would happen. I had thought that I would be strong, that I would be able to take my mind away from what is going to happen to my body, but I can't. I can't. *It shoulda been Jaimy, it coulda been Randall, it mighta been Robin, but no, it's gonna be this.* I look into his face with its tic-torn mouth and wandering eye and I turn from him in revulsion.

"Please, Captain, send me away maiden as I came!" I wail, tears gushing from my eyes. "The very angels in Heaven would sing your praises!"

He puts his hand on my knee and I clap my legs together. He leers into my face. "Tears, is it now? That's fine. And maiden, too? Though I doubt it, I like it that way. I..."

*What . . . What's that?*

There is a rumbling noise overhead.

He looks up at the sound. We both realize what it is: It is a cannonball placed on the Captain's roof, right behind the quarterdeck, and left there to roll around with the motion of the ship. It is another of the traditional signs of impending mutiny.

*Thanks, Mates, but I don't think it's gonna do any good.*

The sound stops and the Captain frowns, but then turns his attention back to me. He kneels next to me and picks up the glass of whisky and puts it to my lips himself. "I told you to have a drink, girl. Open your mouth."

With that he forces the glass between my teeth and pours it back. The spirits hit me in the back of my mouth and I choke and gag and it spews out over my chin and down my shirtfront. He looks at the whisky staining my shirt and says, "You want it rougher, then?" and he reaches over with both hands and rips my shirt open to the waist. I cry out and try to cover myself and . . .

*. . . and it's another cannonball, rolling overhead.*

"Damn them!" roars the Captain, getting to his feet and charging out the door. "Who did that?" I hear him demanding of the helmsman.

"I couldn't see, Sir," says the helmsman, "as I've got to keep my eyes on the course, Sir!" Through my terror, I recognize the helmsman's voice. It is Jared. He must have relieved the other man at the helm after I was taken in the cabin. *You saw, Jared. You did.*

"Blast you! Keep your eye out then, or you'll pay for it with your back!"

"Aye, Sir!"

The Captain plunges back into the cabin, where I am now on my knees, prayin', with my hands up, palm to palm, in front of my ruined shirt, my eyes cast up to Heaven and sendin' out gallons of tears. He glares at me, his chest heaving, his face even redder than it was before.

"What?" he snarls. "Praying for your deliverance? It'll do you no good. Get in that bed."

"No, Sir, I ain't praying for myself 'cause I know I'm a good girl who never harmed anyone who didn't have it comin' and always tried to do right in everything the best I could. No, Sir, I ain't prayin' for me 'cause I know I'm goin' to Heaven when I die. No, Sir, I'm praying for you and your immortal soul and asking God not to cast you down to the lowest pit of Hell for the ravishin' of poor me, like you know He's gonna do if you do it, even if I ask Him not to, Sir!"

He grabs my arm and pulls me to my feet. He puts his face in mine and I feel the rasp of his cheek. "Do you *ever* shut up? I don't care for any of that crap! Now get in that bed!" He flings me over onto the bed. "Get those clothes off!"

"Oh, please, God!" I cry, sittin' up and putting my face in my hands and bawlin' away, my chest buckin', snorts and gasps and...

*There it is again. Two cannonballs this time, maybe three.*

Again he charges out. "Helmsman! What did you see?"

"He scurried off 'fore I could see his face, Sir!" I hear Jared say.

"Marines!" the Captain bellows into the night. I hear the pounding of booted feet.

"Aye, Sir," says one of them, probably buttoning his coat.

"You will station yourselves on the fantail and club into

insensibility anybody you find there rolling cannonballs! Do you understand?"

"Yes, Sir!" say the Marines as one. I hear them tread to their stations. Then I hear something else. I jump out of the bed and go to the door. It is the *Hmmmmmmmmm* sound coming from unseen men in the rigging. The Captain screams. "Mutinous dogs! I will see about you in the morning! Some shall swing! Count on it!"

He comes back in. Any trace of humanity is now gone from his face.

"I told you to undress yourself, girl. Do it now!" He pulls back his arm and backhands me across the face and I go down to the deck. I curl up in a ball, sobbing. I can taste the blood from a cut on the inside of my lip.

*Again the cannonballs rumble across and...*

...and then there is the sound of muffled shouts and a scuffle. Then the Marines appear at the open door.

"We've got 'im, Sir! It's that Midshipman Raeburne!"

*Oh, Robin, no!*

I look out and see poor Robin slumped between them. They are holding him up by his arms, but his head hangs down loosely from his shoulders.

"Have you killed him?" asks the Captain, lurching back to the hatchway.

"No, I don't think so, Sir. Just clubbed him up behind the head, Sir."

"Too bad. Well, throw him in the brig, then. We'll see how he likes the feel of hemp around his neck tomorrow."

*Hmmmmmmmmm...* The sound comes down from the rigging.

"That's right, you hounds! Hum, hum away! First he will

swing, then half of you!" I can see him shaking his fist at the unseen sailors in the night. The sound dies out, and he lumbers back into the room. I get to my feet, my heart in my throat.

*Maybe, if I can get him drunk and he sleeps long in the morning, the officers will be back and prevent him from harming Robin, maybe....*

"Come, Sir, have a drink with me," I say, and get up and go to the table. I try to smile. With shaking hand I pick up the bottle and pour a large portion into his glass. "Here, Sir! Let us be friends! Let us be merry!" I say, but I am sure I sound anything but that.

He comes over to me. He is breathing hard now and must put his hands on tables and railings for support. "To Hell with all this!" He shouts and sweeps everything off the table with his arm. Plates break, glasses shatter. He knocks the drink out of my hand and it spills over me and the glass goes flying off into the shadows. "Come here!"

He lunges toward me and grabs me by my hair and drags me to the bed. "Merry? By all means, let us be merry! Let's have a bit of a kiss, shall we?" He brings my face up to his and he slobbers his lips on my face and then throws me down on the bed again. Then he puts his hand on my chest and pushes me down flat on the bed.

He stands over me, weaving, his eyes unfocused, and he whips off his shirt and comes down upon me, his sour smell reaching me before he does, and I gag and twist and turn and try to get away, but it doesn't do any good. He's on me and he's heavy and the sodden mat of his chest hair is on my face. *Oh, God!* He's got me pinned good. His fingers pull down my trousers and then, when those are down around

187

my knees, his thumbs hook into the waistband of my drawers, and, in spite of all my wriggling, they start their downward journey. *No! Please...*

*WHAM!*

It is a tremendous sound. He jerks his head up, shocked beyond fury. It sounds like we are being fired upon!

*WHAM!* Again. He raises his upper body on his arms.

It becomes plain to me, in spite of my situation, that someone is dropping cannonballs down on the Captain's roof from a great height in the rigging. It's a wonder they don't come crashin' through.

There are shouts and curses from outside and then there is silence.

I look up at the Captain's face, expecting to see fury, but I don't see that at all. What I see is shock, pure and simple. The red has gone from his cheeks and his face is dead white. He looks off at something and then makes a choking sound. And then his arms give way and his chest comes down on my face again and I can hear his heart beat *Thump... Thump... Thump...* then... *Burrrrp...* then nothing.

Everything is quiet. I wait, turning my head to the side to get my nose out of his chest hair.

"Captain?" I whisper. No answer. I listen real good for a heartbeat, but I can hear none. I wait for a while longer, 'cause if he's just asleep, I don't want him to wake up.

There's no more commotion topside, so I guess my friends are resigned to the fact that their Puss-in-Boots has already been done, there being no further sounds of struggle from in here, and there ain't no more use in tryin' to help her.

I can hear no heartbeat and there's no sound of breathing and there's no rise and fall of his chest and I'd know that, I would, bein' right under him as I am. I start to try to wriggle out.

The Captain's bed is up against the starboard bulkhead and I try to roll him over in that direction so he doesn't fall out of the bed, but I can't. He's too heavy. I get my legs free and then squirm the rest of me out from under him and stand up and take some deep breaths. Then I pull up my pants and go back over to him.

His eyes are open and so's his mouth. I put my hand in front of his face, but can feel no breath. I put my hand on his wrist, but I can feel no pulse.

Captain Abraham Scroggs is dead.

I force myself to *think, dammit!* I know I have friends on this ship, but not everyone is my friend. I remember that talk I had with Jared up there in the foretop that day, when he as much as said he didn't know what would happen if discipline on the *Wolverine* fell apart completely. I think of Muck and his crew in this regard. If I tell the crew the Captain is dead, there's no telling what they would do to me, there being no officers aboard to stop them. It would be a cruel joke to have escaped the Captain's vile embrace, only to end up under half the crew. I'm strong, but I don't think I'd survive that. Jared would try to help, as would Harkness and Drake and many others, but I just don't know…

*Ah. Here's what I will do.*

I will let the crew think the Captain has had his way with me this night and is now sleeping in total, satisfied bliss. Maybe he is in heavenly bliss, but I doubt it. The officers will be back in the morning and Mr. Pinkham will be in command and everything will be straightened out. And I'll wager it'll be a happier ship, for all that.

*That's what I will do. I feel better now. I always feel better with a plan.*

Unpleasant stuff first. I close the windows and pull the little curtains that cover them, and then I turn the Captain over on his back and a hard job I have of it, him being so heavy and all, but I get it done. I slide the sheets and cover out from under him. I take off his shoes and put them next to the bed as if he intended to put them on again in the morning. I'm about to pull up the covers when I see there is a key on a short chain dangling from his belt. I take the key off and put it in my pocket. *You won't be needin' that down there in the seventh circle of Hell, Captain.*

I see that he has soiled himself a bit in dying, but it ain't too bad—he always smelled like he'd pissed himself, anyway. I grab his hair and lift his head and stick his pillow under it. Then I pull the covers up to his chin and cross his arms on his chest. Then I close his eyes with my fingertips.

*There, Captain. Sleep tight.*

Then I clean up the mess from the table and the whisky spills as best I can. I put a plate of the food and a bottle of wine aside. There's a tray on a side shelf and I pile the rest of the plates and glasses and food on it and take it to the door. I think about putting my jacket back on to cover my torn and whisky-stained shirt, but no—let them think the worst. That way I'll be able to keep this all secret tonight.

I open the door and step out.

"Call for the Captain's steward," I say to the Marines standing guard, and one of them goes off. I stand there looking all woebegone and sad until he comes back with the steward, whose name I know to be Higgins, in tow. He is a big man, dressed in a spotless white steward's coat. I had spoken to him briefly before and found him to be a very gentle sort of fellow and completely out of place on this ship. I hand him the tray.

"Captain Scroggs does not want us"—here I choke back a sob, a small, maiden-no-more sob—"to be disturbed tonight. In the morning, tap on the door, and I will bring his food in to him. Is that clear?" The steward nods and takes the tray and leaves. With some relief, I think—it must not have been very pleasant being that Captain's man.

I turn to the two Marines. We are alone, except for the helmsman, who I notice is no longer Joseph Jared but is instead John Harper. *Was Jared relieved before or after the cannonballs were dropped from the top rigging? Did I hear "Here's one for Puss, you lousy bastard!" shouted out just before the second ball was dropped? I don't know...* I do know ears are out there listening in the dark and so I speak up for all to hear. "The Captain is worried for his safety because of what has happened here this evening. Therefore, he wants one of you to be on guard here at his door, around the clock. You will let no one but me in this door. One of you go get some sleep now, and relieve the other in four hours."

With that I turn to go down into the midshipmen's berth. Ned, Tom, and Georgie are there, all looking miserable and confused. Me standing there with my shirt ripped down to my belly button and stinking of whisky don't help their distress any. "How's Robin?" I inquire as I go into my cabin to get my seabag.

"He's in the b-brig, Jacky," says Georgie, sounding as if he's about to cry. "He's awake now and his head hurts." He's looking at my ripped shirt and stained pants. "What happened to you, Jacky, what..."

Ned nudges him in the side and says, "No, Georgie, not now. Let her be."

"Jacky, we...we...," stammers Tom, not able to look at me. It seems Ned and Tom have grown up some in the past few hours. They need something to do.

"Ned. Go up and take the watch. You shall be the Officer of the Deck for real now, as there are no other officers left aboard. Tom, you relieve him for the Midwatch. I'll take the Four to Eight," I say. "Just knock on the Captain's door to wake me."

Tom reddens and looks at the floor. I leave the midshipmen's berth and go back on deck. I walk across the fo'c'sle and across Three Hatch with my seabag slung over my shoulder for all to see, and I go back into the Captain's cabin.

The deception is complete.

Later, as I sit on the floor, eating the Captain's food and drinking his wine, I think on the nature of things. I'm munching away, not thinking it overly strange to be eating and soon to be preparing to sleep in a room that also contains a new corpse, as I've got to keep up my strength for what is to come. Plus, I find him a much more charming companion in his current condition, anyway.

Then it hits me....

And it hits me with the force of a blow. I am maybe fifteen years old. I am a girl. I am also an acting lieutenant in the Royal Navy, and, by the Naval Rules and Regulations as regards the chain of command, I am in command of His Majesty's Ship *Wolverine*.

# Chapter 14

I hear the knock on the door at quarter to four in the morning and rouse myself from the floor where I had slept. I dress myself in my jockey gear yet again, 'cause my shirt and trousers are messed up, and my drawers, too, are soiled with the spilled whisky that soaked through to them. I do, however, put my uniform jacket on over the striped top, since it managed to escape harm. As did I, thank God.

On with my boots and out the door, I stop to remind the Marine standing there that the Captain is not to be disturbed, and then go up on the quarterdeck. I relieve Tom of the watch and he goes below, too tired to think of anything to say to me other than the course we are steering and the knots we are making and the time we will turn to the next leg of our patrol.

There is now a different man on the helm, and I don't know him very well, so, other than checking his course, we don't talk. I just plant my feet amidships, look up at the stars, and wait for morning.

I had especially wanted this watch because I wanted to be out in plain sight when morning came so they can all get a good look at me in all my shame. What they *think* to be my shame. I've told the lookout to keep a careful eye out for the officers returning from their mission. Dawn breaks, but he reports nothing.

At six o'clock, I send word to the cooks to fire up their stoves for breakfast. I tell them the Captain has had a change of heart, and so the men wake up to a hot breakfast, one they had no reason to expect. I want them in a good mood.

What will happen to me when the officers come back? I suppose I'll be demoted back to common girl and taken back to England as fast as possible and dumped, which will be all right with me. I'll pick up Judy and we'll figure out something to do. It will be lovely to get the Lady Lenore, Gully MacFarland's fine, fine fiddle, in my hands again and back to playing in the taverns till I get a big enough stake to return to Boston. Who knows, if I work hard enough and am thrifty, maybe I'll be able to earn enough to buy a small boat and get Faber Shipping, Worldwide, started. I will miss Robin and the boys, but I will leave this ship secure in the knowledge that I did some good whilst I was here.

At seven o'clock I wander over by the speaking tube and then suddenly stop, as if I had heard something from the Captain. I put my ear to the tube and pantomime listening to the Captain speak. After a few moments, I put my mouth on the tube and say, "Yes, Sir. Eight o'clock it is." I send word to the Captain's steward for him to have a tray ready for me to take into the cabin when I get off watch at eight o'clock. My Boston acting experience is coming in handy.

I have fun going over in my mind what I will say when the officers come back. I plan to be at the rail when they come aboard and I will have the Bo'sun's Mate trill his pipe and say *Wolverine, arriving...* when Mr. Pinkham's head appears, and he'll look all shocked and say, *What?* because that's how you announce the Captain of a ship when he comes aboard. I'll salute him and say, *I wish you the joy of your command, Sir,* and he'll be all incredulous. And I'll tell him he is, indeed, the commander of the *Wolverine* for the time being, at least, and that Captain Scroggs is dead, and everyone will try to look solemn, but everyone will be jumping for joy inside.

It is so satisfying to imagine this scene that I do it over and over again in my mind... *I wish you the joy of your command, Mr. Pinkham...*

Men are coming on deck to commence their ship's work. Most look at me with pity, perhaps thinking of their sisters and sweethearts, while others can barely keep the leers and smirks off their faces as they pass. *Well, she finally got hers,* I know they are thinking, *and the little busybody sure had it comin', she did.*

That's the expression Muck and his crew have on their faces as they file by. *Let it be, girl,* I say to myself. *Just wait.*

Ned relieves me at eight and I tell him that if he needs anything to just rap on the Captain's cabin door and I'll be right out. He blushes and nods.

Higgins, the steward, comes up with the tray precisely at eight and I take it from him and go in the cabin. I sit down at the table and survey my breakfast. It sure beats what we've been eating, that's for sure. There's two cups of coffee— thanks, Higgins—and a plate of real fresh rolls and butter, some little fishes with sauce, slices of ham—*ham! Can you believe it!*—and eggs! Three of them! Where the hell has this

Higgins been hiding the chickens?

Before I sit down and tuck in, I go and open the windows just a bit, but I do not pull the curtains. Then I sit back down and rattle the silverware as if two people were sitting down to breakfast.

I make the lowest rumbling in my chest, *Grumble rumble ratz...* hoping it sounds a bit like the Captain's surly voice.

"Yes, Sir," I say in my meek little voice. "Holystone and sand, and then exercise the guns. Yes, Sir."

I make other small talk, back and forth, and then I set into eating. I know the ears at the windows have heard, and while they probably wanted to hear the Captain thumping the bed with me, breakfast talk is all they get.

*Lord, that's good!* I exult. How does he afford this on a one-swab captain's pay, I don't know, but I'll take it. Or, rather, *we'll* take it. After I'm done, I find some paper on a shelf and I wrap the leftover food in it. Then I take the tray and my bundle of soiled clothes and I go back out and close the door behind me. Higgins still waits there.

"That was very good, Higgins." I hand him the tray. "Will you see that my shirt is sewn back up and it and the other clothes are cleaned?"

"Oh yes, Miss," he says, seemingly overjoyed at not having to go into the cabin. I guess each of his visits there ended with a boot up his behind. Though he is a big man, he is gentle, and he seems touchingly glad to hear a kind word about his service.

"And, Higgins," I say with a warning look, "none of that stuff that Weisling pulled with my clothes..."

"Miss. Please. I was trained in service to Lord Hollingsworth before I was brought down to…this."

"Well, all right then. Thank you."

I instruct Ned not to disturb the Captain for anything, just send for me and I'll be right up. Then I take my packet of food and go below to the berth. Tom and Georgie are sitting at the table. I go up to them and say "Open." They don't know what to think, and so I pull out one of the delicious fishes and dangle it over Tom's face. He opens his mouth and I drop it in. "Mmmm," he says.

I do the same for Georgie. "See? It ain't so bad. Now cheer up." But Georgie don't cheer up. *Hmmmm…* I give them each a piece of the buttered bread and leave, heading down to the brig.

The light is dim, but I can see Robin lying on the hard bench. There is no guard, as there is no need for one. Even if he got out, where could he go?

"Robin."

He stirs and sits up. Seeing me, he puts his palms over his eyes.

"How is your head?" I ask.

"It does not throb so much in pain now as it does in shame and disgrace."

"Come, Robin, you did what you could—you even put your very life on the line for me, and I will never, *ever* forget that, as long as I may live."

He takes his hands from his eyes and they blaze fever-ishly in mine as he gets down on one knee and says, "Jacky Faber, if you will do me the honor of being my wife, I will be the happiest of men. Please say that you will before that fiend takes me out and hangs me. I do not care what he—"

"You could not have been more noble, Robin Raeburne, but we will not speak of that now. And the Captain is not going to hang you. I have already taken care of that," I say to set his mind to rest. "Come, have something to eat with me."

There is a stool in the corner and I pull it over to the bars and sit down and unwrap my package. His anguish is plain and he seems to be struggling to put something into words, but I stop him by putting my fingertips to his lips. "Just eat, Robin." I sigh, and, reluctantly, he sits down beside me to eat. The heart guides, but the belly rules.

On the way back to the quarterdeck, I meet Jared. He's got a bit of his cocky look, but not all of it.

"Sorry, Miss," he says, "but, hey…"

"'But, hey' is right" is what I say in reply. "Thanks for what you did—taking the helm like that and covering for the cannonball rollers…and for whatever else you did." I am sure he is the one who dropped the cannonballs from the top rigging onto the cabin roof.

I pat his arm and go to the deck and check in with Ned. The turn to the next leg is due at four o'clock. On my watch. Good.

Six bells in the Morning Watch. Still no sign of Mr. Pinkham and the others returning. Even if they were taken out to the flagship itself, and they would have been, considering the grave charges against the Captain that they were carrying, they should have been back by now. Could they have been taken by a French patrol? Are they now in a French prison? Poor Mr. Pinkham, if only you will return, you will find yourself in command of a fine ship. If you don't, a year or so in a dank French dungeon, waiting to be exchanged for a French officer in similar straits, will be your lot. Either way, it'll be better than serving under the late Captain Scroggs, I'll wager.

At noon, Higgins appears with the luncheon tray. He tells me my clothes are drying and I should have them soon. I thank him and take the tray into the cabin.

"Good day, Captain," I say. "I have brought the noon meal," for the benefit of the Marine guard and Higgins, as I close the door.

The Captain doesn't say anything. His mouth has fallen open, but I'll be damned if I'm going to try to close it. Besides, it just looks like he's asleep and snoring.

"*Harrummmph. Gargle snark,*" I say for him, as low and guttural as I can make it.

Then I eat. Once again, the food is delicious, and once again I wrap up the greater portion to take to Robin later. I had thought about letting him out of the brig—sure could use another officer on the watch rotation—but then I thought better of it: The Captain certainly would not have released Robin after what he had done. The crew would know that and be suspicious. *Very* suspicious. Then, too, Robin might make an attempt to kill the Captain to avenge my fallen honor. Couldn't have that. *Nay, Robin, you must cool your heels a while longer.*

At one o'clock I mount the quarterdeck once more, having told Higgins, and anyone listening in, that the Captain was ill again and for him not to prepare quite so much food as the Captain's digestion is upset and he has taken to his bed. This, of course, gets to Earweg, the loblolly boy, and he appears with his bottles of white stuff and his bleeding bowl. I take them from him and say that I will give the Captain his doses. Earweg looks distressed, feeling, quite rightly, that he is losing some status here. I tell him, too, that the Captain does not want to be bled just now. I put the bottles on a shelf in the cabin and wonder about what harm they might have brought to Earweg's late patient and shiver. *First, do no harm…* Isn't that part of the doctor's oath?

I talk to Ned for a bit about the set of the sails and such. Being on these watches has been good for the boys. For Ned and Tom, that is. Georgie, being too little to stand watches, gets no benefit and thus is still without joy. Ned and Tom, being close in age, have each other. Georgie has no one, 'cept maybe me, and I ain't very available just now.

The Messenger of the Watch is standing at the starboard rail, just off the quarterdeck. I go to him and say, "Have the ship's boy, Tucker, lay to the quarterdeck." He knuckles his brow and heads off. Soon Tucker comes swaggering down the deck.

"Yes, Miss Faber?" he asks, grinning.

"You know Midshipman Piggott, do you not?" I say.

"Hard for me not to know him, Miss, as he's powder boy with me in your division."

Such cheek.

"Very well, then, I am going to tell you something. Mr. Piggott is going to be demoted to ship's boy. I want you and Eli and Tremendous to welcome him into your company. I do not want him given any special treatment, but I do not want you to be cruel to him, either. Do you understand, Tucker?"

He nods.

I turn again to the messenger. "Go get Mr. Piggott. He'll be in the midshipmen's berth." He's off again.

In a few minutes, he's back with a mystified Georgie.

"Georgie," I say, "take off your jacket."

He does it.

I put on the Look and say, "You are being demoted to ship's boy. You may go collect your things from the midshipmen's berth. You will string your hammock with the rest of the ship's boys and you will mess with the crew."

His jaw drops and his eyes fill with tears. "Jacky... what..."

"That's Lieutenant Faber, Piggott. You mind your manners. This is Tucker. He will show you the way of things. Dismissed."

Tucker comes up to him and puts his arm around his shoulders and says, "C'mon, Georgie, let's get your stuff and then we'll go up to the foretop and meet Eli and Tremendous, your new mates," and they are gone. *God bless ship's boys.*

Ned, standing behind me with the long glass in the crook of his arm, has watched all this and now looks at me with not much love in his eyes. "That was cruel, *Lieutenant* Faber," he says.

I should say nothing—*Never Complain, Never Explain*—but I can't afford to lose the middies as my friends, so I say, "Nay, Mr. Barrows. I did not mean to be cruel. I just want him to have some time to be a boy, before he has to stand up and be a man."

An hour later, pretending again to hear the Captain's hail from the speaking tube, I again go over and place my ear upon it and pretend to listen.

"Yes, Sir," I say into it when I straighten up. I advance to the edge of the quarterdeck and say to the Bo'sun's Mate of the Watch, "Muster the gun crews for practice."

I run them hard, over and over, till every back is slippery with sweat, till every man wishes me dead a hundred times over, until, finally, each man knows his job.

As we secure from the exercise, I hear it whispered for the first time:

*The Captain's whore...*

I have the Midwatch that night, and as I stand there, I think, *What if the officers don't come back, ever? What shall I do?* The Captain ain't gonna last forever in the state he's in now, that's for sure. True, the days and nights have been cool, but three more days is the best I can hope for before he really starts in to stinkin'.

I must plan. I must turn this to my advantage, somehow. But how? Once again, I see the flashing light on the shore, and I wonder at it.

I think far into the night, and by the time I am relieved, I have a plan.

# Chapter 15

The next morning I'm up at the break of dawn and ready to do or die. I let the men enjoy their breakfast and then I order them to Quarters to exercise the guns again and I leave the deck to Tom.

The first part of my plan is simple: Get them used to taking orders from me. Even though they might think the orders are from the Captain and are merely being repeated by *his whore,* the orders still will be issued by me.

I had started on that course yesterday when it came time to come about to start our southern leg. It was on my watch, me having the First Dog, and I bellowed out, "All hands aloft to make sail!" and all the topmen climbed into the rigging and I gave the command for the helm to be put over, "Left full rudder!" and the ship started her turn and I yelled, "Helm's alee!" and the bow crossed the wind and the sails shook but gathered and stiffened as the wind shifted to the other side, and still we turned, from being close-hauled, to a beam reach, to a quarter reach, to running down wind.

The topmen did their job, adjusting the square sails to

their new positions, whipping the triangular fore-and-aft sails to catch the wind on the other tack. They all came down and everything was fine with the set of the sails...except a corner of the main royal was shaking, luffing-like.

"You there," I say to a sailor on the deck. It is Bishop, a seaman in Third Division. "Be so good as to run up and take that luff out of the main royal."

Bishop decides to be a wise ass. He lifts his hands help-lessly. "Take the what out of what?" He looks around to see if his mates appreciate his humor. They do, chortling away behind their hands. "Oh no, Miss, we can't do that, it's much too far out on that scary yard to fix that awful, awful luff!"

*So.*

I toe out of my boots and leap into the rigging. "You will follow me up and I will show you how to do it," I shout. "If you are unable to follow me up, you will become the oldest ship's boy on this bark!"

I think he suddenly realizes his mistake, and he seeks to make it better by beating me up there, but there ain't no sailor alive who can catch Jacky Faber in the rigging and I'm out on the royal yard way ahead of him. I wrap my legs around the yard and am pulling the line taut as he comes out.

The sail stops shaking.

"There," I say, slapping a few half hitches on the line and pulling it tight. "That's how the job is done. I'll see you down on the deck." With that I stand and leap off the spar into the air. My hands find the main buntline and I swing around it and then go hand over hand back down to the deck. He comes down a little later by the usual way.

"What's your name and rating?" I demand when he arrives, even though I know it.

"Bishop, Miss," he says, miserably, "rated Able."

"*Able?*" I exclaim. "And still you couldn't do that simple thing, and in calm weather, yet? What kind of sailor are you?"

"Sorry, Miss...I guess I was just..."

"Just making fun of me, Bishop, is what you were doing," I say. "Do it again and I'll have you busted down to cook's helper. Do you understand?"

"Yes, Miss Faber."

I took no joy in shaming him, but I had to do it.

When all the men are on station for gunnery practice, I go down into the Captain's cabin and stand there for a while marking time and making noises like he and I are having another conversation. When I come back out, I back out the door saluting and saying, "Yes, Sir, it shall be done!"

I close the door, turn around, and give the order. "Load your guns with live powder and report when ready!"

I hear exclamations of surprise as they go to do it.

Of course, my good old First Division is ready first, but the others are not too far behind.

I call Jared to the quarterdeck. He lifts an eyebrow in question when he arrives, but I don't say anything to him. Instead I go up to Ned and say, "Mr. Barrows, the Captain intends to have some live gunnery practice. We want you to take the ship out to sea, so we cannot be seen or heard from the land. When we get out there, I want you to drop over a barrel as a target. Seaman Jared here will be the Bo'sun's Mate of the

Watch and he will help you. Do you understand?" Ned gulps and nods yes. Jared looks at me with a knowing eye and winks.

Jared leans over Ned and whispers, "All topmen aloft to make sail."

"All topmen aloft to make sail!" squeaks out Ned. Jared nods at me and I leave the quarterdeck to supervise the gunnery. I am, after all, the Assistant Gunnery Officer.

The barrel sits out there about fifty yards abaft the port beam. First I go to my old First Division. "Harkness, fire your guns as they bear."

He grins and leans over Number One. He pulls the lanyard and the gun roars out. We watch. Not bad. About twelve yards wide. He goes to Number Three, squints over it, ratchets left two and pulls the lanyard.

"Good shot!" I say. The ball goes over the barrel at a height of about six feet and splashes in the sea beyond. "If that had been a ship, it would have been hit! Cease fire! Let's give some others a shot." With that I pull out the Captain's pocket watch and press the wand. "Now, let's see how fast you can reload!" But the crew of Number One has already started, and the Number Three's are not far behind.

I see Georgie hauling his bag of powder, but he will not look at me. It hurts me, but I let it go.

Then I have the port quarter guns fire. They are wide and they are high, and sometimes, when they don't gauge the roll of the ship just right, the ball plows into the ocean well short of its target. But I shout encouragement and I clock the time it takes them to reload. So far Division One can do it in under two minutes. It takes the quarter guns four. But they are coming along.

I have them shoot out all their charges and cease their fire upon reloading. My ears are ringing from the noise.

I catch the eye of Ned on the quarterdeck and make a circular motion with my finger in the air and Jared says something to Ned and he says, "Left rudder! Topmen make sail!" and the *Wolverine* swings around and the starboard guns now bear.

These starboard divisions crews have not yet fired live charges, so I take some extra time to make sure no one is being stupid and standing behind the guns to get hit by the recoil, as I want no one to be hurt. When I am satisfied, I let Robin's starboard division have the first shots under John Harper's supervision, Robin still being in the brig, of course. The guns bark out. Again, clean misses, but I am not as concerned with that as with how fast they can reload. They try their best, all of them.

Then there's the starboard quarter guns. "Shaughnessy. Fire as they bear." Their results are similar.

After all have had their turns, and the clouds of powder smoke thin out and drift away, I get up on Three Hatch and say, "All reload and hold fire. Do not set the matchlocks. We will leave the guns loaded. Secure from gunnery practice. Well done, Werewolves, all of you."

It occurs to me that it is Sunday. "Commence holiday routine. An extra tot for all at the noon meal." Whether they think that order comes from the Captain or from *the Captain's whore,* they ain't arguing with it.

---

With lunch, Higgins brings me my clothes, cleaned, ironed, and neatly folded. I thank him and he asks if he might take my jacket for a bit of cleaning and brushing and I give it to him. The day is warm and I plan to ask Drake for a swordsmanship lesson.

Drake has gotten the boys to the point of instructing them in saber, since that's mostly what they'll be doing in the way of sword work—boarding other ships and hacking and hewing at the enemy. On the Field of Honor, the duels between gentlemen, swords have largely been replaced in favor of pistols, and I think it's a pity. With swords, you go at each other for a while, and when blood is drawn, honor is satisfied. Then everyone goes off to have a drink and brag about how brave they were, with maybe a saucy scar to show for it. A bullet is so... final.

Gentlemen still carry swords, of course—they wouldn't feel dressed without them—but they're mostly for self-protection and sort of spur-of-the-moment arguments. I think of Randall Trevelyne and his friends back in Boston, swaggering around with their scabbards clanking on their hips. *Hmmmm... Randall Trevelyne, you proud and arrogant but undeniably beautiful young man, what are you up to now?* No, no, get out of my mind, I'm going to live single all of my life, and that's best.

Anyway, that's for the boys. Drake looks at me appraisingly and says, "No, you're just not strong enough. Someday those boys"—he says, nodding toward Ned and Tom who are lustily going after each other with the dulled practice sabers that Drake has issued to them—"will be strong enough, but you will never be."

"I am quick and strong for my size," I protest.

"I know, but still, a swordsman of even little skill would have your sword arm off at the shoulder in the wink of an eye." He throws me a practice saber and I snatch it out of the air and we go into the en garde position and he says *Now!* and the blades touch for a second and then he feints and I lunge to the side and then I see that he has already laid his sword on my right shoulder, right at the joint.

I look at my still-attached sword arm with a certain fondness and decide to listen to what he has to say.

"If you persist in trying to learn this art, Miss," he says with a heavy emphasis on the *Miss*, "we shall stick to the foil, and then to the rapier. Here. Take this." And he hands me a foil and takes one himself.

He comes beside me and shows me the hand position—the thumb on top of the pommel and the rest of the fingers curled around. "See how by pulling the thumb back and forth and squeezing or not squeezing the fingers, you can control the point of the blade, up or down, and with your wrist, right or left? Good. Now, en garde."

I assume the position.

"Now hold your hand like this and position the point of your blade such that it is directly between your eyes, and the eyes of your opponent. Hold that." He moves back and lifts his own sword and gets in the en garde stance, which is the mirror image of mine. "Now the point is between our eyes. Advance."

I do it.

"Now retreat." I do that, too.

"Put your sword hand a little bit more to the left, but keep the point between our eyes. Good. That is Position

Four. It protects your left side. See, if I lunge in this position, my blade would slide harmlessly off to the side."

He makes a slow lunge to show me, and sure enough, I am able to slide his blade off to the side.

"Now, however, if I were to dip the point of my blade *under* your weapon"—he does it—"then I am in Position Six and your right side, from your breastbone to your right shoulder, is exposed."

He makes a slow lunge and puts the point of his foil on the right side of my chest. He retreats. "Now, to prevent that, when you see my point coming down into Six, you disengage from Four and go into Six—rotate your forearm and pull it way out to the right, still keeping the point between our eyes. Yes, I know it hurts. But it will hurt less than a sword point run through your neck. All right, go back in Four, which exposes my left side, and lunge."

I do it and he lets me touch him on the chest.

"Good. Now we shall have a match. You will advance and retreat and lunge at will, keeping in mind these two positions. They are the most important ones for the rapier, the other positions being ones that protect the legs and feet, but we will get to them later. Put the pommel of your weapon to your face with the point in the air and bow, and I will do the same. It is tradition. Now, en garde!"

And so it goes, for hours, it seems. *Advance, disengage Four, lunge, recover forward, retreat, retreat, advance, out of Six, into Four, lunge, recover. Now, beat parry Four, into Six, lunge! Retreat, beat parry Six, and…*

He parries everything I try, coming back to lay his point on my throat, my breastbone, anywhere he wants, but then, when he sees that I grow discouraged, he lets me through to touch him on the chest.

Finally, we stop. "You did well," he says. "Especially on the envelopment parry. It is not an elegant thing, but it might save your life someday. Good day, Miss. You know what to practice." With that he leaves me standing there, exhausted.

I have the Evening Watch, the Eight to Twelve, one of the sweetest watches to stand, for it guarantees eight solid hours of sleep afterward.

Before going up, I take food down to share with poor Robin, yet again. Tonight's dinner is fine cuts of meat swimming in a sauce made of what I think are truffles. *Truffles!*

He has not cheered up much, but then again, how could I blame him, confined as he is to an eight-by-eight-foot cage, not knowing what is to become of him. Plus, him thinking that I'm being ravished on a regular basis by the loathsome Captain Scroggs must prey on his mind. He has grown wilder, pacing back and forth like a caged animal and raging. He has taken to pounding the ceiling of the cell with his fist, daring the Captain to take him out and hang him, and poor Private Rodgers has to say, *Please, Sir, none of that...*

Robin does not look much like a boy, anymore. He needs a shave.

I have to let him suffer, for if I were to tell him the Captain is dead, then he would demand to be taken out and put in command, being the senior *male* officer aboard, and I cannot have that, not yet, anyway. It is not part of the plan.

After he has eaten, I say, "Come sit over here, Robin, next to the bars. Hold my hand and let me put my head on your shoulder for a bit, as it will give me comfort." He does it and it does give me comfort.

Before assuming the watch, Higgins appears to collect the dishes. He also has my jacket, for which I am grateful, as it has turned quite cool. Good for the Captain's condition, I reflect.

"I trust I was not forward, Miss," he says.

*What?*

I go to put the jacket on and I see what he means. Somehow, from somewhere, Higgins has found some lieutenant's lace and woven it through the lapels, just where it belongs. The lace catches the waning evening light. My chest expands with pride. False pride, I know, but still...

"Thanks, Higgins," I say, and I cannot say more. He bows and disappears in the shadows.

I step up and assume the watch.

# Chapter 16

This will be the last day of this deception and I mean to make the most of it. After breakfast I appear on the deck in my jacket with my new lieutenant's lace woven through my lapels, and I hear some low whistles and *the Captain's whore—lookit 'er all tricked up,* but I choose not to hear. I know it mainly comes from Muck's bunch. I hear a lot more of *there's our Puss-in-Boots, by God,* and that cheers me.

Again I set Jared on the deck as Sailing Master, this time without the pretense of helping one of the boys, as it is my watch and I will be busy.

"Take us out to sea again, Jared. You have the con," I say.

"Aye, aye, *Lieutenant,*" he says, with a not-quite smirk on his face. I know I let him get away with being entirely too familiar with me, so I give him a warning look. He knuckles his brow and shouts, "All topmen aloft to make sail!"

I sense, too, that Jared really likes standing on deck as Sailing Master. His teeth gleam in a wide grin as he barks out the orders for the resetting of the sails as the ship turns out to sea. "Get aloft there, you lubbers! Could you be any slower! Port your helm! Haul on those buntlines! Bring her around! Cleat down the foresail! Now the jib!" He is quite a sight, standing there with his feet apart, fists on hips, his head thrown back and the breeze blowing his curls about his face, his back straight and his striped shirt tight across....*No, girl, you keep your mind on the job at hand.*

"Muster the gun crews for practice," I say to the Bo'sun and he goes off and does it.

I did not do the pantomime at the speaking tube this morning. The Bo'sun took the order directly from me, without notice or comment.

*Good.*

I go and stand on the hatch between the mainmast and the foremast so I can see all four of the gun crews. I have a barrel put over the side.

"Werewolves! Today we shall practice broadsides. Gun captains, prime your guns!" The guns are, of course, still loaded from the day before, as they should always have been. "Report when ready!"

I wait for them to prick the charges and pour in the primer and cock the flints.

"Division One, Manned and Ready, Sir!" barks out Harkness. *Good old First Division, first again.* "Division Three, Manned and Ready, Sir!" I know the "Sirs" are coming automatic and have nothing to do with me, but... "Division Two, Manned and Ready, Sir!" Then, "Division Four, Manned and Ready!" says Shaughnessy, shamed to be last.

"We shall begin with a rolling broadside on the starboard side, fore to aft! Fire on my command!" I wait till the barrel is in good position, then I puff up my chest and yell, "Fire!"

Number Nine barks out its charge, then Ten, and Eleven, and so on down the line till all eight have fired, each in turn. It was most elegant, and most of the shots fell close to the barrel. The starboard side rushes to reload.

"Jared, bring her about!"

He does and the port guns have their turn.

"Fire!" I shout again and Number One cracks, then Two, and so on down the line, each gun thundering in turn. I lift the long glass to watch the target. It is Number Seven that nicks the barrel, I think, but it still floats.

"About again!" I call, and the *Wolverine* backs her sails and comes around. *Nice maneuver, Jared.*

"Full broadside this time, Mates! On my order!" Again I wait a bit and then... "Fire!"

There is a mighty, thunderous blast as all the starboard guns belch forth at once. I know it is small of me, but I find it immensely satisfying for my small voice to bring forth such a tremendous sound. The ship itself rocks back in recoil. I look out and see the barrel tossed in the air. There is a mighty shout from the men and I start chanting, "*Were-wolves! Were-wolves! Were-wolves!*" and all the gunners, both port and starboard, pick up the chant "*Were-wolves! Were-wolves! Were-wolves!*"

Again the ship is brought about and I shout over the din to the port guns, "Full broadside. On my command... *Fire!*" The port guns roar as one and the ship heels again and the barrel disappears in a shower of splinters and there is a mighty roar from the men, "*Were-wolves! Were-wolves! Were-wolves! Hurrah!*"

I put aside the glass and leap up into the jack lines. "You

have done a fine job! Reload, but do not prime, and secure from drill. An extra tot again this day for your fine work, and beef and plum duff for dinner!"

*Hurrah! Hurrah! Hurrah!*

My ears are still ringing from the blasts as I head back into the cabin.

*The last day and night as roommates, Captain,* I think. I look over at him. His white skin has gone a bit gray and maybe a little black about the temples, but still no overpowering reek. At night, he has begun to give off little *pops!* and *pfffffps!* followed by a real stench in the room, but I think that is due mainly to his belly swelling up and then farting and burping itself back down. I will certainly sleep this last night with my nose next to the crack under the door, where a fresh draft works its way in around the Marine sentry's boots.

I force myself to spend some time in the cabin, for appearances' sake. Having this time, I make a last inspection of the cabin. I haven't forgotten the key that I took off the Captain that now hangs around my own waist, and so now I look about in real earnest.

I peer around under the desk and poke around shelves and tables and things, but nothing. Then I look over at the Captain. Of course. He would trust nothing that he held valuable to be very far from him. I see that behind the covers that hang down from the bed there are drawers built into the bottom of his bed, and the middle one seems to have a keyhole.

I don't want to get near him, but I must. I take the key and crawl over on my hands and knees so I won't have to look at his body moldering up there on the bed. I reach the drawer and put the key in the lock and turn it. It works.

I go to pull it open, but there are some of the covers hanging in front of it, and so I move them to the side and when I do his arm comes swinging down over the edge of the bed and flops against my head.

*"Aaahhhh!"* I shriek in terror and fall back on my elbows, watching the horrid arm, all mottled black and white and gray, swinging back and forth in front of the drawer, as if protecting in death whatever the Captain treasured in life.

*Damn!* What if someone heard me cry out? I look at the door, knowing the Marine is standing right there. To get so near the end and to be found out now. No! I must...

"Ahhh, Captain," I say a little less loud than before. Then I pause. Then I giggle. Then I give one of my Captain imitations. *Hrrrummmp graggle.*

"Oh, Captain," even less loud this time, trying to make it sound as if the Captain was now done taking his pleasure with me. I don't know what that sort of thing really sounds like, but thinking back to the sounds I used to make when I was in a clutch with Jaim—with that boy back on the *Dolphin,* I think I've gotten close enough.

At any rate, there's no pounding on the door.

The Captain has made his own bed, in a way. He has made his men so terrified of him that no one wants to risk taking it upon himself to check on his well-being. If any of them have suspicions, they keep them to themselves.

I get up and look about for something to move the Captain's arm, for I'm certainly not going to touch it. *Ah. The Captain's sword.* I take it, scabbard and all, over to the bedside and with it, I lever the arm back onto the bed, tucking

217

it way over so it doesn't come down again. When I do it, I jostle the body slightly and...*purrrrppp*...I almost cry out again as I whip my hand over my mouth and nose in a vain attempt to keep out the awful smell.

I drop back to my knees, trying to keep from retching, and pull open the drawer.

The first thing to greet my sight is an elegant, leather-bound case. I pull it out and open the catch. Inside lie two matched pistols, beautifully engraved and polished. I pick one up and marvel at its workmanship and balance.

I smile and think. How would Miss Clarissa Worthington Howe, my old nemesis back at the Lawson Peabody School for Young Girls in Boston, put this? *Ah do think poor Captain Scroggs would want me to have these beautiful thangs, ah really do.* I feel the same way, Clarissa.

I put the pistols aside and delve deeper into the drawer. There is a bag and I lift it out. It clinks and it is heavy. I undo the drawstring on top and look in. It is full of gold. A *lot* of gold. There are guineas and half crowns and even Dutch guilders and other heavy coins that I can only guess at. I sit back on my heels. How could a mere one-swab captain, one who holds a dead-end command—a brig like the *Wolverine* usually has a senior lieutenant as commander—have this much money? I have an idea, but...

I pull the drawer all the way out and put the bag of gold behind it, in case someone else knows of the Captain's stash.

The rest of the drawer yields some packets of letters with weird groupings of letters on them. Some sort of code. Maybe his secret orders from the Admiralty. I don't know. We shall see.

That's about it. Another watch. Some rings and snuff-boxes and such, but that's it. No letters from a wife. No *Dear Papa* notes. No locks of hair, no miniature portraits. I close up the drawer and lock it and tie the key once again around my waist.

As I come out of the cabin, Higgins is there with the noon meal, with a white cloth neatly covering it. *No, no, I can't possibly eat anything in there.*

"The Captain is sleeping...," I say and glance over at Corporal Martin, the Marine on duty, and he blushes. *Hmm. I see my little act worked.* "...and I don't wish to disturb him. I will take my dinner below."

I go to take the tray but Higgins says, "Please, Miss, let me. I must get some things and I'll meet you down there with Mr. Raeburne."

Now, how did he know I've been taking food down to Robin? *You are turning out to be quite a fellow, Higgins.*

I take a turn on deck and Higgins beats me down to the brig. He has found a small table and placed it next to the bars close to Robin's bench, and he has found a chair for me to sit upon. He pulls it out as I approach, and I sit. There is a clean tablecloth on the table and the settings are arranged perfectly. The glasses are polished and twinkle in the dim light.

Higgins pours the wine and serves the food and retreats to the passageway. I know I have only to call and he will appear.

"Robin. Show some cheer. You are to be released tomorrow. I have arranged it." Hmmm...perhaps not a good choice of words on my part.

"How can you stand it? How can you stand him doing that to..." He looks even more disheveled and wild-eyed.

"Now, Robin. None of that. Come, look at this wonderful dinner Higgins has made for us. A glass of wine with you."

I can see that it all still tortures him and makes him writhe with impotent fury. He eats but seems to take no joy in it. He does throw down the wine, though.

This whole time, since I first went into the Captain's cabin that evening, Robin has not asked me for a kiss or an embrace or anything of that sort, and I think I know why. Though he has said he would still marry me, and I believe him on that, that would be something that might happen in the future. Right now, he can't bring himself to touch something the Captain has touched, kiss something the Captain has kissed, or embrace something the Captain has taken and defiled.

We eat mostly in silence.

Later, as I go out for my swordsmanship lesson, I notice four sets of boyish legs hanging over the edge of the foretop. One set of legs is whiter, less tanned than the others, but the feet are as bare and the pants are folded up over the knees like the others. *Are you looking up at the clouds as they roll past, lads? Are you making plans, boasting of future glory, swearing oaths of eternal brotherhood to each other?*

Even though I am glad to see them so, it gives me a bit of a pang to think back on how my own bare and tanned legs would dangle over the edge of the foretop on the *Dolphin*, not so very long ago.

Ah, thoughts of the past—always rosier than they actually were. My reveries end when Peter Drake steps up on the hatch for the lesson. We bow to each other and lift our foils. En garde!

Afterwards, when the session is about over, Drake says, "You have been coming along. I did not think it possible, but you have attained a measure of skill in a very short time. A small measure, to be sure, but still…" He trails off, maybe slightly embarrassed? "Please wait here, if you please," and he goes off.

*What?*

In a moment he is back, bearing something wrapped in a cloth. "This is for your efforts…in spite of your…troubles…in trying to make this a real fighting ship."

I take the bundle from his hands and unwrap it. It is a sword and scabbard with leather harness.

"Why…why, thank you, Drake," I say, looking in wonder at the thing. "I don't know what to say…"

"I have daughters, Miss," he says by way of some explanation. "Here. Permission to touch?"

I nod and say yes and he takes the belt and wraps it around my waist and cinches it tight. Then another strap of leather goes across my chest, over my shoulder, and back down across my back to attach again to the belt, to support the weight of the sword and scabbard, which Drake now snaps onto a ring on the harness. The sword hangs easily to my side.

"There," he says. "It is to be hoped that someday you shall tell your grandchildren how you once trod the deck of a Royal Navy ship with a proper sword by your side!"

I pull out the blade. It gleams as it comes out of the scabbard.

"The smithy had the forge fired up yesterday. I took a standard rapier and cut it down some in length, then pounded and tempered the blade and sharpened it all the way down until just above the hilt. I shortened the pommel—it fits your hand, I trust?" *It fits my hand perfectly.* I nod. "And I changed the hand guard from the simple bell to a more saberlike protection for your hand."

As always, when someone does anything really nice for me, my eyes start to well up. He sees and says, "None of that, now. We must exercise with your new weapon now. Carefully, though, as I've no wish to lose an eye. En garde!"

That evening, after I stand the Second Dog and turn the ship to the south, I go into the cabin to try to get a good night's sleep. I'll have the Four to Eight and things will change forever right after that.

But before I do that I kneel down and take the sword in my two hands. You shall be *Persephone,* after the Greek goddess who was condemned to spend half of each year in Hell as the consort of Hades, the Lord of the Underworld.

I look over at the shape of my would-be consort lying dead in the bed. You Gods, both Greek and Christian, know that I, too, have gone through some sort of hell down here, so *Persephone* you shall be.

I clutch *Persephone* to my chest as I curl up next to the door, my nose sucking up the fresh air from the outside.

And so the deception continues. Until tomorrow.

# Chapter 17

I step off the quarterdeck at eight in the morning, having been relieved by a very sleepy Ned. I pat his shoulder. *Don't worry, Ned. Your one-in-three watches will soon end, however things go for me.*

The Four-to-Eight watch was uneventful. No flashing lights from the shore, but I learned from Tom that there had been some on his watch.

Good.

I send word to Higgins that the Captain and I will want no breakfast today.

It is a beautiful morning with a nice alongshore breeze. We have just turned to the southern leg. I stand at the rail for a long time, looking out toward France. I wait, and I enjoy the day. I take a turn around the deck. I wait.

I go to inspect the guns. They are in good order. Swabs and wads in place. Everything clean, all lines and carriages taut.

At about ten o'clock, I go back out to the quarterdeck and take a long glass and climb up the ratlines into the maintop and look out toward the coast. The ship rolls along and it feels good under me and...

*There!* Another smuggler has nosed his way out from the coast, seeking, once again, to cross our wake without incident. Why am I not surprised? Did those flashing lights tell me something? I think they did, and if not, they will.

I take a deep breath and turn to the business at hand.

I send word for Bo'sun Morgan and for Higgins.

"Bo'sun, I want you to have the table from the officers' mess brought up and set it there on Three Hatch. I want there to be five chairs. One at the head, two on that side, one on that side, and one at the foot." The Bo'sun looks confused but decides not to argue, and he goes to have it done.

"Higgins, I want the table placed fore and aft. Set the table for five, two places on one long side, one place on each of the other sides. You will set out five glasses and place a bottle of the finest...Madeira, yes, on the table. You may draw the wine from the Captain's stores. Understand?" He bows and withdraws.

Tucker is the Messenger of the Watch. "Tucker," I say, "go get Mr. Wheeler. Wake up Corporal Martin and ask him to lay to the quarterdeck. I'll need Earweg, the loblolly boy, too. Be respectful, but do it. And when you have done all that, tell Jack Harkness and Joseph Jared that their presence is requested on Three Hatch. Oh, and have the Master of Arms bring up Mr. Raeburne from the brig. That is all."

I go down to the cabin, hearing the buzz of curiosity behind me. I know that as soon as my foot touches the deck on my way out, the entire ship will know of the table, and wonder at it.

I go down to the cabin and I strap on *Persephone,* then I go and get the pistols, and after checking that they are loaded, jam one into my cross-chest strap and one into my belt. My trousers are tucked into my boots. So, looking like the perfect pirate queen...*I hope*...I go back on deck.

They are all there: Tom Wheeler, Earweg, Seaman Harkness, Seaman Jared, and, standing between the two Marines and next to the Master-at-Arms Drake is the prisoner Midshipman Robin Raeburne, his hands shackled together in front of him. He blinks at the light and then looks at me. I do not smile or otherwise acknowledge his gaze. He lifts his chin and casts his eyes about, probably looking for the noose. I'm sure he suspects that the reason for all this is that he will be hanged today by order of the Captain for his mutinous conduct, in spite of what I had told him. After all, I'm just a girl. What influence could I possibly have with the cruel and vile Captain Scroggs?

I'm sure the crew also thinks that this is what is about to happen, as there is a low hum of sympathy, I believe, for the young man. Robin takes a deep breath and looks calmly off into eternity, a noble expression on his face.

*Good for you, lad.*

I go to the chair at the head of the table and Higgins pulls out my chair. I sit down, carefully. I know I present quite a sight already and I don't want to look ridiculous by tripping over my sword and sprawling across the deck. My back is to the quarterdeck, which holds only the helmsman and Ned. I face the entire crew, both those on the deck and those in the rigging. That is how I arranged it to be.

Higgins fills my glass with the sweet wine. I don't touch it.

"Mr. Raeburne, you will please sit there, next to me, and, Drake, if you would sit there." Higgins goes over and pulls out the chair for Robin. He looks confused, but he sits down, with Drake, looking guarded, next to him. The Master-at-Arms has to sit next to him because he's holding the end of the chain. I would have Robin unshackled, but I don't have the authority to do that on my own. Not yet, I don't.

Higgins fills his glass and that of Drake. Robin doesn't touch it, but only looks intently at me, me who's trying my best to look calm and collected. With Robin chained the way he is, I don't think he could reach the glass, anyway. Drake doesn't touch his, either.

The ship is dead quiet now, and I don't think there's a soul aboard who ain't listening in to all this.

"Harkness, if you would be so good as to sit here"—I motion to the place to my left—"and Jared, if you will sit there..." and I nod to the place opposite me.

They look at each other with eyebrows raised in question, but they do it. Higgins does not pull out their chairs, but he does pour the wine into their glasses. They do not reach for them.

I say nothing for a while. I look about as if this was just a jolly family outing, here out on the shining sea. Finally, I say, "I must commend the crew and especially you, Jared, and you, Harkness, for your performance over the last few days. I think I can safely say the ship is in fighting trim." They say nothing, only nod in a guarded way.

"That is good," I continue, "for I mean to take, as prizes, those ships that have been coming off the coast and thumbing their noses at us all these weeks."

There is a sharp intake of breath around the table.

"You mean the Captain...," says Harkness, narrow-eyed, leaning toward me.

226

"I mean *I* am going to take those ships and you all are going to help me, and by doing so, will make yourselves rich. Rich in prize money."

I pause, letting this sink in, and then I say, "The Captain is dead. He has been dead ever since that night he tried to have his way with me."

They are astounded. The men on deck and in the rigging let their breath out in one sharp *whoa!* of astonishment. Robin's head snaps up and his countenance undergoes a transformation upon hearing me say the word *tried*.

Before they can do anything else, I continue in command voice. "Corporal Martin, you will take Earweg into the Captain's cabin and verify what I say. Earweg, you will then undress him and examine him for any wounds—you will find none. He died of a brain or heart stroke in the excitement of his desire to wear the mantle of my maidenhead. In which attempt, by the by, he did not succeed." *So much for "the Captain's whore," you dogs.* "When you have done that, you men at this table will verify it and will sign a paper to that effect drawn up by Mr. Wheeler here. *Do it, Corporal Martin!*" I bark out as he hesitates. The Marine and the loblolly boy go down into the cabin.

I notice that men have come down from the rigging and are beginning to make a circle around the table. *Better do this quick,* I think. Even though the day is cool, sweat is trickling out of my armpits and down my sides. My face is dry, though, and I place the Look upon it and hope for the best.

"You men," I say to Jared, Drake, and Harkness, "and all you men"—I raise my voice to the throng pressing ever closer—"have a decision to make. I am Acting Lieutenant

Faber, made so by Captain Scroggs before you all, as you well know. I have been written into the ship's log as such, and, as such I am, and have been for the past four days, by lawful succession in the naval chain of command, the commander of this ship!"

Growls and grunts and disbelieving *ahs!* greet this announcement. The *Hmmmm!* starts up again, this time *not* in my favor.

I lean back in my chair to look all languid and without fear or care, even though my heart is pounding hard in my chest, and I say, "It is simple. Here are your choices: You can stand in open mutiny to my lawful authority, bind me, confine me, do whatever you want with me. When the Court of Inquiry convenes, they will doubtless commend you for your courage in standing up against a foolish woman. They will probably pin medals on you, and then they will most certainly hang you, for you know there are no exceptions to mutiny!" I lean into that one.

I let that little nugget of doubt worm into their brains and then I say, "Or, you can follow me, take lawful prizes, and be happy in your newfound wealth. If there is any problem with all of this later, it will be on my head, not yours. You can truthfully say you were only following lawful orders. What will it be?"

*This is the moment, right here, right now. Whether Jared and Harkness and Drake will follow me and whether they can hold the crew. Whether in one minute I am in command of this ship or in its brig. Or worse.*

"I fer one ain't gonna be followin' no orders from no jumped-up splittail what thinks she's a bleedin' officer!"

*Uh-oh...*

That came from a group of men gathered about the foot of the mainmast. There are growls of agreement. Curses, too. I look over and see that it has come from none other than Cornelius Muck, himself. His crew of ne'er-do-wells, slackers, and Waisters is around him, nodding and mouthing their agreement.

I jump to my feet. "Hear me on this, all of you! When I was child, I was an orphan on the streets of London. I was a member of the Rooster Charlie Gang and we lived in our kip under Blackfriars Bridge. Is anyone here from Cheapside?"

The crew is taken aback by the sudden turn this has taken, but I have known, from their Cockney accents and the slang they use, that there were many from my old neighborhood aboard, and several from the crowd do say, *Yes, I'm from Cheapside,* and one in the rigging says, *Aye, I remember that gang,* and suchlike. They are mystified, but Muck is not. A look of sudden fear crosses his face, and I can see him trying to make his way back into the crowd.

"Then you must know of Muck, the Corpse Seller!" I sing out. "He who gathered us up when we were dead and sold our bodies to the anatomists who cut us up and treated us most foul! Do you remember?"

More calls of *Aye* and *I remembers the bastard!* Muck tries to get back and away, but he can't—the crowd is too close.

"Well, there stands, 'neath that beard and cap, and under the false name of Asa Horner, none other than Cornelius Muck, the Cheapside Ghoul, the Purveyor of Corpses!" I make my arm ramrod straight as I point my finger to Muck's stricken face. He shakes his head *no…no…* but it ain't gonna do him any good.

Hands are put on him and men peer into his face. *Good God, it's 'im! It's goddamn Muck, himself!* says a voice and *'e got me little brother! And 'im not dead but a few minutes!* says another and *a body snatcher! Here, on our ship!* and then, the thing that dooms him...*He's the Jonah! The cause of all our bad luck!*

The babble of voices grows louder and louder. I rise and go to the rail and look out over the water to France. Behind me, I hear the sound of a struggle, but I do not turn to look. If someone wants to take this moment to put a blade between my shoulders and settle this that way, then so be it. My last sight on this earth will be the beautiful ocean slipping by my keel on a beautiful, soaring day.

There are sounds of desperate pleading behind me, cries of *no...please, no!* then a long, long gurgling sound, then silence. Sounds of something being dragged. Then a splash. Then, again...silence.

*So, Rooster Charlie, so...*

I turn back to face the crew. Jared and Harkness are standing at their chairs. Jared is smiling at me. "What's it to be, Lieutenant?" he says.

Taking my seat again, I reflect that sometimes it takes blood to properly seal a bargain. "Please sit, gentlemen. Drake, please unlock Mr. Raeburne's bonds." All sit and Robin's hands are freed. He rubs his wrists and looks at me with real heat in his eyes.

"You, Mr. Raeburne, are to be First Mate. You, Mr. Jared, are to be Master's Mate. You, Mr. Harkness, are to be Gunner's Mate, and you, Mr. Drake, are to be Sub-Lieutenant-at-Arms. Mr. Wheeler, read that into the log." I see their chests swell at being elevated to warrant officer rank. "A glass of wine to seal the bargain." I lift my glass and they do, too, and we all drink them down.

"I will dine with my officers tonight in my cabin. That is, if we are not otherwise engaged. As for now, we are going to take that ship!"

As one my men look out toward the smuggler. A roar of pure greed comes from their throats.

I rise and call out, "Beat to Quarters! Clear for action!"

Feet pound on the deck and the men go running to their stations, joyous as any pack of wolves in sight of helpless prey. I go up on the quarterdeck to relieve Ned who dashes to his station as Fire Control Officer with Tom. I see Georgie and Tucker tumble out of the foretop and head for the port guns, and I confer with Jared and Harkness as to our plan.

"Mr. Jared. I want to continue south for a bit till our quarry goes over the horizon. Then turn east and parallel their course for about a half hour till we are out of sight of land as well. Do you understand why?"

Jared's cocky look is back on his face. It gives me some satisfaction to recall that, during the session at the table, that look was gone for a bit. "You do not want to alarm those on the shore so that they will stop sending ships out?"

"Even so, Mr. Jared. You have the con. Mr. Harkness, you will ensure that all the guns are ready. And I want you to personally make ready the Long Tom up in the fo'c'sle. It's possible it may see some action this day, and, if it does, I want you to do the firing."

Jack Harkness grins and goes to knuckle his brow and

then remembers his new station and bows instead and says, "It shall be done, Lieutenant."

"Thank you, Mr. Harkness."

I guess that is what they have decided to call me. *Lieutenant.* Lieutenant Faber. I think about it and decide that I like it.

Robin comes up to me now. "I am so glad, Jacky, I..."

"So am I, Robin, but now you must go down and clean up. I have put Seaman John Harper in charge of your old division. As First Mate, your place during Quarters will be by my side on the quarterdeck. Go down. We will have the Captain's funeral soon, and you must be presentable." He hesitates, then nods and goes to leave.

"And Mr. Raeburne..." He turns and looks at me. I lay two fingers over the lace in my lapel. "...when we are in public..."

He flushes and says, "Yes, Lieutenant." He turns on his heel and is gone.

*Sorry, Robin, but if you think things are going to be as they were, you are wrong.*

I send the Messenger of the Watch for Higgins and when he arrives I say, "Have Earweg prepare the Captain's body for burial. Then, if you would be so good, see what you can do to fix up the cabin for me. I know it's distasteful...the bed and all..."

Higgins bows and says, "On the contrary, Miss. This is the happiest day of my life. I shall do what I can."

I take a deep breath and go to my usual spot on the quarterdeck, right in the middle with one leg on either side of the centerline so I can get the feel of the ship. I look up at the sails and find that they are perfectly set, and when I look back down, I am astounded to find little Eli Chase, the smallest of the ship's boys, standing in front of me with a drum strapped on his waist, his hands holding the drumsticks poised above it, his eyes fixed on my face should I give an order that requires his drumming. *Oh, my...*

During the chase Captain Scroggs went over the side. Earweg had sewed him up in a canvas bag and his mortal remains were laid upon a plank that was set on the starboard rail. I took the Bible and said the necessary words and the board was lifted and the body slid off.

On my command, the men of the starboard guns pulled their shameful skirts from their belts and threw them into the water, to sink down with the Captain's corpse.

There was not a sorry heart nor a damp eye on the ship.

We come down on the unsuspecting smuggler like the pack of hungry dogs we are.

He is running up there ahead of us, and I take the glass and run up to the foretop and train it on him. Sure enough, the other Captain has his glass trained on us and, from what I can see, is looking mighty worried. *Why is this English ship bearing down on me?* he's probably thinking. *Have not the bribes been paid?*

*Oh yes, Frenchy, you have paid, but not quite enough. Not yet, anyway.*

A suspicion has been growing in my mind that Captain Scroggs had been taking bribes for letting the smugglers through the blockade, a suspicion fueled by gazing at all that gold he had in his drawer. As I figure, he was probably paid off through a middleman in London—the smugglers pay the middleman, who takes his cut, and then gives the rest to the Captain and all are happy. *Were* happy, that is.

I still haven't figured out the flashing lights on the shore, though, and we did see them again last night.

"Mr. Harkness!" I shout down. "Give him one across his bow."

*Crracckk!*

The bow chaser barks out its nine-pound ball. It hits a few yards off to the left of the ship. *Good shooting. We don't want to hurt the prize,* which looks to be a nice little two-masted schooner, maybe ninety feet long. Good and beamy and sure to hold a fat cargo. Little Mary, Cheapside Mary, that greedy little thief who still lives within me and is never very far from the surface, is in full control of me now, and my heart beats in a state of high excitement as we bear down. *Better than rollin' drunks, eh, Mary?* I think.

"Another on his other side, Mr. Harkness!"

*Crraacckk!*

The Long Tom blows out another blast of fire and smoke. *That was quick reloading, Jack Harkness. Good job.*

The ball hits about ten yards to the right of the schooner, but she shows no sign of heaving to. Probably doesn't know anything about that, striking the colors and all, being a non-combatant. *Give up nicely now, Frenchy. This is strictly business, nothing personal. Don't want anyone to get hurt.*

I swing back down to the quarterdeck. Drake had already been told to issue cutlasses and they gleam in the hands of my sailors.

"We'll come along his port side and take him there," I say to Jared. "Mr. Raeburne, muster the Boarding Party, but keep the starboard gun crews at their stations in case..."

*Booommmm...*

There's a blast from the other ship, a high whistle and a neat round hole appears in the mainsail right above our heads. *He's firing on us, the sod! The cheek of the man!*

"Close now!" I shout to Jared. "Man the Boarding Party on the starboard side!" The drummer boy starts his drum roll and I pull my sword.

We're comin' up fast on the prize, only about fifty feet away...now twenty...ten...we are on her!

"Starboard gun crews, hold your positions!" yells Robin, lifting his own cutlass. "Grappling hooks, away!" He gets up on the rail.

The hooks are thrown and the ships are pulled together.

I lift my voice in the chant, "Were-wolves! Were-wolves! Were-wolves!"

And the chant is taken up by the entire crew, until the very sky seems to shake with it.

*Were-wolves! Were-wolves! Were-wolves!*

With Robin in the lead, the Werewolves surge over the rail, waving their cutlasses and yelling like very devils from Hell. Jared and I swing aboard and we find the crew of the smuggler cowering against the starboard rail. Their Captain stands up before them and unbuckles his sword.

"*Capitaine?*" he asks of Robin. The French Captain is plainly enraged by the turn of events, but I guess he intends to do things in the right way with the giving up of his sword and all. Robin shakes his head and directs the Werewolves to disarm the smuggler crew and herd them back onto the *Wolverine,* where they will be confined below.

"*Capitaine?*" he says again, holding his sword out to Jared.

Jared grins his mocking grin and bows low, sweeping his arm toward me, standing there with *Persephone* in my hand. "No, Sir. *This* is the *Cappy-tan*. May I present our own Captain Puss-in-Boots?"

The Frenchman's mouth drops open. "*Une femme! Une jeune fille!*" he says and pulls his sword and I drop down in the ready position, but he pulls the sword to use on himself, not me. Jared comes up next to him and knocks the sword out of his hand.

"You'll get over it, Froggie, count on it," says Jared. "After all, we did."

The French crew of what turns out to be the *Emilie* is taken over to the *Wolverine,* to be put into the brig until we can prepare the fo'c'sle for them. I go to the hatch that leads down into the hold. There is a lock on it. Jared comes up next to me and upon seeing it, takes an ax from its place in a bracket on the mainmast, swings back, and smashes the lock off. We go in.

In the gloom, I see stacks and stacks of cases. As my eyes become used to the gloom, I see what is stamped into the sides of the cases:

H. M. FLETCHER & SONS

IMPORTERS OF FINE WINES

BRATTLE STREET, LONDON

*Oh, my…Jaimy Fletcher's dad…*

Laughter bubbles up in my chest, but I make myself stop thinkin' about that 'cause I got a real problem here. I stick my head back out the hatch and bellow, "Mr. Drake, to me

NOW!" I look again at the cargo. *Christt! Just what I need— a hundred drunken Werewolves!*

Peter Drake comes bounding across the deck and I climb back out of the hatch and stand in plain sight of the crew so that all can hear.

"Mr. Drake. You will secure this cargo. Shoot any man that tries to force his way into it. Do you understand?"

He says he does and motions to some of his trusted men to get chains and locks. Then he gives orders to collect the cutlasses, as they are no longer needed. *Good man.*

I step up on a hatch cover and say to my crew, "Werewolves!"

There is a roar in answer.

"You shall each share in this fine wine with your dinner tonight. We shall plunder the stores of this ship and you shall have the finest of feasts!" I pause. "But if you want to ever see any serious prize money, if you ever want to ever have money to spend when you go ashore, you have *got* to leave the cargo alone. We will take it back and we will sell it and you will all get your proper share. Do you understand?"

There is another roar.

"Good. Now let's get back on station before they know that we have been gone."

I put my foot back on the *Wolverine* and give the orders.

*Captain Puss-in-Boots, indeed... I'll get the rascal for that.*

# Chapter 18

"I wish you the joy of your first command, Robin."

I have called him into the cabin in the morning to give him his orders before he departs with the prize. It is the first time we have been alone together since he was released from the brig.

He comes up to me and takes my hand and holds it to his lips.

"I don't care about my first command. All I care about is you. Why did you not send Jared or Harkness back with the prize? I want to..."

"I know what you want to do, Robin, but we can't do that now. I am the Commander of this ship, however crazy that sounds, and you are my First Mate. We have to keep it that way, at least for a while, till this is all resolved. I do have great affection for you and I do love you, in my way, but...I'm confused...and I do intend to live single all of my life, as I am convinced that would be best, considering the mess I usually make of things."

"That's nonsense, Jacky, and you know it." He puts his arm around my waist and draws me to him, but I push him back.

"Please, Robin. We must deal with the problem at hand. Your orders are to sail the prize back to England and register it with the Prize Court. See if there are any problems. Get a lawyer if that seems wise. It is your job to protect the crew's money. This is our big chance and we are all counting on you. When you get that done, hire a boat to bring you and the prize crew back as soon as possible. This scam won't last forever, and I'll need you here."

He glowers at me. I soften a bit.

"I'll need you here, my *beau sabreur*," I say, and put my hand on the hilt of his new sword that hangs by his side. I had given him the French Captain's sword in the way of reward for how he had handled himself and the men of his Boarding Party when we took the prize. I turn my face up to his. "Now a kiss for good luck, and then go."

Our boat takes Robin over to the prize and he climbs aboard to take command. I had given him the money we found when we ransacked the French Captain's quarters. It wasn't much, but it will probably do to get things started— especially since I added a few gold pieces from Captain Scroggs's stash to it.

Jared has the watch and he comes up next to me to watch the *Emilie* sail off. He, Harkness, and Drake are in rotation as Officers of the Deck with Ned and Tom. I'm off the Watch list as befits my station. Pretty soft, that, but I do need my rest. No telling what is to come.

Jared is clad in his new warrant officer's jacket as befits *his* new station, and he looks good in it. The coat is black with a high collar and the gold tabs of rank sit upon the shoulders, and I know he wears it with pride. I can tell that by the way he takes a deep breath every now and again so as to feel it tighten across his chest. Higgins had somehow rounded up uniforms for the three new officers—probably from the stores of the unfortunate Mr. Harvey and Mr. Smythe. I shall have to make sure they are reimbursed for their loss. I'm sure Captain Scroggs will be delighted to pitch in.

"Why did you send the boy, Lieutenant?" he asks, as usual skirting the edge of insolence. "I could have sent Harper over with that ship."

"Because he's a gent, as well as a fine young man, Joseph," I say with narrowed eyes. Robin has proved he is no mere *boy.* "And we both know that will go a lot farther with the Admiralty than any of us common types showing up on their doorstep. If he runs into trouble, he'll ask his father or some other relative and they'll get a lawyer and things will be said in the right ears and things might work out well for us. You do know it's not a sure thing with prizes?" I ask, watching his face.

He grunts and says, "You mean they may call this piracy instead of prize taking?"

"Something like that. It depends whose ox is being gored in the loss of the cargo. There was someone in England waiting for that ship, you know."

I think back to the jolly time we had with the Fletcher wine company's product last night when I dined with my new officers. It was a wonder what Higgins had done with the musty old cabin. Fresh breezes blew through newly cleaned curtains. The bed mattress had been turned and set out for an airing and then returned to the bedstead and made up with fresh sheets and pillowcases. The table had

been set with a gleaming white tablecloth and the place settings were perfect, the silverware polished and set just so,
and the cabin positively gleamed with new wax.

The glasses twinkled merrily as Higgins poured the fine
wine, and we drank toast upon toast to each other and to
our bravery and to our cunning and we sang songs and told
tales. It was then that I presented the French Captain's sword
to Robin, saying that such a fine young gentleman should
not be flinging himself onto the decks of enemy ships with
a common cutlass in his hand. I gave him a peck on the
cheek as I presented it to him, but that was all he was to get
in that way. I saw him sneaking glances at the newly cleaned,
newly aired, and newly fluffed-up bed beneath the speaking
tube, the bed in which I would later be sleeping. I know he
is picturing me as I looked in my bed in the midshipmen's
berth the last time we were there together.

And that is another reason I sent Robin off—to try to
cool his ardor a bit. It's a touchy thing with Robin. For me
to have actually offered myself to him that time, as I did,
and then to turn around and pull back into propriety, well,
I know it's hard on him. Explaining that the circumstances
are different now doesn't seem to help much, either.

My crew, as well, enjoyed themselves hugely at dinner,
with the booty taken from the *Emilie*'s stores and the ration
of wine set out for them. I announced that singing and
dancing was allowed until six o'clock, and from my cabin I
heard the sound of a pennywhistle, something I had not
heard in a long time, and I vowed to find out who was the
player. He was pretty good.

I rouse myself back to the present and say to Jared, "Keep
a sharp eye out for any more that might try to cross our

wake, Mr. Jared," and I leave the quarterdeck and go below to check on the prisoners.

First off, we had packed them all into the brig, there being only about twenty of them, but they were so packed in there that they could only stand and not sit. Drake worked furiously with the shipfitters and carpenters to fashion a larger prison down under the fantail, on the lowest deck down, and that's where they are now. It's pretty foul but they won't be down here long. They don't know that, though. They probably think they're going to be taken to England to be hanged, and I let them think that, but I won't really do it. Harkness had asked me about it, about why we didn't just send the prisoners back in the hold of the *Emilie,* but I said that they were just sailors like us and I didn't want to see them jailed or hanged just for doing something that we might be doing ourselves someday. He snorted and asked me what I was going to do with them then, and I said I'd decide later.

*Damn! There're so many details to this plundering business.*

I look them over and they seem healthy enough. I ask them in French if they have been fed and they sneer and say that yes, they have been given what we English would call food. It galls them all the more that I am a girl, but I am not down here to enrage them, merely to observe, so I leave. But not before I notice that one of them, better dressed than the others, stays far back in the pack, like he doesn't want me to notice him. He was a passenger and we tossed his room but could find nothing except for some clothing. On his person, he just had a small pistol and a little money, I recall, all of which we took.

Something about him strikes me as curious, is all.

I go back up the three levels to the deck, confident that

the smugglers are secure, and emerge into the light. I hear the sound of chatter and look up and see that the ship's boys are playing follow-the-leader with Tucker in the lead. The little deck apes are going hand over hand over the fore-topgallant brace, high over the deck, goading each other on. Georgie is the third one in line, right after Eli. *A few more days, Georgie.*

"Higgins," I say. I don't see him anywhere around, but as soon as I say his name, he appears at my elbow. I've found he is very good at that.

"Yes, Miss?"

"Will you ask Mr. Drake if he will join me for a little shooting on the fantail? Then bring up my pistols and the bottles we saved from last night's dinner."

Peter Drake shows me how the pistols are loaded and primed and we set up the empty bottles on the rear rail of the fantail, the stern of the ship. He shows me how to aim and asks me if I have ever fired a gun before.

"Only once, when I killed a pirate in a skirmish when I was on the *Dolphin*."

I fire, missing all the bottles. I try the other pistol and miss again.

"It must have been a very unlucky pirate," says Drake, drily.

"He was that," I say. "But then, he was a lot larger and a lot closer."

I reload and try again, trying to hold the gun steady as I sight across the barrel, and this time I get one, shattering it off into the ocean. The fact that it was not the one I was aiming at does not diminish my pleasure in seeing it go.

Peter and I trade shots and I find that he is a dead shot. I would not want to face him in a duel.

I upend the black powder horn and recharge, tamping it down, then ramming down the wad, and then the ball, and then another wad to hold it in. *Much like a cannon,* I'm thinking.

I fire again and hit another bottle and I hear something from the boys in the rigging overhead.

"What's going on?" asks one who was plainly below when we started all this and has just come up.

"The Captain's shooting bottles off the fantail, is what," comes the casual reply from Tam Tucker, as if it was the most natural thing in the world.

# Chapter 19

"On deck there! Sail standing out from the harbor!"

I leap into the rigging with my glass, my heart pounding. Another one, and it's a fat one! I exult with all the larceny that's in me. It's a two-masted brig, a little smaller than we are, but not by much. What could she be carrying?

My Sailing Master is up next to me in a flash.

"Same drill, Lieutenant?" he asks.

"Same drill, Mr. Jared. Let her slip over the horizon, then after her!"

He stands a little too close to me and gives me his cocky look, his face in mine. He's the first man I've met who can swagger standing still. "Like shooting fish in a barrel," he says with a grin.

"May it be ever so, Mr. Jared. But let us not grow too confident. Let us attend to our duties," I say. Then I turn and shout, "Beat to Quarters, boys! We've got another one!" and my Werewolves fly to their stations, every eye fixed on the prize, every greedy heart beating in joyous anticipation of more wealth, more excitement, more...well...*fun*.

———

Her name was the *Jan Wemple* and she was even easier to

take than the *Emilie*. Her Dutch Captain was too astounded to get off even a shot at us when we put a couple over her bow, or to put up any kind of fight as we lashed the two ships together.

We swarmed aboard with me in the lead and all the Werewolves howling like banshees. The completely terrified crew of the smuggler was quickly rounded up and taken aboard the *Wolverine*, and Harkness and I went below to examine the cargo.

Putting my hand on the latch, I feel like a child at Christmas. *Stop that now, you greedy girl. You get giddy and you are lost. You are doing this for your men, your country, and to get yourself out of a tight spot. Now settle down.* I open it and go in.

I see stacks and stacks of boxes. "What is it, Jack?" I ask of Harkness as he pries up a board and looks inside a crate.

"Looks like dishes. Crockery, like. Dutchy stuff," he says.

"Let's get Higgins over here to see what he thinks it's worth. If anyone aboard knows, it'd be him."

"Get the Lieutenant's man over here," shouts Harkness to a man on the *Wolverine* and then follows me down into the cabins to search for more booty.

The Captain's cabin yields a good deal more money this time—probably earmarked for bribes, probably even some meant for Captain Scroggs. I'm just cuttin' out the middleman, I'm thinkin'. It was in a locked drawer that we smashed open, not wanting to stand on ceremony. Some other stuff in there, too. A miniature portrait of his wife. Letters from his daughters. *Dear Papa...*

I take a deep breath and let it out slowly, feeling a bit rotten now. Jared comes in and sees me and what I got in my hands and says, "'Tis the nature of the piratical business, lass, some gains, some loses."

I'm pondering on that when the shout comes from above.

"Captain! Here comes another one!"

In a flash I'm back on the deck, all soft thoughts gone. There is another ship heaving over the horizon!

*Damn! She's seen us take this ship! She'll alert the others!*

"Joseph!" I shout. "Get the men back to their stations! We've got to stop her!" But Jared is already back on the *Wolverine* and the sails, which had been hanging slack, are pulled tight and they fill, and we are again in pursuit.

*Two ships,* I'm thinkin' to myself, *and no lights last night.*

She was fast, but we were faster, and soon we grappled again. This one, the *Heloise,* tried to claw her way back to the shore when she saw us at our cherry-picking work, but we managed to catch her before she got back in sight of land. She tried a few shots at us and Harkness had to put a few balls through her sails to get her to heave to.

When we boarded her, though, the sight of me out front of the howling, cutlass-waving mob—me with my pistols in my belt, my hair flying free, and my own sword in my hand—was too much for the Captain, who swore something and lunged at me with his saber upraised. I managed to parry the blade on its way down, but it narrowly missed my arm as it swished by my side 'cause my parry was too weak. He lifted his sword again, no finesse, just brute male strength is all, and was about to bring it down on me again and I, in desperation, dropped the point of my blade and gathered myself for a lunge at his throat when Jared stepped up and dropped him with a belaying pin to the head.

The unconscious Captain was hauled off with the rest of his crew and we had ourselves another fine ship with its rich cargo of olive oil, cask upon cask of the stuff. I muse that tons of olives were grown in southern Spain, France's ally in this war, then they were carefully picked and pressed of their oil, the oil put in barrels and carried by donkey the length of Spain, up across the Pyrenees Mountains, up through France, onto a boat, and right into our hands.

Funny how things turn out, sometimes. *The best-laid plans of mice and men...*

"A busy day's work," says Jared, as we watch the two prizes sail off toward England.

"Hot work, too," I say. I'm thinking of how I shall dream some nights of that sword coming down and almost taking off my arm, and in those dreams I shall wonder if I really would have put the point of my sword through his throat. I don't know.

Harkness comes up to us and says the obvious, "We're gettin' stretched pretty thin, what with sending off two more prize crews." We sent the *Heloise* off under John Harper's command and the *Jan Wemple* off under Seamus Shaughnessy. Both of them'll be lookin' for Master's jackets soon, too. Too bad I won't be here to put them on their worthy backs.

"I know, Jack. I'm hopin' Robin gets back with the first crew and some word on how things are goin' with the Prize Court," I say, wearily. *Details, details, details.* If I'd have known command would be like this, I'd have stayed a ship's boy.

There's a line of people to report to me.

First is Higgins: Yes, the cargo of the *Heloise* is valuable. "Very valuable. The finest Delft, Miss. I took the liberty of taking a few settings for your cabin? Ummm?"

Then Drake: "We haven't got much more room for prisoners, Lieutenant. I'll have to build another cage. And it's getting pretty foul down there."

*Christ! Like running a slaver!* I think, and then say, "Right, Peter. There won't be many more, if any. And oh, by the way, do you remember that cove who was dressed as a gent on the first ship we took? The *Emilie*? Good. Have him taken out and put alone in the brig. Thanks."

Peter Drake and I go down into the hold where the cage of the brig sits. I am dressed in full pirate queen regalia, and Drake has pistols and sword lashed to himself as well. The formerly well-dressed cove, who had by now divested himself of his finer clothes in a vain attempt to fit in with the other seamen, sits on the bench, disconsolate.

Before coming down, I asked Peter if he would respond "Right away, Captain," to any outrageous request I might make of him. He cocks an eyebrow and agrees.

"So, Monsieur," I say in French, "what were you doing on that ship that tried to evade our noble blockade?"

"I am but a poor businessman, Mademoiselle, only doing my business," he replies, again in French. Something strikes my admittedly tin ear about the way he pronounces *Mademoiselle*, having heard it pronounced by experts back at the Lawson Peabody School for Young Girls.

"A poor businessman, indeed!" I snort. "Come now, Monsieur, out with it! You know you are headed back to England for a noose, do you not? Why not make a clean breast of things?"

"But, Mademoiselle…," he says, shrugging, his palms up.

"Do you speak English?" I demand. I put the Lawson Peabody Look on my face: chin up, lips together, teeth apart, eyes hooded and absolutely devoid of pity.

"*Ah, non. Je ne parle pas anglais.*" Again the palms up, and this time with the supplicating eyes.

I turn to Peter Drake and say in English, of course, "I am done with him and I'm thinkin' the men need a little sport after their work today. Take him out on the deck, cut off his bollocks, and give him fifty lashes. Then bind him up and throw him overboard. Oh, and put an anchor around his neck, 'cause I don't want his body washin' up onshore and warnin' others of his ilk. I'll be in my cabin. Let me know when the fun starts." I go to leave.

"Right away, Captain," says Peter Drake, right on cue, heading briskly to the cage.

The man in the cell crumples to the floor.

"No, no, Miss, please don't," he says. In English.

"Let us start with your name." I say. "And before we start, let me tell you something you do not know. I intend to set each and every one of those French smugglers safe on French soil when this is all over. If you want to be among them, I suggest that you speak plainly to me. You can choose to believe me or not on that score, but your only alternative is the noose. Do you understand?"

I settle down for a long conversation.

He says that his name is Frederick Luce. It turns out that he is an important cog in the smuggling operation and he gives me many names—those exporting, those importing. Those bribing, those being bribed. I take it all down and I lock it in my drawer under my bed.

He says he tells me all, but I don't know....I leave him alone in the cell to fester further.


That night I dine by myself, with Higgins, of course, in attendance. We have the pretty Delft dishes and other pieces of finery that we have lifted off the *Jan Wemple*—Higgins, for all his deference and his obvious education in the finer things, is not averse to a little larceny, it seems, when it is in the service of one's master.

Higgins slides the covered dish in front of me and then takes the silver cover off of it to reveal the sliced meat and savory gravy and grilled potatoes that lie steaming beside it. I had not seen the silver cover before. There is a small white cloth covering my wineglass, I guess to keep the dust out, and he whips that off and pours the wine into it and then steps back out of sight behind me.

"Did you know, Higgins," I say, taking a sip of the wine, and leaning back, "that as little as a year ago I, myself, was in service?"

"Oh yes?" he replies.

"Yes. I was a chambermaid. I made beds, emptied slop jars, served dinners, washed laundry, combed hair, anything I was asked to do. Does that make you think less of me?"

"No, Miss, I could not think more of you were you a member of the royal house. You delivered me from a horrid situation and I will not forget it."

"Um," I say, "that was largely luck, you know."

"Luck that you made happen, Miss," he says and then

we are silent for a while. I turn to my dinner, which is, of course, delicious. Once again I reflect how easily I get used to the finer things, as if they are going to last forever, which I know they are not.

While I'm eating, I think more about those lights on the beach. The night before we took the *Emilie,* the lights blinked at us from the shore, and Frederick Luce was on board, sticking out like a sore thumb amongst the sailors. Then we took the *Heloise* and the *Jan Wemple* and there were no lights the night before and we found nothing out of the ordinary on board, nothing like Mr. Luce. *Hmmm.*

Higgins clears his throat behind me and I say, "Yes?"

"Forgive me, Miss, but may I speak?"

"Yes, of course."

"Did you know that I am not a member of the ship's company but am instead a free hire?"

"Which means...?"

"Which means I was hired directly by Captain Scroggs. After Lord Hollingsworth died and I was looking about for a new post, I thought a sea voyage would be just the thing," he says, letting just the slightest bit of bitterness creep into his voice.

*Ahhh...*

It must have been horrible for him—abused by the Captain and shunned by the crew because of...the way he is. No friends, no one to talk to. I say nothing and he goes on.

"I know you will leave the ship soon, and I wish to go with you."

I think about this and say, "You know, Higgins, I am just as likely to be poor, in jail, singing in taverns, or about to swing for my sins as I am to be in my current condition."

"Yes, Miss, but I will follow you wherever you may go."

"I will, of course, take you with me, but surely you can find a more suitable post?"

"Perhaps. But certainly not one more...interesting."

Well.

"All right, Higgins," I say, looking around at our splendid table. "You may start making preparations for our departure. I suspect it will be in a few days."

That night, as I lie asleep in my bed, *He* comes again for me, the pirate LeFievre with his noose that he puts around my neck and then pulls it tight till I'm choking and this time I look on the ground next to the keg that I'm teetering on and I see my cut-off arm lying there and bleeding with my sword in my dead hand. Then the keg is kicked out from under my feet, the rope bites into my neck, and I scream and I scream and I hear *Jacky! Jacky! What's the matter!* and I think it's Amy and I say, *Save me, Sister, save me!* But it's not, it's the speaking tube that's sayin' that and it's not Amy but Tom up on the deck and it's Private Rodgers who's shakin' me awake and there's Higgins and *oh...oh...oh...*

And then, later, as I have calmed myself and am heading back into sleep, I hear Tom say through the tube, "The lights, Lieutenant. They're back."

I say, "Aye," and lie awake for a bit more.

# Chapter 20

"Captain!" yells Ned through the tube. "Another ship is coming out!"

My eyelids seem glued together but I shake myself awake and plunge out of bed, out the hatchway, and up onto the quarterdeck, blinking at the light. I didn't think they'd try again. I'd thought they had the news that we were waitin' for 'em out here by now, but I'll take this gift, I'm thinkin', however unclearly. Ned hands me the glass and I squint through it. The ship is in full sail and again it looks like they mean to cross our wake as so many did before…before we started nailing them.

It is a fast ship, a brigantine—not as big as the *Heloise* or the *Jan Wemple,* but fast and sleek, and sure to contain some sort of treasure. I think of the lights that were blinked at us last night and I want to know what is in her.

"Beat to Quarters!" I yell, for what I know is the last time, and the feet pound and we are in hot pursuit.

"Take them now, Mr. Jared, in plain sight of the land. Let them know that no more will be slipping out."

He grins his wolfish grin and says, "Aye, Captain, we will take her. You'd best get dressed."

I look down at my nightshirt blowin' about my legs, my bare feet on the deck, my hairy ankles plain for all to see, and I have to agree. I head down to my cabin and find that Higgins has laid out both breakfast and uniform for me, the breakfast being good and the uniform having been cleaned and brushed. He gets the breakfast into me and me into the uniform and then I'm back on deck.

I tell the Messenger of the Watch to have George Piggott lay to the quarterdeck. In a minute he appears. Tucker is with him.

"Mr. Piggott. You are to resume your duties as midshipman. Go put on your jacket. Your duty station will be here with me on the quarterdeck as Junior Officer of the Watch. Do you understand?"

I want Georgie to have at least one action as a middie.

Georgie nods and turns to Tucker, and they exchange a kind of handshake, which I know to be some sort of brotherhood thing, and then both go off, Georgie to the midshipmen's berth, Tucker to his station as powder monkey for the Division One guns.

We wait now, as we close in on the other ship, which is fast, but I think we can catch her. My crew is more experienced, more attuned to getting the last ounce of thrust out of every sail. I can't say it's all due to me, but some of it is.

Georgie appears back on deck, buttoning his jacket and pulling it down tight. I notice that the coat is a bit looser in the waist, a bit snugger in the shoulders now. I go up to him and smooth the jacket over his back, brushing it off a bit.

He looks up at me. "When I was demoted, it was you that did it, wasn't it? Not the Captain..."

I sigh and say, "Yes, Georgie. It was me." I see his hurt

look. "But I never really took you off the books as midshipman. You've been one all along, and now it's time for you to resume your duties."

He nods but says nothing and takes a few steps away from me and assumes the Parade Rest stance.

The ship, which I now can see is named *L'Emeraude,* carries four guns, which look to be twelve-pounders, two on either side. She is well armed. She probably has a stern gun, too, since a ship this small would be more used to running than chasing. I am proved right in this when we see a puff of smoke from her fantail and a ball whizzes overhead.

I feel Georgie jerk by my side and he ducks his head. I remember what he had said about not being able to stand up when the time came. *Steady, Georgie, steady...*

Harkness on our bow chaser puts a shot over her bow, and, honor being satisfied, *L'Emeraude* strikes her colors. After all, what merchant captain in his right mind, with five, maybe six guns, would fight a King's ship, even a small one like the *Wolverine* with eighteen guns, all manned with crack Man-o'-War's men? I wouldn't do it, that's for sure.

The men set up their *Were-wolves! Were-wolves! Were-wolves!* chant as we close with *L'Emeraude.*

"You have the deck, Mr. Piggott," I say, and climb into the netting on the starboard side. Jared brings her in perfectly, and I leap onto the deck, followed by my Boarding Party. Again an astounded Captain stands there, but he doesn't hand over his sword. He just spits out the word *Brigand!* Then he spits for real on my boots and says *Pirate!* and then Drake hits him and then he ain't saying nothin'. Not spittin', neither.

Harkness goes to check the main cargo, but I go down into the cabins.

*The lights last night—I wonder what I will find?*

I go to a door and try it, but it is locked. I smell smoke. Could someone be trying to scuttle the ship? I lift my foot and slam my booted heel into the door by its latch and it flies open. I'm little, but I'm strong.

Charging in with sword drawn, I see a well-dressed man hurriedly stuffing papers into a cloth sack. There is a small fire on the desktop into which he has already thrown some letters. There is a pistol on the desk next to the fire and when he sees me, he picks up the pistol and aims it directly at my face.

My mouth drops open and there is the roar of a pistol firing, but it is not that pistol, no, it is the pistol in the hand of Joseph Jared, which he has just fired next to my ear.

I'm seeing all this as in a dream. A small hole has appeared in the well-dressed man's forehead. He stares sightlessly forward for a moment, then crumples to the deck, the pistol falling from his hand. I stand stunned, my mouth still open.

Jared whips me around and puts me up against the bulkhead. He grins his damned cocky grin and says, "That's at least three times I've saved your life, Puss-in-Boots, and now I'm gonna collect some reward." And he kisses me hard on my still-open mouth. *Long* and hard.

Finally, he backs off and looks at me, smiling. "First time you've ever been kissed by a man, Puss? A *real* man?"

I come back to my senses and say, breathlessly, "Put out the fire, Jared."

"If you mean the fire down below, Jacky, that will never go out...," he says, coming for me again.

"The fire on the desk, you fool!"

He turns and looks and then smothers it with a pillow from the man's bed. While he does it, I go over and grab the bag the man was stuffing with papers. I have to pull it from under his body. I lift it and discover the bag is weighted, like it's designed to be thrown overboard and sunk with its contents.

I look at the papers. Some are letters in English, some in French. Some are meaningless collections of letters. I think on this.

*Codes. Spies. The blinking lights on the beach. So, along with everything else he was, Captain Scroggs was a traitor as well. The lights signaled that a spy would be crossing the next day and the* Wolverine *had to be kept well away.*

"Gather up this stuff, Joseph. Miss none of it. This is very important. This is more important than me or you..." *or anything else you might have in mind, Joseph Jared.* "This is going to be of great interest back at the Admiralty, and this is going to guarantee our prize money!"

He's right. It is the first time I've ever been kissed by a full-grown man. Kissed that way, anyway.

I should have bitten his tongue...but I didn't.

The cargo of *L'Emeraude,* aside from spies, was French perfume—there were boxes and boxes of tissue-wrapped bottles of the stuff. I had it all taken over to the *Wolverine* and stowed below. 'Course I took some for myself—enough to last several lifetimes, probably.

The dead spy is stripped of his clothes and a chain with a weight attached is wrapped around his neck and he is thrown overboard without ceremony. I take the papers back to my cabin and tell Private Rodgers that I am not to be disturbed by anybody, and then I go through them carefully. I compare them to the coded things I had found in Scroggs's safe, and they look mighty similar. Some of the letters are in code, some not. I am able to cipher out reports of English troop movements, descriptions of shore fortifications, and things of a like nature. *Things an invading army would want to know.*

It seems our spy had several names. Kopp. Boland. And his code name was *Defiant.* I think for a bit and then I go get a few selected men and some equipment. I coach these men in their duties, set them up, and then go down in the hold to see my supposed smuggler, Mr. Frederick Luce.

I wear my pistols down for this interview, as well as my sword, and, for good measure, I tie a large kerchief around my head. Luce looks up at me from the bench, and he doesn't look at all happy to see me.

I cross my arms on my chest above my guns and just look at him for a while. Then I say, "We caught a spy on the last ship we have taken and…"

*NOOOOOOOOaaaaaaaaaaEEEEEEEEEaaahhhhh!*

The ear-piercing shriek comes from someone just beyond the closed door of the hatch, and then a muffled plea, *No, no, please, no!* and then another shriek. Mr. Luce goes white. There is the sizzling sound of red-hot metal touching bare skin and then the smell of burnt flesh comes under the door. Another scream.

"…and we are interrogating him. I thought I might tell

you that so you do not take alarm." With that, I turn and go out the door, leaving him openmouthed with horror.

In the next room Peter Drake is leaning up against a bulkhead placidly smoking a pipe and a grinning seaman named Ozgood is sitting in a chair. I had asked the crew if there were any actors among them and all said that Ozgood was just the thing, him not being good for much else in the way of seamanship, that's for sure. He had been doing *Hamlet* last year in London when he had stepped outside into an alley during intermission for a little hanky-panky with Ophelia, and he was set upon by a press-gang. The ragged remnants of his costume still cling to him. He has taken the whole thing with relative good humor, but he feels certain that his understudy had set him up to be taken by the press-gang and does intend to kill him when he gets back.

I cover my ears and nod and Ozgood roars out *FOR THE LOVE OF GOD, MISS, NOOOO!* then Seaman Langley takes the hot poker from its bed of coals in the little brazier and puts it on the hunk of salt pork lying on the deck next to the bottom of the door. Then Ozgood screams again. *My God, what a pair of lungs!* Guess he never had trouble in being heard back in the cheap seats.

I signal to him to tone it down some and he trails off in a welter of moans and pleas and small cries of despair. He's really pretty good, if a bit of a ham.

I wait awhile, then signal Ozgood to do some hopeless whining and weeping and he certainly sounds like a soul in deep despair. I open the door and go back in to Mr. Luce.

He sits there ashen.

I dust off my hands. "That was distasteful. It is a shame

that I will have to do the same to you. You see, your Mr. Kopp—or is it Boland?—has given you up as a fellow spy. *Defiant* didn't turn out to be very defiant at all. He named you and many others…" and here I reel off a list of names I had culled from the captured papers, looking at him as if he were the scum of the earth, which, of course, he is.

"What are you?" he whimpers. "What kind of monster are you…"

"I'll show you," I say, without a trace of emotion. I call back through the open door, "All right, in here now."

Ozgood troops into the room, hunched over with a coil of rope on his shoulder, his face now transformed into that of a gleeful and demented torturer. He is followed by Drake, jiggling his keys to the cell, and followed, in turn, by Langley, who carries the smoking brazier in which is buried the red-hot poker.

"We will first open the cage, then strip him, and then tie him to the chair. Then we'll get started. Come on, let's get this done."

Luce gapes at us as Drake singles out a key and puts it in the lock. He looks at my expressionless face. He looks at the hot poker. He looks at Ozgood, who looks at him and giggles and drools.

"Wuh…wuh…wait…I'll tell you everything I know."

I go up to take a turn about the deck to clear my head. I look out toward the west, hoping soon to see Robin and the prize crews returning. I open and close my right hand several times to get the cramps out of it. I had spent an hour sitting next to the cell, writing down what Luce had to say. He did have lots to say—*Better the noose back in England than what the fiendish Captain Jacky Faber, Piratical Scourge of the Coast of France, had in store for you today, hey, you poor fool?*

I pull the kerchief off my head and let the breeze blow through my hair. I don't like spies and sneaky stuff, and I didn't enjoy doing what I just did, but I felt it had to be done. As usual, the sight of the sea and sky and scudding clouds soothes my mind, if not completely scrubbing my soul free from guilt.

I shake my head free of these thoughts and go see that things are all well with the quarterdeck watch, and then I go back toward my cabin. I must make my final preparations. Maybe a little snack, a glass of wine. That was hot work today.

When I enter, I'm startled to see Higgins standing there holding a razor. There is a bucket of hot, steaming water placed next to a chair, and the washstand has on it a shaving mug and brush all soaped up and foamy. He strops the razor back and forth on a belt that is hung on a hook by the washstand. Always wondered what that hook was for, and now I know...but *what*? He's going to shave himself in my quarters?

I should have known better.

"Your ankles, Miss. We must do something about them. If you would take off your trousers and sit down?"

He notices my lifted eyebrows.

"The Misses Hollingsworth, Esther and Ruth, and other young ladies in Lord Hollingsworth's household. I used to perform this task for them."

I take off my jacket and drop my trousers and sit down. I pull my drawers up over my knees and put my left foot in the bucket. He kneels down and takes the shaving brush and soaps it up and applies it to my ankle and calf. It feels wondrous good, and it won't hurt my feet any to get washed, either.

He gives the razor a few more sharpening swipes and then sets to work. He is very skilled and is soon done.

It was not at all unpleasant.

"Now if you would remove your shirt and lift your right arm?"

*What?*

"If we are going back into Society, Miss... The new fashions, you know, will require it."

"Higgins, you gotta know I ain't much of a lady."

"You'll do, Miss. You'll do just fine."

I doff my shirt and lift my right arm.

Newly hairless in some parts, I have my three senior officers, Jared, Harkness, and Drake, to dinner. We have eaten and are well into the wine when I ask Higgins to bring over a certain tray. There are four leather bags on it.

I take the three smaller bags and toss one in front of each of them. The bags clink and the men pick them up and heft them. They know what they are.

"This is the money we have taken from the passengers and captains of the prize ships. We do not know what the Prize Court will do and I want you to be rewarded for your loyalty. We all know I could not have done this without the help of you three.

"You will keep this secret—what the Admiralty doesn't know won't hurt it. This larger bag, I want divided up amongst the crew, so they will at least have something to jingle in their pockets when next they hit port. Tomorrow is Sunday, and I intend to hold Church. We will have inspection, and then we will divide up these spoils. Agreed?"

All three pouches disappear inside jackets.

Jared, of course, has to grin his cocky grin at me. "The Captain of *L'Emeraude* was right, Captain. You do have the heart of a pirate."

I take a sip of wine and let that go, mainly 'cause he's right.

I see Peter Drake regarding me for a long while. "What is it, Peter?" I ask.

"Do you really believe the Admiralty will give you a Captain's share?"

"I am not so stupid, as I hope you know by now. No, and here is how I intend to take my rightful share."

And then I lean in and tell them.

# Chapter 21

I'm not halfway through my morning eggs when I hear the call go out, "Sail ho! Two points on the port quarter!"

I grab my long glass and rush outside. Port side! We're on the northern leg of our patrol so that means the side toward Britain! Maybe...

I shoot up to the foretop, scattering ship's boys to the outer edges, and train my glass. It is a small cutter... getting closer... closer... is that a midshipman's jacket on that man standing by the mast? Can't quite see...

"What is it, Captain?"

"Don't know yet, Tucker, but I hope... Yes!" I exult. *It's Robin and the prize crews!* I slide back down to the deck.

"I'll be below, Jack," I say to Mr. Harkness, who has the watch. "Send word to me when they are alongside!"

Higgins stands next to the remains of my breakfast.

"Higgins! We must prepare! This is our last day aboard!"

He is calm and pulls out my chair.

"Plenty of time for that, Miss. For now, you must finish your breakfast."

---

I stuff down the breakfast and then open my drawer. I take out the packet of papers concerning the spies and say, "You must wrap these in oiled paper and then oilskins. You must guard them with your life, Higgins, as they are the most valuable thing we have, even more valuable than this." And with that I pull out Captain Scroggs's money bag and thrust it into his hands.

He takes it, but says nothing, he only nods, but I think I see emotion writ on his face, that I would trust him with such wealth.

"Hurry! Not a moment to lose!"

"Now, Miss. We have plenty of time. You take care of your duties and I will take care of mine."

"Mr. Raeburne! You could not be more welcome! Come, tell me the news!" I say as he comes over the side and we go down into the cabin.

Robin storms into the room and puts his arm around my waist and twirls me around and then bends me over backwards and brings his face down toward mine...and then he notices that Jared, Harkness, and Drake are standing in a line beside the table, and Higgins is pulling out a chair for me to sit in. Robin looks hard at me and then lifts me back up to my feet.

"*Harrumph*," he says, and bows, all red in the face. "Forgive me. I hope I did not give offense."

"None taken," says I briskly, sitting down. Higgins pulls out the chairs and seats Robin and the others.

Jared looks at Robin with ill-concealed contempt, the disdain a self-made man feels for the man born to wealth and privilege. Were it not for the fact I was here, that feeling would never have been shown outright, but…I give Jared a look and a kick under the table.

"So," I say, clasping my hands together and placing them on the tabletop in a schoolgirl way. "We have all of us here together. What news, Robin?"

Robin glares at Jared and says, "All of the prizes and their cargoes have been registered with the Prize Court. As always, there are problems—you have stepped on some toes, Jacky, make no mistake about it."

I do not miss the use of my first name. Neither do the others.

"However," he continues, "I have engaged the services of a lawyer well known to my family who will represent us to the best of his ability. I have every reason to hope for the best."

Glances around the table. For a bunch of common sailors, they are well versed in the ways of the world. I am glad of my packet of letters.

"You have done well, Mr. Raeburne. A glass of wine with you. To Robin Raeburne, for having gone off and done a thankless task, while we had all the fun!"

"Hear, hear!" say all and raise and drain their glasses. Robin is not fooled. He does not exactly glower at me, but he doesn't really beam, either.

"Now," I say, and lean forward, "this is the plan of the day. We are going to release the French crews ashore. Mr. Drake, I want you to handle that—and be careful, the prisoners are quite testy by this time. At noon, I am going to send a boat off to the Flag telling them of the situation. We

267

will then muster the men for Inspection. After that, I have some things I wish to say to them and we will then go to holiday routine.

"By tomorrow morning the Flag will have had time to run around in circles and finally decide on a new Captain and some new regular officers for the *Wolverine* and send them over...no, no...we knew this could not last forever and this is the perfect time to end it. We will muster the crew again and have a Change of Command, and I will leave the ship. I will go back to London and continue Robin's good work in securing for us and the crew the prize money we so richly deserve. That is all. Anything else? Good, then. Let's get on with it."

Sub-Lieutenant-at-Arms Drake brings the first batch of prisoners out into the air. There are at least thirty pistols trained on them as they crawl down the netting and get into the boat.

I had previously gone down into the hold, dressed in my full rig with pistols, headband, and sword, and addressed them in French. I told them they are not going to be taken to England to be hanged, but instead will be put back on French soil. Some listen in stony, disbelieving silence, some fall to their knees in gratitude for their lives. I tell them we will take them over in three shifts, that being the capacity of our two boats. They will be placed on the spit of land that sticks out into the sea and all must wait there till the last of them are landed. The last ones to be landed will be the Captains and Mates, and they will be put on their knees and shot through the head if the terms of the release are not observed to the letter by those on shore. *Vous me comprenez?*

It seems they do.

I go to visit the miserable Mr. Luce in his cell.

"I am releasing the French crews this morning."

The doomed man sighs and nods, not lifting his head.

"Do you have a wife?"

He nods.

"Do you wish to write her a last letter?"

He nods again.

Now it is my turn to sigh and drop the farce. "You were not a very good spy, Mr. Luce. In fact, you were pathetic. Did you know the whole torture thing next door was a sham? That Kopp was killed cleanly in the taking of the ship he was on, killed by one of my men when he drew a bead on me?"

He looks up, incredulous.

"I am going to put you ashore with the others." His mouth drops open. "Do not think I am doing it for you, as I am not—I hate spies of any stripe, French or British— spies make friends with people and gain their confidence and love, and then betray those very same people. It turns my stomach to think of it."

He looks up with a glimmer of hope in his eye. I continue.

"No, I am doing it for myself. I do not want your death on my head. I do not want you joining the host of ghosts who line up at night to destroy my sleep."

I pause and then dig a coin out of my pocket. It is a small gold coin, French, and it has about the worth of an American ten-dollar gold piece. I flip it in the air to him. It lands in his lap.

"Take that," I say, "and take your wife and run away, run away as far as you can, for when the French spies learn how much you have told me, your life will not be worth a farthing.

I suggest Italy. America. Or Russia. Anywhere but France or England, for count on it, the Admiralty shall know your face."

I hold up the charcoal portrait I had done of him. It's a very good likeness. He blanches and nods.

The prisoner transfer goes smoothly. We do not have to shoot any Captain or Mate. Both the *Wolverine* and I are heartily glad to be rid of them. Standing in the rigging, with my glass to my eye, watching them finally scatter, I wonder if they will tell tales of the Gallant Female British Officer.

Nay, no chance. There will be tales of the Cruel Girl Pirate, if anything.

The Bo'sun blows the whistle and Eli beats the drum and the men go to quarters for Inspection, and while they are doing it, I write the letter to the Flag.

*Commodore Shawcross*
*Squadron Fourteen*

*My Dear Sir:*

*It is with regret that I must inform you of the death by natural causes of Captain Abraham Scroggs, late commander of the HMS* Wolverine.

*However, it is with great pleasure that I inform you that since taking command, as ranking officer aboard, I have taken three French merchant ships laden with cargo as prizes. I wish you the joy of your share of the prize money.*

*Although it has been a great honor to serve the King in the way I have done, I know that you are sure to want to replace me as Captain of the* Wolverine *with an officer of higher rank. I await your word on this.*

*Your most humble and obedient servant,*

*Acting Lieutenant J. M. Faber*
*Master and Commander, HMS* Wolverine

I had told the Bo'sun that after the prisoner drop he should leave one boat in the water alongside and ready to go. I also sent word for Midshipman George Piggott to make himself ready to take command of that boat for the delivering of a letter to the Flag officer. We are at the southernmost tip of our patrol and so the boat should reach the flagship in a short time—maybe in as little as four hours. So they'll get the word and have time to make preparations and be here tomorrow, but will not have enough time to do it today.

I take my folded and sealed letter topside and go to the rail and look down at the boat. The crew looks up expectantly. I feel something against my leg and look down and find George Piggott standing by my side.

"Make us proud by your behavior, Mr. Piggott. Stand up straight and strong. Show the Flagship what a true Werewolf looks like." I put my hand on his shoulder and leave it there.

"So you are going to leave?" he says, very quietly.

"Yes, Georgie. Tomorrow, sometime. Depending on when the Flag sends someone over."

"What are they going to do to you, Jacky?" he asks. He looks off into the distance.

"Oh, don't worry about me, Georgie. I'll be fine. I always am." I reach over and ruffle his hair. "I always bob up, somehow."

"I'll never be brave like you, Jacky. I…I should have stayed a ship's boy." He looks down at his feet.

"Come, Georgie. I know you liked being a ship's boy—so did I, when I was one—but you can't stay a ship's boy forever. Tucker and Eli and Tremendous will be seamen in their own right soon, you know that, don't you?"

He nods, takes the letter and puts it in his jacket, salutes, and goes down into the boat. The sail is lifted, pulled taut, and they are off.

The Bo'sun's Mate comes up to me and says, "All ready for Inspection, Lieutenant."

I nod and follow him to make the Inspection, but I do not inspect, as I know everything is in order. Instead, I look into the eyes of each man and shake his hand and thank him.

*Shaughnessy…Wilson…Grimes…Harper…James… York…Bowdoin…* the list goes on and on, all one hundred of them, bless 'em…*Scott…Irwin…Corbett…Coughlin… Reilly…*

Finally it is done, me havin' already dissolved into tears by about the first twenty of 'em.

There is a podium and I mount up behind it and wipe my eyes. I look out at them at their stations on the deck and in the rigging, and when I think I can speak, I do.

"Werewolves!"

There is a roar in reply.

"Tomorrow I will leave this ship, and I want you to know that I will do everything in my power to see that you get your rightful shares in the prizes we took!"

Another roar. I lift the bag of money and put it on the podium.

"Right now, we have this bag of money that we took from the captains and passengers of the prizes. We have totaled it up and divided it, deciding not to wait for the Prize Board to decide on the rightness of it, for did we not stand on board as brothers? Did we not?"

A roar. *Werewolves! Werewolves! Werewolves!*

"Well, this little bit comes to five pounds six per seaman."

There is a great sucking in of breath. That is *quite* a sum of money to a common seaman. 'Course I had added a bit from the Captain's stash, to sweeten the pot, like, figuring the men had it comin', putting up with Scroggs for all that time like they did. And the spies were carryin' a good bit of change, too. They certainly were.

"This will be entered by your name on the ship's log, along with your regular pay. You will receive it when you go off the ship."

We can't give it to them now, for they would certainly gamble, even when told not to, and all the money would end up in the pockets of a few of the sharper ones.

"As I am going off the ship, if there are any of you who wish this money to go to your wives or families, and they live near London, tell the Purser, and I will be happy to see that it happens."

I pause and look out at them for the last time as Master and Commander of the *Wolverine*. "As for now, there will be a special dinner prepared from the stores of the last ship, an extra tot, a bottle of perfume for each of your wives or sweethearts, and holiday routine for all!"

Another roar.

"And an extra shilling for the man that first puts a pennywhistle in my hand!"

# Chapter 22

*James Emerson Fletcher, Midshipman*
*On board HMS* Essex
*On station off France*

*My Dear Jacky,*

*Although I despair of ever hearing from you again, much less actually seeing you and taking your hand in mine, I shall continue to keep corresponding with you in this manner as it does give me some comfort in that I feel that I am communicating with you on some level, spiritual or otherwise.*

*I am still studying for my lieutenancy, though I take no joy in it, my real interest in this life having taken to her heels and run from me, and I am back on board the* Essex, *on patrol off the French coast.*

*I have sent word throughout the fleet concerning the possibility that you were somehow contained in it, though in what capacity I cannot imagine. If you are here, could you be posing as a boy again? No... not likely. What would be the point? Could some unscrupulous officer have... no, I will not think of that possibility.*

*If you could read this, you would be happy to know that I have placed your Judy and my Hattie with a lovely old woman, Lady Chumbley, who is greatly in need of their company and care. Judy and Hattie have been getting along famously. It is a good post, and though it will not last forever, I believe all concerned are happy.*

*Judy had told me, in vivid detail, a good deal of your life on the streets, before you had joined the company of the Dolphin, and while I took her wild tales with more than one grain of salt, I did enjoy hearing stories of you, however fanciful. However, I was disabused of the notion that the stories were exaggerations, to a great extent, when Judy, before being conveyed to Lady Chumbley's residence, asked that she be permitted to visit your old "kip," as she put it. I agreed, of course, but only on the condition that I be allowed to accompany her. She protested, thinking that not at all wise, but I persisted and she finally agreed.*

*Upon gaining the place, that dank place under the old bridge, it was all I could do not to draw the handkerchief soaked in cologne water that I kept in my sleeve as protection for my nose from the smells of the city, and putting it to my face and keeping it there. In deference to the children living there in that place, though, I managed not to do it. Even so, I was aghast at the thought of you, my brave but still frail and fine flower, living here in this squalor all those years. I truly cannot put my mind around it all.*

*The urchins received Judy as an old comrade and there were expressions of great joy as she doled out portions of her meager earnings into each hand, money, I then realized, that she had been saving up for just such a purpose. I, however, was viewed with the greatest of suspicion. I suddenly felt ashamed of my own wealth and position.*

The excited conversation flowed and I was astounded to hear from the girl Joannie that you had visited here on your arrival back in Britain. It seems that all the whole world has had the joy of your company, all except me.

Judy informed me, upon our taking leave of the place, that, had I ventured in there and had she not been with me, I would have been clubbed, stripped, and left unconcious and naked in the street in under two minutes, but I cannot quite believe that. They are just children, after all.

So, to sum it up, Judy and Hattie seem content and contemplate their futures with happiness, but that same happiness, however, continues to elude me, as word of you and your whereabouts are still unknown to all. In desperation, I had written to your school in Boston and have received a reply from your friend Miss Amy Trevelyne to the effect that you have not returned there and she is frantic with worry over your safety. I fear I have done wrong in alarming her, but I saw no other path in trying to find you.

In addition, I have sent…wait…there is a knock on my door…

It is with a shaking hand that I report that a boat has just pulled up alongside bearing a very small midshipman with a letter from one of our smaller patrol ships. My Captain informs me that it concerns events that have recently occurred on HMS Wolverine. It seems that its Captain has died, its officers are missing, and the ship is being commanded by a J. M. Faber, Acting Lieutenant.

Good Lord.

We leave in the morning,

Jaimy

# Chapter 23

We are not far into the Morning Watch when we see the boats approaching—both our lifeboat, which I assume carries Georgie and my boat crew, and a larger boat that bears a commodore's flag.

*Well.* It looks like we're going to get the royal treatment here.

"Beat to Quarters!" I say for the last time. "Let's look sharp for the Flag, his own self!" The Werewolves fly to their stations.

I go over to the large table, which once again has been set up on Three Hatch. There are chairs set out and plates laid with the finest delicacies from both the Captain's stores and those of the prizes, along with bottles of rare brandies and vintage wines—burgundies, Bordeaux, ports, sherries, and Madeiras.

When I had Higgins set it up, he had asked discreetly, "Not in the cabin, Miss?" and I said, "No, Higgins. I know that would be the usual place for this sort of thing, but I don't want to be anyplace where they could take me quickly, and bind me and confine me and stuff me in a sack, out of sight of my crew," and he nodded and said, "Very wise, Miss," and then he set about his task.

The boats draw closer. I take my long glass and see that the *Wolverine* boat carries just my small midshipman, our original crew, and a few other sailors—probably the new Captain's coxswain and other enlisted staff. I swing the glass to the other boat and see much gold on lapels, shoulders, and hats. That will be the new Captain and Commodore Shawcross. Why is he, himself, coming over here? Probably for a little excitement—patrol duty is as boring for a commodore as it is for a seaman. There is one man with one swab of gold on his shoulder—that will be the new Captain of HMS *Wolverine*. I hope for the sake of my crew that he is a good and a fair man. We shall see. *Hmmm.* There seem to be only two more officers in the boat with him. That is good. I want to try to get the new Captain to keep Jared, Harkness, and Drake as warrant officers, as, by God, they have earned it.

I swing the glass back to the smaller boat and see Georgie standing up in the prow, directing the approach. *Good boy, Georgie! The gangway is down, waiting for your arrival, but let the Flag boat get there first, that's a good boy...*

I swing the glass back to the Flag boat one more time before putting it down and...

*Oh...my...*

The glass starts trembling in my hand. There, standing next to the mast on that boat, is none other than...*him.*

*No. Get hold of yourself, girl. You have been good and strong, you have not thought of him even once since he proved false. You have done well. You have survived without him.*

*Treat it just like meeting another old shipmate...the same as when I saw John Harper, another man from the* Dolphin... *just another old shipmate...no less, and certainly, no more... It does not matter...Calm, now. Calm.*

I advance to the place where they will come aboard and inspect my quarterdeck crew. Tucker, Eli, and Tremendous are fitted out as side boys, looking nervous, but they'll do all right, I know. Then there's Ned and Tom and Joseph Jared and Jack Harkness and Peter Drake all drawn up and looking fine, and then there's me with Midshipman Robin Raeburne standing straight and true by my side as First Mate.

I'm not wearing the pistols—I had Higgins pack those, figuring that my mere presence in tight white trousers tucked into shiny black boots would be scandal enough— but I do have *Persephone* strapped on and I am wearing my Lieutenant's jacket with gold lace woven through its lapels over a new dress shirt that Higgins had somehow found, with creamy lace spilling out at my throat and wrists. And, by God, I have the Look on my face—eyes hooded, chin up, lips together and teeth apart, as Admiral Shawcross, Commodore of Squadron Fourteen, steps upon my ship. Following close behind him is the new Captain, and, I suspect, the new First Mate of the *Wolverine.* Then...and only then does Midshipman James Emerson Fletcher step onto the deck of the *Wolverine.*

The Bo'sun starts his shrill trill and the side boys whip up their hands in salute, as does everyone else on the quarterdeck.

I step forward and take off my hat, a cocked hat that we had taken from the Dutch Captain that Higgins had somehow altered to fit me. It is all dark blue and gold and I feel ridiculous with it on and am glad to take it off. I bow and tuck it under my arm, as I have been instructed by Higgins.

The Commodore merely looks me over and does not return the bow. A definite snub. *Very well, Commodore.*

"You would prefer this, then, Sir?" and I dip down in my lowest curtsy, pantomiming the holding out of an invisible dress. The Look is hard upon my face as I rise. If they were expecting a pipe-chewing harridan as a female Captain, they do not get it. If they were expecting a simpering, frightened female, they don't get that, either. What they get is a Pimm's girl, pure and simple.

This time he barks out a laugh and gives an offhand salute. He looks about at the ship—the newly scrubbed decks, the shining brass. "This is Captain Trumbull," he says, gesturing to the new Captain. "He will be taking command of this ship."

I bow to Captain Trumbull. He does not bow back. He is a dark cove, of slight build and a long, blue-jawed face. He does not seem to be possessed of a great amount of humor and he certainly does not seem to approve of me.

"Shall we get on to the business at hand then? Will you take refreshment?" I say and motion Commodore Shawcross and the others to the table. He greedily surveys the spread on the table. His girth shows him to be a man of some appetite, and he wastes no time in going to the head of the table, and, after a seaman pulls out his chair, he sits down. After many months on station, even the stores of a commodore must be growing lean.

"Some wine with you then, Sir," I say, nodding at the Weasel, who has been pressed into this service by Higgins. He has been cleaned up and put in a white steward's uniform, and we have promised him a grisly death if he messes up. He shakily pours from a dusty old bottle of extremely rare amontillado, which looks like it came straight from the catacombs of Rome. The other officers come to the table and are seated, a specially selected seaman behind each chair. It is then that I, too, sit.

The Commodore smacks his lips over the wine. "Ahhhh...," he says, unabashedly, "it's been a long time."

"I hoped you would like it, Sir, and I took the liberty of setting aside a crate of it for your own personal use," purrs I. "I'm sure the Admiralty would not mind. There is also some French perfume for your lady, Sir, as well as many foodstuffs that would surely spoil if not used right away." The Commodore looks at the pile of stuff to the right of the quarterdeck, the most prominent of which is the box of wine plainly stamped H. M. FLETCHER & SONS, IMPORTERS OF FINE WINES. BRATTLE STREET, LONDON on its side, and beams his pleasure.

"I'm beginning to like this girl," he says. "How many prizes, then?" he asks, smiling in anticipation.

The man who will become the next Captain is not smiling. The slight, dark man does not look like he has spent a large part of his life in idle pursuits. He has a sharp face, with prominent nose and piercing black eyes. He is not drinking the wine. Instead, he is looking around at the rigging, the trim of the sails. As well he should. That's what I would be doing, were I in his place.

"Three ships and four full cargoes," say I, quickly, stressing the *four* and not the *three*. "Wine, perfumes, china, silks, cheeses, hams, the list is endless, Sir."

"Good, good," says he, contentedly.

I gesture for the serving men to fill his plate.

I do not look at Mr. Fletcher directly, but I observe him out of the corner of my eye. He is seated across from me, staring intently at my face. He appears to be struggling with the desire to say something, but, of course, he cannot. *Rules, you know. But you know, if it were me, I would say something and damn the consequences. I would jump across the table and wrap my arms around your neck. But, then, that's always been the difference between you and me, Jaimy. Always.* I do not allow our gazes to meet.

"Ah, but now we must get down to it," sighs the Commodore. Another truffle slips down his throat. "The matter of the dead Captain Scroggs. Would you care to explain how that happened? And how you happen to be sitting here in the uniform of a Lieutenant in His Majesty's Service, addressing in familiar terms a Commodore of the same service?"

I lean back and take a sip of my wine and begin. "I was taken by a press-gang in London, Sir. They mistook me for a man because I was dressed as a jockey at the time—it was a lark, a prank I wished to pull on a former friend of mine, a prank which, as you can see, backfired upon me. At any rate, I was brought aboard here and read into the ship's company. Since it was apparently well known that I had been made a midshipman by Captain Locke on HMS *Dolphin*, Captain Scroggs appointed me as such."

"Did he know you were a girl when he did that?"

I think back to the vile Scroggs groping my chest that day on the deck. "That fact was known to him, yes," I say.

"And still he read you into the ship's company?"

I pause and look around. "Do not think that in any way

that I believed he had either my best interests or the best interests of the Service in mind when he did this. I think you all know exactly what he had in mind."

I look off into the clouds and then I look back at them. "At any rate, I assumed my duties and I did them as best I could." I say this hotly, looking especially at Captain Trumbull. "What else could I do? You tell me. You tell me now."

The Captain speaks up for the first time. "You could have thrown yourself on Captain Scroggs's mercy. I'm sure his sense of decency would have preserved what is left of your virtue, girl."

*Hmmmmm!* This from my crew.

"What's this, then?" wonders the Commodore, looking about at the men in the rigging. "Mutiny?"

"It is not mutiny, Sir," I say. "They are merely looking out for me, that I not be hurt. They are a good and loyal crew, as you will find out. It was on their mercy that I threw myself, and they are the ones who proved true."

They say nothing to that and I continue. "I performed my duties as midshipman in charge of the First Division Port Guns. I exercised them to a high degree of proficiency, and when the *Wolverine* was attacked by a French gunboat, my gun crews were the only ones able to fire and sink the attacker. As a consequence, Captain Scroggs appointed me Acting Lieutenant and Assistant Gunnery Officer." I motion to Tom, who is nervously standing by holding the log. "Mr. Wheeler, please show the Commodore the entries in the ship's log concerning this. You will notice, Sir, that the entries are signed by Captain Scroggs."

The Commodore glances at the book, shaking his head. He waves Tom away.

"I believe he did it to humiliate his officers and crew, Sir. It was something he enjoyed doing," I say, giving them an explanation they might believe.

"He must have been insane," says Commodore Shaw-cross, "but that is for the Court of Inquiry to decide. Now, how did he die?"

"Captain Scroggs died of what I believe is called apoplexy. His heart attacked him."

"And how did you know this?"

"I was there at the time. In his cabin."

"When was this and was anyone else there in his cabin?"

"It was the night of the fifteenth of October, and, no, there was no one else in the room."

"You were alone with him?"

"Yes."

I notice Mr. Fletcher stiffens at this, but I do not meet his eye.

"Where are the other officers?"

"Captain Scroggs sent them off with a message to you, Sir."

"I never received them. Why did he send them?"

"I believe he was looking forward to an uninterrupted night of sport with me. I must now say that those officers did their level best to look out for me, Sir, they were most honorable and I hope they are safe. They were also taking to you an account of Captain Scroggs's recent behavior for your judgment on his suitability for remaining in command of this ship. I assume they were taken by a French patrol."

"Hmmm. Lamentable, that," says the Commodore. "And his death was occasioned by..."

"The excitement of his anticipation of a night of revels

with me, Sir." *That, a bad heart, and several rolling cannon-balls served up by my loyal friends.* "I have here an affidavit signed by Earweg, the loblolly boy, and my officers to the effect that there were no wounds on the Captain's body."

He looks at the paper and says, "This may be as you say, but I still must take you into my custody until a Board of Inquiry convenes."

At this, my crew once again sets up the *Hmmmmmmm!* of warning.

I stand and sing out to my men, "It is all right. Let it be. It is over now."

To the Commodore I say, "I wish to take leave of my officers, now, if you please." He nods.

The warrant officers, Drake, Harkness, and Jared, are lined up first. Then the midshipmen, Tom, Ned, and Georgie, with Robin last, over by the far rail.

I go up to Drake and take his hand. "Peter. Thank you for my sword and for teaching me how to use it. May you have fair winds and prosper in this life. And you, Jack Harkness, my strong and solid gunner, the same fair winds to you." Harkness bites his bottom lip and nods.

Then I stand in front of Jared and take his hand and look into his eyes and say, "Good luck, Joseph, you piratical rogue. Thank you for my life."

He grins his mocking grin and says low so none but me can hear him, "Good-bye, Puss. When you are done playing with boys, you know where to find me."

I grin back at him and give his hand a squeeze and move on to Georgie. I take his hand in both of mine and bend over and kiss him on his forehead. He looks like he's going to cry, but he doesn't. "Good-bye, Georgie. You are going to make a fine young man.

"And Tom. And Ned. My two noble Knights Errant, who slept outside my room on that first night to protect me from harm. Ah? You did not think I had noticed? I did, and I will never forget." I shake their hands and put a kiss on each forehead, and they nod and I move on to Robin.

I stand before him and I take his hand and look into his face. "Good-bye, my brave and gallant corsair, who stood up in the face of evil to save me. No, no, don't say it. Someday you shall find a good girl to stand by your side and she will be a lucky, lucky girl, indeed, and I mean that with all my heart, Robin. Now kiss me good-bye."

With that I lift his hand and place it on my left breast and lift my face to him and kiss him full on.

*How does it feel, Jaimy? Tell me, how does it feel?*

I break away from Robin and say to the Commodore, "Do you recognize me as a lieutenant in your service, Sir?"

He shakes his head, sadly, I believe.

"Do you consider me in any way to be part of His Majesty's Royal Navy?"

Again he shakes his head.

"Well, then," I say, "I am not bound by your rules!" And with that I dash to the far rail and hook my leg over the side. "Good-bye, Werewolves," I calls out to my shipmates. "You were the best of men!"

There is a final roar of *Puss-in-Boots!* as I drop over the side into the waiting boat, cast off the line, throw over the tiller, and pull in the mainsheet. The sail fills and I am off. Astounded faces appear at the rail of the *Wolverine*, but I don't care. They shan't catch me, I know, 'cause Barnes, the coxswain of the boat that brought Georgie back, had been told to contrive to foul his lines with those of the Commodore's boat, so I shall be far over the western horizon before they can even get sorted out.

Yes, I shall be far over the horizon where lies my share of the prize money, where lies my jewel, where lies my *Emerald.*

As soon as I am taken aboard, the sails are dropped and trimmed and we head to England. Higgins has prepared my cabin and good smells are coming up from down below, but I do not go right down but instead linger on the quarter-deck next to the helmsman.

I run my hand over her polished rail and look up at her perfectly white, perfectly trimmed sails. I look at her wake foaming behind us and her decks all clean and gleaming and I think: *You lovely, lovely thing. You used to be French and now you are not. You used to be called* L'Emeraude *and now I name you the* Emerald. *You used to belong to others and now you do not.*

*Now you belong to* me.

# PART II

# Chapter 24

I'm poundin' through the night and it's startin' to rain and this horse I'm ridin' ain't exactly happy to be sharing this evening with me and it takes constant kicking of my heels to keep him up to pace. He's a big black gelding and he's game enough but he's had just about enough of me by now—the damned nag has been fighting me every step of the way for the last hour. I had hired him back at the last village and had gotten directions and set out. There were some low types smirking about, so, before climbing aboard and setting out, I made sure my cloak blew open and they saw my pistols loaded, primed, and in my crossed belts.

The cottages flash by in the darkening evening, small, mud brick, straw and wattling dwellings, right up on the road, with the fields beyond, rolling off in the distance toward the mountains that lie all misty at the horizon.

It's raining for real now and I pull my cloak tighter around me. This ride has given me plenty of time to think of the events of the past few weeks. Like finding Judy. Like finding a crew to get my ship across the Irish Sea. Like the confrontation with Sir Henry Dundas.

———

We had brought the *Emerald* into Brighton without incident, warping her alongside an open dock and mooring her tightly. I paid off the prize crew and they disappeared into the city. They were a crew that Jared had put together for me to get my *Emerald* back to England, at least, and they were generally men who had been pressed and were desperate to get back to their families or sweethearts at any cost—desperate enough to take a small payoff instead of waiting for their share of the prize money. At least the money in their pockets was sure, and we can't be sure of the prize money.

I had drawn up discharge papers for them so they wouldn't be hanged for desertion should they be caught and charged with that crime.

One of them was Ozgood. I figured it was not a disservice to the Royal Navy to deny them the services of No-Good Ozgood, a sailor famous for his ineptitude. I gave him his money and his discharge paper and warned him to be careful.

"Don't worry, Miss, I'm a man of a thousand faces. And besides, Ozgood ain't my real name."

He lit off into the town and I was sorry to see him go. He was a merry sort, a big strapping fellow with a wide, toothy grin, and dead handsome to boot—would have to be, considering his profession, I suppose. And actually, on the trip over, he proved quite useful as a sailor—it seems that a lot of his incompetence was again just an act to get him out of any serious work, and to make sure the Navy was not sorry to see him go, whenever he went.

Higgins was having a glorious time fitting out the *Emerald*'s cabin and galley, while I went off to see about the prize money. He had taken virtually all of the late Captain Scroggs's stores, as well as a good deal of the choicest of the wines and foodstuffs from the stores of the captured prizes. He left the Captain's place settings to Captain Trumbull, but resupplied us with Dutch plates and French silver and Austrian crystal that he had been...*requisitioning*...from the prizes. It seems that Higgins, for all his fine manners, also has the soul of a pirate.

After Higgins had settled in and had arranged everything to his liking, I gave him a few jobs. One was to take the prize money that the men had given me to give to their wives and sweethearts and to get it to them. *A most pleasant task, Miss,* he said as he took the pouch and the list of addresses. He had taken off his white steward's coat and was dressed in a fine suit and vest—*My uniform when I served Lord Hollingsworth, Miss.* Another job was for him to go to Jaim—Mr. Fletcher's home on Brattle Lane and find out what happened to my Judy.

Then I dressed in my uniform, wrapped myself in a cloak that Higgins had purchased for me in a store right off the dock, and went to see Sir Henry Dundas, the First Lord of the Admiralty.

'Course he doesn't see me right off. Why should he, him being the highest man in the Royal Navy and me being a mere girl? Ah, but a girl with a packet of very important papers.

I had gone in the front door of the place and there were crowds of men standing about in various degrees of military finery. Elegance everywhere. Fine legs, fine bows. And a definite frost when I, pulling back the hood of my cloak, marched in and went up to the secretary and said, "My name is Jacky Faber. *Lieutenant* J. M. Faber. I wish to see the First Lord."

Snorts and snickers all around. The secretary bows to me with great insolence and says with a smarmy smile, "Perhaps you'd like to place your name on a list…"

I whip open my cloak and reach in my jacket front and pull out a letter and stick it in his face. "Perhaps you'd like to give the First Lord this letter? You might first run it by his Intelligence Officer if you are afraid to approach the great man himself." I look out at the clock on the Tower of London and see that it is 11:45. "I will wait for fifteen minutes, no more. If the First Lord reads this and then finds that I have already left, then you will be in serious trouble. Count on it."

He stands there and thinks on this. I take off my cloak and throw it over a chair. No, I am not wearing the white trousers I wore on the ship—I didn't want half the room to faint away—no. Higgins had procured for me a blue lieutenant's jacket, a real one this time, with a high collar and gold piping with military lace threaded through the lapels with a riding skirt in navy blue to match. Lace foams out at my throat and at my wrists. The skirt is flat in front but gathered in the back so that the folds sit up on my rump and then spill down in a graceful way. The toes of my boots peek out beneath.

The secretary shrugs and hands the letter to a man next to him and the man takes it and leaves the room.

I look out the window and down on London. Funny… Three years ago I was a penniless orphan running around those streets below and now…Now, what, exactly? I don't know, we'll see. And thinking this, my knees start into shakin'. I suddenly am gripped with fear—*What am I doing here? I ain't much different now from that urchin I was then! They'll see through me, they'll…* Calm down. Calm down *now*. If they see you weaken, they'll eat you alive. Pretend you're acting a part, like you did with Mr. Fennel and Mr. Bean's acting troupe back in Boston. *Portia!* That's it! From *The Merchant of Venice* when she went into the men's world dressed as a lawyer to save Antonio's life. That's it. An act. This is just a play and everyone here is just an audience, like any other. *Good, my Lord.* No, that's Ophelia…too old-fashioned… *Thank you, My Lord…* That's better… Breathe… in and out…slowly…there.

The letter I gave the man described the happenings on the *Wolverine* and the dealings with the spies. It mentioned the names Kopp, Luce, Boland, *Defiant,* and some of the French names contained in the various papers: Devereaux, Caillbotte, Dufy…but nothing else. The remainder of the papers rest with my lawyer, a Mr. Worden. If I do not return to his office by tomorrow morning, he is directed to turn the papers over to the newspapers on Fleet Street, because in that case I will almost certainly be dead and no longer in need of them.

In ten minutes, another man comes into the reception room and says, "Miss Faber?"

I turn around and frost him with the Look. "Yes?"

"If you will come with me?" and he bows low and directs me through an open doorway. There is a disappointed and highly resentful hum from the other gents waiting to gain an audience. Before going through the doorway, I turn and give the room a deep curtsy and my most insolent Look. Then I turn and sweep through.

I am led up endless hallways and finally into an office, wherein sits a large man behind a desk piled with papers.

There is another man in the room, thin, and dressed all in black. He wears spectacles and looks at me with what appears to be no interest at all.

"Where did you get these names?" rumbles the man at the desk. He is large and florid and has a Scots accent. A thick Scots accent.

"A well-born Scottish gentleman does not rise when a lady enters a room?" I ask in a musing sort of way. "And no introductions? Why, I fear the culture is being debased." I ask myself how I could be talking in this way to so noble a personage and I tell myself, Hey, you've talked to captains and commodores and such, so what's the difference? They are merely men, after all. *And these men need what I got.*

He glowers at me for a while and finally stands up and bows slightly. "My name is Henry Dundas, First Lord of the Admiralty, and this is my adviser on matters of intelligence, Mr. Peel. Will you be seated, Miss?"

In answer to his bow, I whip off one of my grandest curtsies—this is, after all, the first Lord that I have met—and, after the black-clad gent pulls out the chair, Jacky Faber, formerly Little Mary of the Rooster Charlie Gang, places her bottom in that same highly polished and doubtlessly very fine chair, the chair of Sir Henry Dundas, known also as Viscount Melville, the First Lord of the Admiralty.

"I will now tell you what happened on HMS *Wolverine,* my Lord," and I do it.

It takes me about twenty minutes to finish. Then I sit back and wait for their questions. They are not long in coming.

"Why do you think these papers would be of value to us?" rumbles the First Lord.

"Well, my Lord, for one thing, I know you recognized many of the names on that paper I have given you, or you would not have invited me up. Further, I think that you would like to know more about the names on the list that you *don't* recognize."

"Ummm...," he says, without saying either yes or no, not giving an inch.

"And," I say, puffing up a bit and looking him square in the eye, "I think what is contained in those papers is nothing less than the early plans for Napoléon's invasion of Britain."

"What?" he snorts. "And what makes you think that?"

I think for a moment on what I had read in several of the papers, then I say, "I know, for instance, that Lord Bellingham's Regiment of Foot has taken up quarters at Dover—out of sight behind the cliffs but not out of sight of spies. And I know that the Highland Regiments have been given secret orders to decamp from Peterborough to Folkstone next month. Somewhat secret orders..." I finish with a slightly insinuating smile.

*That* gets a reaction. Lord Dundas shoots a look at Mr. Peel. "Damn traitors!" he snaps.

"I believe the enemy would find that information very useful, don't you? The Dover area being the narrowest part of the Channel, and it's plain he'd take his army across there. In barges, it seems to be planned, after Boney's fleet manages to destroy ours, or so he hopes."

"How much have you read of these papers?"

I cock my head as if I'm thinking. "I've read all the stuff that's in English and French. I can't read much Latin or any German and some of it seems to be in that. And much of it's in code."

"*Hmmm…,*" he says, and looks again at the man in black.

"Does that seal my death warrant then, Sir?"

He doesn't answer the question. Instead, he asks another: "Where are these papers?"

"They are sealed and in the care of my lawyer. He is directed to give them to the newspapers in Fleet Street if I don't return from this interview by five o'clock today."

"You had reason to think we would harm you?"

"You would harm me, or any thing or any body you had to harm in order to win this war. I know that. I am not stupid." I gulp and take a shaky breath. "But if you were to tie me to this chair and torture me to find out the location of the papers, I believe I could hold out till five o'clock. I believe I could."

Viscount Melville is quiet for a while, just looking at me, and then he gives out a short bark of a laugh and says, "I believe you could. Now, what do you want in return for these papers?"

"Besides the joy of knowing that I have served my country? Nothing, except for the matter of the prize money for my men. You can authorize that with one stroke of your pen, Sir. Do it and you shall have the papers on your desk in the morning."

"And that is all? Nothing for you?"

"Will you say, 'Well done, Lieutenant Faber! You are a credit to the Service and good luck on your next posting!' Will you say that?"

He snorts. "No."

"Will you give me my share of the prize money? A Captain's share, for that is what I earned?"

"I cannot."

I shrug. I expected nothing more. "Well then. Just a Letter of Marque, then. It is nothing to you to grant such a request."

He barks out a laugh. "A Letter of Marque? A document authorizing you to be a privateer? Whatever will you do with it?"

"I just might find a use, Sir..."

Sir Henry Dundas looks at the other man. He shrugs and nods. The First Lord looks back at me. He is silent for a while, sizing me up, I think, and then he says, "That is quite a tale you tell. Do you know that you are not unknown to us? That we have received word of you and your actions?"

I am shocked. "Commodore Shawcross has already made..."

"Not Commodore Shawcross. We have been getting reports from our French contacts...reports of one Captain Jacky Faber, the Female Pirate, who wears a sword and two crossed pistols and who is the Scourge of the Normandy Coast."

My mouth hangs open—*it's been less than a week!* He goes on.

"*La belle jeune fille sans merci,* 'the beautiful young girl without mercy,' they call her, she who laughs as she tortures and kills prisoners..."

"That is a lie! I told you what I did there! And I wasn't a pirate. Those were legal prizes!"

"Rumors, Miss, rumors that become stories, stories that become legends." The First Lord of the Admiralty leans back and smiles. "We will meet all your demands, Miss Faber. We shall have all the necessary paperwork drawn up by tomorrow. Please bring the papers you have in the morning. You have my word of honor that there will be nothing untoward done as regards your personal safety."

His smile deepens. "I have a feeling we will be seeing more of you in the future, Miss Faber. Good day to you, now. It has been a pleasure."

I delivered the spy papers the next day and received my Letter of Marque and a letter signed by the First Lord that the prize money for the Wolverines would be paid and paid quickly. I examined the Letter of Marque and it looks genuine—and why shouldn't it be? They figure I'll never be able to use it 'cause I don't have a ship and ain't likely to get one, neither, so why not give it to me? Just humor the silly girl, is all.

I dispatched my own letter to Robin on board the *Wolverine* that all was set regarding the prize money and took a coach back to the ship and was greeted by a blur of pink cotton.

"Mistress! Oh, Mistress Mary, I thought I'd never see you again!" wails Judy, throwing her arms about my neck. I see Higgins behind her, holding my old seabag and the fiddle case that holds the Lady Lenore. I am very glad to see all of them.

"I found out from the Fletchers' butler where she was, Miss, and went to fetch her," explains Higgins.

"Thank you, Higgins. Now, Judy, dry your eyes. You can see I have a way of popping back up. Let us have a bit of lunch and you can tell me all that has happened to you."

We go down into my cabin, my lovely cabin, which sparkles and gleams under Higgins's care, and have a fine reunion.

I am told that the kind gentleman, Mr. James, Mr. James Fletcher, that is, *and oh, Miss, what a kind gentleman he is!* had gotten her and Hattie a fine post caring for a dear sweet old rich lady and Judy herself would have been most happy if it weren't that she was so worried about her Mistress being gone and she would have spoken more of Mr. Fletcher, saying, "*You should give him one more chance, Miss, he seems so…*" but I forbade her to speak his name and she obeyed me, even though she didn't want to.

I tell her some of what has happened to me and about the *Emerald* and all and it's decided that she should stay in Lady Chumbley's service till the dear old woman goes off to her reward and then Judy would join me again. It's best that we get things settled with the *Emerald* first, as there is a lot to do on that score—it's going to be hard enough getting a crew with one woman aboard, let alone two.

I had given the Admiralty the packet of information on the spy network, but I did not give them the information on the smuggling operation, figuring why get a lot of people in trouble over a little under-the-table importing? Especially Mr. Hiram Fletcher, Jai—*his* father, that is. I mean, it's one thing to steal a man's wine, quite another to get him slapped in jail. Or worse.

And, of course, I didn't tell the First Lord about the *Emerald*. It's such a small thing, considering everything else he has on his mind. Who's gonna miss a little ship like her in this great big war?

I've cast about, trying to hire a crew for my ship, but I've met with no luck—even men in the worst of circumstances, men desperate for work and money for their families, will not serve under a woman, much less a girl who still doesn't look much more than fourteen.

I know that men will not follow what they call a "petti-coat captain" and so I will have to find a Captain for the *Emerald*. It irks me, but what can I do?

I am standing on the unmanned deck of my ship, pondering the problem, when who should I see but my future Captain come running down the street, looking over his shoulder in fear that something might be following him. He is dressed in tights, jerkin, and doublet, and he ducks by the side of a building, peers out when he sees no one coming, and then makes a dash for my gangway and storms up the ramp and jumps aboard.

"Ozgood," I say. "What now...?"

"No time for that, Miss," he says, and dives down the center hatchway. "You ain't seen me now, mind?"

I stand there in astonishment for a moment and then a mob comes round the corner at the head of the street. They are dressed in a motley fashion—some in modern dress and some in tights and doublets—and all shouting and waving swords and clubs. One, who is dressed as a king, has a scepter...and is that a two-handed broadsword?...a battle-ax? There are several women, too, each seemingly as outraged as the men. One, in a costume I take to be that of Ophelia, is very much with child.

They stop and look about, and, not seeing the object of their hunt, they see me.

"You there! Girl! Did you see a man running by here—big, with black hair?"

I put on the waif look. "Oh, Lord, yes, Sir, and 'e scared me most terrible and so I scampers up here so as to get away from 'im! He run down that street there, Sir!" and I point down a street that I know goes a long way.

The crowd roars and heads off in the direction of my point.

When all is quiet, I go below to see Ozgood. I find him hiding behind a cask in the main hold. "Now, Miss, it ain't as bad as it looks, y'see…"

"Don't bother, Captain Daniel Ozgood, Master of the Ocean Sea," I say, smiling down at him. "Higgins! To me!"

"You do not have to *be* a Captain, you only have to *act* like a Captain, something I am sure you will be very good at. Treat it as a part, a part for which you will be paid. I will be by your side at all times and I will tell you what to say and do."

My bold sea Captain looks dubious, but he gets into the mariner's uniform that Higgins had gone and got. Black pants, big black boots turned down on top, and a black jacket with two rows of gold buttons and a high, stiff collar. Two thick belts cross his chest and another goes around his waist. It is all topped off with a black cap that has a shiny leather brim. The more Ozgood gets into the gear, the more he gets into the part. When all is done, he puts hands on hips, throws back his head, and roars, "Avast there, me hearties! Splice the main brace! *Arrrrr…*"

He will do just fine. If we can just shut him up.

Last night I did a performance at a local tavern, The Full Fathom Five, just to get my hand back in. Higgins didn't want me to do it, but I told him just how many times I had done just such a thing, and so he relented but insisted on coming along, so the crowd was treated to the spectacle of a small female performer attended by a large gentleman's gentleman in full fig. It went well, considering that I'm a bit out of practice, and it was wonderful to have the Lady Lenore back under my chin, and my dear pennywhistle back on my lip, and my feet tapping out the steps. I put out the word then, during breaks, about the *Emerald*'s taking on hands, assuring the sailors that we would have music and good times as well as hard labor on that fine ship.

When we did the actual hiring, Ozgood glowered at them and I listened to what they had to say in the way of their character and experience. I sat off to the side, the good Captain's daughter who would be along on this trip, doing a bit of sewing, like a good girl. If I scratched my right eyebrow, the man was hired. If I touched my nose with my knuckle, not.

Soon we had our crew, and two days later, thanks to Captain Scroggs's stash of gold, we were supplied, victualed, and off on the tide.

Because of foul and contrary winds, it took us three full days to get across St. George's Channel and to the Irish port city of Waterford, during which time the crew figured out Ozgood for the fraud he was. When we got there, the entire lot of them left in a manly huff—*Serve under a bleedin' female, I'll be damned, I will… What kind o' fool did she think we was, what with 'er telling the big lout what orders to give like we couldn't see it?*—but that's all right. Getting the ship here was all I really wanted them to do.

I paid off Ozgood and reclaimed the captain's gear I had bought him back in England. I also gave him a letter of recommendation to Messrs. Fennel and Bean should he ever get to the States and need employment.

"Thank you, Miss," he said as he went happily off toward Dublin with his money jingling in the purse that hung about the waist of his *Hamlet* costume. "That was the easiest role I ever played and the easiest money I ever made! Good-bye, Captain, and good luck to you!"

*Good luck to you, too, Ozgood, you merry fool, for I enjoyed your company greatly.*

So I have a ship with no crew, no captain—and with no captain, I know I shall find no crew. But I do think I know where to find a captain. And a fine captain at that.

*A clap of thunder brings me back to where I am now, which is in the rain, on the back of a cantankerous nag, and I'm aching with a sore bottom from three hours in the saddle. According to my directions, though, I am approaching my destination. There's the bridge over the small river, a large bend in the road, a stretch of moor, then a hill and then…a small cottage, low, with a thatched roof and a dim light glowing in the window.*

*I rein in the horse and he stands there puffing and blowing. I believe I see a face at the window as I dismount and tie the reins to a pump handle. I reach up and unbuckle the saddlebags and slide them off the horse's rump and go to the door. With water dripping off the end of my nose, I knock.*

*The door is opened a crack and a pair of very suspicious eyes peer out.*

*"Yes. What do you want?"*

*"Your pardon, Ma'am, but my name is Jacky Faber and I was told that I might find Liam Delaney here."*

# Chapter 25

James Fletcher, Midshipman
HMS Wolverine
On Station off the Coast of France
November 3, 1804

Miss Jacky Faber
Somewhere in the world, yet again

Dearest Jacky,

Well, at least I got a glance at you for a moment. Not that it settled my mind in the slightest. I still think about that encounter—when you would not meet my eye, when you left the ship without even speaking to me, and when, just before that, you kissed that damned midshipman and let him put his foul hand on your...I can't allow myself to think of it...let alone to write of it.

I will, however, write of what happened on the Wolverine after you took yourself off, should you read this at some future time and find it interesting.

Commodore Shawcross departed, soon after you left, with

his booty, which included a good deal of Fletcher wine, I noticed. I know you thought that would hurt me, but it didn't, Jacky, not really. I don't care about that sort of thing—money and all. Ah, but the other things you did, and said, though, that did hurt me. If that was what you wanted, you certainly succeeded.

When you left, you might have thought that I was calm and collected on the deck of the Wolverine, but, oh no, far from it, as your Bloody Mister Midshipman Bloody Robin Bloody Raeburne soon found out.

After the Commodore was gone, Captain Trumbull wasted no time in bringing the Wolverine back under real Royal Navy discipline. Those men you had made warrant officers were examined and interrogated as to exactly why they agreed to be led by a girl.

The first of them, the stolid Harkness, stumbled around a bit and came up with, "Well, Sir, the way she explained it, it seemed so...reasonable...like."

And then the man Drake said, "It was a gradual thing, Sir. First Captain Scroggs made her a lieutenant, then the Captain got sick and the men got used to taking orders from her. And when we found the Captain was dead, why, she was still a lieutenant, so...mutiny is mutiny, Sir, how could we have done any different?" He said this with a helpless shrug. Clever, he is. You chose well in your officers, Jacky.

And lastly, there was Jared. Now, there's a proud one— when Captain Trumbull addressed him with "What's your name?" this Jared started unbuttoning his Master's jacket and said, "Joseph Jared, Sir. Seaman. Rated Able. Captain of the Top" as if to deprive the Captain of the satisfaction of demoting him to his former rank. When asked why he agreed to follow you, he paused as if collecting his thoughts and then said, "Why did I follow her? If you must know, Sir, it was easy. Pound for pound, Puss-in-Boots was the best commander I ever served under."

The Captain, having only myself and Lieutenant Beasley as officers, decided to let the three keep their warrants. I think he was wise.

So that is how you did it. You got the three most respected sailors on the ship to subscribe to your scheme, and the rest of the crew followed along. That, and appealing to a sailor's natural greed for prizes. A remarkable achievement, Jacky, even for you and your cunning ways, I must say.

And, of course, the younger midshipmen would have fallen immediately under your spell—they are afraid of me, as the new Senior Midshipman, but they still will get on their hind legs and bristle at me if a word is spoken against your name.

Which brings me back to the matter of Mister Cock Robin.

The moment the Captain left the deck on other business, Raeburne and I did not lose a moment in expressing our mutual loathing for each other. We came up nose to nose and I cursed him to hell for defiling you with his touch, and he said he did a good deal more than touch you, and I roared out that I was going to kill him where he stood. And we drew our swords and were well into it, each intending to do nothing less than kill the other and to hell with the consequences, when the Captain came upon us and ordered us to stop or, by God, he'd hang us both.

Captain Trumbull, seeing how things stood between us and desiring to make an impression on the crew, directed a bo'sun's chair to be rigged up to a boom on the port side of the ship. He ordered Mr. Raeburne stripped down and placed in it, securely tied. He has him swung outboard and then asks me if I would do the honors.

With pleasure, I say with clenched teeth.

"Down!" I order, and down, Jacky, down goes your dear midshipman to disappear under the icy water. And I'm thinking, with no small degree of satisfaction, "That'll cool your ardor, Mister Cocksure Lusty Bastard Raeburne." I count to six and yell, "Up!"

He comes out of the water with his hair plastered over his face but with his eyes staring right at me. "You're a poor excuse for a man, Fletcher, leaving…"

"Down!" I yell, and down he goes again. I wait longer this time before shouting, "Up!"

"…her to fend for herself alone in this world!" The water streams off him and he is turning a shade of blue that gives me a grim sort of pleasure.

"Down!" The nerve of the son of a bitch! Count of ten for you this time. I wait the count of ten. A slow count of ten. "Up!"

He takes a great gulp of air and finds my eyes again and smiles a knowing, insinuating smile. "I was that close to having her, Fletcher, closer than you've ever been, closer than you ever will…"

"Down!" Damn you to hell! You'll stay down there forever, you miserable…

"Up," says the Captain, ending the game. "We don't want to actually drown him, Mr. Fletcher. I'm sure he is quite chastened and will not again challenge your authority as Senior Midshipman."

Raeburne comes up out of the water and is pulled over on the deck and his bonds are loosed and his body sprawls across the deck, seawater spewing out of his nose and mouth. Unbidden, Midshipmen Wheeler and Barrows collect him and haul him down to the berth. As they go, they fix me with looks of the purest hatred. I do not care. They can all go to Hell.

I stood on the deck for a long while and I felt my fury slowly fade. I began to think more clearly, and the more I thought, the more I was ashamed of my actions, or inactions, both then and in the past.

Raeburne was right. I am a poor excuse for a man. I should have gone back and gotten you as I said I would. I cannot blame the Service—when the Dolphin was broken up, I could have postponed being reassigned to another ship and gone back and gotten you. I had enough money. I could have done it. But I didn't. I thought it would be best for both of us if I were to assume my new post—and now I have lost the thing dearest to me in the world. Now I have nothing.

I went to my new cabin and got a bottle of brandy I had brought with me when I came aboard this ship and I went down into the midshipmen's berth. Mr. Raeburne was seated shivering in a chair, wrapped in a blanket, with Wheeler and Barrows and Piggott about him plying him with hot coffee. All turned and looked daggers at me.

"You three. Out," I said. They didn't move. "Do not worry. I have come to apologize to Mr. Raeburne for my conduct," and I bowed to Raeburne when I said that.

The three boys looked to him and he nodded and they left. I placed the bottle on the table and looked about for glasses.

"In that cabinet," he said, still looking wary. I got the glasses and put them on the table and then sat down across from him. I poured a good portion of the liquor in each.

"Come, have some brandy with me. It will warm you." He didn't move. "I do beg your pardon for my behavior. It was inexcusable. You were right in all your accusations. Now have a drink." I raised my glass to him and then knocked it back.

He reached for his glass and lifted it.

"She is gone and we two have to get along," I said as he drank it down.


One-third of the way through the bottle, I tell him fondly about our days on the Dolphin. Halfway through it, he tells me everything of the events of that night when Captain Scroggs called you, dear Jacky, to his cabin. Everything...in both your own cabin and that of the fiend...Poor girl, to be faced with such a horror—although I am no longer in your heart and have no right to an opinion as to your virtue, I do see the wisdom of your actions of that evening and rejoice in the fact that you emerged unscathed. Three-quarters of the way through the bottle, I draw out an account of Robin's heroic actions in your defense, and, when we find the bottom, we are as brothers.


Today I sit here with quill poised above this paper and think: What would you and I be doing now, right now, if we had gone off together in Kingston that time and not gone back on the Dolphin? Probably raising crops of sugarcane and little fat babies.

Idle thoughts. Worthless, idle thoughts...I wonder even if you will get this letter...

Jaimy

# Chapter 26

That night, after I had knocked on the door of Liam Delaney's cottage and was reluctantly admitted, I said, "My name is Jacky Faber and—"

The woman who had let me in crossed her arms and looked at me standing there dripping on her floor. "I have heard Liam speak of you," she said with deep suspicion in her voice. "Mairead, go get your father." A girl of about fourteen, maybe fifteen, with curly hair the same shade of deep red as her mother's, looked me over with open astonishment and then whirled and left the room.

The room had a hard-packed earth floor, with a large, rough table in the center, exposed roof beams low overhead, and a fireplace on the other wall. It also had in it a number of children, ranging in age from about five to twelve, both boys and girls, all with big eyes and all trained on me. I could see from their clothing and the scant portions of potatoes set out for the little ones that things were not going well for them.

I dropped the saddlebags on the floor, pulled back my hood, and wiped off the drop of water that was hanging on the end of my nose. I was neither invited to take off my cloak nor to sit down, so I just stood there.

"Liam is just in from the fields. He is cleaning up. I am his wife. My name is Moira," she finally said.

I took the sides of my cloak and I dipped down into a deep curtsy. "I am very honored to meet you, Missus Delaney," I said, and as I came back up, Liam came into the room. *Oh, Liam...*

I had not expected to choke up upon seeing him, but I did. Tears poured out as I cried out, "Father" to the man who had looked out for me back on the *Dolphin*, he who was my sea dad, he who taught me the ways of a sailor, who took care of me when I had been beaten senseless, and, finally and most important, he was the one who pumped air back into my chest and started me breathing again after I had been hanged. "Oh, Liam," I cried as I stretched out my arms.

"Jacky! Is it really you?" he asked as he wrapped me in the bear hug of his embrace and I put my head on his shoulder and wept there for a moment. "You could not be more welcome! Here, here, take off your cloak! Moira! Set a place for her!"

The girl Mairead had come back into the room with her father and a young lad of about sixteen years, he having the same red hair as hers.

I stepped back from Liam and unfastened my cloak and took it off and handed it to Moira, who didn't look much like she enjoyed taking it, nor was she overjoyed at setting a place for me.

Then hearing a gasp from both Moira and Mairead, I looked down at myself.

In my excitement at seeing Liam again, I had forgotten all about my pistols. They were held, as usual, in the leather belts that cross over the chest of my blue and gold lieutenant's jacket.

*Ooops...*

"I'm sorry, but I was coming alone and I didn't know what to expect...," I said by way of explanation for the guns. I didn't know how to explain away the fact that I was wearing boots and trousers, which are now quite speckled with mud, so I didn't try. The boy looked just as astounded as his sister.

I came right out with it. "Liam. I've got license to be a privateer. I have a fine ship and I want you to be Captain of her!"

Before any could reply, I reached down and picked up the saddlebags. "I hope you don't mind that I brought some food and drink along. Perhaps we could speak of this over something to eat. Maybe some sweets for the children?"

I began bringing the things out of the bags—fresh loaves of bread, butter, cheeses, sausages, a roast beef, cakes, puddings, sweets, and several bottles of the finest wine. The wonder on their faces over my words about the ship was replaced by wonder over the food. When Higgins was putting this feast together I told him not to spare the expense for I wanted to make it as grand as possible because I wanted my mission to succeed.

It did.

The last thing I pulled out of the basket was a small leather bag that clinked when I tossed it on the table in front of Liam. "An advance on your pay as commander of the *Emerald*, Captain Delaney."

I think that's what really did it for Liam. The name, that is, more than the gold.

It was decided that Liam would be Master and I would be Owner. He would have all the authority of a Captain, his word being law in matters of discipline, operation, and safety of the ship, while I would direct where the ship went and what it did. I told them of my time on the *Wolverine* and the easy pickings to be got by nailing those smugglers that had gotten through the blockade—*Money, Liam, real money! And it's patriotic to boot! We'll be doing our bit by disrupting the enemy's shipping, upsetting his commerce, like. This chance won't come again! That blockade won't be there forever!* Moira wrung her hands and protested, but it did no good—*The potato crop is failing, Moira. My brother John has no land and he can farm this place and bring in what he can from it.*

Liam will pick the crew but the seamen would have to know that I would be aboard and am an eccentric—pants and swords and all—and then Liam's son, whose name is Padraic, spoke up and begged to be part of the crew, and this got Moira really wailing, and I say, *It ain't like they'll be going off for years, Missus, we'd be back every few months or so.* And an angry Mairead pipes up with *Well, if he's goin', why can't I?* It doesn't take much to see that the girl is sick to death of changing dirty nappies and is sick of waiting around to be married off so she can have a batch of babies of her own and so can change even more dirty diapers. She was told to hush and to leave the room. She ran off in a huff, but was soon back.

When all was decided, and all had eaten and drunk their fill, I took the saddlebag again and this time pulled out the

Captain's uniform I had bought for Ozgood's temporary use and I gave it to Liam. Higgins had brushed it up and added a bit of gold here and there.

In the morning, Liam was wearing it when we left for the *Emerald*.

"Ain't she beautiful?" I exclaim, bouncing up and down in the saddle and pointing at the *Emerald*, lying there like a jewel in the harbor.

"Aye, she is that, Jacky," says Liam. "As fine a ship as I've ever seen. Looks right new, too."

"Sound as a drum, with new copper on her bottom," says I. "Come on! Let's go aboard your new command, Captain Delaney!" And I give my heels to the horse and down to the ship we clatter.

"Haul away, there. Careful," says Liam. An eighteen-pound cannon is being hoisted in the air by crane and swung aboard the ship. I had felt, and Liam agreed, that we needed two more guns on each side and a Long Tom up forward for the job we mean to do, and those are being hauled aboard and blocked and rigged under his watchful eye.

"Padraic. Go see Nader and see if he can rig a better chock for Gun Number Six there. It looks like that one might slip if the work gets hot."

"Yes, Father," says the young man, so delighted to be here that he can scarcely contain himself. He gets a warning look from his dad and says, "I mean, Aye, Sir!"

Padraic dives below to find the shipfitter, while Mairead stands with me on the deck watching all the confusion. Liam has brought his family down here to Waterford for the fitting out. Mainly, I think, to set Moira's mind more at ease, and further, I think, to show her what a little money in the pocket can do. While it may not have made much of an impression on Moira, it certainly made one on her eldest daughter.

"I'm not going back to that dirty little farm and I'm not going to marry that dirty Loomis Malloy like he thinks I'm gonna and you think I should just because he's got that scabby little bit of land!" she shouts at our stern Captain Delaney, who's trying to maintain a bit of dignity here on the quarterdeck of his new command.

"Your time will come, Mairead," I say, trying to smooth things over for Liam, who looks about ready to have her dragged bodily off the ship. "You'll just have to wait a bit."

She shakes her curly red locks and glares at me. "*You* didn't wait. Why should I?" I ain't got no answer to that. She breaks away and climbs up the ratlines to the maintop to pout and sulk. I recall that when she came on the ship three days ago that it wasn't five minutes before she found her way up into the rigging. Ah, well...

Higgins stands by the gangway and checks off items in his notebook as dockyard laborers haul aboard stores for our upcoming foray—barrels of salt pork, kegs of rum, sacks of flour, and the like. John Reilly, an old man-of-war's man who Liam has picked for First Mate, is directing the stowing of bags of powder. There are also new cutlasses, muskets, wads, and ball—we hope we will not have to use them, but we do have to have them. Grappling hooks, too. And, since the *Emerald* is too small to have a brig, some sets of leg irons, just in case.

Liam takes a deep breath of the salt air and looks about with satisfaction. *Aye, Liam, your farm was lovely, but you ain't no farmer, that's for sure,* I'm thinking as I look at him.

Liam looks at me sideways. "You're becoming a young woman on us, Jacky."

I blush and say, "Nay, Liam. It's just the clothes."

"No. It's more the way you carry yourself now."

"You mean this?" And I rear back and put on the full-bore Lawson Peabody Look, the same one I had just used to put a chandler in his place a few minutes ago when he was trying to overcharge us for rope.

Liam laughs, and I say, "Well, I've been to school, is all."

The crew has been signed on, good Irish men and boys all. There are thirty-six of them in our company—enough to handle the guns and the ship in a fight, but not enough to be crowded and bring on an epidemic of jail fever, typhus, which has killed many more poor sailors than war ever did.

The families of the crew who came down to watch our preparations depart. Liam sends Moira and his own brood off, Moira in tears over the leaving of her husband and son, Mairead furious at not being allowed to come along. The girl sits in the coach with her arms crossed over her chest, staring straight forward and not saying a word to anyone when both Liam and Padraic kiss her cheek good-bye. Moira will certainly have her hands full with that red-headed fury, now that the girl has seen the bustle of the harbor town and has had a taste of freedom.

Such a lovely girl, Mairead—and such a lovely name she has... It is spoken *mah-Ray-ad,* though it is spelled many different ways.

Everything is rigged and set, everything is stowed. All the

stores are in. The upper edge of the *Emerald*'s hull, wherein lie the gunports, has been painted green to honor both her name and the country from which she sails.

Tomorrow we go adventuring.

# Chapter 27

The tide is right and the wind is fair for the channel.

"Shall we get under way, Miss Faber?" says Liam, coming up next to me on the quarterdeck. He had taken off his fine black uniform during the dirty work of fitting the ship out, but now it was back on, the black jacket with the broad leather straps, newly polished, crossed on his chest. He is a fine figure of a man, every inch the Captain of his ship.

"Yes, we shall, Captain Delaney," say I, and the order is given to cast off the lines that bind us to the land.

I had made a flag, about the size of a Captain's command ensign. Against the field of white was emblazoned a blue anchor with line twined about it—what we sailors call a fouled anchor—and when the last line slips from our ship, I have the flag cracked out at the top of the mainmast. The *Emerald*, the flagship of the Blue Anchor Line, Faber Shipping, Worldwide, is under way.

We clear the harbor and the wind catches her sails and my beautiful ship leans over ever so gracefully, and her elegant bow cuts cleanly into the increasing chop of the waves. I take a deep breath and my chest expands and my heart starts thumping so strongly that I fear that others might see it beat through the cloth of my jacket. I face into the wind and my lips peel back from my teeth in a grin of pure joy.

"She's a fine ship, and I wish you the joy of her," says Liam.

"Thank you, Liam," I say, looking up at the fine spread of white canvas above me. "And it is good being back at sea, is it not?"

He does not have to answer, for I know it to be true.

We tear out into St. George's Channel and then up into the Irish Sea. We sail 'round and around and up and down and back again to season our sailors. We sail up to Dublin, then further north to Dundalk, and then down to Cork till every man jack aboard knows her ropes and how to handle her in a light breeze or in a howling gale. The new men get seasick and cry out loud for Jesus to come deliver them from their misery and why, oh why, did they ever leave their dear little farm. But they got over it, just like I got over it when first I went to sea. I felt for them in their misery, though, as I know there's no worse feeling in the world.

There are some experienced sailors aboard and they quickly bring the green hands up to snuff—everyone knows that the lives of each of them depend on the skills of the others. Any slacker will be put off in the next port, without doubt or pity. There will be no slackers, not on my ship, there won't.

All the men work hard but none is more eager to learn the craft of the seaman than Liam's son Padraic, beautiful, red-haired Padraic. He has cast what he thinks are secret glances my way, but I think the gulf between us is so great—

me being Owner and all—that I won't have to tell him that I have decided to live single all of my life.

We have gunnery practice every day—Liam drilling the port guns and me the starboard—and we blast away at barrels, we blow up rafts, and we roar out broadsides at innocent rocky islands to the amusement of curious seals. The men start out inept and clumsy, falling over one another in confusion, but soon develop a gratifying smoothness in the operation of their guns. After they get good at it and feel proud of themselves, the gun crews take white paint to name their cannons—mostly in Gaelic, but I was told by Liam what they meant: *Thundercrack, Widowmaker, Firespitter, Old Murder,* and such. It is good. It builds team spirit.

At first it takes awhile for the crew to get used to me being aboard and walking around in my old sailor togs, or, on Sundays, my lieutenant's coat and white trousers and boots. But they do get used to me—after a bit. Especially when they find out that I know my business and that I know it better than they do.

These Irish boys follow me 'cause they've got an example in their own Irish history of Grace O'Malley, she who first went to sea by cutting off her hair and pretending to be a boy, just like I did. Now *she* was a real pirate—she captained not just one ship but commanded a whole fleet as well. She even met Queen Elizabeth one time and managed to survive the encounter. Sometimes I've even heard the crew call me their own Grace O'Malley. And I can't say as I mind. Like I really didn't mind Puss-in-Boots.

Like Grace's boys, our Boarding Parties are drilled on what they are to do when we come alongside a prize, like how to swing a grappling hook and such. Liam shows them the hacking and hewing art of the cutlass and I teach what I know of the parry and thrust of the rapier. There is practice with the muskets, with speed in reloading being stressed as much as accuracy. The rifles are too heavy for me, so I work with my pistols.

When I am not needed on deck for drills and such, I take to crawling around the insides of my ship, putting my hands on her knees, the massive timbers that support the thinner planks of the hull, marveling at the craftmanship that went into building her—the carefully shaped pegs and wedges that are pounded into her and hold her together—how like a delicate eggshell she is, yet she is able to keep out the raging sea and keep us safe inside her. I go to the lowest deck and watch the tiller ropes slide back and forth as the wheel above me is turned by the helmsman—sometimes just a little bit, sometimes a lot. The ropes, which are attached to a drum at the base of the wheel, come down through the floorboards of the decks, go through pulleys, and attach to the rudder, and so the ship is steered. If anything happens to any of this rig in a fight or a storm, then the ship has to be steered from down here, and it ain't an easy thing. I sit way down below the waterline and listen to how she creaks and groans as she weaves and twists her way through her watery world. To my ears it is music of the finest sort.

The *Emerald* is a brigantine bark, in that the mainsail is a fore-and-aft sail called the spanker rather than square rigged. She's a bit too long for a proper brigantine, but with her sail rig she has to be named as one. Besides, I think *brigantine* is ever so much more elegant than mere *brig*. A brigantine is a Thoroughbred, a brig is a nag, from the sounds of them. Course, the *Wolverine* was a brig and she wasn't bad, not bad at all, once she had proper command.

Higgins serves me my meals in my cabin and he keeps me and my clothes neat and tidy. He also serves Liam and supervises the cooks in the preparation of the food for the men. I invite Liam to eat with me sometimes, for dinner or maybe lunch, but not all the time—I find more and more that I like to be alone, alone in my lovely cabin, alone with my thoughts.

Our shakedown cruise is over. All the men are now able seamen. The gun crews can fire and reload in under two minutes. The men can handle their muskets as well as any Marine. They are ready to go and they are hungry for prizes. The order is given and the wheel is turned and the *Emerald* heels over and points her bow for the coast of France, in search of her prey.

# Chapter 28

"It is a small brig," says Liam, his eye to his long glass.

"Aye," says I, my own eye pressed into the eyepiece of my own glass. "And it looks like a fat one!"

He and I are not the only ones looking greedily at the small ship standing out from the shore. Every man on the *Emerald* is either at her lee rail or in her rigging.

"Do you see any guns?"

"No, but she probably has one in her stern—to fire at someone chasing her... it's not the kind of ship that chases others."

"Not like us, eh, Liam," I say with a grin. "Shall we go to Quarters?"

"All hands to Quarters! Clear for action!" bellows Liam, and with great whoops the men leap to their stations.

I go below to have Higgins strap on my cross-belts and pistols. "Be careful, Miss," he says as he puts my sword belt around my hips and pulls it tight.

I tell him I will be careful, then I go back up on deck. I make sure I don't show it, but I'm a little bit nervous—this crew has been drilled, but there's a big difference between practicing something and actually doing it for real. This is not a Man-o'-War and this crew is still green. But I hope for the best and shake off such thoughts.

"Let her get far enough out from the land before we turn to cut her off," I say to Liam. "We don't want to give her room to double back out of our reach." He nods and we wait, keeping our course to the south while the quarry continues beating to the west.

We had come up to this spot on the coast, which was a bit north of the *Wolverine*'s old patrol area, for we thought that this is where the ships would be forced to try to come out. The *Wolverine*, with a new Captain, one who doubtlessly intends to do his duty, unlike that miserable Scroggs, ain't going to let any smugglers through. And the *Wolverine* being about the most northern ship on patrol, this is where they have to come out.

We have stayed well out from the coast because I don't want to run into any of the blockade ships—they wouldn't bother us, because I have the Letter of Marque, but still, someone in the Royal Navy might start wondering just where I got this ship and I don't want anybody wondering about that.

"I think she's past the point of no return now, Jacky," says Liam.

"Then let's go get her, Liam."

"Topmen aloft to trim sail! Left full rudder!" roars Liam, and men fly up into the tops while others on deck take up the lines to trim the canvas in this new point of sail. The *Emerald* turns smartly to her new course and her sails shake and shudder till they are brought stiff and hard again. We are heading directly toward the merchant and my heart starts to pound in the excitement of the chase.

The Captain of that ship must have wondered what we were about when first he spotted us, but now he knows for sure we're after him, for he has crowded on all the canvas he can get up. He is pretty fast, for a fat merchant, but nothing is faster than my *Emerald,* and the distance between us gets steadily smaller.

Padraic, standing next to me as part of the Boarding Party, is about to jump out of his skin with excitement.

It has been agreed that, during an engagement, Liam would con the ship, bringing her alongside the prizes, and I would command the guns and the Boarding Party, so it is me who shouts, "Sullivan! Give him a shot!"

Sullivan, who runs the crew of the bow chaser, leans over the long barrel of the twelve-pounder, sights, and pulls the lanyard. There is a *crack!* and a puff of smoke and we watch to see where the ball will land. *There!* About twenty yards to the right and fifty yards short of the ship.

"Good shooting, Sully," I call out to him, standing at his gun. "We certainly don't want to hit what we're very shortly going to own, do we?"

This gets a roar of laughter. Sully shakes his head as if it was expected that he actually hit the target. Good. Maybe those on the prize will hear and their hearts will fail.

Their hearts do not fail. There is a puff of smoke from their stern, a distant *boom* and we wait and see the ball skip by our starboard side, in plain view of both Padraic and me. I can sense him quiver.

I look over at him and say, "A very dear friend of mine, a New England girl, used to quote to me some of the sayings of their Dr. Benjamin Franklin. Would you like to hear one of them that I think speaks to this situation?"

He grips the rail and looks at me and nods.

"'Nothing in this world is more exhilarating than being shot at...'" I pause. "'...and missed.' Do you agree with that, Delaney, now that you have been shot at...and missed?" I say this, leaning all unconcerned against the ratlines and looking at him from underneath my lowered brows.

He looks back at me and laughs and says, "Yes, Miss. Yes, I do."

With that I turn back to the business at hand.

"Captain Delaney, bring her up broadside to broadside as quick as she'll do it. Mr. Reilly, ready the Number Two Gun Port Side and lay one across his bow as soon as it bears. Mahoney, ready Gun Number Eight to put one at his stern when you hear Number Two fire."

Silence. Everyone understands what they are to do.

We pull up alongside and I can see the sailors on their deck frantically diving for cover.

*Crack!* Number Two fires, and a moment later Number Eight. There is a splash in front of his bow and then another behind his stern.

He falls off and the Captain—I can see him plain now—pulls down his flag and goes to stand beside his mainmast...what used to be his mainmast, that is, for it is ours now.

The *Emerald* comes up and the grappling hooks are thrown over and pulled tight. The ships come together, and I pull out my sword and leap over onto the other deck. I hear the thumps of feet as Padraic and the others join me.

The Captain has his sword in hand, ready to hand it over, but when he sees me, he sighs and slumps to the deck.

*What?*

"Delaney, O'Brian, Parnell...see who's down below! Sully, check out what they're haulin'!"

The men dive through a hatch and go down below. In a minute they are back, hauling up some people from what they thought was the safety of the hold.

It is three men and a young woman and it is she who takes one wide-eyed look at me and screams, "*La Belle Fille sans Merci! Nous sommes perdus! Perdu!*" She wraps her arms around a small child, a boy of about two.

*What?*

I take a step toward her. "*Non!* You are not lost!" I shout. "*Ce n'est pas vrai!* It's not true!" I sheathe my sword, but her cries go on unabated, tears streaming down her terror-twisted face.

"Please! Please do not kill my baby! I beg you! Please do not kill my baby!"

She looks wildly about, first at me, then at my men on the deck with their wicked cutlasses and then at my musketeers in the *Emerald*'s fore- and maintops—they are there with their guns pointed straight down at the sorry group huddled around the mast. She tries to wrap herself even more tightly about the child, shielding him from the threatening guns with her own rather small body.

*Christ!* Just what the men need on their first foray—a terrified young mother brought to her knees in fear for her child. Already I see looks of doubt in some of my men's faces. They signed on to fight, yes, but not this...Padraic, standing next to me, stares at the woman, aghast. Now the kid is crying, too....

"Put up your muskets!" I order, and they do it. I kneel down by her side and put my hand on her shoulder. She shrinks away from my touch.

"Listen to me," I say in French. "*Ecoutez moi!* No one is going to hurt you or your child or anyone else here. You will collect your things and be put in a boat and you will go back to your land in perfect safety, I promise it. Now, please, *please*, stop the crying."

Gradually she subsides into a quiet sobbing. I stand back up and ask Padraic, "What's in the hold?"

"Wine. Lots of it." He still can't take his eyes off the woman at his feet.

"Good. I wish you the joy of your first prize. Now, Padraic, take two men and get their lifeboat in the water." It is well the boy has something to do, to occupy his mind. He turns to go do it, and I plunge down into the hold.

It ain't surprising that much of the contraband I have taken so far has been clarets, burgundies, and Bordeaux—making good wine is one of the few things that we can't do well in England. That and perfume. I run my hand over the crates and read the names burned into the sides. This time the cargo doesn't belong to...*go ahead and say it, I dare you...* to Jaimy's family. There. I said his name to myself and I had said that I wouldn't, ever again. Steady down, girl. It's probably because you know he's on patrol not twenty miles from here. That's it. But don't do it again because there's nothing there for you. And, for sure, he ain't thinking of you.

I go back up into the light to find that the prize's boat has been lowered and the people are in, ready to cast off. I go to the rail and look down at them. "When you get back to shore, you may curse my name to the high heavens as much as you want for the taking of this ship," I say, again in French. "But you must also tell everyone that you meet that Jacky Faber is not without mercy nor have I ever hurt a captive. I am not a pirate, I am a lawful privateer. You will tell them that, will you not?"

They look back up at me and I know they won't.

"Cast them off!" I shout, heartily sick of this batch of Frogs. I hop back on the *Emerald* and shout to my crew, "You have a rich prize, you gang of piratical rogues! Let's have a cheer!"

And cheer they do, any lingering thoughts of the French woman's distress drowned in thoughts of their prize money and how they're going to spend it.

That evening I have Liam into my cabin for dinner and to discuss the disposition of the prize. I would have had First Mate Reilly join us, but he is commanding the prize, which is called the *Topaz*, and which is sailing a hundred yards off our port beam as we both head back for England. It had been decided before that, when we took a prize, we would all head back across the Channel to dispose of it, for we could not spare the prize crews for very long because we were so few in number. That, and the fact that we would have to sell the prize and her cargo ourselves and not just turn it over to the Admiralty Prize Court. Or rather, I had thought with greedy satisfaction, we *get* to sell it ourselves and keep all the money.

I slip a truffle down my throat, take a sip of wine, and spear a piece of tenderloin dripping with mushroom sauce off the platter that Higgins has placed in front of us. These Frenchies for certain know how to stock their galleys.

Higgins had wasted no time at all in going through the *Topaz*'s stores to find the finest of things for my table. I have tried my first caviar today, and I find I don't like it. *Yuck. Salty fishy eggs. The Frogs can keep that stuff,* I say. *An acquired taste, Miss,* says Higgins. *I recall that you once did not like olives...*

"Well, Liam. We've got a prize. Where shall we go to sell it? I don't want to go anywhere near London." I hold my glass up to the lamplight, marveling at the rich, red color of the fine claret that swirls about in it. I had given orders that each man was to have a half bottle of the best with their dinner, and, given that they had their usual tot of rum in addition to that, I'm thinking that they're feeling right mellow about now. Which is good. I have another olive.

"Hmm," says Liam, chewing thoughtfully, "perhaps we should slip up to Scotland. It's still pretty wild and untamed up there."

Higgins refills both our glasses. "Forgive me," he says, "but if I might interrupt?"

I give him the go-ahead with a questioning eyebrow.

"When I was in Lord Hollingsworth's service," he continues, "His Lordship would rant and rave far into the night about the scoundrels that abounded in a place called Harwich. It is a port that is frequented by smugglers and other sorts whose pursuits of livelihoods do not rule out the... well, slightly irregular. Lord Hollingsworth's estates were concentrated in the Colchester area, which is nearby to Harwich, and I believe he suffered some losses at the hands of denizens of said Harwich. It is likely that not many questions would be asked of us there." Higgins reaches down and pulls the napkin that was supposed to be in my lap from the tabletop and puts it in its proper place.

I look at Liam for his reaction. Although he knows I have the Letter of Marque, he also knows just how I got the *Emerald* and why I'm shy about people asking questions as to her origins.

"It's only about eighty miles from here. If winds stay fair we could be there in three days," he says. He leans back in his chair and considers. "I've been there. It's an active, well-protected port. Before the war it was the main port for mail packets running back and forth to Holland. It would be easy to sell the ship there. And there're several good taverns... the men would have a good time, without getting into too much trouble, I think."

"Also, it is entirely possible," says Higgins, "that the *Topaz* was headed for that very port with her cargo of contraband. We might be able to sell the wine to the intended receivers."

I feel a smile spreading over my face. *Ain't you just the cleverest fox, Higgins, ain't you just?*

"Harwich it is," I say.

Later, after the lamps are put out and I am in my bed, I lie there looking off into the darkness. I listen to the creak and groan of my ship, sounds which are usually like lullabies to me, but this night they comfort me not, for I cannot rid my mind of images of that poor, terrified woman, begging me for the very life of her child. I pull my knees up to my chin.

Sleep comes neither easily nor quickly to me this night.

# Chapter 29

Higgins was right. Harwich is an excellent port in which to do our business—except for one thing. They don't let us tie up alongside the quay. They make us anchor a couple hundred yards out and the *Topaz* farther out still.

We don't dare ignore the orders, for when we came in, we had to sail right under the big guns at Shotley Gate, which guard the entrance to the harbor and which we know could blow us all to bits before we could even think about firing back with our puny cannons. The brutish guns sit up in a stone bunker and we looked right down the barrels as we passed, at point-blank range. Well, that's all right. We'll be good. We'll just have to use our boats to get back and forth from the ship to the dock.

It also turns out that Higgins was right about this being the destination of the smuggler and it is not long before a meeting is set up between us and the owners of the cargo... the once-owners of the cargo, and a sullen bunch they turned out to be.

We receive them in my cabin. They are shocked by the sight of me seated at the head of the table in my officer's rig, but let them be shocked. Higgins, dressed in his fine suit of clothes, sits next to me, pen poised over a ledger. There are four of them and they pull out chairs and sit down. No nice manners here. Liam and Reilly stand next to the wall and all of us are armed to the teeth. I wear my sword and pistols so that there is no mistaking our seriousness of purpose.

Higgins begins, "We have a consignment of wine worth, in our estimation, one hundred and fifty-seven pounds sterling, which..."

"Which we already own, you blackguards!" says one of the merchants, his face red and his eyes bulging.

"And which, I might point out," says Higgins without expression, "you entrusted to the care of a ship owned by an enemy power with the express intent of transgressing His Majesty's laws..."

The man shuts up.

"Let us continue," says Higgins. "In consideration of the fact that you once held ownership of this cargo, we are willing to accept the sum of an even one hundred pounds. You will still make a profit, in the end."

"And if we don't accept that offer, you damned thieves?" fumes another of the merchants. Liam and Reilly put their hands on the hilts of their swords.

"Then, Sir," says Higgins with a slight smile, "the damned thieves will drink it themselves, or else we will pour it into the harbor to the delight of the mermaids and fishes, before we drop the price one farthing."

They pay the price. And, after much haggling, they buy the *Topaz*, too. Higgins turns out to have not only the soul of a pirate, which I already knew, but also the keen and calculating mind of a hard-nosed businessman.

The men are in a high state of excitement, as they are suddenly richer than they have ever been before, each of the crew having been given two guineas, six shillings so as to have a good time ashore and maybe buy some gifts for those back home. Liam and Reilly and I had sat down and divided the crew into two in-port watch sections, one section to stay on the ship while the other was allowed to go on liberty. Liam would head the Port Section and Reilly the Starboard, and in each section we evened out the numbers of older, experienced men with the younger, more green sailors. Men known to be good friends were put in the same watch. That way the ship is properly protected, and that way maybe the grayheads would be a good influence on the youngbloods when they hit the taverns at night. Calm them down a bit, like.

With me on one side and Reilly on his other, Liam addresses the assembled crew and gives them warnings about how to conduct themselves onshore. My ears burn a bit when he tells them that no women are to be brought aboard the *Emerald* and not a few merry eyes glance my way—all of them know of my past on the *Dolphin* and the *Wolverine* and figure I'm acting quite the hypocrite, but so be it—I'll not have my ship turned into a floating brothel. A flip of a coin decides that the Starboard Watch has liberty today, the Port tomorrow, and then we will head back out to resume our raiding.

Higgins and I take a turn about the town and again I'm hit by the strangeness of being on the land and how firm it feels underfoot after having been at sea for a spell—*got to shed your sea legs, girl, so you don't roll down the street like any old tar.*

I poke about in the stores while Higgins goes to an iron-monger to buy a strongbox to bolt to the deck under my bed—that's where we will keep our new riches till we get back to Ireland. I buy a new bonnet and some handker-chiefs, and then I walk by a goldsmith's shop, but there I stop. In the window, on display on a piece of black velvet, are gold hoop earrings, placed there so as to catch the eyes of young sailors who think they are now salty enough to wear one with pride. I think about my own lost gold earring and that goldsmith's shop in Kingston and I start to tear up but I shake my head. *You stop that now!* And then I make myself not think about that anymore, and I go to find Higgins and return to the ship—to my ship, my *Emerald*, which is now the love of my life, and the only love I need.

As we lie out at anchor, a good hundred yards from the dock and the town lying there with all its enticements, a swarm of bumboats cluster about us, offering their wares to my sailors, my sailors who open the gunports and look down, the better to deal with the waterborne vendors. As most are selling food, trinkets, souvenirs, cloth, and other harmless things, I don't interfere with their honest trade. After all, we are in the same sort of business, and it goes on in every port. But I see also that some of the things for sale are not quite so harmless—I see that some of my young men, like that young rascal Arthur McBride and his friend Ian McConnaughey, right down there on the deck below me, have already used some of their money to buy certain things from the bumboats, but not fine presents for their mothers, nor the best Dutch tobacco for their fa-thers' pipes, nor soft cloth for their sisters to sew into pretty dresses, nay, not any of that, but instead cheap versions of gentlemen's swords for themselves, which they now buckle about their waists. It looks like they mean to go swaggering off into the town looking for trouble, a couple of hotheaded Irish lads just waiting for some Englishman to insult them. Insults that they will, no doubt, receive. I must speak to this.

I get up on the quarterdeck and call for their attention, just before the first liberty party goes to leave the ship.

"Pray, listen to me, my brave and noble lads! If you have any affection for me at all, and I *so* hope that you do, then you will keep yourselves from trouble while you are here in this town. If you are put in jail, I will be unable to get you out, so please, *please,* if someone here in town offers a slight offense, let it go, for God's sake. If a chance for a fight comes up, do not put your fist in the other fellow's face but instead clap him on the back and buy him a drink in friendship. I tell you this not only as your friend who fears that harm will come to your dear bodies, but also I tell you this as Owner of the *Emerald* that you will get no more prize money if we have to leave you here behind to rot in an English prison!"

I hope they take my words to heart, but telling Irishmen not to fight, well, it could be a forlorn hope. Maybe, though, by telling them that I, myself, a girl that they maybe admire a bit, will think more of them for being good and less of them for causing trouble, it will make them behave. We'll see.

"Would it be out of place for me to recommend some restraint tonight, Miss?" says Higgins. He has laid out and spruced up my riding habit, which I intend to wear out this evening.

"Are you telling me to be good, Higgins?" I ask, arching

my brows and grinning at him. I imagine that it's plain from watching me bounce up and down on my toes as I get dressed that I have a bit of mischief in mind.

"It is obvious from the raffish glint in your eye that you are up for a bit of fun, Miss, and I hope you have it. I only hope that you will also exercise some caution," he says, and I think I hear a note of fatherly concern in his tone.

"Oo-ow, don't ye worry yerself, 'Iggins, luv," I crows. "An old Cheapside scrapper loike Jacky Faber ain't loikely t' get 'er arse in no trouble that she can't get it out of."

"Hmmm...," says Higgins, unconvinced and disapproving. "Very colorful language, Miss. It is not surprising that you were on the stage."

*It warn't the stage that taught me to talk like that, Higgins, it was the streets of London.* I peel off my white stockings and pull on the black pair. Then I stand and Higgins opens the corset like a clamshell and I step into it and the sides of it clutch my ribs. He laces it up behind and says, "Deep breath now, Miss," and I puff up and hold it, and he puts his knee in the middle of my back and pulls hard on the cords, which takes all the middle part of me—my ribs and half my guts— and shoves it all up to my top and makes my waist about twelve inches around and then he ties the cords tight. I can breathe out then. Now he holds out my ruffled-front white shirt, the one with the lace at the sleeves, and I put my arms into it. He buttons up the back and then holds open my dark green skirt and I step into it. He tucks the shirt into the waist of it and then cinches it up in back, under the folds of cloth that are gathered into pleats and fall down off my tail. Then he puts the strap of the lace collar around my neck, up high under my chin so that the lace spills down over my chest, and makes it fast. Last comes the deep maroon jacket with its stiff gray lapels that curve out and turn back, the buttonholes through which Higgins has threaded a lieutenant's narrow gold lace.

I stand before my mirror, all trim and tucked in harness, as Higgins smooths the jacket over my back and gives it a final tug and brush.

"How old are you, Miss?" he asks, and the question takes me by surprise.

"Why...fifteen, I think...Maybe closing in on sixteen. Why do you ask?"

"Nothing, Miss. Just be careful."

I tell him not to wait up for me, but I know he will.

I approach the Blow Hole Tavern on the arm of my First Mate John Reilly, and I look up at the sign that swings overhead. It pictures a whale like none I ever saw on my whaling cruise and probably like none that ever swam the ocean, blowing a great spout of water out the top of his head while mermaids cavort about. Liam said this was the place we should go to, and I hear the men from the *Emerald* inside already working up to a fine pitch of gaiety.

We enter and the old familiar smell of spilt ale and beer and dark rum soaked up in sawdust and into the very timbers of the place hits my nose like the greeting of an old friend I ain't seen for a while. There's a cheer when I'm seen by all, and I look about for the landlord or -lady. There she is, her brow knit together, thinking about whether or not to toss me right back on out for being a brazen hussy.

I pull out my purse and call out, "A drink for every man and woman in the house, compliments of the *Emerald,* the finest privateer ever to sail the ocean sea!"

That gets another great cheer and soothes the landlady's mind, for she beams and starts drawing pints.

I go to the biggest table of all and am seated next to Padraic, which is as it should be, as we are the ones of a common age. John Reilly sits to my left, which is as it should be, too, as we are similar in rank. I know this is Padraic's first time out in a place such as this without being under his father's watchful eye and he is flushed with pleasure. Liam had agreed to have Padraic put in the other section from his, thinking it was, as he said, time to loosen the leash on the boy. I look carefully at Padraic and say to myself, *Careful, me lad,* but he seems to be handling himself all right. He sips at his pint without slamming it down as young men are wont to do their first time out.

"A glass of rum with you, Miss Faber," says young Arthur McBride from across the table. Now there's one who ain't being careful at all. I sense John Reilly tensing up as Arthur ain't supposed to be quite so familiar with me, but I put my hand on my First Mate's arm to quell his urge to put the youthful sailor in his place.

"Nay, Mr. McBride," I say. "I have taken a vow never to taste strong spirits again. But I will take a glass of wine with you." A glass is poured for me and I hold it up to him and take a sip and then I look away from him. That's the way it is done, according to the Lawson Peabody School for Young Girls.

"No strong spirits, Miss? It seems a mighty stern vow," says John Reilly.

"Aye, John," I say. "But I took spirits one time to great excess and not only did I disgrace myself but also I lost the love of my dearest friend. It was then that I took the vow on the brow of one fine soul named Millie."

"Did you take the vow in the name of some saint, like Saint Bridget or Saint Brendan, then?" says Arthur McBride, who is plainly not going to be kept out of the conversation.

"No, I took it in the name of Saint Millie, a dog, actually, but one who saved my life at risk of her own, and whenever I am tempted to let rum or whisky slip twixt my lips, I think of her loving and trusting and loyal countenance and I cannot do it."

"Well said," says John Reilly, and there are murmurs of agreement all around. These Irish lads, they do love their saints, but they do love their dogs, too.

*Well, enough of being good,* I think, and look out across the table.

A great platter of cold raw oysters is laid out in front of me. I reach out and take one and lift the shell and tip it toward my mouth and Padraic, who sits next to me, must look away. Padraic, poor farm boy from the interior who has never even seen an oyster let alone eaten one, must look away as I tip the shell and drop the gray glob into my open mouth. The devil is in me, I can feel it now for sure, and I pull his shoulder around to make him look at me as I open my lips and tongue the oyster and then swallow it and say, *Ahhhh... surely you'll join me in some, Padraic.*

There are slices of lemon there and I grab a wedge and squeeze the juice of it on top of a few of the oysters and they are so fresh, I swear I see them jerk as the juice hits them. I send several more to their graves at the bottom of my gut and then I look about with great satisfaction. I've found that a good deal of the pleasure in eating oysters is in watching the disgust on the faces of people who do not enjoy them, as you hoist them up and slide them down your neck.

More platters are brought and I turn to the offerings they bear—smoked salmon, grilled perch, and, *oh yes, Padraic, you must try these, the baby octopus from Spain... see the little tentacles there? They are quite chewy and good.* I take one up and wiggle it at him. *Wait, now you. Stop teasing him, as he is a fine boy and just off the farm. What can he know of these exotic things? Here, a bit of trout with you then, my bold and noble sailor,* and I pick up a piece and push it to his lips and he lets it in.

"A song please, Jacky!" says some bloke who's forgot his place. They've seen and heard me play my fiddle and whistle on board ship, but I have never yet sung, nor have I danced, for the sake of discipline. Now, though, I stand at my place and toss back my head and sing out:

> *"Come cheer up, me lads, and banish all fear*
> *For on our ship the* Em-er-ald
> *'Tis to Glory that we steer!*
> *To Honor She calls you, as free men not slaves,*
> *For none are so free*
> *As the Sons of the Waves!"*

I messed a bit here and there with the lyrics to "Hearts of Oak," but they get it and come roaring back with the chorus, roaring fit to shake the windows:

*"Heart of Oak is our Ship!*
*Hearts of Oak are our Men!*
*We are always ready—STEADY, BOYS, STEADY!*
*We will fight and we'll conquer and do it all again*
*Singing the Emerald's song of Freeeeeeeeedom!"*

They messed with some lyrics there themselves, and they really came down hard with their mugs on the tabletops with *STEADY, BOYS, STEADY!* but I guess it goes with the song. I pop back up with:

*"Come all you quick young Irish Lads,*
*Who soon will come home,*
*With presents in your pockets and money to your names.*
*The girls will bob and coo and blink their eyes at you,*
*For who's the bravest of them all*
*But the Emerald's gallant crew!"*

That nails them down for sure and they go and hammer out the chorus, and then Arthur McBride stands up, a bit unsteadily, and holds up his hand and, when all is quiet, sings out in a clear tenor:

*"Now Gracie was a wild one,*
*Anne Bonny was the same,*
*But our Jacky of the Emerald*
*Puts both of them to shame!"*

Well! The boyo's got a bit of the Irish poet in him, I see. There's more cheers and they finish up with another turn of the chorus and I stand and raise my glass, "To Arthur McBride, the *Emerald*'s very own Celtic Bard!"

More toasts are lifted and drunk and then someone bellows out, "Give us another song, Jacky!" "Yes, a song!" says another and there are claps all around, so I put down my glass and pull my pennywhistle from my sleeve and place it on my lips. What to play for these Irish lads? Ah, what could be more Irish than this? I play the melody through once and a sailor cries, "Why, 'tis 'Whisky in the Jar'!"

And indeed it is. I put down the whistle and lift my head and sing out the first verse.

*"As I was a-going over Killgarrah Mountain,*
*I spied Colonel Farrell and his money he was countin'*
*Quick I drew me pistols and I rattled forth me saber,*
*Sayin' Stand and Deliver! For I am your bold deceiver!"*

As I'm singing this, I come around the table and stand in front of Arthur McBride and I come down hard on "Stand and Deliver!" and extend my hand that holds my whistle and I point it at his breastbone as if it were a sword. He plays his part by broadly pantomiming shock and anger. Then I do the chorus:

*"Musha ringum duram da,*
*Whack! for the laddie-o,*
*Whack! for the laddie-o,*
*There's whisky in the jar!"*

Now I leave the newly robbed Mr. McBride and skip around the table to stand behind Padraic. I put my hands on his shoulders and sing out:

*"He counted out his money and it made a pretty penny,*
*I took the money home and I gave it to my Jenny,*
*She sighed and she swore that she never would betray me*
*But the Devil's in the women and they never will be easy!"*

And when singing the last line I put on my most evil opened-mouth smile and run my fingers slowly up each side of Padraic's smooth young face. Whoops from the crowd and I lean over to see that the lad's face is as red as his hair.

I belt out the chorus again and this time the crowd joins in, bringing their tankards down hard on the tabletops with each *Whack!* And, with each *Whack!* the landlady is beginning to look a little more worried. More verses, two in a row and skip the chorus, I'm thinking...

*"The next mornin' early as I rose to travel,*
*Up stepped a band of footmen and likewise Colonel Farrell,*
*I flew to my pistols, but, alas, I was mistaken,*
*For my Jenny'd wet the powder and a prisoner I was taken!*

*"They put me in the jail with a Judge all a-writin',*
*For robbing Colonel Farrell up on Killgarrah Mountain,*
*But they didn't take me fists, so I knocked the jailer down,*
*And bid a farewell to this tight-fisted town!"*

I lifted up my puny fists in front of my face like a prize-fighter on this one, got a laugh, and went to the chorus again, and then motioned for silence so I could sing the last verse at a much slower, more dreamy tempo, and when all are quiet and waiting, I slip myself into Padraic's lap and put my arms around his neck and sing, all whispery and low…

> "Some take delight in the fishing and the bowling,
> Others take delight in the carriages a-rolling,
> But I take delight in the juice of the barley,
> And courting pretty boys in the morning so early!"

With that I plant a kiss on Padraic's blushing cheek and then pop back up, fist in the air, and we roar out the final chorus…

> "Musha ringum duram da,
> WHACK! for the laddie-o,
> WHACK! for the laddie-o,
> There's whisky in the jar!"

And this time the windows shake and threaten to shatter with the raw power of our voices raised together in song and good fellowship. Through the cheers and hoorays and applause I go to the center of the room and call out, "Now give me room as I means to dance!"

# Chapter 30

"Would you like a cold compress for your forehead, Miss?" says Higgins the next morning. I crack open an eyelid and I think I catch a note of primness in his voice.

"Whatever gave you that idea? I've never had a headache in my life, 'cept once, and I didn't drink any spirits last night," I say, turning over and groaning. "But put it on anyway." I lie back on my pillow and I must admit the cool, wet cloth feels good.

"I didn't do anything wrong. We ate, we drank, we sang, we danced. And we all got back here by midnight. What's the matter with that?"

"You got back here before midnight because you were all thrown out at eleven thirty."

"That landlady was damned ungrateful, if you ask me, for all the fine custom we brought her."

Higgins doesn't say anything for a while and then he says, "After you've had some breakfast, you might speak with Captain Delaney."

"Did it ever occur to any of you that sometimes I just want to act like a frisky young girl? Just sometimes?"

*What next?*

I go out on the quarterdeck and Liam is standing there all massive against the morning sky. I walk up beside him but he doesn't say anything.

*Hmmm.* I don't say anything, either.

He turns and goes to the other rail.

"All right, Liam, what's the matter?"

"Nothing is the matter. It is your ship. You act the way you want to act."

*Ah.*

"Out with it, Liam. I will have nothing between us."

He takes a breath and says, "Padraic is just a boy, but he is a fine boy. He sees you as the very picture of action and adventure. That is all right. But I do not want you to toy with his affections if you have no thought to carry on with such an alliance."

*Oh, Lord. Time for the knees. A girl's gotta do what a girl's gotta do.* The knees hit the deck and the hands come up under the chin in a prayerful attitude. "I'm so sorry, Father, and I won't do it again. It's just 'cause I'm young and wasn't brought up proper. Didn't get the proper guidance, like. And I really do like Padraic, he's a fine lad, it's just that I've decided to live single…"

"Aye. I've heard you say that before. Now stand up, you young fool," he says and pulls me to my feet, but now he is trying to keep from grinning. I am forgiven. Again.

This evening I will go out again, for it wouldn't be seemly for me to socialize with one-half of my crew and not the other, but I vow to be more restrained this time. I'll take my fiddle and play more tunes—more dignified-like, with not so much wild dancing as last night. And I'll dance only on the floor, not on the tabletop.

Was I too familiar with Padraic last night? I heave a heavy sigh. I'm afraid I was and now I'm going to have to frost him out for a while to show he has no chance with me in the way of love, as I do intend to live single all of my life. But did I really sit in his lap last night? Oh, my.

Ah, well, tonight I shall be good. Liam will be my escort and that will make me be good.

But it didn't work out quite that way…it never does, and it is a bleary-eyed gang of Emeralds, myself included, who set sail on the next morning's tide.

# Chapter 31

The two-masted schooner tried to slip out of a little harbor just north of Calais at dusk. He managed to slip through the blockade, but he didn't slip through us. We came in behind him and cut him off from the land, and he started to make a run to the west. We heeled over and the chase was on. It had been three weeks since we had shipped out of Harwich and we were hungry.

Liam and I each have our eyes pressed to our long glasses, our usual posture when a prize is in sight. The ship seems low in the water, like maybe he's carrying a good, heavy cargo.

"Looks like a choice one, Liam," I say. I make no effort to keep the greed out of my voice. I'm hoping we can catch this smuggler, as the men are getting restless—I mean, the food is good, better than on any warship or merchant that I know, and we have music and dancing and stuff, but I know the men want plunder, money for their pockets and for their families—this being the first real chance of a capture since we left Harwich, as ships like that one are growing ever more wary of rascals like us.

"Aye," he replies, "but he's got a bit of a start on us. Let's hope we can catch him before dark." We both look up at the fast-darkening sky. Then he calls out the order to get up all the canvas the *Emerald* can carry, and we try to close the distance.

Half an hour later it is plain that we ain't gonna catch him before dark, and I don't see any moon rising, either. Damn!

Ten minutes more and it's full dark and we're still way out of cannon range. Lights are beginning to be seen on the ship up ahead and his stern lantern is lit.

Liam leaves my side and goes to the foot of the mainmast and addresses the crew in a strong voice, but not one so loud as to carry across the water to the quarry.

"Men. Listen to me and listen to what I say. I want *complete* silence on this ship as of right now—no bells rung, no talking, no sneezing, no belching, no farting, no coughing, no stomping around, no footfall, no sound at all. If any of you are wearing shoes, take them off. If you see a block knocking against a railing, then wrap it in canvas to muffle it. If you hear a gun carriage squeaking, then grease it. Anything you see that you can do to lessen the noise of this ship, then do it."

He pauses and then continues, "Furthermore, I want no light to be seen on us—no lanterns, lamps, not even flint sparks to light your pipes. Knock your pipes out now and careful you don't burn down the ship in doing it."

*Damn right be careful,* I'm thinking, *and mind you don't mar my polished rail when you tap out your nasty pipes.*

Liam ain't done yet, though, and he goes on. "I hope you understand what I say, for if any man causes us to lose this prize, he will be sent back to Waterford and never again sail on this ship. Understood? Good. Now get to it, lads."

Hatches are closed so the cooking fires down below can't be seen, and I can see the coals falling from pipes into the water alongside. The ship goes dark and quiet. Liam comes back next to me. It is pitch-dark now and on the other ship, all the lights are winking out, too.

All except the stern lantern.

"Is he stupid, Liam?" I whisper. Could the Captain of that ship have forgotten about that light hanging off his tail? Could it be that he cannot see it from where he stands?

I hear a very low chuckle from Liam. "No, he is not stupid," he whispers, "but he thinks we might be."

I am mystified but Liam will only say, "Just wait, Jacky, just wait and watch." And so we watch the light bobbing up ahead, growing ever closer and closer.

"I think he'll do it very soon," whispers Liam in my ear. We have been watching the light for such a long time that it becomes weird—like it's not a ship's stern light at all but rather is a low star rolling about in the inky darkness. I shake my head to clear it of such thoughts.

I shake my head again, 'cause it seems to me that the light has shifted a bit to the right. *What*...

"Ah," says Liam, "'tis time."

Suddenly the ship ahead is veering hard to the right and...

"Left your rudder," says Liam, very quietly to the helmsman.

"*Left?*" I say, pointing out at the prize turning to starboard right before my very eyes. "He's going ri—"

Liam's hand comes over my mouth and he leans down and hisses, "The silence goes for you, too, Missy. Now look."

He takes his rough hand from my mouth and hands me my long glass. "Keep an eye on your prize. I must go have the sails trimmed for our new course. Quiet, now."

*Right,* I growl to myself, fuming. *I'll watch our prize all right. I'll watch it get clean away.*

The light is now abaft our starboard beam, which means that's as close as we'll ever get to this prize, dammit, and I bring up my long glass and focus it on the light. It is fuzzy for a bit, but I turn the end piece and it comes in sharp and clear and...oh, my...

I put down the glass. *Scammed again.* My prize turns out to be a small rowboat with a lit lantern sitting jauntily on the middle seat.

Liam comes back onto the quarterdeck.

"I'm sorry I doubted you, Father. I am a perfect fool."

"Nay, Jacky," he whispers back, "you are not. That trick is an old one, but it is a good one. It's one that has fooled many captains more experienced than you in the past and it will fool many more in the future. Come, let us go below where we can have a glass of port and talk. It's going to be a long night."

We have our glass of the thick, sweet port wine in Reilly's cabin, it having no windows, which allows us to light a candle. Men have been put in the rigging to listen for the other ship, some of them with speaking trumpets with the mouthpieces held to their ears rather than to their mouths. All I can hear right now is the sea rushing alongside a scant four inches away on the other side of the hull. Reilly's room is at the waterline.

"My guess is that he will do what I would do in his case—hold on a westerly track for about an hour, then turn north again to the original course. I figure we've got about one chance in four of seeing him come dawn."

"Maybe his men are not as disciplined as ours," says Reilly, his face swimming out of the darkness into the circle of candlelight. "Maybe we'll hear them in the night."

I take a sip and say, "Well, at least we have a chance at him. If it had been up to me, we'd have taken a fine rowboat as a prize, and, split thirty-eight ways, we'd each have a fine splinter onto which we could carve an account of our glorious exploit for grandchildren to admire."

Low laughter all around. I do not mind a joke at my expense, 'specially when I'm the one doing the joking.

There is a scratching at the door and Reilly says, "In."

The door opens and Dennis Muldoon sticks his big head into the circle of light. "We heard a cough or two off the starboard bow and we thinks it weren't from no mermaid sittin' on her rock, as those darlins' ain't prone to colds from the damp as we poor mortals are."

"How far off?" asks Liam.

"About two or three hundred yards. And them coughs had a definite Frenchy accent," says the grinning fool. "Through the nose, like."

"All right, Muldoon, get yourself back out there and be quiet about it. Let us know if you hear any more. Try to judge the distance on any other sounds, as we don't want to get too close to him in the dark. I'll be back on deck in five minutes."

We divide up the night watches between us—Liam now,

Reilly for the Mid, and me for the Four to Eight. We knock back our glasses and get up to leave.

"Looks like the odds just got better, Captain," I say.

"We'll see, Jacky. A prize ain't a prize till it's in your fist."

I go back to my cabin, fumbling in the dark, and flop down on my bed in my fighting clothes, 'cause no telling what's gonna happen. I don't think I'll sleep with all the excitement of the chase, but I do, and sometime before the Four to Eight, Higgins comes in and throws a blanket over me.

I'm on watch at dawn, and sure enough, there is our prize, sitting out there to the north. Liam comes up from down below, sipping a cup of coffee.

"The luck of the Irish," I say by way of greeting.

Liam smiles and stretches. "Aye," he says. "The luck was with us. There's no getting away from us now, and there's no more reason for silence." He takes a deep breath. "CLEAR FOR ACTION!" he bellows, but the men are already scampering to their stations.

Higgins comes up, bringing me a cup of coffee and some cake. I eat it gratefully, and it helps ease the tension of the night—all those hours spent listening at the darkness till, finally, the growing light of dawn revealed the outlines of the schooner. She is putting on all the sail she can, but she is doing it in vain—she can't get away from us now.

Higgins brings up my pistols, newly charged with fresh loads, and he straps my sword harness around my waist. "I suppose begging you to exercise caution would be a waste of my breath?"

"I am *always* the soul of caution, Higgins. Wherever did

you get the idea that I am not? And besides, what would you have me do? Hide down below? Stay in port? What kind of example would that be to my merry band of brigands?"

"Hmmm," he says, "I had expected a response such as that. But do be careful, Miss, as there are many here who both love you and fear for your safety, and question your evident lack of a sense of self-preservation." Saying that, he takes his tray and goes below to take his station in the surgery.

*Come on, Higgins. If you, yourself, had any sense of self-preservation, you sure wouldn't have teamed up with the likes of me, that's for certain.* I've the sense that Higgins has a little bit more of a taste for the life of adventure than he lets on.

First Mate Reilly comes up and reports that the ship is manned and ready.

"Then let's have Long Tom send him a good-morning salute, John," I say, and raise my voice so the men at the forward gun can hear, "Sullivan! Fire one off to his side!"

There is a pause of a moment and the long nine-pounder barks out its greeting. The ball hits to the left of the schooner, abaft her beam.

"Well, we are within range," I say, and that fact is brought back to us when there is a puff of smoke from the stern of the prize. The ball whistles through our rigging, but hits nothing.

"Seems he's gonna put up a fight, Liam," I say, my knees starting to tremble a bit, like they always do when someone is shooting at me. Now they're shooting at my beautiful ship, too, and I've got that to worry about as well.

"Right," says Liam, squinting at the ship through his glass. "And it looks like he might have something serious mounted amidships. At our speed now I don't think he'll be able to bear on us again with the stern gun. He's lost the angle on that one."

We continue to gain on him and I call out to the starboard guns, "Chock 'em up as high as you can so you hit only the rigging! Don't hurt the hull! Sully, you may fire as they bear! Let's show him what an *Emerald* rolling broadside feels like! Boarding Party to the starboard rail! Crouch down out of sight!"

They do it and there is a *crack!* as that serious gun on the prize fires.

The ball hits the bowsprit of the *Emerald*, smashing part of her walkway and cutting loose both her jib and forestaysail. They flap wildly in the wind, but nothing can be done now, not in the heat of this encounter.

"Musket men!" I yell to the men standing in the foretop. "Pepper the ones around that cannon as soon as you can see them!" Muskets are lifted to shoulders. Soon I hear the flash and *pop!* of the rifles. That oughta worry 'em....Hurt my *Emerald* will you?

We're almost broadside to him now and we could smash him to bits and put him down under the sea, but we don't want to do that, no we don't.

I put my hands on the shoulders of Ian and Denny as they crouch there behind the rail, cutlasses in hand. "Steady, boys, steady…"

There is a tremendous flash and *boom!* followed instantly by a *crack!* as the prize again fires his amidships cannon and the ball strikes a spar right behind me.

"Ow!" I cry as somebody slaps me on my butt, prolly that cheeky McBride, but I don't pay it any mind for it's time for me to shout, "Let's get him, lads! Get the hooks on him!" I draw my sword.

We get closer yet and Sully fires another of our guns, and the top gaff of the Frenchy's foresail shatters in a shower of splinters and the Captain gives it up. He goes back and pulls down his flag. *About damn time,* I'm thinking.

"Cease firing!" I bellow.

The ships are pulled together and over the rail we go. The Captain is on his gun deck—he's holding his flag and his sword. He looks at me with shock and, suddenly, real fear. *La Belle Fille sans Merci...*

"Padraic. Arthur. See what she's got," I say, and they plunge down into the hold.

I bow to the Captain—I think a curtsy would be a bit out of place here—and recite, in French, the little speech I had made up for these occasions to try to tone down my growing reputation as a bloodthirsty pirate.

"I am Jacky La Faber. Perhaps you have heard of me. I am a privateer who takes ships and their cargoes, but I neither harm nor rob the crews or the passengers of the ships I seize, no matter what you may have heard. You and your men will be put in one of your lifeboats and allowed to return to France."

I thought the "La Faber" was a nice touch.

He bows back and looks relieved, which is good. He presents his sword to me.

"*Non.* Please keep your sword. You led us on a merry chase and you fought gallantly."

Several more bows and back to business. The lads have come back on deck and Arthur McBride crows, "It's full of champagne! Enough for a hundred English New Years, or ten Irish ones! And we found this, too."

They have between them a well-dressed man of about fifty years, who don't look happy, no not at all. More spies? I would have thought they'd have learned their lesson by now. Well, must do my patriotic duty.

"Shake him down and see if he's got anything suspicious on him. I..."

There is a footfall as someone jumps down on the deck behind me, and I hear John Reilly cry out, "Jesus!"

I turn to see what the matter is and notice in passing that my right pant leg is bright red and my right boot is filling up with blood. How strange...

"Higgins! Come attend to your mistress! She's hurt!" Reilly roars out, and he scoops me up and jumps back over to the *Emerald*.

Higgins appears from the hatchway to the hold, takes one look at Reilly and his burden, and says, "Take her to her cabin. Put her on the table. I must get the bag." With that he ducks back down below.

Reilly carries me across the deck past Liam who says *Damn!* and follows us down into my cabin. My pistols are taken and I am put facedown on the table. In a moment I see Higgins come in bearing the medical bag I had put together back when we were rigging out the *Emerald*. He also has a pail of steaming water.

"Thank you, gentlemen," says Higgins. "Now I believe it would be best if you left us alone." Liam and Reilly nod grimly and leave, closing the door behind them.

Higgins goes around behind me and I feel him pulling

off my boots. Then he unloosens my sword belt and slips that off.

"Excuse me, Miss," he says as he reaches in under my belly and undoes the buttons of my pants and then the drawstring of my drawers. Then I feel both pants and drawers tugged down off of me.

"How bad does it look, Higgins? I hardly felt anything."

"We'll see, Miss. Here, let me put this pillow under your middle...there, that's it. Now, let's look."

Putting the pillow under my hips puts my bum up in the air, but I suppose that's what he wants, so as to get a clear shot at the problem. I wait. Then I feel a hot wet cloth cleaning off the area under scrutiny.

"Hmmm...," he says. "It is a splinter, but the end of it is visible, which is good, as we won't have to go digging for it, if it comes out all in a piece. One moment..."

I hear him rummaging through the medical kit for what I know will be pliers, and then he comes back.

"Steady now," and I feel the cold pliers against my cheek. "It would be better if you don't clench your buttocks when I do this, and now..."

"*Yeeeoowww!*"

I had intended not to cry out as an example to my crew as to my bravery, but I did anyway. Higgins carefully puts the withdrawn splinter on the table next to my nose. It is about two inches long and sits there glistening wetly.

"It seems to be relatively smooth and free of burrs. I think it all came out in a piece."

"Good *Emerald* oak," I manage to say.

"Indeed," he says, drily. "I am sure you will have it

mounted on a bronze plaque, given your usual sense of the dramatic." I think about the joke I made about splinters last night down in Reilly's cabin. Strange how things always come back at me.

"The wound is deep, but not wide," he continues. "I think it will heal up quite nicely. The bleeding has already stopped. I don't think there will even be a scar, so when you present yourself to your husband on your bridal bed, I am sure he will not even notice." His tone is joking, but I know he's just trying to put me at my ease—he's worried about infection, as am I. I've heard of people who've died of a mere blister on their heel.

"Dammit, Higgins, I told you there ain't gonna be no bridal bed and no...oh, the hell with it. Get the spirits of wine...right there in the brown bottle. Pour it on." I grit my teeth again.

"I suppose that is good, Miss. Then you won't have to explain to him about that tattoo."

"*EEEEEEEeeee...*" I keen as the pure alcohol hits. I don't know for sure that it helps keep off the infection, but I hold that if it hurts, it's got to be good. It's the Puritan in me. Higgins takes a cloth and is cleaning up the mess of blood and water and spirits when there's a knock on the door.

"Jacky," comes Liam's voice from outside. "Are you all right? We've got a situation here."

"Not yet, Captain," pleads Higgins. "Please, we've got to get a bandage on this first."

"No, Higgins, we've got to take care of business first. Just throw something over me and open the door." I can tell from the feel of the ship that we haven't cast off the prize and gotten under way yet, and that puts us in a precarious position. We ain't the only privateers about—there's French and Dutch and even Danish ones, too—and it would be a shame to lose both our prize and ourselves by being surprised in a weak condition like this.

When I feel the cool sheet float over my backside, I call out, "Come in, Liam."

The door swings open and Liam enters, followed by Padraic and Arthur holding the French passenger between them. I get up on my elbows.

Upon seeing me stretched out on the table with my legs spread out and my bum in the air, Liam reddens and says, "Put him in the chair and then get out, both of you."

The boys push the man down into the chair at the head of the table and then leave. As they go Padraic looks at my face with great concern, and Arthur looks at the rest of me with great merriment, as if he can barely keep from making a fine joke concerning my current state. *I'll get you, Arthur,* my glare tells him.

"What's this, then?" I ask.

"This is what it is," says Liam. "We found these on him."

Liam opens a leather bag and pours its contents out onto the tabletop in front of me and I gasp and gape in wonder. *Are those rubies, diamonds? And can that big one be an emerald?* I look up at Higgins who is himself looking down at the pile of glittering stones. "A king's ransom, Miss," he murmurs.

The French gentleman, for gentleman he plainly is, sits straight in his chair, but there is a look of utter defeat on his face.

"No other things on him? Nothing that looks like spy stuff?"

Liam shakes his head.

The man looks up, surprised. "I am not a spy," he says in English, looking offended at the notion. Then he looks back down. *Ah. That will make things easier.*

"How came you by these baubles?" I ask, carelessly running my finger through the pile. "I am sure you will tell me they are nothing but glass."

"No, they are not. They are very valuable. For a long time, I felt desirous of leaving my native land and so I cashed in all my assets into this form. I am, or I was, before the Glorious Revolution, the Marquis de Mont Blanc. I had sent my family to England while I remained behind to settle our accounts. And now I have lost everything."

"Why did you wish to leave?" I ask.

"I do not like the present government of my country. My family was aristocratic and we lost many of our members to the guillotine...to the mob. We haven't forgotten. And with Bonaparte's latest outrages...we had to go."

"And where were you going? Surely you wouldn't stay in Britain?"

"No. Only to book passage. Then on to America to make a new life."

It strikes me then that I, so lately a girl of the streets, a mere beggar, really, could right now bring down this man and his whole family, they who have been parading around as high-and-mighty lords and ladies for a thousand years or so, and bring them down, right down to the ground. It is a mighty temptation.

But I sigh and say, "You have great good luck, Monsieur de Mont Blanc. We are honest privateers and take only the cargoes and ships of enemy countries. We do not rob passengers or crew of their personal belongings. You may gather up your jewels and return in the lifeboat to France. Good luck to you and your family."

I see Liam stiffen at this. *Steady, Liam, and see how this plays out. I know how you feel about aristocrats and such, but maybe we can have our cake and eat it, too. Maybe we can hold to our honorable vow, and yet prosper...* I don't take my eyes off the Marquis de Mont Blanc.

He looks at his hands. "There is a problem with that. Were I to go back now, I would not be received... well, with kindness."

*Ah, I thinks. It's either me or the guillotine, eh, Monsieur? And what kind of choice is that?*

I smile and say, "You would book passage with us, then? Ah, well... Higgins... please... hand me my shiv." Higgins's hand, bearing my knife, appears in my vision. The Marquis stiffens when he sees me take it, *but, don't worry, Sir, the blade is not for you.*

I use the knife to separate the jewels into two equal piles. Then I make sure that there are equal amounts of rubies, diamonds, and emeralds on each side. I hum a little tune as I do this. Could it be "La Marseillaise" I'm humming? *Allons enfants de la patrie-eeeeeeee...* I don't know... The biggest emerald of the lot I do not include in either pile—that I put separate, close to my chin. I point with my shiv to the pile on the left.

"You shall keep those jewels, Monsieur, and I wish you and your family the joy of them. There is surely enough there to get you a fresh start in America. Your sort always rises back to the top, anyway, eh?"

He doesn't say anything.

"And this pile here," I say, gesturing to the jewels on the

right, "will pay for your passage. We will get you safely to Harwich and we will provide you an escort to take you to the bosom of your family. Your escort will be strong and well-armed, I assure you—there are many thieves abroad in this world, Monsieur, as I am sure you know."

He looks at me steadily. "That is surely the most expensive fare ever paid for crossing the Channel," he finally says, but he doesn't look quite so hopeless now.

"That may be so, but I believe it is your best option. Besides, it is not only a fare you are getting, but also our kind protection. And if you decide to go to Boston in America, I can even give you a letter of introduction to le Comte de Lise, a very high-placed Frenchman there. I went to school with his darling daughter. It will give you a leg up in Society."

I wait a bit for him to juggle the odds and then I say, "Agreed?"

He gives a shrug and says, simply, *"Oui."*

"Good. Then, as my honored passenger, you shall join me for dinner tonight, and you will find that I set a fine table," I say, bestowing on him my best grin. "But, wait... there is one more thing..."

His eyelids droop and he looks warily at me, waiting for the ax to drop. I continue.

"The ship you hired to spirit you away from France did fire on me and did hurt me sorely. For my pain and suffering I will take this emerald for myself and my poor bottom... or how would you have it? ... *mon derrière faible?* Till this evening then, Monsieur, I bid you *adieu.*"

Three days later and we are back in Harwich with our hard-won prize.

# Chapter 32

"You went to school with the daughter of a French count?"

"Try not to seem so surprised, Higgins. Am I really all that crude that you cannot believe that I went to any school at all?" He's got my head down in a basin washing my hair and so has me at a disadvantage, as I have to be careful not to snort in any of the suds. We are back once again in Harwich, so as to sell the prize and get Monsieur de Mont Blanc off.

"No, Miss, you are the very soul of elegance and refinement and I am sorry, as I did not mean to offend."

"*Hmmph.* I bet you didn't." I sniff. "Well, yes, actually, I did. It was the Lawson Peabody School for Young Girls in Boston. Not much of what they tried to teach me took, but some did. Would you like to hear of my adventures in America?"

"Yes, I would, actually. I had wondered about it but did not intend to pry."

"All right, then. I will tell you of it at dinner, but only if you sit down and eat with me this once, as it's a long story."

---

We had hired out horses and got Monsieur de Mont Blanc delivered to his family all safe and sound, if a bit lighter in the purse. He is not going to Boston but instead to New Orleans, where they've got a bunch of French people, which is just as well, as my letter of introduction to Lissette's folks would have gotten him tossed right out into the street. *What? A letter from the des-pis-ed Jac-Kee Fay-Bear! Non!* Now, Mademoiselle Claudelle de Bourbon *does* live in New Orleans, but I really don't think that she and the Marquis would travel in quite the same circles....Never can tell, though—not with men, you can't.

The Marquis turned out to be good company after all, and we had a merry time at our dinners. He had a good baritone singing voice and I learned two good French songs from him—"*Plaisir d'Amour*" and "*Jolie Blonde*"—lovely songs, and I'm sure they'll come in handy someday. The man was not cheerful over his loss, but now he didn't have to worry about running the blockade anymore, and I'm sure that put his mind at ease.

We came back into Harwich port with our second prize in tow, and again we sailed under the grim and threatening guns of Shotley Gate. The first time we came into this port, Liam had looked up at the guns and said, "I'd hate to try to get out of this harbor without their permission," and left it at that. This time Liam gave me some sobering instruction in gunnery. He gazes at them looming above us as he says, "They are forty-two-pound carronades—cannons designed to crush at short range, and short range they got. The channel is only about one hundred yards wide here and a ship has no choice but to go right by these brutes at point-blank range. Their gunners would not even have to aim the guns—just wait till the ship pulled into their sights and *wham!* There goes your bow, then the second gun caves in your midsection, and the first one after being reloaded gets your after section—that's if you're still afloat, which would be very doubtful."

I look at the bunker and have to agree. We couldn't even shoot at the gun crews with muskets because the guns are housed in a big stone building with only the muzzles sticking out.

It is something to remember.

Higgins got to work and had the prize, the *St. Moritz,* and her cargo sold right quick—I swear the merchants were standing on the Point when we entered the harbor, just rubbing their hands in anticipation of profit—and after that was done and the money was in hand, we held an accounting with the men. I had decided, and Liam had agreed, that we should go back to Waterford to repair our ship and to let the men see their families and spend their money. At least in Waterford we could tie up at the quay and not have to take boats back and forth from our dear old *Emerald.*

We called them to gather about the quarterdeck and they knew what we were about, make no mistake about that, and their high spirits could scarcely be contained. I may have to have that Arthur McBride flogged at some time. It was too much to hope that this crew would line up in ranks like a disciplined King's ship, but Liam and Reilly managed to get them in some sort of order and settled down. Higgins sat at a table set at the foot of the mainmast and fussed with a ledger in front of him as he got ready to read from it. I, being in port and being good as regards my attire, am dressed in my riding habit with skirt, and I stood behind him.

The ship's company knew when they signed on that the shares of the money would be divided thusly:

50 shares for me and the *Emerald*—after all, I have to pay for all the food, the powder and shot, and all the other supplies, and the refitting and repair. And, it's *my* ship.

10 shares for Liam Delaney, Master and Commander.

5 shares for John Reilly, First Mate.

1 share each for 35 men.

"I am pleased to announce that the privateer *Emerald* has taken two prizes, and the total amount realized from the sale of those prizes and their cargoes is such that each share is worth ninety-one pounds."

There is a sudden silence. *Ninety-one pounds!* For a six-week cruise! Ninety-one pounds is what they could only hope to make in three years at any job they could find in Ireland! Every man aboard is now a confirmed privateer, if not an outright pirate.

There is a great cheer from the men and I step forward to address them.

"You have been a fine crew and you deserve every cent of what you got. I only hope you spend it wisely."

Arthur McBride comes forward and drops to his knees before me. "I love you, Jacky Faber! Marry me and you shall have all of my riches!"

"Get up, you fool, for we all know you shall never have me at all, nor your riches for very long!"

Another laugh and a cheer and the men line up for some of their money—again, enough for a good time and that's it. I want the real money passed out in Waterford so their wives and mothers can get their hands on it for the benefit of themselves and their children before it's gambled or frittered away on drink and loose women. If there's one thing I know in this world, it's the ways of sailors when they are ashore with something jingling in their pockets.

Of course, Higgins's accounting also means that me and the *Emerald* got 4,550 pounds—five years' pay for a captain of a first-rate. My, my... It was the diamonds that did it, I know. I know also that I've got to talk to Higgins.

"Do you know of a bank you can trust?"

"Yes, Miss. There is a Bank of England branch in Colchester. Lord Hollingsworth used it and was never disappointed in its services."

We are seated in my cabin talking about this, but I still ain't convinced.

*Ouch!* As I shift my lower self on my chair I reflect that I sure as Hell ain't gonna be riding horses for a bit yet. Things look good on that end, though—the infection did not set in and I did not die. The worst of it was having to put up with the pitiful looks of concern I got from the oafs I have surrounded myself with.

"You are sure of this bank?"

"The Bank of England has the entire treasury of Great Britain behind it. It cannot fail as long as England exists. If you bank your money in the branch in Colchester, you will be able to draw it out in any of its branches—London, Ireland, Scotland—anywhere. I highly recommend it. You can't keep that amount of money in a box under your bed."

*Hmmm…* The gutter girl in me has great suspicions about banks and such, but Higgins says that it's all right, so…

"All right, Higgins. Take it all tomorrow and bank it. And take two hundred pounds as your own pay out of my shares."

"That is most generous, Miss. Thank you. I will take the opportunity to visit with Lord Hollingsworth's family and my own father who lives nearby."

Higgins, being written onto the *Emerald*'s books as chief steward, gets a share like the others, but I know that somebody like him don't come that cheap and I intend to see that he gets what's coming to him.

"Of course, Higgins, and please, take an extra day with your visits and give my regards to your dad."

"…And that's the end of Jacky Faber's adventures in the New World. After that, I hopped aboard a whaler and you know the rest," I say in finishing my story. "And I sure hope you ain't handy with a pen, Higgins, for I know I ain't ready to have another book out there about me and my free and easy ways."

Higgins had returned from Colchester and I had a bank draft in the amount of four thousand pounds sterling in my strongbox. I didn't bank all I had—we do have to re-victual in Waterford and the bowsprit repairs ain't gonna be cheap—and I still have my money belt with its stock of gold coins that encircles my waist every moment that I'm not in bed. That, and my emerald, of course.

Higgins's aged father was well and was even better after his son had laid some coin of the realm on him. His visit with the Hollingsworths was joyous, with all the girls tugging at his sleeve and begging him to come back to them and stay, but Higgins said he told them that now that he was a bold sea rover, it would be quite impossible, however charming were their entreaties.

"Quite a tale, Miss, and I enjoyed it hugely, for you are, without a doubt, without equal as a storyteller. And rest assured that I shan't abuse your trust in a literary way," says Higgins, dabbing his mouth with his napkin. "I suppose Boston and its inhabitants have by now recovered from your visit?"

"I guess so, but Boston was burning right cheerfully as I left."

Higgins laughs. "You, Miss, are nothing less than a modern Visigoth, lacking only a two-handed broadsword. Perhaps the next item we should purchase for you is a Viking helmet, shiny gold, for sure, and complete with fur-trimmed horns."

"Well, I hope I'm not as bad as all that. I try to be good, but sometimes things don't seem to work in that direction."

"One mystery, though, if you don't mind?"

"Shoot."

"How did you learn to speak French so well in only three-quarters of a year? I know you received some instruction when you were on the *Dolphin* but that could not have been much. And I know you are a quick study, but…"

I consider this. "Well, the Boston winter was long and my friend Amy and I would have contests, dares if you like, wherein we would speak only French to each other for a certain period of time. Sometimes for hours, then for days, and once for a whole week. You learn a language fast that way."

"Ah," says Higgins, "I see. I also see you miss your friend Amy from the way your eyes mist up when you talk of her."

"Aye, but that's over. Like a lot of things," I say. "But now, let us be merry." I lift my glass. "Thank you for coming back to me, Higgins, and I really mean that."

As I get undressed for bed, I wonder how they are on the *Wolverine* tonight—my friends, I mean, Robin and Tom and Ned and Jared and the rest of the Werewolves. I hope they are well. Yes, and Amy, too.

When all of my clothes are over a chair, I take my emerald out of the money belt where I have made space for it. I hold it up and watch the facets glimmer in the lamplight. Beautiful...I try to get the emerald into my belly button and, by stretching the skin around a bit, I do force it in so that it stays. I look at myself in the mirror. *Well, my girl, if you ever fall out of favor with Dame Fortune again, and I'm sure you will, you can become a hoochie-coochie dancer.* I mean, I do all those other dances—Irish jig, Scottish sword dance, English hornpipe—why not hoochie-coochie as well?

I go over to the wardrobe and take my white shawl and I tie it low down on my hips like a Hindoo belly dancer might wear it and go back to the mirror. I put my palms together over my head and try out a few wiggling moves, and as I do it, I hum the tune to the song that those rascally boys back on the *Dolphin* used to sing when they wanted to get themselves worked up over the thought of women with no pants, and further thought that they were sounding like Indian snake charmers when they were singing it. *There's a place in France where the women wear no pants. And the dance they do, it is called the hoochie-coo...* Hmmm. I puff out my belly, but that still doesn't seem to do it. *Well, better stick to buccaneering, Jacky.* I don't think Hindoos prize scrawniness highly in their nautch dancers.

I read once in a newspaper that Lady Hamilton, love of the great Lord Nelson's life, started out as a hooch dancer, dancing naked behind sheer curtains, on the other side of which old men would lie in beds hoping to be cured of the ailments of old age by the dancing of young girls amid braziers smoking with aromatic herbs. Men sure are strange, no matter what the age.

You'd think the press'd be a little nicer to Lady Hamilton, she being the consort of the Great Lord Nelson, him who's the darling of the British Fleet and the one most likely to keep Napoléon's feet off of British soil, but they ain't. They're downright mean, showing her in cartoons as a strumpet and as fat and ugly, which she once wasn't. I've got some respect for her, though. She started out no better than me and now she's Lady Hamilton, can you imagine that? Married to a Lord...Well, not exactly married, for she ain't Nelson's wife, but she might as well be—she's got a daughter by him. Go figure.

Well, enough of this...I tighten my belly and out pops the emerald and on goes the nightshirt and so to bed. Tomorrow we will weigh anchor and the *Emerald* will head back to our home port of Waterford, on the Emerald Isle, to refit and replenish.

# Chapter 33

Waterford is a fine, bustling port city and it bustled even more when the *Emerald* came in on the morning tide with her loot and her boisterous crew. We warped her in next to the pier and soon the ship swarmed with workmen repairing the bowsprit damage and loading new stores aboard. The ship swarmed also with the wives, children, and sweethearts of the crew, and a proud lot they were, those boys and men of my crew proud to be able to put money in the hands of their wives and mothers, proud to know that their children would not starve through yet another cold, miserable winter but would instead have good food in their bellies and new clothes on their backs.

The repairs are going slower than I hoped and, of course, are costing a lot more because of it. Liam has been overseeing the work while Higgins has been watching over the money end of it—to make sure we are not swindled by those cheatin' weasels.

Those damned cheatin' weasels, damn...No, wait. Calm down. Take a deep breath...I've got to put that out of my mind and let others handle it. I've got enough other stuff to think about, like noticing that Higgins doesn't go ashore any more than he has to when he's here in Waterford. In Harwich he was all over the shops looking for neat new things for the *Emerald*'s living spaces and such. I ask him right out about that, and he says the people here are very cold to him and so it is not pleasant to go out so he doesn't. Hmmm. That steams me a bit, but Higgins doesn't seem to want to talk anymore about it so I drop it.

But I don't drop it for good.

"Liam, Higgins tells me the people in this port have been mean to him—look at him with narrowed eyes and such. I won't have it. There're other places we could spend our money. Is it because he's...the way he is?"

Liam and I are at the rail looking out at all the activity on the wharf. There're barrels being rolled and hogsheads being hoisted and crates being stacked, and there's Arthur McBride strolling by in a new suit of clothes and a girl on each arm—'tis plain that lad will not have his money for very long, but he will have some tales to tell, I'm sure, and I'm sure his mates will listen to those tales and admire him for both the doing and the telling.

Liam takes a long drag on his pipe and says, "No, lass, that ain't it. We've got as many like him as any other people. No, it's that he's British and he is so plainly British—the way he dresses, the way he speaks, the way he carries himself, even. To the people here he looks like the very picture of an English nob."

"So?"

"So, about six, seven years ago there was a big uprising— it was called the Rebellion of Ninety-Eight, when the Society of United Irishmen rose up to throw off the yoke of their

British oppressors. A lot of the battles were fought here-abouts, especially up around Wexford, about twenty miles north of here, up near where I lived."

His pipe makes burbling noises and works up a great head of smoke as Liam pauses, looking out over the roof-tops of the town. I know he's thinking back to those troubled times. I don't say anything, not yet. I just wait.

"Terrible, terrible things were done. The British put down the rebellion, and they put it down ruthlessly...without any mercy. Thousands were killed...tens of thousands...there was scarcely a pike or fence post here-abouts without a severed head stuck on it for the beaten Irish to look on and admire."

His voice has taken on a real edge. His eyes narrow, but it is not against the smoke from his pipe. *Geez...I think, how did I get from Higgins being uncomfortable to this?* Liam goes on.

"Did you ever wonder, Jacky, just what I was doing on the *Dolphin*, in the British Navy, as I was?" He manages a rueful smile at this.

I figured that he was there out of poverty as I was, or that he had been pressed, as so many others were, and I tell him this.

"Nay, Missy, it was to keep my own head from resting on a spike. I had to hide out for a bit and it seemed to me that the best place to hide from the Beast was in his very belly. And so I joined as a man-of-war's man and met up with you and here we are. Ain't life strange?"

"It is that, Liam," I say, and I put my hand on his arm. "I am sorry for your poor friends and for your poor country."

Liam puts his hand on mine and pats it, gently. "Now,

girl, banish these thoughts from your mind. 'Twas none of it your fault. And tell Higgins it's nothing personal, just politics...just bloody politics."

I think on the things that Liam has told me. Many things are plain now—how the older men like John Reilly are uncomfortable in an English port like Harwich, and how the younger ones like Padraic and Ian and Arthur are always ready for a fight with the Brits. And 'tis plain now why Liam's wife, Moira, did not receive me with open arms when first I burst into their little farmhouse all those months ago. Why should she—to her I was English, and girl or not, kin to the murderers of her kin.

Sad thoughts as these are dashed from my mind as I see a flash of red curls sticking out from under a bonnet down below on the pier.

"Jacky!" she cries out, waving. "I've been let out!"

"Mairead!" I call back and wave in turn. "Come on up!"

In a moment she is dashing up the gangway and onto the deck. She sees her father and gives him a kiss on his grumpy cheek and then clasps my hand and we dive down to my cabin to plot out the afternoon. Away, dull care!

Liam had moved his family from the farm and into the town as soon as we arrived back— and why not? He had the money and the potato crop, what there was of it, had already been brought in. Mairead and I lose no time in becoming fast friends in the short time we have been here together in Waterford—it is natural, after all, as we are of the same age and temperament, and sometimes I don't want to be the Owner of a Fine Ship or a Lieutenant in the Royal

Navy or a Pirate Queen, *La Belle Fille sans Merci.* Sometimes I just want to be a kid, out on the town with a friend. Being out with Mairead reminds me of being out and being bad in Boston with Amy or Annie and Betsey and the other girls of the Sisterhood.

Mairead is such a delight, too, in all her country-girl wonder at the sights of the big town, and it was great fun seeing her decked out in new clothes and eyeing the boys and seeing the boys eye her, with her sparkling green eyes and flaming red hair. And, because she is Liam's daughter, she is musical with a fine voice and can dance, if not rings about me, at least as well. She plays a mean pennywhistle, too, so we lose no time in getting an act together.

Of course, I have Liam and his family to dinner in my cabin right off and Higgins serves up a fine feast and we have a grand time, but I don't think Moira will ever really love me—she sees me as too much of a threat to her family, and I have to admit she's right. Already I've taken off with her husband and her eldest son, and now I'm working on Mairead. Why wouldn't she view me with suspicion? When I'm thinking straight I have to admit I see her point—I *am* a bad influence on her Mairead. If I had my way, we'd be putting on our act in the local taverns at night, which is probably why Mairead is *not* allowed to stay the night with me in my cabin. Pity, I could have used the company. Liam knows me, too, and what I'm likely to do if I get my blood up, so, regrettably, I spend my nights alone.

We have found a teahouse where we are allowed in, so we go in and are seated. Mairead sits stiffly, not knowing what to do right off, but I say just relax and they will bring us stuff to eat and drink. When they do, I say, "Put that napkin in your lap and then put your left hand in that same lap and leave it there. Pretend it doesn't work anymore, for all the good it's going to do you here. Reach for your teaspoon with your right hand and put some sugar in your cup. Stir it up. Put the teaspoon on your saucer, like this. Now take a sip. Put the cup back down and take a piece of cake. Bring it to your mouth and eat it—small bites, now. Now, another sip of tea, put the cup back down, and say, 'I say, Miss Faber, is it not the most *deliiiiiiightful* day?'"

By this time we are both convulsed in giggles, but we soldier on and do not make complete fools of ourselves.

"Jacky, I gotta say this's been the best part of my life so far and if anybody thinks I'm going back to that dirty little farm and marry that dirty little Loomis Malloy, they're sadly mistaken." She takes another cake and drops it down. She shakes her head and the red curls dance, her green eyes defiant. Mairead, like her brother Padraic, has red hair—not orange hair, not ginger hair, not carrottop hair, but *red* hair. I've never seen the like.

"Come, Mairead, he can't be as bad as all that," I say, munching my own bit of cake. It's good and I have another.

"Well, if you, Miss, are partial to lads what ain't got no foreheads or necks and whose knuckles drag on the ground as they walks, then Loomis is just the man for you! I'll set up an intro-duck-shun, like," she says. I have to clap my hand over my mouth to keep from snorting tea and cake out my nose and onto the nice tablecloth.

"Loomis, I'd like you to meet Miss Faber. She is a lady. Miss Faber, I'd like you to meet Loomis. He is an ape."

I manage to swallow my cake without choking.

"His talk is all about his hogs and how the sow is about to have piglets, and then he looks at *me* and *my* belly when he says that, and I about die of the pure mortification, I do."

"Ah, but he has some land, I hear. That's got to count for something," say I, playing the devil's, or rather, father's advocate, just for fun.

"Land!" she snorts. "Jacky, land is nothing but dirt, and all the dirt in Ireland grows nothing but sorrow. I notice you ain't had much use for it, dirt that is, always being out on the nice clean ocean and being Captain of your own fine ship and all."

"You wouldn't use the word 'clean,' Mairead, if you ever smelled our bilges after we've been out for a month or so... and besides, I ain't Captain, your father is."

"Aye, but everyone knows who's really the boss."

"Boss ain't the same as Captain, Mairead, and you should know that." To change the subject I ask, "Surely, Mairead, Liam would not marry his beloved daughter off to someone she did not love?"

She sniffs and looks off out the window. "Dad didn't send Loomis away, like he did the others...like he did Arthur McBride..."

*Jesus!* I think. *I sure don't blame Liam for that!*

"Or..." And here her voice softens, "like he did Ian McConnaughey."

*Ah. The things you learn when you just sit and listen.*

"I am sure the real reason he took Arthur and Ian on your *Emerald* as crew, them being farm boys who had never been to sea before, was to keep them away from me when he was gone out on the ocean."

"Well, let's finish up here and head out into the town,

and if we meet up with Arthur and Ian and I find myself on Arthur's arm and you on Ian's, then what's the harm?" I say, tidying myself up and getting ready to get to my feet. "We have two more days before we sail, so let's make the most of it."

Two more days, which we fill with music and song and wild romps through the town. Yes, she does meet up with Ian, and I let myself be led around by Mr. McBride for a bit, rascal though he be. He spends most of his talk on telling me what a fine fellow he is, but he is fun and good company and so we get along.

On our last afternoon in port, Mairead and I put on a performance on the main deck—all of the men are back on board and since she and I ain't allowed to put on our show in one of the pubs, 'cause Moira would crucify us both, her daughter in the regular way and me upside down like poor Saint Peter, it seems the only place we can do it.

We do the usual sad Irish songs like "The Mountain of Mourn," some comic ones like "Galway Bay," and then rip into some fast reels like "The Green Groves of Erin" and "The Merry Blacksmith," with me on the fiddle and Mairead on the whistle, and then Liam can't stand it anymore and decides not to be the grumpy dad and pulls out his concertina and plays a hornpipe and Mairead and I link arms and dance to the delight of all. Then Dennis Muldoon, of all people, takes the Lady Lenore from me and he and Liam go into my favorite "The Rocky Road to Dublin," which I had sung all alone on the shores of South America and on the road from Boston and now sing here in Ireland, and when I finish the last verse, Mairead and I stand side by side, with

Padraic by me and Ian by Mairead, and we all four pound the deck of the *Emerald* like it's never been pounded before. Glory!

Mairead was good as any dutiful daughter at dinner that last evening. We all had a fine feast in my cabin and she left with her mother, without complaint, when night had fallen and it was time for them to go. I think my time with Mairead has settled her down a bit and she seems reasonably content. Easy in her own skin, like, and looking to the future with more assurance. She waved to me as she left and I waved back. *It will be all right, Mairead, you'll see.*

Then we put away the charms of the shore and it's out to sea to raid once more.

# Chapter 34

We hold a Council of War in my cabin—Liam, Reilly, me, and Higgins. We've been out for four days and ain't seen nothing yet, nothing worth taking. We boarded some fishing boats and all they had on them was fish so we bought some and let the boats go. Never let it be said that Jacky Faber is a common thief, not nowadays, anyway.

"I say we head south and go worry the Dagos off the coast of Spain. The Frogs know us too well around here and are laying low it seems. Else we got 'em all," I say.

"Well, it sure would be warmer," says Reilly, "and I wouldn't mind that." I hadn't really thought about it till now, but it is getting on into late November and there's a definite chill in the air.

"Any prizes we got would have to be brought a farther way back, to sell at Harwich," says Liam, leaning back and plainly thinking it over. "Sure ain't no places down in Spain we could sell 'em without us getting hanged for it. Have to protect 'em on the way back up, too, as well as ourselves. Lots of Spanish privateers down there. Thanks, Higgins." Higgins has our silver coffeepot and is refilling the porcelain cups we got off that second ship the *Wolverine* took. "But it's all right with me," says Liam, finally, and the plan is approved.

John Reilly and Liam leave the cabin, and from outside I hear them give the orders to come about for the south. I settle back in my chair and prepare for some reading, or maybe some practice on the Lady Lenore, but, oh no, it is not to be.

"Miss, if you would have a seat," says Higgins, "I think we need to redo your hair."

*Uh, oh.* That's Higgins's way of saying, *Sit down, you ignorant slug, I want to talk some sense into what passes for your brain.*

I sigh and plunk down. The Continuing Education of Jacky Faber...

He takes my pigtail and unbraids it and begins to brush my hair. *Uummmm, that does feel good...*

"You might consider, Miss," he begins... *And here it comes,* I think... "now as you grow in wealth and will no doubt soon go into Society, that you might consider avoiding using such words as Frog and Dago, as many people find them offensive."

*What?*

"But they're the enemy, Higgins, why not call them what we want to call them and bugger their feelings?"

Higgins sniffs. "'Bugger' is another word you might profitably drop from your vocabulary, Miss. But I digress. I have come to know you to be a young lady who is pure of heart and free of prejudice, but sometimes you seem to... without thinking, I believe... express yourself in a manner rather rude as regards another person's origins."

"All right, Higgins. I'll listen, if you keep brushing."

"Very well. Now, there are many in Britain who can

claim either French or Spanish ancestry. Your own Captain Delaney proudly claims descent from the Spanish Armada. Many, many people have relatives across the Channel—after all, we have been living next to each other for thousands of years, even though we've been at war for most of that time."

"Hmm," I hum, unconvinced. Once again someone is telling Jacky Faber to clean up her mouth. It always seems to be the thing to do, don't you know...

"And as for being enemies, does not one honor one's enemies and accord them a measure of respect if they act in an honorable manner? Does not a captain in any service, French, English, or Spanish, put on his finest uniform before a battle as a gesture of respect to his enemy?"

"They *say* that's why they do it," I snort, "but I thinks it's 'cause they want to have their best clothes on their back if they're captured and so their best duds can't be stolen by some snot-nosed sublieutenant or, if they're killed, they want to leave a good-looking corpse."

"Well, we all want that, don't we? But is that why you dress up each time we attempt to take a ship?"

"Higgins, you know damn well I do it to prance around and show off," I laugh, but I take his words to heart. And well I should, for who knows better than I from my time at the Lawson Peabody School for Young Girls that words can pierce the heart as surely as swords? I know I didn't like being called "the Tory" back in Boston, or "the little fairy" on board the *Dolphin,* or "the Captain's whore" on the *Wolverine,* and for sure, there's been more front teeth lost to the word "Mick" than to any dentist's pliers. I sigh a great sigh and resolve to take his advice and be good.

"All right, Higgins, I will do it. No more Frogs, Dagos, Spics, Yanks, Blackamoors, Portagees, Hunkies, Polacks, Russkies, Chinks, Japs, Hindoos, no more…"

"All right, Miss. I think I know your intent and I am glad of it."

It's two hours into the noon watch and I'm sitting up in the maintop, scanning the horizon for something interesting and finding nothing save a few seabirds floating high overhead. *Should save myself the trouble,* I think, *the lookout high above me would see anything before I did.* I lean back against the rail and look up at my sails all white and tight up there, as they should be, and I relax in the sun.

Spread across my lap is a length of black cloth, about four feet square, for I am making yet another flag and I am almost finished. On it I have stitched a cutout piece of white cloth, shaped in the form of a grinning skull, very much like the Death Angel heads I saw in the churchyard next to the Lawson Peabody School for Young Girls back in Boston, and under this I have put two white, crossed bones. I would not think of using this flag for ordinary prize taking—the people on the ships we take are scared enough already and I find my reputation is going in a way I don't really like—but suppose, just suppose we run into a French or Spanish privateer or any kind of pirate for that matter, who might want to bag us? If we crack out this flag at the mainmast when he comes close, well, maybe he might just think twice and slack off, as he would then know that we are not helpless prey, and he would most surely get his nose bloodied if he attempted to take us.

Putting the last stitches in around the teeth of the skull, I reflect that Mistress Pimm, she who tried to teach me embroidery, among other things, might be proud of my effort here. Maybe.

I put up my needle and look out over the water again. We've had a good breeze and the *Emerald* is fairly tearing along. We'll be down in Da—down in Spanish territory before too long and perhaps we'll find something choice, maybe we'll...*what?*

There is a commotion down below and I throw the flag aside to go see what is the matter. When my feet hit the deck, I see Sheehan, one of the older hands in the Port Watch Section, coming out of the forward hatch, dragging someone by the neck.

"Here!" I cry, and hop down on the main deck, "I'll have no fighting on my ship, Jack Sheehan!"

Sheehan, a big man, grins from ear to ear and says, "No fightin', Miss! I just caught me a big rat! A stowaway!"

*What? Who would...*

The rat in question has its head down 'cause of the way its neck is being held by Sheehan's mighty paw. Looks like it might be a boy—barefoot with white trousers and shirt and a large floppy cap.

"Bring him here!" I order and Sheehan pushes the stowaway forward and stands him up in front of me and I look into green eyes and...*Oh. My...*

"What's going on here, then?" says Liam, coming up next to me. The stowaway's large floppy hat chooses this time to fall off her head and the red curls tumble out. The entire crew is up on deck now and there is a common gasp.

Liam cannot say anything for a moment—he can only stand and stare, openmouthed and goggle-eyed, then...

"Mairead!" he roars, loud enough to wake up half of Spain, if not China, too.

I've seen Liam Delaney truly, truly crazy mad only twice—once when that Sloat come at me with wicked intent back on the *Dolphin,* and right now, when he glares into the green and defiant eyes of his eldest girl.

Sheehan, who has just realized he is holding his Captain's daughter by the throat, jerks his hand away as if he suddenly found he was holding a snake. Mairead falls to the deck, gasping for breath—that Sheehan does have hands like a vise.

"I'll not go back! I'll not marry that awful Loomis Malloy! If you send me back, I will run away again!" she cries, tears running down her face as she gets to her feet. Liam starts rolling up his sleeves. "I don't care!" she blubbers. "Beat me to death if you want, but I won't go back! I'll run away again and again!"

"You are going to get the thrashing of your life, you are..."

I go and put myself between Liam and Mairead, and I see Ian McConnaughey coming forward, too. *No, Ian, not now...*

"Please, Liam, do not beat her," I say, putting her behind me. "Let's go down in my cabin and talk this over." I feel Mairead's hands on my waist, keeping me between her and her completely maddened father.

"Who put you up to this? Was it a man? A member of my crew?" he shouts at her, ignoring me. "McBride! Get up here!"

Arthur McBride, who I've got to agree would be the one most likely to hatch such a prank, steps forward, a barely suppressed grin on his foolish face. "Sir?" he says, plainly getting in a good look at Mairead in her less than modest outfit.

"Did you have anything to do with this?" asks Liam through his bared and clenched teeth.

"Nay," says Arthur McBride, who *never*, it seems, knows when to keep his lip buttoned. "She's Ian's piece, anyway."

"Ian's *piece*, is she," growls Liam. "McConnaughey!" I hope Arthur realizes just how close he came to being thrown overboard and drowned. Probably the fool doesn't, 'cause he merely stands there grinning.

Ian presents himself, a bit shakily. He looks over at Mairead with big moonstruck calf eyes and she back at him in the same sort of way.

"Did you know of this?" again comes the question from Liam.

"No, but I wish I did," says Ian, who must be taking lessons in foolishness from his boon companion, Arthur McBride. "But, no, I did not know and would not have allowed her to do it if I did." Well, there's some sense being spoken here at last.

The lad crosses himself when he says this, whether as proof of the truth of what he's saying, or in anticipation of his coming death, I can't tell, but Liam sure ain't convinced. "You and your friends've been sniffin' around her like dogs in rut and don't think I don't know it, you miserable sneaking little cur!"

Ian's face goes white with anger. He's scared of Liam, true, but he's Irish, too, and he won't take that from anyone, and he spits out, "'Tis true I love Mairead with all my heart and soul, and I respect you as her father and as my Captain, but call me a dog again, man, and I will..."

"Take her down and put her in the leg irons. Clamp her to the bulkhead in the foulest part of the bilge. Do it NOW!" roars Liam.

I stay in front of Mairead. "She'll slip out of the leg iron, she will. It's too big for her ankle and too small for her neck, and we don't have a brig for a cell. Please, Liam, let her stay with me. For company, like. It gets a bit lonely for me sometimes when we're under way and I would welcome her company. We'll look for one more prize, then take her and everybody else back to Waterford for the winter. It'll be fine, you'll see. She'll get this seafarin' stuff out of her system and settle down—not with Loomis, maybe, but with some good man—you'll see...now calmness, Liam. Please, Father, do this."

I make hand signals behind Liam's back for Arthur and Ian to make themselves scarce. Arthur makes sure he gets in a last look at Mairead's rump in her trousers and then goes down the hatch. But Ian doesn't, he just stands there looking at Mairead.

"Please, Liam, down in my cabin, now. Please, Father, down in my cabin, now please, both of you!"

# Chapter 35

Peace has been restored twixt the warring Delaneys. Somewhat restored. Mairead is allowed to stay with me in my cabin, but on deck she is forbidden to go forward of the aftermast and all of the men, save Reilly, Liam, and Higgins, are not to go aft of that same mast, else they will face the wrath of Liam Delaney.

I fit her out with one of my skirts, as Liam will *not* allow her to be seen on deck in the trousers she wore when she snuck aboard in the middle of the night and dived down into the hatch, where she had stashed a bag I had seen her bringing aboard on that day, a bag I stupidly thought was laundry for Padraic. That bag had held food and a blanket and other things for her to get by on till she was ready to show herself. I found out later that she had gotten on board that night by tossing a can full of pebbles on the fo'c'sle, and when it rattled around up there, the man on watch went forward to investigate. While he was checking for the source of the noise, she scampered up the gangway and down the hatch to hide. I took down that watchman's name to make sure he would never again be on watch in a tight situation.

Liam fully intends to lock her up and throw away the key when he gets her home. For her part, Mairead remains stubborn and holds to her promise to run away again first chance she gets, but we'll see. I'll work on Liam a bit, maybe point up Ian McConnaughey's more admirable qualities.

Both Liam's plans for her and her own ideas as to her future depend, of course, on Moira not murdering her outright on our return. Funny thing to remember now, but on the morning we left Waterford, I was on the fantail and happened to look back at the dock we had just left. There stood a figure that I knew to be that of a woman, frantically waving a handkerchief over her head. I couldn't make out who it was but figured it was just some tearful sweetheart waving a last good-bye to her brave sailor boy, out to make his fortune. But it wasn't, I know now—it was Moira, trying desperately to signal that her daughter had fled the coop and was, without doubt, on board with us.

The weather turns warm as we make our way south, and Mairead and I loll about in the maintop and talk and sing and dance and play our whistles, and I'm really glad she came along, if only for this one trip. It ain't very military, the way we act, but what the hell, I am the owner of this bark, and with that comes some privileges.

The maintop is a small platform that goes all the way around the mainmast, the mast that Mairead is supposed to stay behind, about thirty feet up. I have her go up the ratlines and through the lubber's hole—no sense teaching her the real sailor way since it involves being upside down for a moment, and she being with a skirt on, it would present quite a show to any who might be looking on, and many are looking on, make no mistake about it.

At times, when we have been up in the top, I have seen her wave off to someone up forward and it is not too hard for me to figure out that Ian McConnaughey is up in the foretop waving back at her—out of Liam's sight, of course. Actually, she does just that, right now, smiling and dimpling up and dancing on her tiptoes. I forgive her, for I know that one does not hear a proclamation of love from a proud young man delivered in front of his friends and all, like Ian did on that day, without it having some effect on a young girl's heart.

"Jacky," she says, still looking off at the foretop, while I, like any cat or kitten, lie down below warmed by a patch of sun. "If *that* part of this maintop is in front of the mast, then would not Ian be allowed to stand right *there*?" She points at the decking in front of her.

"Maybe," I say, shading my eyes and turning my head to watch her, "by the very letter of the agreement, but I wouldn't push it if I were you. Let your father get used to things as they are. After all, it's only been three days since you were found out. If he catches you and Ian spooning up here, there'll be hell to pay, count on it."

She takes a deep breath and puffs out her chest, puts on a pout, and shakes her hair, all wavy and red so that it flows out and floats on the wind. *Poor Ian,* I think to myself, *you are one done-for lad.*

"...and besides," I say, a little stuffily, as owner of the *Emerald,* "Ian has work to do and playing 'Chase the Colleen Through the Rigging' ain't part of it."

After Higgins is done with dinner and fussing over us, we spend our evenings doing the same singing and talking and fiddle playing and such, but also I read to her and we work on her studies. I have assigned her some work—I cannot help myself—whenever I discover someone in need of schooling, out come the ABC's and let's get down to it. It seems I have a need to do this. It also seems that Mairead has had some schooling and can read enough to get along. I am impressed and I tell her so.

When I ask how she came by this learning, she being out on the farm and all, she says, "Well, they had what was called Hedge Schools and what they'd do is set up benches in a field next to high hedges so we could hide and classes would be held and we'd take what we could from the lessons and go back home and study and show the little ones. On slates, or roofin' tiles, like."

"But why ever did you have to hide?" I ask.

"Why, it's against British law to educate Irish kids, surely you know that?" she says, amazed at my stupidity.

"I cannot believe what you say," I say, firmly convinced that my country would not do such a horrid thing. "England would not do that." I had heard from Amy back in the States that it was forbidden to teach slave children to read, but *here?*

"Believe what you want to believe, Miss," she says, puffing up, "but I was the one there with me butt on the bench and Padraic was the one standing at the back peerin' over the top of the hedge, him both listenin' to the teacher and keepin' an eye peeled for the magistrates. The teacher was dressed as a hog butcher in case anyone should come upon us. Bloodstained apron and all. And him a university man, too. That was the way of it, Miss Faber."

I am astounded.

---

Later, when I am in my nightgown and Mairead is wearing an extra one of mine, we climb up on my bed, turn off the lamp, rutch around, and settle in.

After a while, she sniffs and says, "I ain't goin' back to that, I ain't."

"Even if it's with Ian?" I ask back quietly in the dark.

She doesn't answer for a long time. I can hear only her breathing. "On a farm? I don't know," she finally says.

I find her shoulder and pat it. "Don't worry. Just go to sleep. I'm working out a plan and maybe you can be a part of it. We'll see. Sleep now. I've got the Four-to-Eight watch, you know. They'll wake me by calling down through that tube there," I say, tapping the shiny brass tube that snakes down over me, "but you can sleep through it. So good night, now."

*I am working out a plan. I just need some more money before I can act on it.*

# Chapter 36

Liam stands with crossed arms on the fo'c'sle, just forward of the bowsprit, staring resolutely aft. He has a mighty scowl on his face 'cause he doesn't approve of this at all, but I had insisted and won out in the end.

The weather was warm and so was the water, and the netting under the bowsprit had been rigged and made secure. Some of the young ones had stripped down and gone into the netting to splash about in the water just as young men—and boys—always have done when on board ships with understanding captains. On the *Dolphin,* me and the other ship's boys—Davy, Tink, Willy, and...*him*—used to do it every chance we could. Course I could only do it till I started to change into a woman, and then I couldn't do it anymore 'cause I'd have been found out as a girl and put off the ship.

So, figuring I'd be damned if the boys were going to have all the fun—listening to Ian and Padraic and Arthur and some others whooping and hollering up there was too much for me—I got Liam to clear the fo'c'sle and stand guard when the boys were done so's Mairead and I could have a turn at it without having our modesty compromised, like. Fair's fair, after all.

"And tell 'em to stay out of the Head, too. We don't want to be lookin' up at any nasty hairy butts hanging overhead," I order, as we go past Liam, wrapped in our cloaks, under which we have on our drawers and light undershirts.

Liam grunts in answer and we go out on the bowsprit walkway. The net below is really there not for fun but to catch any unlucky sailor who might fall off while tending to the fore-and-aft sails that are attached there. But fun is certainly to be had on it, as Mairead soon finds out.

We doff our cloaks and I show her how to climb down into the netting. It's a scary thing the first time you do it, but she's a game one and soon she's next to me down below in the belly of the net. Then the *Emerald* comes on a mighty rolling wave, lifts her nose high in the air. "Hang on, Mairead!" I shriek, and then down she plunges, right into the heart of the wave and everything is cool and green and bright.

We come up wet and gasping and I point and shout, "Look there's one!" and she looks over and is astounded to see a large dolphin swimming right next to us, eyeing us merrily, it seems. Dolphins always have this smiley look on their faces and they seem to enjoy this sport as much as we do.

"And another over here!" exults Mairead, looking like a veritable Irish mermaid with her red hair plastered about her laughing face.

"Open your eyes when we go down again and you'll see more of them!" I say, and down we plunge again. Sure enough, there seems to be about a dozen of the creatures gamboling about down there in the misty green depths below us.

The sea provides us with a fine set of rolling swells, but then calms down a bit, as it always seems to do, and Mairead and I climb back up a little higher in the netting and turn over on our backs to catch our breath and await the next batch of good waves.

Looking up we are treated to the sight of the bottom of the latrine. If I had my way, each man aboard would use a chamber pot like we ladies do and dump it demurely over the side, but, no, that is not the way of men. And so we see right above us, as we lie laughing in the netting, the round holes of the Seats of Ease as they are called—the latrine holes that are set out from the side of the head of the ship and so are called the Head. Mercifully, the hull of my *Emerald* has been scrubbed clean by the waves that crash about Mairead and myself, tumbling us about in their grasp, or else we should be disgusted.

"Oh, my God!" cries Mairead suddenly, crossing her arms across her breast. She frees one finger and points... and there, not six feet away, is the grinning head of Arthur McBride, sticking upside down out of one of the Head holes. This apparition is soon joined by the face of Ian McConnaughey hanging in an adjacent hole.

"The cheek of the rascals!" I shout and cup a handful of water and throw it at Arthur's face. "Away with you now!"

The water hits his foolish face and he sputters and laughs, saying, "Do it again, Jacky, please, as water that comes from your own dear hands is like the very nectar to me face!" I stand up wobbly in the netting and put my finger in Arthur McBride's face.

"You get yourself and your face out of there, Arthur McBride! Ain't you got no sense of decency?"

"Oh, ho, I do, Jacky my love, and I do think you look right decent right now!"

I'm trying to keep a stern look on my face, but I ain't succeeding. The two idiots must be doing handstands on the benches up above and...

Suddenly Arthur McBride's face registers comical shock as he and his head are jerked upward. I suspect John Reilly or some other responsible member of my crew has discovered the prank and is taking care of it. I hear cries and sounds of struggle from above, but before Ian McConnaughey can be hauled back up to his own destruction, Mairead reaches up, grabs him by the ears, and plants a great, wet, salty kiss on his mouth. A moment later, he, too, disappears from sight, jerked up from above. Ah, but jerked up a much happier man than he was when first he stuck his head in that hole.

Mairead and I hug each other and howl with laughter. The *Emerald* dips down again, and again we are submerged in the green water. When we come back up, gasping, someone is yelling something at me.

"Sail, Jacky! A ship is coming through the Strait!"

I'm up on deck in an instant, my wet feet slapping on the deck as I run back to my cabin, with Mairead right behind me.

"Clear for action!" I call out just before I go through my door. "Higgins! Towels! Get my fighting rig!"

I rip my wet shirt off over my head and take the towel

and rub myself with it, then off with the drawers and dry my lower half, then on with the gear. Within three minutes Higgins is strapping on my sword belt. Stuffing my pistols in their holsters, I say, "Mairead, you stay down here!" and head back out on deck.

"Ooooohhh, just look at him, so plump and helpless," I marvel. "Is he asking to be taken by such as us?"

"He probably was in convoy with an escort," says Liam, "but I suspect the escort was called away to deal with Nelson's fleet and this one decided to chance it and keep going rather than duck into port."

"Bad luck for him, then." I put down my glass and shout, "Muster the Boarding Party port side! Sully, fire when you get close enough!" The ayes come back quick and sharp— this looks to be a nice prize, maybe our best one yet.

"He came out hugging the African shore, I suppose to stay as far away from the guns of Gibraltar as possible."

"Is he Spanish?"

"I think so, from the shape of him. He changed flags a little while ago—I think that's a Maltese one he's got up now—he did it when he saw by our change of course that we were interested in him, but that ain't gonna help him. We'll find out what he is when we board. If he's a friendly or a neutral, we'll let him go with our compliments, but I don't think so..."

There's a *crack!* and a puff of smoke, which blows back over us as Sully fires the bow gun. I've come to like the smell of gunpowder—it smells to me of money.

The ball falls short, but not by much. The prize turns to the right, and when we see that, Liam gives the order to the helm and sees to the new set of the sails while I holler out, "Boarding Party to the starboard side! Get ready, boys!"

The prize is trying to run, but he's just too slow, and *yes!* there's a golden crucifix on his mainmast! He *is* a Spaniard!

The crew of the prize is running about in total confusion—I don't think they even have a single gun mounted—what did I do to deserve such good fortune? A moment later the prize slacks its sails and heaves to under our lee and waits for us to board, which we waste no time doing. The hooks are thrown, the ships pulled together and I'm up on the rail and over, sword drawn and looking for the Captain.

There he is, looking grim over by his helm, as my lads swarm over his ship, taking possession. He takes one look at me and says *Dios!* I bow to him and manage to make him understand that he and his men will not be harmed, and then there's a flash of red hair at my side and it is not Padraic's. Mairead is standing there with the hilt of a cutlass held in both hands. She points the thing at the amazed Captain.

"Stand and Deliver!" she says, and then grins at me. "I always wanted to say that."

# Chapter 37

I rein in the horse and look out over the port of Harwich, where my beautiful *Emerald* lies at anchor a few hundred yards off the quay. I can never look upon her without my chest swelling with joy and pride. I know that pride is a sin, and Pride Goeth Before a Fall, but I can't help it.

The prize lies off to the left of us, in the hands of her new owners, who are fitting her out for the transatlantic trade, this time with guns. *Smart move,* I'm thinking.

The gelding, which whinnies and blows beneath me, is grateful for this short rest, as I have been riding him hard. I had Higgins rent him for me for a day's outing, with the regular saddle. Higgins protested most vigorously, but I prevailed—*I know how to ride sidesaddle, Higgins, I just don't like it. When we go off into Society, I promise I'll do it all the time—ride to the hounds in the silly female rig, even, but for now, please get a regular saddle. I'll wear my cloak over my uniform and trousers so there will be no scandal. Pleeeease, Higgins…*

I win again.

On the day we took that prize, it was not long before Mairead, stripped of her cutlass, was hauled squalling back aboard the *Emerald* over her father's shoulder and the Spaniards were in their lifeboat and heading for the coast of their native land and we were headed north with their former ship following behind us. The *Santo Domingo*, for that is what she turned out to be, was newly back from the Orient and was filled with spices, rare silver treasures, and fine silk. There will be presents for wives and sweethearts from this load, that's for sure. Maybe something for my cabin, too. *And* money for our pockets.

It's been a long time since I sat a horse and I felt the need to get out and away, alone. Mairead is not allowed off the ship, and besides, she is not a lover of horses. So *I found myself in bad company, even though I was alone* as the song goes. I have my pistols strapped to my chest, 'cause Higgins insisted, not totally trusting the ethics of the locals.

I mounted the horse in the stables down by the docks, burst out the doors, past the church, and pounded up here to the High Road, leaving a cloud of dust and not a few irate citizens behind me. Hey, I've been working hard and need a bit of fun, I figure. Besides, I've been bringing a lot of honest commerce to this town, so I'm owed.

*All right, horse, you've rested enough.* I pull his head up off the grass and around to the left and dig in my heels and we're off again. He is a good horse, with a sort of merry glint in his horsey eye, but I know he will never love me like my dear Gretchen loved me. Or even that Sheik of Araby. Or me him.

I ride up the road to the north and I bring Bucephalus, for that is his name, back up to a full gallop again. I've loosened the front of my cloak and it flies out behind me like a cape—like any highwayman come riding—and I'm whooping like a banshee when we come to a turn in the road. As we round it, I'm astounded to find myself in the midst of a gaggle of young girls, all dressed in white frocks and plainly out for a church outing of some sort. There're blankets laid out and there're baskets of food placed upon them.

I pull back on the reins to keep the horse from trampling them, and he rears back and screams in fright. The girls scatter like a flock of geese and I hear one of them cry, "It's her! She's the one!"

I leap off the back of the horse to pat his neck and calm him down so he won't hurt any of them, and it's then that I realize that my cloak is hanging down my back and there I am in my lieutenant's uniform and my white pants and black boots and, of course, my pistols sticking out of my harness all brazen.

The girls stare at me aghast. One of the braver ones trips up to me, backed up by several of her friends, who hide behind her skirts, and asks, "You are the one, aren't you? The one on the ship with the Irish boys?"

I nod in the way of a bow and say, "I suppose I am. But you needn't be afraid of me. I'm sorry I disturbed your picnic, I was only out for a ride. Please forgive me. I'll be gone now," and I go to remount.

"Wait," says the brave girl in the front. She is a neat and pretty thing, with light brown curls sticking out from under her bonnet. "The boy with the red hair..." Those behind her collapse in giggles.

*Ah.*

I smile and say, "That would be Padraic Delaney. He is a fine lad...and...he is not married."

There is a great shriek from the brave girl's friends.

"And if you would like to be introduced, Miss, come down to my ship and have a tour. Come, all of you. I can—"

Two older women burst into the clearing, take one look at me, and gather up their charges, covering their eyes as best they can, and hustle them away. The brave girl is the last to be hustled off, and she looks back at me with a kind of defiant longing.

The old woman in charge looks at me with undisguised loathing as I throw my leg over the horse. I give her a bit of a salute and turn to go on my way.

We trot up the road and soon woods close in on either side and the road tips upward and eventually we come out into an open place, where lush grasses grow between smooth flat rocks. There is a place to the left where the woods open up enough to see the harbor again and now my *Emerald* looks like a tiny toy boat down below. A perfect place for the picnic that Higgins has packed for me.

I hop down and tie the horse to a tree, but slack enough so that he can get at plenty of grass. I choose a nice rock, throw my cloak over it, and plop myself down upon it. I pull out my whistle, to have a few tunes to see how they float in the air hereabouts—it's my feeling that the tunes on the pennywhistle sound different in different places, whether in the foretop on a stormy day, in a cozy tavern, or here on a windswept heath. Having done my duty there, I open the basket that Higgins has packed for me. Dear Higgins, I have become quite spoiled, I know, as I pull out the chicken pieces, the potato pie, the hard-cooked eggs seasoned with the spices we took from the *Santo Domingo.* I think he is trying to fatten me up, for what I don't know, me living single and all. With that I look off to the south again. Then I shake my head—got to stop doing that.

Having eaten like a pig and drunk the little half bottle of claret that Higgins had packed, I stretch myself lazily in the weak but warm fall sun to think and plan and daydream. I am lulled by the drone of the bees buzzing about doing their last work of the year, and I doze in and out of sleep.

*And the warm sun on my face makes my dreaming mind think of the Caribbean and Kingston, and Jaimy and me rolling around with our arms and legs wrapped around each other in the foretop and, Oh, Jaimy! and in that way that dreams have, suddenly I was off and gone and dragged away and he was in a small room, a box, really, writing me letters, letters that he lifted up and held to the wind and the wind had borne them away like fluttering white doves…And then he puts down the pen and he's standing over me as I lie as if dead and he's crying… But Jaimy doesn't cry—not that easy, he doesn't, not over my poor dead bones anyway, and he sees me and says Nancy! Nancy! It's you! And I think, Wait a minute, Jaimy—my name ain't Nancy—why, you, I'll give you Nancy, I will, you false…*

My nose itches and maybe that's what wakes me up—or maybe it's that horsefly—I groan and stretch again and bat at the fly and crack open an eyelid. There, leaning over me, is an old man holding a walking stick and crying.… *Crying? Christ! It ain't a dream, it's a lunatic!*

I scramble to my feet and lunge for my horse, leaving the remnants of my lunch scattered on the heather, but still the old man comes after me.

"Nancy!" he cries. "Nancy! Don't you know me? Don't you..."

But that's as far as the crazy old coot gets, 'cause now I'm up on my mount and off. I leave him standing there in the dust and calling after me. *Damn! You take a little nap and you wake up with a crazy old man standing about you!* I'm getting back to my ship, I am.

I ride for a bit and then slow down, knowing that the old man couldn't possibly catch up with me. *Damn! I left my cloak back there!* Oh, well, I sure ain't going back for it now. *Stupid! To fall asleep all splayed out and unprotected like that! You deserve whatever happens to you, girl! Damn!*

That night, I stay in. The Port Watch invites me out to the taverns but I say, *Nay, I cannot,* for Mairead is not allowed off the ship, and in the spirit of true sisterhood, I must stay with her. And besides, later, when we are put up for the winter, there will be lots of time for the pubs and taverns. And besides, that Arthur McBride needs the damper on his ardor turned down, and besides...there are lots of besides.

After dinner, as a special treat before turning in, we take out this book I had bought back in Waterford. It is called *Laugh and Be Fat* and it is a bunch of stories and jokes and is just the most obscene, dirtiest thing I have ever read, and, as I tell Mairead, I *have* read the *Decameron* as well as *The Canterbury Tales,* mind you, and so, of course, we are soon snorting and burying our faces in our pillows, we're in highest gross hilarity and rolling around in the bed in pure hellish joy.

It is good that we have the laughter 'cause it eases me off to sleep—it keeps me from thinking about that crazy old man on the road today. Something about that nags at me, I don't know why. Probably 'cause I was so stupid as to let myself be surprised like that—helpless and all. That's gotta be it, and I won't let it happen again.

We snuff the lamp and stifle giggles and poke about and *Get your cold feet offa me! Cold feet? I'll show you cold feet! Yow! It comes from eatin' cold potatoes all yer life and you got it coming, Brit! Take that!* and we settle in for the night.

# Chapter 38

Noon of the following day finds us in the Golden Rudder tavern—Liam, Mairead, Padraic, and me. Higgins had been dispatched to the bank in Colchester and would be back shortly, but since he was not there to make my lunch, I invited the Clan Delaney out to lunch at this local pub. No singing or dancing at this time of day, just eating and knocking back a few pints. A fragile peace exists between Liam and his daughter—and between Padraic and his sister. Padraic was none too pleased, either, when Mairead was found aboard—but now he knows we're sailing back to Waterford tomorrow and he can stick her back in Moira's care. During this meal, at least, Mairead keeps her mouth shut about running away again and that's good, for even though I know she intends on gaining her freedom, it's best that things lie calm for a while.

The food was good, but now it's done and time to be gone, so we get up, pay both money and compliments to the landlord, and go back out into the bright light of day. Just as we are heading down the road and back to the ship, the midday coach from Colchester pulls up and Higgins gets out.

"Ahoy, Higgins!" I say. "That was quick. We hardly had time to miss you."

"Yes, Miss," he says, as he joins our little group. "I had good luck in..."

"Nancy!"

I whip my head around and there he is again, the dusty little old man who stood over me yesterday as I lay asleep on the hillside. Again, he comes at me with his hand outstretched, tears running down his face. "Nancy," he wails again, "oh, don't you know me, Nancy?"

"Crazy old beggar," says Liam, fishing a coin out of his pocket and holding it out to the man. "Here's a penny, old man. Now off with you."

The old man, who I now notice is wearing a churchman's collar and an old-fashioned frock coat, once fine but now threadbare, ignores Liam and his coin.

"No, no," he says, never taking his eyes off me, "I don't mean Nancy, I know you can't be her, because she's...she's dead, my child is dead. I'm sorry, I'm sorry...I got confused because you look so much like she looked is why I got confused...I'm sorry..."

Liam makes a move to hustle him off. A chill runs up my spine and I put my hand on Liam's arm to hold him back.

"Wait. Wait, let's hear him out," I say, feeling myself start to tremble. From out of the half-forgotten past it comes to me now and I know why I was so uneasy yesterday when first I saw this old man—*My mother's name was Nancy.*

"You are not Nancy," the old man says, nodding as if getting his mind in order. "You are her daughter Mary...Mary Faber...and, as such, you are my granddaughter."

———

We have taken him back to the ship and sat him at my table. Liam, Higgins, and I stand frowning down on him like agents of the Spanish Inquisition looking down on a hapless heretic. He looks around in wonder at the richness of my cabin and then he begins.

"My name is George Henry Alsop. I am, or I was, the Vicar of Saint Edmund-Standing-in-the-Moor, up in North Allerton, just north of Leeds..."

I look at Higgins and he says, "A considerable distance—over two hundred miles."

"With my dear wife, Rosemary, now sadly departed and much missed, I had but one child, a daughter, Nancy. When Nancy grew up, beautiful and wild, she married one Jack Faber, a poet, scholar, and a bit of a rascal. They were well matched, for Nancy, always a cheerful child, had grown into a young woman of independent mind and adventurous spirit."

Here Liam and Higgins turn to look at me.

"At any rate, they had a child, Mary, and then later another, Penelope, and after that they decided to decamp for London, for there was certainly nothing in St. Edmunds for a penniless scholar like Jack Faber, and nothing to contain the spirit of Nancy. Jack believed himself in possession of a teaching post in London and so they all set out. Jack, Nancy, Penny, and Mary. I never saw any of them again, till now, with you."

"I know all that," I snap, without much warmth. "How came you to hear of me, here in this place?"

"I was teaching Sunday School one day and found that two boys, two very naughty boys, were giggling over an assignment, one of the book of Job, which I never found

particularly funny, and upon peering at their book from behind them, I found something quite different therein…"

*I know what's comin' here…just like Ned and Tom and*
*their navigation book…*

"What they had was a copy of a penny-dreadful book
called *Bloody Jack: Being an Account of the Curious Adven-*
*tures of Mary 'Jacky' Faber, Ship's Boy.* I would have immediately thrown the thing away and given the boys a swift
smack for their inattention to their lessons, but the 'Mary
Faber' caught my eye. I wandered off and read the first page
and it was like the very heavens opening up. What was described there was nothing less than a description of the end
of my own dear family, the thing most precious to me in
the world. But through the misery of reading of my own
lovely daughter's lifeless body being dumped in a cart, I
saw that glimmer of hope—the hope that one of you had
survived."

He sniffs and looks down at his hands, which are worry-
ing each other on the tabletop, and he continues. "It became
an obsession with me—it was all I could think of—could
the child in that book be my own daughter's daughter?
When I heard from a traveling tinker that the girl who was
the heroine of that book was known to make port in Harwich, well, I had to know, and so I packed up what little I
had—and it was not much, even my books belonged to the
vicarage—handed over my post to young Reverend Stewart,
who always wanted it so much anyway, and I put my foot on
the road and came here."

"You walked the whole way?" I ask.

"Aye. Shank's mare, mostly, but sometimes a kindly
farmer would give me a lift on his hay wagon. And once I

rode for ten full miles on the back of a plow horse next to a cheerful plowboy riding the other member of the team." He pauses to collect his thoughts and smiles a small smile and then goes on. "You know, I've never felt better—since that time... when all that I held dear was lost—I had in my mind a mission, which was to find out what happened to the one member of my family I could not absolutely account for—you."

"Why didn't you come looking for me back then? Why didn't you try to find me back then... back then, when I needed you?" I bite off the words and I've got my haughty Look on my face—I don't know why, but I do.

"I did. As soon as the letters from Jack and Nancy stopped, I went to London. I feared the worst—and the worst is what I found. I learned that they had died and had been buried in a common grave and that about you and your sister there was not a word. And that..."

"They were not buried in a common grave... that's too nice a word for it. They were stripped and thrown into a lime pit at the edge of town. I saw that pit once when the gang and I were out that way. Arms and legs stickin' up through dirty white powder, that's your common grave. And as for Penny, she was sold to the anatomists to be cut up and put in jars."

*Why am I being so cruel? I don't know...*

He nods his head and looks down at the floor. "I know. I know. I read all of the book. Penelope... Little Penny... was only one year old when they... you... left for London. I can still see you sitting up on the wagon, all gay in your new bonnet, all sparkling with excitement over the coming journey, all..."

"Did you come to Cheapside when you made your inquiries?"

"Oh yes," he replies to me. "I had the address of their flat from their letters. I went to the flat, but..."

"You probably went right by me, then. I was the one in the dirty shift and snotty nose with my grubby hand held out to you."

He nods again and says, "I know. I know."

I think for a minute and say, "So what do you want from me now?"

He seems startled. "Oh, nothing. Just the joy of knowing that you are alive and..."

"Good. You have your joy, then. Higgins, if you would be so good as to take this gentleman out and buy him a new set of clothes and then give him a bit of money and send him on his way back to Saint Edmund-Standing-in-the-Bloody-Mucky-Moor. I bid you good day, Sir. I found our talk most interesting."

With that, I end this reunion by turning and leaving the cabin. I'm up in the maintop in a mighty sulk before they can even leave the cabin.

*What the Hell do I need with a grandfather, now? Ain't I got enough men about me tellin' me to be good without a bleedin' gramps doin' it, too? And him a goddamn preacher to boot! Nay, go back to Saint-Who-Cares-What's-Squattin'-in-Some-Bloody-Cesspool or wherever the hell you come from! Jacky Faber is a wild and free rover who takes none of this... oh, the Hell with it!*

I put on my maroon riding habit, and, with bonnet on my head, I leave the ship and go out into the town. It is not long before I see Higgins and Reverend Alsop emerging from a tailor's shop.

I take the edges of my skirt and give a deep curtsy and say, "I am sorry...Grandfather...it was just so sudden for me. Pray, please return with me to the ship and we shall have dinner and talk."

A spark of joy lights the old man's eyes. He nods and says, "Thank you, dear. Thank you. I—I know it was sudden for you, but can you imagine what it was like for me—to have lost a child and then to see her again walking toward me? I..."

I go to him and open my arms and fold them around him. By holding his form, I find him to be a trim and upright little man. I also know he is trying hard to keep from weeping.

I see Higgins beaming at me with that look that says, *I knew you would do the right thing, Miss.* Well, I don't always do the right thing. In fact, I almost *never* do the right thing, and I wish people wouldn't expect that from me.

"*Ahem.*"

I turn from my grandfather's embrace to see that a group of women has come up to us. I give them a glance and figure them for churchwomen looking for a donation for some worthy cause—a new bell for the belfry or something like that. Well, they know I got money, so who can blame them for asking?

"Yes?" I ask, all stupid and innocent.

A thin woman with a disagreeable look on her face marches forward. It is plain she is the leader and it is plain, too, that a donation ain't what they got in mind. "We wish you to leave this town immediately and never return," snaps this biddy. "Find some other port in which to do your dirty business. We know you to be a bad influence on the good girls of this place with your whorish ways, and we will not have it!" Her mouth snaps shut. I recognize her as the woman at the picnic who shooed the girls away from me.

I feel Higgins stiffen beside me, but I put out my arm to hold him back. I don't need no help in fighting this fight. I lower my eyelids to half-mast and wipe the pleasant look off of my face.

"Do you know that I had thought that you were going to ask me for a donation to some worthy cause, or to invite me to one of your services, or to welcome me into your Christian fellowship? But, no, that was not your intention at all. Instead, you come up unbidden to me and call me a whore in front of my own grandfather."

Her mean little eyes dart over to my now well-dressed grandfather with his unmistakable vicar's collar.

"The way you dress, the way you carry on..." She is not to be stopped. Neither am I.

"I, Madam, am an agent of King George the Third, by the Grace of God, *King* of England, Scotland, Wales! I hold a personal commission from His Majesty to harry the trade of the enemy, an enemy, I might add, who could very likely land right there on that very beach and sweep over your land and all that you hold dear. What would your good girls do then, as they were thrown over the shoulders of Napoléon's soldiers? How will your teaching help them when their skirts are lifted and their drawers hauled down?"

I think she's going to faint away. Good for her, stupid old biddy. What does she know of bad influences?

"If anyone here is a bad influence on the minds of young

girls, it is you, with your failure to welcome a stranger in your land."

She recovers and throws back her head and spits, "For all your fine words, you are naught but a common thief!"

"For all your fine airs, you are naught but a common scold! I bid you good day, Madam!"

Later at dinner I think about things and say to my grandfather, "You know...what that woman called me? I hope you know that I am not one...a bad girl, I mean. I am free and easy in my ways, but..."

He reaches out and pats my hand and looks at me with a serene expression. "I hope you are a good girl, Mary, and I think you are one. But it is not for me to judge you. I care only that you are alive and in the world."

*Well, good,* I'm thinking. "Now tell me about my mother when she was little, and how she grew up and all."

"I will," he says. "And gladly, but first..." He puts his hand into his waistcoat and pulls out something carefully wrapped in velvet cloth. He hands it to me.

I unwrap it and find that it's a miniature portrait. It's of a young girl wearing a blue collar trimmed in lace. Her sandy hair is tied back with matching blue ribbon, and from the look on her merry face, it looks like she's been up to some mischief.

"It's her," says my grandfather. "That's my Nancy."

*It is like looking into a mirror...*

And then he starts to tell me about her.

# Chapter 39

The bell of St. Nicholas peals off its seven notes at seven o'clock like always. It's getting to be the time of the year when that's around dawn. We're up and having breakfast for there's lots to do on this, our last day in port.

Mairead is looking a bit grumpy, I guess from knowing she's going back to face the wrath of Moira. Grandfather, however, is quite cheerful and in high spirits. Our talk last evening went far into the night, so far, in fact, that we went out on the deck so Mairead could turn in.

One thing I found reassuring was that, even though my mother looked exactly like me, she managed to have two children without dying. I always imagined that I would probably die in childbirth, because of my narrow hips and all, and it was a bit of a relief to find out that I might not. Not that it matters, for I intend to live single all of my life, but still...

"So what will you do now, Grandfather?" I ask. "Will you go back to your parish?" Higgins refills our cups, and I nod my thanks.

He thinks for a moment before answering. "No, I have been on the road and have had a taste of adventure and now

I have no desire to go back. I'll leave the vicarage to Reverend Stewart. I don't suppose you'll let me join your crew?" he says, smiling, already knowing the answer. "No, I thought not. Well then, I think I will go to London and set up as a letter writer as Nancy's Jack did before me. Maybe I'll get some tutoring jobs. I am not so old that there is not another adventure in me. I believe I will set up near to where my child died so that I might feel a bit closer to her."

I put my hand on his arm and am unable to speak for a moment. Then I do.

"Grandfather. I have a much better idea."

But I do not get to tell him of my Grand Plan, not yet anyway, as there comes a pounding on the door and John Reilly's voice calling out, "Miss! Come quickly! There's trouble!"

I fly out the door, followed closely by Mairead. The look on Reilly's never-cheerful face does not bode well.

"What happened?"

"The young men of the Starboard Watch. They were taken by the police late last night. There was a fight."

"Who?"

"Delaney, McBride, McConnaughey, Duggan, Lynch, Hogan, and O'Hara."

"Where's Liam?" I demand, fuming. *The idiots!*

"He's below, loading his pistols," says Reilly, darkly. "He says he won't let his son rot in no English jail."

*Damn!*

Just then Liam comes out of the hatchway, armed to the teeth and a look of grim determination on his face.

"Liam! Stop! We've got to talk!" I say, stepping in front of him.

"Get out of my way, girl," he says through clenched teeth. He pushes me aside and heads for the gangway.

I leap up and get my arms around his neck and hiss in his ear, "Liam! You've got to calm down! We've got to plan! Get in my cabin, now!" But he keeps on going. "Liam! Hear me out! Then if you still want to go commit suicide, then do it, with my blessing, but hear me out first!"

Liam stops and he lets his shoulders sag.

"I was happy," he says in a low voice. "I was back at sea and making money. I was able to put food on the table for my wife and family. Now my own two oldest children are conspiring to drive me stark-raving mad."

"Ah, Liam, and just how happy and content did you make your own parents, going off and being a bold rebel and all? Now into my cabin. All is not yet lost."

We get him down into the cabin.

"All right. How did it happen?" I ask when all are gathered about my table.

"Apparently Padraic was seen talking to a local girl in the afternoon—out on the quay—they went walking for a bit...," begins Reilly.

*Great, just great, Jacky, you idiot: "Oh, do come down to my ship for a tour, girls, it will be ever so much fun." It was the brave girl from the picnic, I just know it—I guess she decided to come for her tour. Damn!*

"...and they were seen by some local boys. Last night at the Bull and Rooster some of the local toughs told our young hotheads to leave their girls alone. McBride then got up on his hind legs and told them that he and his mates would kiss what girls they wanted to and if the local boys had nothing to kiss, well then they could kiss his fine Irish ass, and the fight was on. Not just with fists, either—swords were drawn and used. None of our boys were hurt, but some of the locals were cut. Nobody's died yet."

*Uh-oh...* more serious than I thought. Not just a simple bar fight. If someone dies...I think of that gallows tree...and a judgment of five hundred lashes, where a man is turned into a bloody side of beef—that can be a death sentence, too.

I shake those thoughts from my head. Action now, not worry.

"Higgins. Take money—lots of it. Go up there and see what can be done to buy them out. It's Saturday, so they can't be brought up before a judge till Monday."

Higgins nods and goes over, pulls out the money drawer, and unlocks the strongbox. He loads up his pockets and prepares to leave.

"Use all your charm and cunning, Higgins," I say.

"I will try, Miss," he says, and he leaves on his mission.

I flop into my chair. "If he is successful, each of those stupid...*boys*...shall work a year for nothing!"

But he is not successful.

"I am sorry, Miss, but it can't be done. I did use a few shillings to pry a little information out of the jailer, though," says Higgins. He puts back the money and stands up. "They will be arraigned on Monday, and charged with aggravated assault, if not murder. A primary reason that money won't work its usual magic is that a Mrs. Constance Grindle, wife of Reverend Grindle, has insisted that the letter of the law be met."

*Hmmm...I know that one, too. She's the old biddy who called me a whore.*

"There is also a bog-draining project on the outskirts of the town that they are having trouble finding laborers for. Apparently it is nasty work, and it is for that place the boys are headed, if not for…" He lets that go in deference to Liam.

Liam starts to get up, but I put my hand on his shoulder and push him back down.

"What is the lay of the land in there?" I ask.

Higgins considers, then speaks. "There is an outer chamber, where the jailer sits. Behind him is a locked cage. Behind that is another locked cage and that is where the lads are. Such is the power of this Mrs. Grindle, that the jailer has only the key to the outer cage, and not the inner, so as to keep him from temptations such as ours. It is a pity, for he seemed perfectly willing to yield to that temptation, and was, in fact, somewhat miffed at being denied his lawful graft that goes with the territory."

"How far is the outer door to the inner?"

"About eight feet."

"Describe the main cell itself." I get up and go over to one of my cabin windows and look out. I can see the jail up there on the hill where our lads are held. Mairead joins me and I give her hand a squeeze. *Steady down, girl. I know that he's in there.*

"It is about twenty feet square. Only the front of it is iron bars. The rest is the stone masonry of the building itself. No windows."

"Are there beds? Benches? Mattresses?"

"Benches around the perimeter of the room, and what appear to be rough straw mattress pads."

"Were you allowed to talk to them?"

"No, Miss. But they did see me there, and I gave them the thumbs-up sign to show them we were doing what we could. Ian McConnaughey stood and gave a thumbs-up back to show they were in good spirits." Mairead lets out a whimper on this.

"Hmmm…" I think for a bit and then say, "Well, we've got to get them out, and to do that we've got to get a message to them. I think that naught but a priest could get close to them now, so a priest we shall have."

I go briskly around the table and start counting off on my fingers. "First, we need a Roman collar. Higgins, if you could find one or make one up?" Higgins nods and says consider it done.

"Then we'll need a Bible. Try to get an old one, one that looks like it's been used, and you're not liable to find *that* on the *Emerald*."

"I have a Bible, Nan—Mary. I am surprised that you do not," says my grandfather.

*You would be surprised over a lot of things about me, Grandfather. One of which is that I seek the face of God in the sky and in the waves of the ocean, not in some book or on my knees in some dusty church.*

"I know, Grandfather, but I don't want you to lose your Bible in this endeavor. And, Grandfather, it might just be easier if you call me Jacky like everyone else."

"Well, all right…Jacky," says he, "but it's a shame you didn't keep your given name, it is such a beautiful one."

"Well, I had my reasons. Now, listen up, Grandfather, and everybody else, too. Here's what you're going to do…"

———

Higgins has jury-rigged a collar such that a Roman Catholic priest might wear—it's close enough for all these Anglicans know—and he has fitted my grandfather out in it.

"Liam, show him how to do the sign of the cross."

My grandfather turns white—that he should be doing this, he of all people, a vicar of the Anglican Church. I see that he might faint straight away.

"Grandfather, you must think of this as an adventure," I say, my hands on his shoulders. "You will be playacting. It will not be real."

"You know, my Nancy was a headstrong girl—that's why she and Jack went off to London, to seek something different than same-old Saint Edmunds," he says, straightening his back. "I'd like to think she got that independence of spirit from me. What do you want me to do, dear?"

"Well, first I want you to give me an apt quotation from the Bible, concerning prison…"

"Hmmm. How about Isaiah forty-two seven…*I have given a light to the nations…to bring out the prisoners from the dungeon, from the prison those who sit in darkness.*"

"Good enough," I say, and I turn to that passage in the Bible and I begin to write, very lightly, in the margin with my pencil…*Tomorrow, at dawn, on the first stroke of the Saint Nicholas bell, you will make yourselves ready. On the second stroke, you shall casually pick up your mattresses, and on the third stroke, you shall place your miserable carcasses up against the wall farthest from the harbor, and on the fourth and fifth, you shall cover up your worthless selves with those mattresses as best you can, and on the sixth, you shall wait for our signal.*

"Now," I say to Mairead, who is still standing by, both Liam and John Reilly having gone off to make the new chocks that we will need, "teach my grandfather how to say, 'Page seven hundred and fifty-three, you ignorant Irish clods' in Gaelic."

She sits down and does so, very patiently, repeating the phrase over and over till he gets it down perfectly.

Higgins now throws a sheet around my poor granddad, fastens it at his neck, and picks up the scissors from the barber's kit laid out on the table. In a few minutes my grandfather, who only this morning had long flowing locks, is now closely shorn.

"Sorry, Granddad," I say, "but you've got to *look* like a priest."

"It is my joy to be doing my part, dear," says my gallant grandfather. He does have a fine profile, I'll give him that.

We give him his instructions and when all is done, we put the newly minted and ordained Father Francis X. McSweeney into our liberty boat and he is rowed ashore to do his duty.

It is two hours later and we see the boat returning with him. He is not halfway up the ladder when we are on him with our questions.

"Don't worry, dears," he says, waving his hand in a Shake-spearean actor sort of way. "The job is done, and, I hope, done well."

Down in my cabin, he regales us with what went on in the jail.

"Well, when I first went in, I was greeted with the utmost suspicion by the jailer, who called me a damned Papist, but, clasping the faithful Bible to my breast, I began blessing everything in sight, the jailer, the desk, the spittoon, and praying out loud in Church Latin, and I think I was able to wear the superstitious man down." Here he pantomimes making the sign of the cross in the air and saying some things that I know to be Latin but that I don't understand.

"Then, I requested that I be allowed to see the boys. That request he denied. But I pleaded, 'Some of these lads might be going to meet their maker soon and shouldn't they be havin' the solace of the Bible, now?'"

John Reilly casts his eyes heavenward at the crudeness of the Irish accent, but Grandfather goes on.

"'All I want to do is give them the Bible, sir,' I say, and I hand the Bible to the man. 'See, there is nothing in it but the Word of God. Surely you don't want that on your soul, that you denied the Gospel to men who might be condemned?'

"The man looked confused, but he took the Bible and riffled the pages and saw that there was no gun contained therein, and I said, 'You shall see Saint Peter at the Pearly Gates someday and what will he say to you then?' and he said, 'All right, all right,' and he opened the outer cage and walked in and put the Bible in the outstretched hand of the red-headed boy...your son, I believe?" says the mock Father McSweeney.

Liam nods.

"A fine boy, I'm sure," says Grandfather. Liam glowers and reserves judgment on the fineness of one Padraic Delaney until he can once again get his hands around that fine neck.

"Anyway, once the Good Book was in the lad's hand, I lifted my hand and pronounced in Gaelic just as Mairead had taught me, 'Page seven hundred and fifty-three, you ignorant Irish clods.' The boys looked up, Padraic thumbed through to the proper page and gave me the thumbs-up sign behind the jailer's back."

My grandfather settles himself in his chair. "All is in

train, I believe, and now I'll have a spot of sherry. A 'bit of the creature,' as you Irish will have it."

He's my granddad, all right. Make no mistake about it.

Out on deck in the afternoon, we make our preparations. Muskets are cleaned and reloaded. The sails are hung and held with slipknots for instant loosing. And the smoke canisters are put on deck alongside the forward and after guns.

Liam looks down at the canisters and says to John Reilly, "Smoke, hey, Reilly? Shall we make some Holy Smoke, then, for these Brits?"

"Aye, Liam, we shall," says the dour Reilly. "We'll make some Holy Smoke for Father Murphy, that we shall."

Liam turns and leaves the deck to tend to the business at hand.

"What's that all about?" I ask Reilly, but he shakes his head and goes about his business.

"It's about the Father Murphy thing," says Mairead, close at my left hand. "You don't know about it?"

"Nay," I say, "tell me."

She collects her thoughts, looking up at the prison where both her brother and her young man lay, then she says, "It was back during the Uprising. One of the leaders of the resistance, Father John Murphy, the Hero of Oulart and Enniscorthy, was captured in a town called Tullow, in County Carlow. My dad, who with John Reilly, was hiding out in an attic in that very town, knew Father Murphy and had great respect for him as a leader."

More pauses, then, "The Brits hauled Father Murphy out to the center of the town, stripped him, flogged him, hanged him till he was almost but not quite dead, and then forced him to his knees and cut off his head with a dull ax. They stuck his head on a pike to stand by the entrance to the town."

I am struck dumb.

She continues, quite calmly. "Then they put the rest of his body in a barrel and filled it with oil and set it afire, and when it was burning, they forced every Irish family in the town to open their windows to let in the 'Holy Smoke' from his pyre, and to *smell* it."

Once again, I think to myself, *Why do people and the governments who govern people constantly do to each other that very thing which can never be forgiven nor forgotten? It is one thing to stand a man up and kill him, it is quite another to demand the Executioner's Tax from the man's family—to demand from them the cost of the bullet used to kill him before they can claim his body. Why do they do that when they know that the deed will never be forgotten, not this generation, nor the next, and down through the centuries? I don't know. I know nothing about this world.*

I get a nudge from Mairead, who, I suspect, has been looking at my burning eyes. "Hey, I've been hearin' that story all my life. Come on, get over it."

All the preparations are made. We gather on the quarter-deck. "There is nothing left to do," I say to my assembled shipmates. "Everyone will have an early dinner and get some rest, it being daylight or not, for we shall get no rest later this night. We must be fresh if we are to have success in this venture. I bid you good evening."

Mairead and I go to bed. Higgins has instructions to wake us at midnight.

We believe that we will not sleep, but we do.

# Chapter 40

"Now two of my children are at risk," says Liam in the gloom of the night, "instead of just the one. Three, counting you." He looks at me, readying myself on my quarterdeck. It is a little after midnight. The town of Harwich lies dark and quiet over there and here on the ship only the creaking of the rigging can be heard. I shiver a bit against the chill, then make myself stop.

"Dad, this is something that has to be done and can only be done by me and Jacky," says Mairead, laying her hand on her father's sleeve. "You know that, don't you?"

Liam, looking grim, nods and says, "But if you're not back in two hours, we're coming after you. Count on it."

I'm dressed in my serving girl outfit from back at the Lawson Peabody School for Young Girls. I've got my shiv stuck in my vest in case things get dicey, and Mairead has been fitted out with one, too. She's got on one of my skirts and that sort of brocaded peasant top she had on the day she was discovered as a stowaway. A couple of mobcaps on our heads and we're just a couple of simple country girls.

We go over the side and get into the skiff. Jack Sheehan is the coxswain and he hands us down. We settle in and Sheehan dips his muffled oars in the water and we creep silently for the shore in the deep dark of the night.

"Over at the far end of that wharf there, Jack," I whisper. "Right at the foot of that street...right there. Good." We bump up against the wharf and Mairead scrambles out, followed quickly by me. "Hand me up the bottle. Thanks, Jack. You'd better lie off a bit in case someone happens by. We'll give a couple of owl hoots as a signal to come pick us up when we get back."

Sheehan bids us good luck and warns us to be careful as he slips back off into the darkness. Mairead and I put our feet on the road and begin the walk up the hill toward the guns of Shotley Gate.

The darkened houses thin out quickly as we get farther and farther out on the Point—no one wants to build a home way out here where the full fury of winter storms would pound without mercy. There is only the looming bulk of the battery up ahead now.

"Here we are, girl," I whisper when we get up to the back of the building where there is a closed door and an open window. "And here we go."

We throw our arms around each other's shoulder and start laughing and giggling. "Lesh do 'Roll Me Over,' Sister!" I say.

"Lesh do it," slurs Mairead, all mush-mouthed. We sing.

> "Roll me over, in the clover,
> Lift me up, roll me over,
> And do it again, again, again,
> Lift me up, roll me over,
> And do it again!"

"*SSSShhhhhh!*" I stage-whisper, putting my finger over my lips. "We'll wake up the whole…*hic!*…town."

"Oh, shush your own self and gi' me another drink!" orders Mairead, grandly.

A light appears in the window. Someone has lit a lamp. I think I see a face peer out, and then the front door opens and a man looks out at us.

"Now you've gone and done it, you've woken up the good people of this 'ere 'ouse!" I say, and lift the bottle to my lips.

"Bob, come look at this," says the man at the door, who appears to be clad only in a pair of long underwear and a nightcap. Another man, pulling up his suspenders, appears in the light of the doorway. Like his friend, he appears to have been asleep, but he ain't asleep now, that's for certain.

I weave and peer at him as if I'm trying to focus my eyes.

"G'evening, gennulmen, we hopes we ain't disturbed yer rest, we hopes, we do," I say.

"Ain'tcha a little out of your way, girls?" says the first man. "You ain't from around here."

"Me and 'er is from Harkstead, out in the country, like… Our mum…*buuuurp*…sent us down to town to sell Bessie our milk cow and sold 'er we did," I say firmly. "Yessir, we sold 'er and got money for 'er and we spent it, sir, yesh we did. Didn't we, Sister?"

Mairead collapses to the ground, laughing and crowing out, "Won't our mother be shurprised? *Haaaaaaaaaa…*" Mairead rolls over and gives them a fine view of her white underdrawers.

The men look at each other. They have just died and gone to Heaven it seems—kind Providence has just delivered two young dames to their very doorstep, two young dames who have plainly lost their way and who are, without doubt, very drunk. Unbelievably good luck.

Mairead, still guffawing over what our mum's gonna say, gets unsteadily back to her feet and clings to me.

"Wanna hear a joke?" I slur. "A really *dirty* joke? Shuuuure you do...," and I proceed to tell them one of the awfullest jokes from *Laugh and Be Fat*, punctuated by assorted burps and hiccups. Great lusty laughter all around when I am done. I catch the two men looking at each other again, and this time winking.

"Come in, ladies. You'll catch your death out there. My name's Bill and this 'ere is Bob," says the one named Bill, gesturing us in. Mairead and I look at each other, put *why-not?* looks on our faces, and stumble through the door. We are inside. Across the large room squat the butt ends of the two big guns.

"I can tell by the light in yer eyesh that you have great— *hic*—affec-shun for little...*burp*...me," I say to Bill, the man who has plainly picked me to be his darling this evening. What I can really tell from the light in his eyes is that he cannot believe his good luck.

"Indeed I do, girlie. Let's have a kiss, then." He pulls me to him and is about to plant a great slobbering bristle-chin kiss on my mouth, but I draw back.

"Before I would kiss such a...*hic*...handsome man, I believe I'll take a drink," I say. "To shweeten my breath, like, for thy shweet kiss." And I pull out my bottle and put it to my lips and pretend to drink. He is *not* a handsome man. He don't smell very good, neither.

"Here!" says Mairead, reaching out her arm for the

bottle. She is in the clutches of the other bloke, who is angling her toward his cot. "Don't drink it all, you greedy pig! You always get everything! It's not fair! Hand it over here! It's mine, too!"

But she doesn't get the bottle, the man holding me takes it from my hand and says, "All for you girls and nothing for me and poor Bob? For shame!"

"Hey, that's ours!" protests Mairead.

"Let's all have a drink then!" Bill shouts as he lifts it up and takes a long, long pull at the bottle. "Man!" he says, when he brings it down, "that's damned good!" He takes another huge swallow. "Whoo! It tastes just like candy, it does! Here, Bob, have a haul at it."

Bob grabs the bottle and upends it. "Lor'! That's good!" he agrees, after he's drained the rest of the bottle. "What *is* this stuff?"

"The stuff dreams are made of, gunner," says I, straightening up as Bill's hands fall from my shoulders and he slips down to the floor. Bob looks at his mate lying there with a certain bleary amusement and then his eyes roll back in his head and he, too, hits the deck. Each of them had drunk enough of the Tincture of Opium to bring a very large racehorse to its knees.

"Quick! Turn the lamp down low!" I say, and Mairead does it.

"Are they dead?" she asks, looking down at the two men sprawled on the floor.

"Nay, Sister, I assure you they are not dead, but they are having the most wonderful dreams of heaven itself. Can you imagine the good time they are having with us right now?"

"Disgusting," says Mairead, imagining.

I look up and see the dangling rope that goes up through the roof to the big alarm bell that hangs above. I pull over a chair and climb up on it and pull out my shiv and cut off the rope as high up as I can. Somebody'd have to really work to ring that bell now.

The bell was the big reason that Mairead and I had to do this job alone. Liam had wanted to send up a bunch of armed men, but our newly found beaus Bill and Bob would have just sounded the alarm and that would have been it. Liam was forced to see the wisdom of my plan, for, even though he hated the thought of his daughter and me doing this, he knew it was absolutely necessary.

I hop back down. Mairead is tying the hands and feet of my Bill and her Bob, using the lengths of light line she had tied around her waist under her skirt for just that purpose. We can't have them waking up too soon and spreading the alarm.

Now, for the guns.

I have a variety of metal spikes with me, fashioned by our shipfitter O'Donnell, tucked into my vest and I go up to the mighty guns lying there all sinister and black in the night. By putting my finger on the guns' powder holes, I am able to choose the right size spikes for the job. I take the hammer I have tied about my waist and, as quietly as I can, I pound the proper nails down into the powder holes till they are flush and cannot be pried back out.

The Guns of Shotley Gate are spiked.


Before we left the bunker, Mairead insisted on arranging Bill and Bob side by side, face-to-face on the floor. She placed the now empty bottle of opium and alcohol between them and, from outside the doorway, she found a sprig of clover to put in the bottle's neck. It ain't a shamrock, but it's close. Then we headed back down the hill to Sheehan waiting below. A couple of low hoots and we were back in the boat, and then, back on the *Emerald*, where Liam said, "Thank God!" and embraced his daughter with great relief. Me, too.

"Come down to my cabin," I say to my officers. "A cup of coffee with us and we will tell you the tale. At five o'clock we'll start warping her in. The moon should be down by then."

There will be no more sleep this night.

The moon was indeed down as we started moving the *Emerald* into the quay. We secured one of our lifeboats with a short line to the bow of the ship and the men in the boat began quietly rowing. It is slow and tedious work for the boat men, but the *Emerald* slowly, silently, and surely edges toward the shore. At least there is no breeze to be against us.

Eventually, at about six thirty, we nudge up next to the wharf.

We are tied starboard side to the pier—two lines only, one fore, one aft. The starboard guns have had hastily made chocks put under the front wheels of their carriages to get higher elevation, for in their regular positions, they couldn't be brought up high enough to bear on the target. Two of the port guns were brought over in the night and one placed on the bow and one placed aft on the fantail. These will launch the first smoke canisters. All of the guns are loaded and primed and ready to go, matchlocks in place and cocked.

There are punks lit, to back up the matchlocks, in case they misfire.

Our nose is pointed out the harbor. All the sails are rigged and held up by slipknots and are ready to drop and take the air at a mere pull of the line.

A gray dawn is breaking.

We have quietly put down the gangway, something we have never been allowed to do in this town. I direct that water barrels be put on the dock to make it look like we are innocently taking on water in preparation for our departure, should anyone be curious. *Don't mind us, just a little water, mind you.*

Liam will stay on the ship so as to be ready to get her away instantly. He is our best seaman and he can't be allowed to join in the shore action. He protests, but he is overruled by all. No matter what happens ashore, the *Emerald* must be able to shake free of this place.

I am strapped into my fighting gear and I stick two extra pistols into my belt. Higgins looks grim but says nothing, for he knows it will do no good.

I go back on deck. I see that the Boarding Party is ready, armed with muskets all. Instead of a musket, my hand is on a flagstaff and on it is furled a flag.

It is now almost full daylight. Still, no one has come down to question our presence at the dock, but, after all, it is Sunday morning and all the good citizens of Harwich are abed.

"When they come, shoot over their heads," I say in a low voice to them. "We don't want to hurt or kill anyone. Understand?"

Nods all around.

I go to check the aim of the guns. I sight over them and they look good to me.

Liam stands at the rail with his long glass in hand, to watch for my signals.

"All right, lads. We're ready," I say to all.

Now we wait. And wait. And wait. Then...

*Bonnnggg!* The first peal of the church bell. All tense and take a deep breath.

*Bonnnggg!* The second peal. The jailed lads will be walking over and picking up the mattresses.

*Bonnnggg!* The third. Now they will be up against the far wall.

*Bonnnggg!* The fourth. Now they crouch down.

*Bonnnggg!* The fifth, and they should be covered up as best they can.

*Bonnnggg!* The sixth...

"FIRE!" I scream and *CRACK!* the *Emerald's* entire broadside roars out, and nine eighteen-pound balls hurl themselves at one spot in the side of the jail.

"Let's go!" I shout and head down the gangway with the musket men behind. As planned, half of them cross the quay under the reloading guns and follow John Reilly up to the right of the jail, while the other half follow me up to the left. We will be needed to cover the retreat of the boys once we get them out.

I've got my eye on the side of the jail as I pound up the slope. The cannonballs had made a cloud of dust when they hit but now it clears away and I can see that the wall is cracked but not yet breached. Smoke canisters have landed and ignited on either side and are pouring out thick, black clouds of smoke. I take my flagstaff in both hands and turn back to face the *Emerald,* and I put it straight up and then straight down, twice. It is the signal to fire again.

Instantly, the ship's guns spit out smoke and flame again. The sight of their flashing is followed immediately by the crashing sound of the balls hitting the jail, now not twenty yards away from me.

Townsmen are pouring out of their houses now, some with guns in their hands. My musket men fall to one knee and fire, the *pop*s of the rifles sounding puny after that of the great guns. Most of the townspeople flee back into their houses, but not all. There is a puff of dust at my feet, and I try to peer through the dust and smoke at the jail....

There! The wall is breached! There's a jagged, gaping hole in the side, big enough for a man to crawl through.

I turn and unfurl the black banner and swing it back and forth over my head in great, sweeping arcs, the wicked skull of my Jolly Roger grinning evilly as he looks out over the mayhem. It is the signal to cease firing cannonballs and commence loading smoke canisters to fire randomly and create confusion.

Confusion we have. Smoke is everywhere. The canvas canisters make little *poof!* sounds as they hit the ground and turn into smoke, and soon it looks like the whole town is ablaze.

I turn to go to the broken jail and I see Mairead... *Mairead? Damn that girl!*...standing next to me with a cutlass in her hand, her eyes blazing with excitement. At the same time the jailer comes bursting out the door of the jail with a pistol in his hand, which he aims at my face and fires. The ball misses me by a good half inch, and I return the favor by drawing a pistol and laying one next to his own ear.

It smacks into the side of the jail as he drops his gun and ducks back inside, his duty, as I am sure he sees it, done.

"Mairead! Go get the lads out! I'll cover you!" I pull out a fresh pistol and look about for anyone that would trouble us.

Mairead leaps over the rubble that now covers the ground around the jail and pokes her head in the hole. She yells out something in Gaelic and a great cheer is heard from inside the prison and Kevin Duggan comes out of the hole, blinking at the sudden light, followed closely by Lynch, Hogan, and O'Hara.

Mairead waves them down to the ship with her cutlass, her hair flaming in the light of the rising sun. "Get on with you! Move it! Come on, Duggan, you run like me grand-mum and she ain't got but one leg! Quickly! We can't cover for you all day now!" She gives Arthur McBride a swat on the tail with the flat of her blade as he emerges grinning into the light. "We should leave you here, boyo, for all the trouble you've caused!"

I regret that I cannot be right there to give him my boot, also, but we've got trouble—a line of townsmen has drawn up and leveled their muskets at us. I fire off a shot to make them duck, but though they wince at the sound of the ball whizzing over their heads, they do not break ranks. It is only a lucky cloud of smoke that comes between us for a moment that prevents a slaughter.

"Come on! Let's go!" I shout, turning and going back to the hole in the wall. Ian McConnaughey is out and he looks wonderingly at Mairead waving her cutlass, and then, finally, Padraic Delaney is the last one out, as I knew he would be. "Down the hill! They're gonna fire!"

I see down below that the first men out, O'Hara, Dug-gan, Hogan, and Lynch, are almost to the *Emerald*. McBride, to his credit, turns and stands and gestures for us to hurry, but he doesn't have to 'cause we're all running pell-mell down the slope as fast as we can.

Behind us there is a shout, like a command, and then there is the rattle of musketry and bullets kick up the dirt around our feet and then...*oh no!*...Mairead cries out and drops her cutlass. She pitches forward on her face and rolls head over heels down the hill till she gets to the bottom, and there she lies still. *Mairead! No!*

Ian gets to her first. "Dear girl! Oh, please God!"

"Pick her up, Ian!" I shout as I come up. "Get her on the ship!" He scoops her up in his arms and we keep running. We've got about twenty yards to go when I see Mairead's arms go around Ian's neck such that her head lies on his shoulder facing me as I run behind. *God, I hope she ain't hurt bad! I didn't see any blood, maybe...*

Maybe, nothing...She pops her eyes open and, seeing me, grins and gives me a huge wink.

*Of course*...Someday, when all are around the fire and the children are being told of the Great Deeds that their parents did on that day, the day of the Grand Battle of Har-wich Port, it cannot be said that *she* saved *him*, now could it? Nay. The conniving minx closes her eyes again and nestles her face into the crook of Ian's neck, and so she stays till we charge up the gangplank. Imagine, bullets popping up dust around our feet and she thinks of that!

"Pull it up!" I shout as my feet hit the gangway, the last one on. "Let's get the Hell out of here!"

But Liam is way ahead of me. My foot scarcely hits the

deck, when the plank is up, and the sails are dropped and filling. The lines are cast off and we begin to move away from the dock.

Mairead is placed on the main hatch-top where the poor dear recovers consciousness. She raises the back of her hand to her forehead as if in a swoon and says that she had stumbled and then was stunned by the fall and *if it hadn't been for that gallant Ian McConnaughey, well, I don't know what...*

Our musket men are lined up at the rail, peppering at those townspeople brave enough to come down to the dock for a parting shot at us.

"Quickly, Liam," I say. "I think we have worn out our welcome in this town."

But he ain't listening to me, oh no, for the light of pure rage still burns in his eyes. The newly freed boys make as if to run for their stations but Liam stops them in their tracks. "You men that were taken and caused us this grief!" he roars, "Over to the rail! You, too, McConnaughey! And Padraic! McBride! Especially you!"

They look confused.

"NOW!" Liam shouts, and they can tell he means business for they can see it in his face. They do it. They scramble over each other to line up at the rail.

We have just about cleared the Point and have all sails up and filled and soon will be in open sea when we approach the Guns at Shotley Gate. Some of the men of the town and some of the women, too, have run out on the Point to shake their fists at us, and pointing up at the Guns of Shotley Gate like they're saying, *Yer gonna git it now, you rotten Irish scum.*

But, of course, the Guns of Shotley Gate are curiously

quiet and do not say a thing against us. We can see the door to the bunker being pulled open and the unfortunate Bill and Bob dragged out, holding their heads and, I suspect, moaning. They are kicked down the slope, and do my eyes deceive me, or is that Biddy Grindle, still in her nightshirt, who's doin' the kickin'? I believe it is.

Liam looks up at the townspeople who have gathered on the Point to witness our destruction. Though we are out of musket range, the two sides are clearly visible to each other. Liam now turns back to the wayward young men of his crew, those so newly freed of their shackles. They stand wondering at the rail, awaiting Liam's wrath.

"Face this way and stand at Attention!" he thunders.

They do it.

"Now drop your pants! That's right, both trousers and drawers! Do it now, or by the living God that made me, I'll have each and every one of you sorry sons a bitches keelhauled!"

The pants come down. Most look shamefaced, but that Arthur McBride is not the least bit shy about showing off his equipment, oh no, he isn't. He grins in my direction. *Not all that impressive, boyo...*

The now completely recovered Mairead is behind me, rolling around the quarterdeck howling with laughter and delight.

*Ah, Padraic. I have often wondered if boys who have flaming red hair up top also have...yep.*

"When I say three," he orders, "bend over and touch your toes!

"One...two...THREE!"

And they do it.

Liam comes over and places his hand on the back of his son and on the back of Arthur McBride bent over next to him, and bellows out to them on the Point, loud enough for the Lord God above to hear him, "TAKE THAT, YOU EGG-SUCKING ENGLISH DOGS!"

The good men of the town, and yes, some women, too, are astounded to be presented with the sight of ten bare Irish bums pointed their way as a parting salute. And now, above the row of white bottoms and upon a raised hatch cover, are two girls, one with sandy hair and one with red, each with a hand on the other's shoulder, dancing a demented Irish jig.

# Chapter 41

We have come full out into the English Channel now, and Liam and I stand on the fantail and watch the plume of smoke that rises over Harwich fade in the distance.

"Makes you feel rather like a Viking, doesn't it, Liam?" I say.

He laughs. "For sure, lass, and for sure we will not be welcome in that town ever again."

"Aye, we'll have to find another port to sell our wares, but we will."

There's a great hustle and bustle about the deck as the guns are manhandled back into their regular places, cleaned, swabbed, and reloaded. Everyone is in great spirits, not only over the rescue but also over the fact they are going home for the winter.

I turn to Liam.

"Liam, will you join me in a victory glass of claret in my cabin as soon as everything is put right? There's something I want to talk to you about."

He nods, looking interested. "Of course. I'll be down in a minute or two."

Mairead is hanging about making eyes at Ian Mc-Connaughey and he back at her from where he's working.

"Mairead," I say, "up into the maintop with you till I say you may come down. As punishment for joining the battle unbidden." I give her a significant look.

She pouts but climbs up into the top.


Liam puts his glass down on the table and Higgins immediately refills it. I have laid out my plan to him and he is thinking hard on it.

"You know she'll just run away again as soon as we get back. She has said she would. You won't be able to hold her, no matter what," I say.

"Moira will kill me if I return without her."

"Moira's gonna kill you, anyway. Me, too."

"My own girl going off, though... I don't know."

"She'd be under the protection and guidance of my grandfather. He is a vicar, you know, and even though he's a Protestant, she would be better off with him rather than alone as a runaway. In the short time we have known him, I think he's shown himself to be a fine man."

"Aye. And maybe he'd do better with her. God knows I've failed."

I put my hand on his. "Nonsense. She's a fine, brave, high-spirited girl. You ought to be very proud of her."

"Ah, well. If Mairead agrees, I will give my blessing."


I think it would be best for me to talk to Mairead alone. Liam nods, knocks back his glass, and leaves. Higgins goes to call in Mairead. I wait and drum my fingertips on the table.

Presently Mairead comes in, does a mock curtsy, and says, "You called, Mistress?"

"Knock it off, Mairead, and sit down."

She does so and folds her hands on her lap, putting a blank expression on her face. I know, since she just saw her father leaving, that she thinks she's going to get a lecture on being a good girl when she gets back to Ireland, something she has absolutely no intention of being.

That *ain't* what she's gonna get.

"Mairead. I have a plan. It is, I think, a good plan, and I want you to be part of it."

Now she looks a bit mystified.

"You already know that as a young girl I was an orphan and lived in the streets of London," I continue. "You also know that I have recently made a lot of money."

She nods.

"I have asked my grandfather if he will help me set up a small orphanage in Cheapside, my old neighborhood in London, to help the homeless ones there."

When I had broached this to my grandfather, he went positively radiant with joy. I had known, even though he did not mention it, that he did not entirely approve of the way I was making my living. But now, with this...*Oh, joy!* he exulted, and clasped his hands together in an attitude of thankful prayer. He probably had been praying pretty heavily over my somewhat spotted soul for a while now. Well, nothing like giving a man a mission, I say.

"He agreed, wholeheartedly."

Mairead looks up at me confused.

"I want you to help me in this thing, Mairead, I really

do," I say and drop to one knee beside her. "I want you to be Mistress of Girls at the London Home for Little Wanderers."

Now her mouth pops open for real.

"Hear me out," I say, pressing my case. "You won't have to go back to the farm and you won't have to marry that Loomis Malloy. You'll never smell peat smoke again. You will have a respectable post and you'll be paid and you'll be able to buy fine clothes and you being so beautiful—oh, yes, you are—you'll be the toast of London! And oh, Mairead, London is such a city, you cannot even imagine—it's the very center of the world!"

"But what about Ian?" she asks, her eyes wide.

"You know damn well that if you go back to Waterford and then back to the farm that your mother ain't gonna let Ian McConnaughey within fifty yards of you. Besides, it ain't like you'll be worlds apart. It'll be a good test of Ian's love...his constancy, like."

*...and I can tell you all about male constancy, I can...*

"But, my dad...what..."

"Your father says he'll agree to let you go, but only if you swear on your sacred honor that you will place yourself under my grandfather's guidance as regards your personal behavior, and I agree with him on this—I know, I know, I sound like a hypocrite—but there are many pretty boys in London and boys lie, oh, yes, they do. I know 'cause I've met a few of 'em. Even good boys lie. I know, I know, I'm sounding like your mother and you hate that, but it's only 'cause I care for you that I'm saying this, and I'll say it once and I'll say it no more as it's your life and you've got to lead it. There. That's it."

She looks at the floor, stunned with the turn of events and the choice she is given.

"You will have a position and respect, and, no, you'll never have to change a diaper again, unless it's for one of your own."

Her head lifts.

"And, Mairead, if later on, if you find that the seafaring life still calls to you, then we'll go a-roving again, me and you. This war can't last forever, and when it's over I plan to set up as an honest merchant, and then we'll sail to the South Seas and China and the Japans, and we'll see Bombay Rats and Cathay Cats and Kangaroos and..."

"And Hottentots, too?" grins Mairead.

"And lots and lots of wild Hottentots!" I say, and the bargain is made.

# Chapter 42

We have a War Council, the staff of the London Home for Little Wanderers and me, in my cabin before their departure. Higgins will go with Grandfather and Mairead to find a suitable place and set things up. He has the papers that I have signed granting him power of attorney over my money, which he will give to my lawyer, Mr. Worden. My grandfather is a sweet man, but the sharpers in Cheapside would smell "country rube" all over him and we'd get fleeced right quick. Nobody, however, fleeces Higgins.

"You will go to Cheapside, right around Blackfriars Bridge, and look for a place there. You should be able to find something cheap but clean. Something that can house about forty children. We can expand later, if things go well. I don't want any more than half my stash of money used for this, 'cause we'll need the rest to keep the school running—and I do prefer to think of it as a school, and not a charity house. See if you can find the girl Joannie. She's probably still living with her gang under Blackfriars Bridge. She will know every orphan in the neighborhood and be able to tell you which kids can still be saved. I don't want any bullies in my school, and I want the girls to be educated just like the boys in music, art, arithmetic, science, reading, and writing."

I take a breath. I get so worked up about this.

"Mairead, you will handle the girls and teach them sewing and their early letters. You will make them be good, but I want them treated fairly and with respect—after all, they have managed to survive where many have not. Grandfather, you will be the Schoolmaster and you will handle the boys and teach the older children philosophy. Look about you when you set up. There will be plenty of penniless scholars that can be hired as teachers. Hire them, but let them know there will be no flogging. If a child is bad, give him a warning. If he continues to be bad, throw him out. There will be plenty of others to take his place. Let them all know that."

Another breath.

"Attorney Worden will be in charge of the money when Higgins returns to me. You will both submit your accounts to him"—*and here I think back on Mistress Pimm's class on Household Management and the Ledger We Must Keep for Our Husband*—"and I will brook no sloppy bookkeeping."

I think that's about it.

"Make your preparations for departure. Higgins has all the papers. All is set in train, and...Higgins, stop beaming at me."

"I can't help it, Miss," he says. "This is such a fine thing you are doing."

*Well, how much money do I need, anyway? Never let it be*

*said of Jacky Faber that she wouldn't stand her mates to a treat when she had some jingle in her pocket.*

We are going to put them in a boat and land them at Brighton. It will be but a short run up to London. Before we do that I say to Liam, "You've got to give them two minutes."

He grumps and says, "Two minutes, no more."

And Mairead Delaney and Ian McConnaughey are allowed two minutes alone in my cabin. When we tap on the bell, they come up, looking flushed. She wipes her eyes and goes to her father.

Liam embraces his daughter at the rail before she steps off.

I nod to Arthur McBride and he shouts, "HIP, HIP..."

And the rest of the crew, all standing in the rigging, replies, "HOORAY!"

Again he does it. "HIP, HIP...HOORAY!"

And finally for the third cheer, "HIP, HIP, HOORAY!" and hats are thrown, and Mairead Delaney goes tearfully over the side.

That night, as we run back toward Waterford, the *Emerald* cutting through the waves like the fine nautical shiv she is, I prepare for bed.

Before I put my nightdress on, I lie back and feel my new silk cushions and sheets, made of the finest damask, cool against my skin.

So, now, Tonda-lay-o, once a castaway and Queen of the Jungle, lies in her own silk bed aboard her own dear ship and is now Tonda-lay-o, Queen of the Ocean Sea!

She has what she always wanted. A fine ship and a fine crew and the whole wide wonderful world to roam. She has money, and, since she has decided to live single all of her life, she is free. She calls no man master.

I am content. I really am.

Really.

# PART III

# Chapter 43

And so, we passed the winter in the port of Waterford, Province of Leinster, County Waterford, Ireland.

Or, rather, the *Emerald* did, after fixing up the few things that were wrong with her—plucking musket balls out of her dear sides and making everything right with caulk and varnish and all, and making a few changes to the rigging that Liam and I thought might make her a bit faster. Lord knows, she already is the fastest thing ever, but it never hurts to keep pushing—after all that, we posted a guard on her and my crew scattered, to meet back again in the spring. Liam and his brood took off for their farm, Moira steaming but mollified that her wayward daughter Mairead had a good, safe post, at least, and I was off for London. I know that Moira probably said, "Good riddance!" Well, you can't please everybody.

I took passage on a ship from Waterford to Bristol, and coach from Bristol to London. We had a joyous reunion, even though I had been gone scarcely a month, and I found that Higgins and the Vicar had indeed found a suitable place—a cozy little building on Brideshead Street, not far from the Admiral Benbow Inn and my old stomping grounds. It has three stories and a big great room with a fine fireplace on the first floor. The cost was within our means and the deal had been closed. I can't really believe it, but we *own* a house. I know it is true, but to me it is still a great and most amazing thing.

I was gratified to see Joannie there, she from the Blackfriars Bridge Gang, dressed in clean clothes, well fed, and helping with the younger kids. She had been found right off and was a great help in bringing in just the right group of children from the surrounding neighborhoods. As I had thought, she knew the ones who would benefit the most from the Home, and the ones who would prove difficult. We can't save the whole world, but we have a nice batch of thirty-two, for starters, half of them boys and half girls, and they range in age from two to twelve. All have their studies, but all work as well—there's constant laundry to be done and the place has to be kept clean, too. When I arrive and am introduced, they are lined up as if to thank me, but I will not have that. *You can thank me,* I say, *by being good and studying hard and doing well in your studies.*

Joannie said she almost didn't come in—the pull of the street was awful strong. Zeke, the last leader of the Blackfriars Bridge Gang, did not come in. As she reported it, "He stood there thinkin' to 'imself, considerin' the freedom of the street and all, and then he said to the Vicar, 'Sorry, Guv'nor, but I'll be on me way. You take care o' the little ones, now,' and he took the shilling that was offered him and went whistlin' down the street. I thought about doin' the same, but I knew that Zeke could go off and be a soldier or a sailor or he could apprentice himself as a laborer, but I knew I didn't 'ave none of them choices, so I come here. And I'm glad I did."

Mairead has gotten right into the running of the place, too. She is brisk with the children, but not at all unkind, and they grow to love her very quickly. She knew of a widow woman back in Kilkenny who didn't have anyplace to go once her man died and she sent for her and hired her on as cook. "Can't have a Brit making my colcannon now, can I?" says Mairead. Mrs. Kinsella is a very good cook, I find, and seems happy in her new job.

I don't stay at the Home. Higgins and I have taken rooms at the Admiral Benbow. I tell Grandfather that I don't want to disrupt the routine of the school, but it's really 'cause I want to come and go as I please, and I don't want to be asking anyone's permission.

On Sundays we all have to go to church, of course. Grandfather is a vicar, after all, and the services are not all that bad—no ranting and raving like I'm used to back in Boston. I enjoy looking around at the great space of St. Paul's Cathedral, the vaulting in the ceiling high overhead, the beautiful stained-glass window. It reminds me of the last time I was in this place, but back then I sure didn't come through the front door. Us street kids weren't allowed in because they thought we'd steal the money from the poor box, and, of course, they were right in thinking that. Plus we were filthy and ragged and smelly. No, but there are other ways to get in here...plenty of ways...

Higgins has everything set up, moneywise, and I leave that all to him and Lawyer Worden. Higgins has enlisted the aid of Lady Hollingsworth and her daughters in this enterprise, and that is good because expenses are beginning to mount—including some unexpected ones. Last week we had to hire a wet nurse because a baby was left on our doorstep one cold night, and we do not expect this baby will be the last one, either.

We have Christmas at the Home for Little Wanderers. The holly and the ivy garlands are hung in our hall and in the great room and a wreath is put on our door. We go about the neighborhood on Christmas Eve, when a light snow is falling, singing carols and wassails, and on Christmas Day we have a huge spread of goose and ham, with potatoes, gravy, pudding, and sweets. And gifts, too, for which Mairead and I have combed the shops—dolls for the girls, spinning tops for the boys, and pennywhistles all around.

Mairead has been good about taking moral guidance from my grandfather, but now that I'm here, we two have a chance to go out on the town together and be, well, not quite so good...*Mairead will stay over with me tonight, Grandfather, all right? We are going to the exhibit at the Royal Academy and...*We put an act together—whistles, fiddle, songs, and dancing—and are well received at several of the better taverns. And there's the theater, and expositions, and lectures, and all that glitters in this wonderful town.

The time passes very quickly.

When spring comes, Higgins and I go back to Waterford to ready the *Emerald* for her next cruise. We need to get the victuals on board, fresh powder and water and countless other things.

It is not long after we get back that I find that I have lost a member of my crew. Ian McConnaughey has gone off to London, and he does not come back. *Good luck to you, Ian. You are a fine young man and we will miss you.*

———

Now that I have a fixed address that I can use, I write a letter to Ezra Pickering, my good friend and lawyer back in the States.


*Jacky Faber*
*On Board the Ship Emerald,*
*Moored at Swett & Daggett's Wharf*
*Waterford, Ireland*

*Ezra Pickering, Esquire*
*Union Street*
*Boston, Massachusetts, USA*

*Dearest Ezra,*

*I hope this letter finds you healthy and happy and that you prosper in your business. I know that you are just the best of lawyers, so you must be doing well.*

*Well, like that bad penny, here's Jacky Faber turning up again. And this time she's got a ship, if you can believe that! That's right, Ezra, I have a ship! She's named the Emerald and she's one hundred and ten feet long, thirty feet in the beam, displaces two hundred and fifty tons, has a crew of thirty-nine, counting me, and is absolutely the most beautiful and graceful thing I have ever seen. Please enter her onto the books as an asset of Faber Shipping, Worldwide, and register her as American, since our company is based in Boston.*

*It is rather a long story as to how I got the Emerald and I would rather tell it to you over a couple of pints down at the good old Pig and Whistle. For now, suffice it to say that I have managed to get a Letter of Marque from the British Admiralty* and have used the ship as a privateer to seize some very good prizes.

I have made a lot of money, and I have put some of it to use in setting up an orphanage and school in my old neighborhood of Cheapside in London. Knowing my past as you do, you will understand why I would do that. Should you wish to write to me, address me there:

> The London Home for Little Wanderers
> 24 Brideshead Lane
> London, England

We sail soon to resume our raiding, but letters sent to me there will eventually get to me.

My funds are in the Bank of England and my lawyer here is a Mr. Worden of Newgate Street, London. Should you ever recover my money from Mistress Pimm, please forward it to Mr. Worden, as he is in charge of finances for the Home.

If you continue to see Miss Amy Trevelyne and she allows you to speak of me, please tell her that her book has made me go right famous in the nautical world and I wish her joy and success in that book and anything she might write in the future—I just hope it's not about me next time. I think I'm about as famous as I need to get. I know, though, that it is not likely she will do anything connected with me, it being that I brought disgrace to her and her family. I hope that she does not still hate me, but when I think back on how she betrayed me to Preacher Mather's men, I despair in that hope—not that I didn't have it coming, I mean. I generally do have it coming.

Anyway, give her my greetings, for what they're worth.

Thank you, Ezra, for all you have done for me in the past

*and I hope to see you soon. Maybe when this war is over I will turn my ship to the transatlantic trade, and then I will see you often.*

*Until then, I remain,*

*Your Dearest Friend and Most Devoted Servant,*
*Jacky*

We will go again to the coast of France, where last year we found the best pickings. If the pickings are scant, then we will head south to bother the Spaniards again, maybe even venturing into the Mediterranean, if we have to.

It will be good to get back to sea after the long winter, to feel the roll of the waves slipping under the *Emerald's* keel again, to once more look up at the white of the sails against the blue of the sky. It is good for a sailor to be at sea, for on shore we get soft.

It will be good to get back, too, for now I've an orphanage to maintain.

# Chapter 44

The *Emerald* could not be in better form, every sail tight, every line humming, as the good ship fairly rips along, the bow lifting and then crashing down into the waves to send spray over the fo'c'sle and into my face. Ah, it is good to be standing in my usual spot on the quarterdeck, the wind in my hair and my long glass under my arm, one booted foot on either side of the centerline, the better to feel the action of my beautiful ship.

"On deck there! Sail off port quarter!"

*Ha!*

Yes, it's good to be back.

And we did roam the sea, that spring and summer of 1805, a sleek, green, waterborne wolf on the prowl. We roamed and raided and plundered and sang and danced and roamed and raided some more. We began in our old hunting grounds and bagged us a few fat prizes, but the French soon grew wary and we headed south to bother the Spaniards again. When that grew tame, we became bolder as we pushed on into the Mediterranean and lurked around the Spanish ports and nailed ships coming out of their harbors and we sold them in

Algiers, where no questions were ever asked. We pushed up to the east coast of France, to Nice, to Marseilles, and made many a captain sorry he had ever set sail and crossed our wake. We rocked and rolled across the waves, we chased ships and we caught them, and other ships chased us, but they never caught the *Emerald*, oh no, not my fast and nimble *Emerald*. We went to Italy, to Malta, and Corsica, and we changed our flag at the masthead from the British Union Jack to the American Stars and Stripes and, yes, even to the Jolly Roger, himself, anytime it suited us. We plundered the north coast of Africa and when things got too hot for us, we crossed the big pond and went to the Caribbean and came back with more Spanish gold. We drank and danced and caroused in ports from Kingston to Saint Vincent, from Palma to Naples, from Rome to Palermo, from Gibraltar to Cork.

In short, we prospered.

When September came we headed back to the west coast of France, from whence we had started. We prowled but came up with nothing. Then, when we were about to give it up, there came that welcome call from the masthead:

"On deck there! A ship! Off the starboard bow! A merchant by the looks of her!"

"Let's get her, Liam," I shout as I run to the rail to gloat over my next prize. "Higgins! My sword!"

We run her down without too much trouble and soon are aboard. The passengers are lined up on the deck, most of them, as usual, quivering with fear.

Most, but not all. One of them is definitely *not* scared. She is a little old woman, very much bent with age, but looking at me with such pure and unabashed hatred that I almost have to look away. Curiously, she has a rolled-up newspaper under her arm.

"Now, *grand-mere*," I say in French, "there's no need to be afraid. We don't rob passengers of their personal things and we will not hurt you."

"Don't give me that *grand-mere* stuff, you piece of filth!" she snarls at me in accented English. "You, you take our boat, you take our life! We were only trying to get our tulips to market."

"All right now, Granny," says Padraic, taking her arm and leading her to the boat. She rips her arm out of his grasp and points the newspaper at my nose. I think she might even try to swat me with it.

"They're going to catch you and put you up on the gallows, you damned pirate! And I hope you twist a good long time before you go off to Hell!"

I put my sword back in its sheath and cross my arms over my chest. "But won't the French prefer to use the guillotine if they happen to catch me, *n'est ce pas?*" I say with a wide grin. "But, as the famous recipe for rabbit stew goes, 'First, catch the rabbit...'"

"The French? It won't be the French, it will be the English! Your own people will kill you, *chienne*, and then you won't be laughing."

I know the meaning of the things she is calling me and I am growing weary of this game. "Get them in the boat," I say to Padraic and turn to Liam. "What's in the cargo?"

"Tulip bulbs. Tons of tulip bulbs."

"Ah, good," I say and mean it. Tulips are the very rage of London.

But it seems the old woman is not yet done. "Here, *putain*," she spits, and flings the newspaper at my feet. "Read your doom."

I am now *very* tired of this old woman. "Get her gone," I say to Padraic, and he hustles her off, spitting and cursing.

Carelessly, I pick up the paper and glance at it. I'm surprised to see that it is a London paper, *Lloyd's List and Shipping Gazette,* and only about two weeks out of date. The *Gazette* is full of nautical news—merchant ship departures and arrivals and such, and it also has news concerning the Royal Navy, promotions, sailings, policy, and the like. It's read religiously by Naval officers to keep an eye on who's getting ahead and who ain't. I look over an account of Lord Nelson chasing the French and Spanish Fleet to the Caribbean and back...and Captain Locke has been made a Vice Admiral and that cheers me—*Good Captain Locke! I wish you the joy of your Flag, Sir.* And then my eye gets to the bottom of the page, and...

*Good Lord!*

"Liam! Get the men back on board! All of them!" I shout.

"But what of the prize?" asks Liam, looking confused.

"To Hell with it! Cast it off! Let them go!"

"What..."

"We have been betrayed. We've got to get out of here, fast!" I leap back on board the *Emerald.* "All men aloft! Make all sail! Liam! In my cabin!"

The men, mystified, do what I say, and the ships begin to drift apart. I see the old woman, in command of her boat again, standing with feet apart on her deck, fists on hips, laughing. "Run, *saloup*, run for your worthless life!"

Liam and I pile into my cabin and I tell him what the paper says.

"But what of your Letter of Marque?" he asks, "Surely…"

"Worthless, now," I growl. "Gather the men."

Liam leaves the cabin and I hand the paper to a mystified Higgins. He reads it and looks up, greatly concerned. "We'll have to get lawyers on this," he says.

"First, we have to get away, then we'll see about lawyers," I say and go out on deck. The men have assembled and I read out the notice posted in the *Gazette:*

AN ORDER TO ALL OF HIS MAJESTY'S SHIPS :
A Warrant is hereby issued for the arrest and containment of one Jacky Faber, a Female, and her crew aboard a ship calling itself the *Emerald,* this ship having been taken unlawfully from His Majesty's Prize Court by said Female. She has in her possession a Letter of Marque that was obtained under Fraudulent Circumstances and has been revoked by Order of The First Lord of the Admiralty. She has been seen harrying ships in and about the Channel. She is to be considered a Dangerous Pyrate, and a reward is offered for her Capture:
Alive, Two Hundred and Fifty Pounds Sterling.
Dead, One Hundred Pounds.
Either she, or her Head, is to be delivered to the Admiralty for trial or disposition.

The men stand stunned when I am done. There is more to the notice—a description of me right down to size, weight, scars, and tattoo, but I don't bother to read that.

Then the rumbling starts…*Damned two-faced English bastards…too good to be true, I knew it all along…try to take our Jacky, will they…over my dead body…*

"Men," I shout, "we have to keep calm, and we've got to keep our wits about us, but most of all we've got to get out of here and away from the English fleet. When we've got some sea room, we'll have some time to think about what we're going to do. As for now, bend on all the canvas we've got—skysails, scudders, anything she'll hold!"

She will hold quite a lot of sail, it seems, for even as I shout the order, the wind dies and the sails hang limp and there we sit, becalmed, not twenty miles from the British fleet on the blockade, every one of them now knowing that my ship is a pirate and that there is a price upon my head.

# Chapter 45

*Lieutenant James Emerson Fletcher*
*On Board HMS* Wolverine
*On Patrol off the Coast of France*
*September 23, 1805*

Dearest Jacky,

If ever I had thought that news of you, my wild lost girl, would always be a welcome thing, I was dead wrong. Today we received a message from the Flag informing the entire fleet that there is a price on the head of one Jacky Faber, Female Outlaw and Pirate, and that she is to be hunted down and destroyed with all dispatch.

It seems that when you were, incredibly, in command of the Wolverine, you took four French ships as prizes but turned in only three of them to the Admiralty. How clever of you, but then you were always oh so very clever, weren't you? You have certainly outdone yourself this time, though—a ship, Jacky, an entire ship! How could even one such as you, willful, headstrong, reckless, and wildly impulsive as you are, have thought you would get away with something like that? Did you not think that the Admiralty would eventually find out about your deception? Did you not think the First Lord could do simple math? And piracy to boot, my God…I choose not to believe the Belle Fille sans Merci stories, for I know you to have a good heart and could not have done those things. But the taking of prizes on very shaky grounds, well, I have no choice but to believe that, as it is so widely reported.

Could you not have just quietly gone back to school or to some other worthy and peaceful pursuit after leaving the Wolverine, having already had many more adventures than any man has in a lifetime, let alone a girl of your tender years? No, I suppose not…

Oh yes, and the sum of Two Hundred and Fifty Pounds is offered for your head, if that stupid head is still attached to the rest of you; One Hundred Pounds, if it is not. Interesting, that—apparently the Admiralty would like to talk to you before they hang you, but they will take the head either way, it seems. Two hundred and fifty pounds is a princely sum. I am sure every captain in the fleet is licking his chops. You will be actively pursued, count on it.

Jacky, I can only hope with all my heart that you get wind of this before you are caught and that you take both yourself and your ship to the other side of the world and live out your life happily there, for there is no life for you here. Not a long one, anyway.

Oh yes. I passed for Lieutenant.

Despairingly,
Jaimy

# Chapter 46

Morning finds us in very light winds and a very heavy fog. I am extremely uneasy. I don't like the feel of this at all. I shush all on deck to be silent and I listen. I hear only the creak of the riggings, and not much of that, it being so still and quiet. I climb into the ratlines and lean out, straining to hear. Did I just hear something off to port there...maybe not. If there is a ship out there, he's trying to be just as quiet as me. Was that a tiny *ding*? Was the clapper of a ship's bell not properly secured? *Probably nothing*, I think. Just getting jumpy. Best go get my breakfast.

I had plenty of time to think these past few days, sitting here becalmed and nervous as hell, hearing phantom noises out in the mist. I thought about the Admiralty. Why the difference in the reward for bringing me back—two hundred and fifty pounds alive or one hundred pounds for my head in a sack? That's a lot of money, two hundred and fifty pounds—that's a captain's pay for a year. They must want to talk to me for some reason...maybe they think I know more about the spy ring than I told them? But I told them everything I knew. They couldn't get anything else out of me even with torture. I shiver at the thought of being tortured. I know I could never hold up under something like that. If it's just that they want to shut me up about what I know, why don't they just put up a reward for me dead and be done with it? My head delivered to them in a bag would certainly be more portable, and I would certainly be very, very quiet from then on. I don't know, I just don't know.

I do know, though, that every captain in the fleet is licking his chops, thinking about laying his hands on me and claiming that reward. I swear, if I get out of this, I'm going to carry rum from Barbados to Boston and granite from Boston to Jamaica. In the summer I'll ferry Irishmen across the ocean to work in Boston—that's it—I'll take their indenture for the passage and get paid when they find work—and there's plenty of work there. That's it. That's what I'll do. I promise. It won't be as exciting, but at least it'll be steady and I won't get hanged for it.

Before going down to my cabin to the breakfast that Higgins has surely laid out, I gaze into the fog in the direction of the French coast for a few moments more, but I don't see anything but gray. The breeze quickens on my cheek as I swing down to the deck and I jerk my head around. *Thank God! Maybe the wind is coming up! Maybe...* The sails give a hopeful flap and start to fill...but wait...is there something out there? Did I hear a noise? Wait...

The breeze gusts again and then it roars right in and sweeps away the fog like it was a dirty rag, and there, *there,* not a hundred yards away is HMS *Wolverine,* all her sails set and bearing down on us like the very wrath of God, Himself.

"Port your helm! Hard alee!" I scream. "Let's get the Hell out of here!"

*Damn!*

We fall off and our sails fill again but the wind had hit the *Wolverine* before it hit us and we have lost precious time and even more precious distance between us!

The *Emerald* finds her feet and claws her way through the water.

"Heave to and prepare to be boarded!" comes the call from across the water.

*Not just yet, Captain Trumbull.*

Liam comes up next to me, looking mighty worried.

"Crowd on all she's got, Liam, or we are lost!"

"All aloft to make sail!" he calls out, and men scramble to the top. "Set the skysails, the stuns'ls, the scudders! Every scrap of sail!"

They do it and the *Emerald* leaps forward, every board, every line groaning under the strain, but the *Wolverine* had gained so much ground, she having caught the new wind first, that I just don't know...

Then I hear it, from across the water:

*Were-wolves! Were-wolves! Were-wolves!*

*Damn!*

There is a deep boom and a puff of smoke from the *Wolverine*'s bow chaser. The ball whizzes through the rigging. They've got us in range, that's for sure, but they can only bring the Long Tom to bear—if they swing around for a broadside and miss, then we will get clean away. *Do it! We'll take our chances!*

But they don't do it. What they do is crowd on more sail and keep coming.

*Were-wolves! Were-wolves! Were—*

The chant cuts off abruptly. The men of my old crew must have just found out that it's me that they're chasing.

"Will we fire on them?" asks Liam, coming up beside me.

"No, we can't. Those are my friends over there. And besides, it will go harder on us if we are captured and we have shot at them. I think we can outrun them."

And, indeed, the distance between us seems to be widening. *Good, good, fleet* Emerald! *Show them your tail!*

There is another shot from the *Wolverine*. Liam and I watch the ball fall short. It skips by our starboard side. We grin at each other.

Then we ain't grinning.

*Uh-oh.*

The *Wolverine* has come about in a last-ditch effort to stop us. She means to give us a broadside. My old Division One will fire on me! She brings her port guns to bear, and I hear Trumbull yell *Fire!* and I hear Eli beat the drum. I hear the thunder of the guns and I watch for the shots to fall.

Most fall short, and two bounce by our port side, but one, one which the gun captain had wedged to shoot high, almost like a mortar, arcs high, and we watch in fascination as it drops down toward us. If it hits our deck, it will do some damage, but the wound will not be mortal. And then we will be away.

But it doesn't do that. What it does is hit our mainmast square on. The mast splinters and comes crashing down to the deck, mainsail, royal, gallant, and all.

"Cut it away!" I scream, leaping on the tangled wreckage

and hacking away at the lines with *Persephone*. Liam and the others take axes to the mess. If we can get it off, we might yet get away!

But it is not to be. The sail drags in the water, slowing us down to a crawl. The *Wolverine* heaves alongside with her starboard guns pointing right into our sides. There is a mighty crash as the Werewolves fire the full broadside right into my side, and right at the waterline. The *Emerald* reels from the blow and starts to settle. I know the wound is mortal. It is over. We are lost.

I go back to the fantail and strike my colors, so that they will not pound us anymore. The red, white, and blue curls around me as I run back forward and down into my cabin. I get my Letter of Marque and put it in my jacket and I look about at my cabin...*oh, I loved you so*...for the last time and lift my seabag and go back on my quarterdeck and wait. I have told Liam to pose as a member of the crew, as it will go easier for him that way. I shall be Captain in these, the last moments.

It does not take long. First it is a few seamen over my starboard side, seamen I recognize, and who, with a shock, recognize me. Then Captain Trumbull, then Jared, then... Jaimy. They see me standing there and come over to me. As they approach, I pull out one of my pistols.

"You struck your colors, damn you!" shouts the Captain, stepping back. But the pistol is not for him.

I put the barrel under my chin and say, "What will become of my men?"

"Jacky, no...," says Jaimy.

"They are all prime seamen," I continue, the barrel cold

against my throat. "Will you press them and nothing more? I cannot bear to see anything happen to them."

The Captain considers. "We need the men," he says.

"On your honor as a gentleman, you will press them and nothing more?"

"On my honor."

I point the pistol to the deck. The Captain comes up and roughly pulls the pistol from my hand. Then he yanks the other one from my belt, and I watch both clatter to the deck.

"What will happen to you, however, is another matter entirely," he says. "Bind her and take her back. Check below for cargo. Save what you can."

Heavy hands are put on me, and I am bound and taken away.


I am put to my knees at the foot of the mainmast of the *Wolverine,* so that I can fully enjoy the proceedings, I suppose. What they can salvage is taken off the *Emerald* and put below. My men are read the Articles of War and are signed on the ship's roster. All the boats are brought back and loaded aboard. My former *Wolverine* shipmates, my loyal midshipmen, all gaze at me in wonder and pity.

"Well, then," says the Captain with some satisfaction, as he comes up to stand next to me. "Mr. Fletcher. Since it was your gun that brought down her mast, I give you the honor of sinking the pirate. Fire at will."

*Oh, Jaimy...*

Jaimy nods and goes to the Number Six gun. He lifts the matchlock line and leans over the barrel. He ratchets two over and winches one up. He pulls the cord and the gun barks out its noise and flame. The ball crashes into the side of my dear *Emerald*, splintering the green and white checked top of the hull I loved so well.

He is a good shot. He moves to the next gun. His next round catches her in her flank at her waterline and she begins to heel over. His next goes in my cabin window and out the other side. I hear her glass shattering.

My beautiful ship is going down. My jewel. Jaimy ceases firing and stands at attention.

I try to keep the Look on my face and my head high, but I can't, I can't, I just can't. Tears slide over my cheeks as my precious *Emerald* sinks.

Her bow goes first, and then her tail lifts up, pauses a moment, and then she slips down beneath the waves. She always was the most elegant thing, and even in death she is graceful.

The last thing to go under is my brave little flag. Faber Shipping, Worldwide, is once again reduced to one rather small, and very scared, girl.

The Captain leaves me slumped there at the foot of the mast with orders that no one speak to me while they finish stowing what used to be my cargo. I will not meet Mr. Fletcher's eyes. *You sunk my ship, Jaimy, you did, you did. And it was a good one, too!* I try not to let black despair overwhelm me. I try not to let my head fall to my chest and my body sag in the ropes that bind me, but it is hard. I keep my head up somehow and look out over the sea, so I don't have to see the pitying looks from my former crew.

"Call the Marine detachment," orders the Captain, finally. The two Marines march forward and stop in front of him, and me.

*Uh-oh.*

The Marines have their rifles at port arms, held across their chests. The Captain is between the Marines and me, and he turns to gaze upon me for a moment. He shakes his head and then steps out of the way.

*I have heard of this! A summary trial! Drumhead justice! I am undone!*

My knees turn to jelly and I start to slip down. "Please, Martin, Rodgers...If you love me, in the heart, please, not in the face." I say this to the Marines and, crazily, I try to struggle to my feet to present my chest and try to make a good brave show of it for the sake of my crews, so they'll think well of me in years to come, though I don't know why I should care, but my mind is numb with terror and I see Jaimy...*Good-bye, Jaimy, I loved you...*and Jared coming toward me, but someone beats them both to it.

Georgie Piggott is standing in front of me, his arms held straight out from his shoulders, all of him shaking as he faces the Captain. "You're not going to sh...shoot her, are you, Sir?"

The Captain lets out an exasperated sigh. "What a ship...," he says under his breath. Then he says, "No, Mr. Piggott, I'm not going to shoot her. I'll let others dispose of her. Although I should shoot *you* for impertinence." He turns to the Marines. "Corporal! Take her below to the brig and keep her under twenty-four-hour surveillance. Her head is worth two hundred and fifty pounds in its current condition, and I intend to collect it. Be careful. I've heard she's a slippery one." I am untied and thrown down into the brig.

*Guess I was born to hang, after all.*

# Chapter 47

I am taken and tossed down into the brig.

I look around. The bench. The ratty blanket. The chamber pot. That is all that is to be had at the Hotel *Wolverine,* except for dark despair—first it held poor Robin, then the unfortunate Mr. Luce, and now me. Corporal Martin stands guard at the door to the hatchway.

I sit down on the bench and try not to bury my face in my hands and weep, but it is hard, very hard. *What will become of me? And what will become of the Home…oh, Lord…*

I am not down there twenty minutes when I have my first visitor. It is Captain Trumbull. He clasps his hands behind him and gazes at me through the bars.

I jump to my feet. "My Letter of Marque," I say, pulling it out of my jacket front and thrusting it at him. "I believe you will find it in order, and that a grievous mistake has been made, one that has done me great harm."

He opens it up and reads it. He smiles slightly. "Very nice, but worthless," he says. "This has long since been revoked. Its only worth now is that it keeps your crew from being hanged as pirates. We are sure that when they signed on with you, they thought the Letter to be genuine."

"So everything I did will be seen as piracy and I will go to the gallows, even though I sailed in all innocence, thinking only that I was doing good for King and country?" I ask, chin up. "I, too, thought the Letter to be genuine."

"How innocent were you when you absconded with a prize ship that belonged to His Majesty? When you did not turn that ship in to the Prize Court?"

*Well, there's no good answer to that, is there?* I'm thinking. *None that's gonna do me any good, that is,* so I don't reply.

"And just how innocent is this?" he says, and unfurls my Jolly Roger flag and holds it up in front of my face.

I ain't got nothin' to say to that, neither.

"But never mind," he continues. "It is not my job to judge you. My job is to deliver you to the proper authorities and they will dispose of you as they see fit. And I *will* deliver you, Miss Faber, count on it. We will be relieved on this patrol in about a week, and we will then proceed to London. I do hope you will enjoy your stay with us."

I think on this and start to steam, but I hold myself back and reply, "I do wish you the joy of your capture, Captain. I am quite sure you will put the two hundred and fifty pounds to good and worthy use."

"You may rest assured the reward will be put to good use. As for now, if you have a dress in your bag, please put it on. That is, if you have any sense of decency at all."

*I guess I don't. I wasn't raised proper,* I think all hurt and surly. *No. Don't. You've got to be good. Think.*

"I may not have a sense of decency, Sir," I say, "but I do have a request."

"What? If you think you are going to get any special treatment you are sadly..."

"No, Sir, but if you were to take my man Higgins as your steward, you would find your life much changed."

This startles him a bit. "How?"

"He was personal valet to Lord Hollingsworth and is very skilled in social things. Who do you have serving you now?"

"I have been getting along with Weisling," he says, drily.

"The Weasel," I snort. "He's not even good enough for the Midshipmen's berth, let alone for the Captain of a British warship."

I watch for a swelling of the male chest and I get it. This is his first command and he is very proud of it.

"*Harrumph*," he says, "I will consider it. Now I will take my leave of you. If you have any needs of a...personal nature, please let me know."

"Thank you, Sir. I shall," I say, and give him the full Lawson Peabody Fine-Lady-Though-Without-Skirt curtsy. Startled to see it, he almost bows back. Then he *harrumphs* again and leaves.

I ask Corporal Martin to hand me my seabag so I can get out a dress and so comply with the Captain's order, but he ain't that stupid. I have to tell him where it is in the bag and he pulls it out, blushing all the while, what with his hand in amongst the lacy things, the smell of Frenchy perfume wafting out of the bag and up his nose. Then I make him turn around while I change into the dress. I choose my black school dress—it seems appropriate.

Then I sit in silence for a while and think on my condition. I heave a deep heavy sigh. *Full fathom five my* Emerald *lies, of her bones is coral made...*

A little later, the door to the hatchway leading down into my hold opens and...*he* comes in.

I jump to my feet and turn to face the wall and don't say anything.

I hear him come up behind me and he, too, says nothing, but I know he's there, looking at my back, which I make as straight as I can.

When the silence becomes unbearable I say, "You gonna marry that girl, Jaimy? You should. She's very pretty."

He still doesn't say anything.

"Not that it matters to me, since they're gonna take me back and hang me and soon I won't be carin' about anything. So if I were you, I would marry that girl. You will have beautiful children, I know you will, she bein' so beautiful and all and such a fine lady. Not like me. I ain't ever gonna be a lady." I give a short laugh. "'Specially not now."

I pause and worry my hands. "We were just babies, back there on the *Dolphin*. I should not have expected more than childhood friendship from you, Jaimy, I know that now. I don't blame you. I really don't. Now go away."

Still he says nothing.

"Did you enjoy sinkin' my ship, Jaimy?" I heave a long sigh. "I really loved that ship. I loved it more than I loved anything in this world 'cept for my friends, which you ain't one of, that's for sure. You smashed her and sent her to the bottom. Was it fun? Will you gain advancement from it? I do blame you for that, Jaimy. I'm sorry, but I do. I notice that you're a lieutenant now. My congratulations. I am sure you will go far in the Navy."

Still he says nothing, and I've had about enough of this. "Why don't you just go away now..."

He speaks for the first time. "Jacky. Please," and he goes around to the side of the cage and reaches out his hand for me.

"Don't you touch me!" I flee to the other side. "Don't you *ever* touch me! Corporal!" I call out.

Poor Corporal Martin doesn't quite know what to do, and he looks confused.

"Get Mr. Raeburne! Please!" I say to him. I'm gonna start cryin' here soon, I know that.

"Raeburne is no longer here." I hear this from Jaimy.

I spin around, and, though I can hardly bear to do it, I look at him. "Why? What did you do to him?"

"We came to sword's point immediately upon your departure and Captain Trumbull thought it wise to get him off the ship. He was transferred to the *Revenge.*"

"Captain Trumbull made a mistake." I puff up my chest. "Robin Raeburne is worth ten of the likes of you. He is twice the man you are, in *all* ways! Believe me, I know!" says I, thinkin' I'm twistin' the knife.

Jaimy does not change expression. "Mr. Raeburne had the decency to tell me what happened that night with the Captain, so I choose not to believe you on the subject of Mr. Raeburne's manliness." So much for the twistin' knife.

"Damn you, get out!" The tears are comin' fast now. "Get out!"

Jaimy takes some papers from under his arm and puts them through the bars and onto the floor of the cell.

"These, Jacky, are letters that I have written to you since that day at the track when you threw my ring at my feet and ran off. They are letters to you, the lost you...a journal, really. I will leave you to think on these, Jacky, if you choose to read them. If you want to speak to me again, please send word. If not, rest assured I will bother you no more in this life."

"Good. Go away," I blubber. "You proved false and I ain't reading any of your lies!"

He bows and leaves.

I look at the pack of papers. It's going to be a long night.

# Chapter 48

I study the key that hangs on the wall next to where the Marine guard stands. It is about twenty feet away from my cell and it is very simply made—it's about five inches long, with a tab on the end and another tab about an inch and a half in on the shaft. The other end is a circle so that force can be applied when it is put into the square lock on the door of the cage and turned. I have watched the lock being opened when the trays bearing my meals are brought in. The lock mechanism does not seem complicated. Why should it be? After all, where could an escapee go?

I arise this morning to see my breakfast being brought in by the Weasel, dressed in a white steward's uniform. Private Rodgers opens the cell door and the Weasel comes in under his watchful eye and puts the tray down on the bench. Then the chinless little bastard smirks at me, showing his brown teeth.

"Ain't so high and mighty now, are ye, Missy?" hisses the Weasel. "And you ain't gonna be high and mighty at all when they drops you through the trap and snaps that pretty little neck o' yours, are ye?"

I swing my right arm and catch him across the face with

the back of my hand and he cries out and falls away, and I fetch him a kick and he goes pitching forward out of the cell.

"Here! Here!" says my Marine. "We can't have that here!"

The Weasel starts to get up and I take the chamber pot and turn it and clap it over his head, its contents running down his neck and into his jacket. The pot makes a slight *dong* as the inside bottom of it comes to rest on his vile noggin.

"Clean that up and bring a fresh one back, you miserable piece of crap!" I spit. The Weasel staggers away and out the door, wearing his new headgear without a great deal of dignity.

"Please, Lieutenant!" pleads Rodgers, forgetting himself.

"Calm yourself, Jeffrey, and you'd better lock the door. And you know I'm not a lieutenant anymore, so you needn't call me that." I turn to my breakfast. It is burgoo, of course, and I would eat it, except that I am sure the Weasel has spit in it and the thought of that curbs my usually fierce appetite.

Private Rodgers secures the door, probably surprised that I knew his first name. "I'm sorry, Miss, for the misfortune that's befallen you," he says.

"Don't be. I brought it on myself." *I know I tried to grab too much, too fast, and now I've got nothing. Nothing 'cept maybe a noose.* "But you could do me a favor, Jeffrey, if you would. Could you have someone come get this tray? I cannot eat this, for I fear that the Weasel has spat in it."

Rodgers gets red in the face and takes the tray. "If he did, it will be the last thing he ever spits in, the dog!"

He takes the tray out to the passageway and I see light through the hatch. Then I hear him say, "Mr. Jared! Beggin' your pardon, Sir, but a word with you!"

I am sure my meals will be pure as the driven snow from now on. I even manage to find a bit of pity in my heart for the poor Weasel, who's about to have a very hard time of it, I am sure.

When Private Rodgers comes back in, with a fresh pot of burgoo and some biscuits and tea, I thank him and say, "Oh, and would you please tell Lieutenant Fletcher that I will speak with him after I finish my breakfast?"

I, of course, had read his letters.

I have been studying the ways of my two Marines. One or the other of them is always standing over by the door, keeping an eye on me, *except* in two cases. One, when I am changing in and out of my nightshirt, in which case he turns away until I am dressed, and two, when I use the chamber pot. Then he steps out of the hold, out of the room completely, until I call him back in. *That* is my only time truly alone.

I look again at the key hanging there and I am still looking at it when Jaimy comes in.

"Hullo, Jaimy," I say. "Seems like old times, doesn't it? Me in here, and you out there. Bars in between." I'm seated at my bench and he stands facing me. "It is nice of you to come see me, considering the trouble I've caused. My other friends have not..."

"No one besides officers is allowed to visit you. Rest assured all your friends have you uppermost in their thoughts and all desire me to convey their best wishes to..." He smiles slightly. "...to Puss-in-Boots, as it were."

I let silence hang in the air a bit and then sigh and say, "Your cousin, hey?"

"Yes. My first cousin Emily. My uncle Jeremiah's daughter. A very sweet girl, actually. It is too bad you did not stay to be introduced, but I know you had other, more pressing business to attend to."

"I know, I know. I read it in your journal…So sweet…I have been so stupid." I scoot over on the bench so as to be close to the bars. "Please come over here and hold my hand."

He steps around to the side of the cage and reaches through and takes my hand.

"Jacky…"

"Please don't be stern with me, Jaimy. Don't yell at me, even though I've got it coming. I know what I did was mad, stupid even, but it didn't seem crazy or stupid at the time it was happening. Trust me. But all that don't matter now 'cause we have so little time, and I just want to sit here and hold your hand. Do you know how often I so wanted to hold your hand when I was off in America, when I was…when I—"

I am crying now. I bend over and put my hand over my face and start bawling, my back bucking, my shoulders shaking, and the tears coming out from between my fingers. *Oh, Jaimy, I missed you so much!*

"Jacky. Please. All is not lost. I have already sent a letter back to London. The best lawyers will be hired to keep you from…that awful possibility. My family is not without influence. We can hope for the best, with transportation to Australia as a possibility." I snuffle and look up at him as he goes on. *He really is the most beautiful boy.* "The fact that you are obviously guilty of the crimes that you are charged with will not aid us in our endeavors, but we shall try. You did actually have a Letter of Marque for a time and that will help, as will the fact that you didn't kill anyone."

I nod. *Yes, there is always hope. Perhaps in Australia I will see my Kangaroo, after all.*

"We have some time. It will be a few days before we are relieved to take you back to London," he says.

"Then come stay with me during this time, Jaimy, as much as you can. And if I am taken back to be hanged, knowing that you did love me all this time will make it easier for me. It will give me great comfort that I did not die unloved. And that is the truth, Jaimy."

We stand for a while in silence, and then we hear the bell toll for noon.

"I must go up on watch now, Jacky, but I will be back," he says. He reaches for something in his pocket. "Put out your hand, Jacky, please."

I do it, and I see that he has my ring, the one I threw at his feet that day at the track. He must have gone back to get it.

Here come the tears again.

"Do you, Jacky Faber, promise never to doubt me again, no matter what?" he says, intently serious, his dark eyes looking deep into mine. He has the ring poised over my shaking finger.

I can only nod. He slides it on, as tears slide down my face.

"Thank you, Jacky. You have made me very happy, once again, knowing that I'm back in your heart…I…I…" He gropes for words.

I turn to the Marine who has been watching us. "Private Rodgers, if you'll give us a moment please." I give him my most hopeful and beseeching look, one embellished with teardrops hanging from my eyelashes.

He looks doubtful, knowing full well what his orders are, but it's the tears that get him, I know. He says, "Mr. Fletcher, do you swear you won't pass her anything or do anything wrong?"

"Yes," says Jaimy.

"All right. The count of twenty-five." And he turns his back on us.

I put my face up against the bars and close my eyes.

"Come kiss me, Jaimy, if you love me."

He does, oh yes, he does.

# Chapter 49

I am not dead yet, nor am I going to place my fate entirely in the hands of Jaimy's lawyers, nor will I throw myself completely on the mercy of his family's influence. I snort to myself on thinking of the Fletcher family as regards the fate of one Jacky Faber—his father would probably love to see me swing for stealing all that wine from him, and Jaimy's mother? Oh yes, I've no doubt Mother Fletcher, if anything, is helping to build my gallows right now. I can see her with hammer in hand, nails held in her teeth, pounding in the very boards herself.

I continue to study the key and I try to think of ways to duplicate it, since it's plain that I will never be able to get at the key itself. The trouble is, I need metal and metal is what I do not have. My Marines bring me my trays of food but it is the now very careful and respectful Weasel who picks up the dirty dishes afterward, and he always counts the silverware when he does so. I have asked my Marines to let me play my pennywhistle that's in my seabag, and they do it, but they always make sure it goes back in the bag when their watch changes. I don't think I could twist the tin whistle into the proper shape, anyway.

My plan, of course, is to fabricate a key, then ask the Marine to step outside while I use the pot, open the cell door, strip to my drawers, and bolt out the open door of the hold and over the side and swim for the French coast, just like I did that first day on the *Wolverine*. If it's too far away and I die in the attempt, well, so be it. I'd rather breathe my last and sink forgotten to the bottom of the sea, than be taken back to London and put up on the scaffold to be hanged for the joy of the mob.

I know that's where we are, right off the coast of France, and this time I think I'd make it, 'cause I don't think my Werewolves would pursue me very hotly—'cause I think they still love me some.

The only problem is the damned key.

Today, when Jaimy comes back down to see me after his watch, I am able to control my emotions a bit more than I did yesterday and I take in the news he has to tell.

"Your men from the *Emerald* are being transferred to other ships in the Fleet. Captain Trumbull thinks their love for you might cause trouble. He knows that you've been in command of both these crews and it would not take much of a spark to put you back in command of all of them again."

"Ah."

"He has said that you might bid them farewell as they go."

I notice now that Jaimy has a small coil of light line in his hand. "That is very kind of him," I say. "Will he put me on my knees again? If so, I won't do it."

"No. He says only that you cannot wear the uniform you were captured in."

I smile. "He can't bring himself to say my 'lieutenant's uniform,' can he?"

"No, but that is the only condition, other than that your hands must be bound. He has heard the account of you jumping overboard and swimming for shore that time."

I nod and stick out my crossed wrists and wait for the rope that will bind them.

"Sheehan, good sailing to you. You, too, O'Hara, Doyle. Good-bye, John Reilly, good-bye, Farrell, Denny, Sean..."

I stand by the railing of the *Wolverine* as the crew of the *Emerald* files by me and, one by one, goes over the side into the waiting boats below.

"God be with you, Ryan, Kinsella...not so glum there, Brian, cheer up. Good-bye, Kelly, Lynch..." *Make things light now, heads up, don't let them see you cry.*

Then up steps Arthur McBride.

"Now here's one Arthur McBride, off to serve his King. Now ain't that just a sight?" I say, in my bantering way. "Now who do you think got the best of things, you or your friend Ian McConnaughey?"

That gets the old familiar smile flashing again. "Aye, the sod," says Arthur McBride. "Him all snugged up with Mairead and me about to enter the hairy embrace o' some cruel monster of a Bo'sun's Mate on a British Man-o'-War. Life sometimes just ain't fair, is it, Jacky?"

"It is not, but somehow I think you will fare well. Good-bye, Arthur. You always brought me cheer."

He goes and then Padraic stands before me and I lean forward and kiss him on his cheek. "Fair winds, Padraic Delaney, you were the sweetest of all the lads and you were ever so kind to me. I will always think fondly on thee."

He gulps and nods and goes over. Liam is the last one. He stands in front of me looking very big and very glum.

"Didn't we ramble, then, Liam, didn't we ramble?" I say, stepping up close to him.

This brings a bit of a rueful smile to his face. "Aye, that we did, Jacky, that we did."

I figure I can let the tears come now and it doesn't matter what I figure 'cause they're gonna come anyway, and down they do trickle. "Put your arms around me, Father, please."

He takes me in his big embrace and I put my face up next to his and I whisper in his ear, "Liam, tell the others not to despair of me—I have a plan and I'm not dead yet!"

I hear a *harrumph* behind me and I know it is Captain Trumbull, so I stand back from Liam and say, "Fare thee well, Liam Delaney."

"Fare thee well, Daughter," says Liam, and he goes over the side.

Captain Trumbull has indeed taken Higgins as his steward and for that I am very glad. I don't think he would have fared very well as a common sailor.

That night Jaimy and I sat and talked long into the night and held hands through the bars. I had the opportunity to explain exactly why I did what I did when I did it and I think he understands and is easier in his mind concerning my impetuous nature. I mean, he's got to see that I had reasons. And when it was time for him to go, the Corporal gave us another count of twenty-five.

I think on that fondly and then snap my mind back to the present. We leave in two days for England and trial for me, so that doesn't give me much time. *How can I make a key? Come on, girl, your life depends upon it! Think!*

# Chapter 50

I see a way to the key opening up on the afternoon of my third day of captivity. We are due to leave tomorrow for England and doom, and I am beginning to despair, when George Piggott, of all people, comes down into the hold and stands stiffly in front of the cell.

"Georgie! How good to see you," I exclaim, reaching through the bars to take his hands in mine. "I so wanted to thank you for being my bold defender that day I was taken!" I haul him to me and plant a between-the-bars kiss on his forehead.

Georgie blushes and says, "With the Captain's compliments, will you join him and his officers for dinner this evening in his cabin?"

*Come on, think! This might be your chance! Your last chance. Ah! I think I see a way…*

"You may tell the Captain, Midshipman Piggott, that I would be delighted, but I will not come unless I am given the chance to bathe and clothe myself in private and not in plain view as I am here!" I say. "You tell him that, and then come back and tell me what he says."

Georgie nods and goes off on his errand. I make myself

ready. I have a scrap of ribbon and I tie my hair up on top of my head. Then I wait.

Presently, Georgie comes back and says, "Captain Trumbull's compliments and it will be all right for you to—"

"You heard the Captain's order, Private!" I cry, cutting Georgie off before he can say that the Captain had said it would be all right for me to hose myself off in some scupper or somesuch. "Now release me and let me get my things out of my bag and take me to...yes, to one of the officers' berths. There will be a washstand and will be private enough for what I need to do." The Marine stands astounded. "Female things, you know," say I, blushing and fluttering my lashes. He blushes even more deeply and takes the key and opens the cell.

The officers' quarters are in the next hold, and I stride out and lead the way, with Georgie and a sputtering Private Rodgers following.

The doors are open to the berths and I look in one and know it is Jaimy's room for I see up there on the wall, next to the bunk, the miniature that I had painted of myself and had sent to Jaimy by way of Davy. *Aw, how sweet...*

"This will do fine," I say, as I sweep in and close the door behind me. I slosh some water from the pitcher into the basin and run my hand through it to make enough noise for them to hear. Then I start going through Jaimy's chest of drawers. Shirts. Drawers. Letter-writing stuff. Damn! Nothing yet! Handkerchiefs...Stockings...and *Hah!*

There, wrapped in a cloth, is his old mess kit from the *Dolphin!* Jaimy, the nob, had a *fork* when all the rest of us had just knives and spoons. Just the thing.

I take the fork and bend it around on itself and stick it up in my hair. I use the ribbon to bring my hair around it to hide it. There. I look in Jaimy's little shaving mirror and it looks fine. It looks just like an ordinary bun.

That done, I strip down and begin to actually wash myself. I quickly finish and dry off with a handy towel and while I'm doing it, I look over at the bed. *Hmmm...*

There is still a very good chance I'm not going to survive this latest trouble I'm in. I think hard for a moment and then I open the door and stick my head out and say, "Mr. Piggott. Go get Mr. Fletcher. I'm having trouble with the wash basin." Then I close the door.

I pull back the cover on the bed and wait. *He's not getting away this time, by God.*

I do not have to wait long. There's a tap on the door and "Jacky?"

I reach out an arm and pull Lieutenant James Emerson Fletcher in by his collar and close the door and throw the latch. Jaimy looks at me and I throw my arms around him and we both fall toward the bed and then we're in it and *Jaimy, I'm so glad to be back in your arms again, I'm your lass and always was and always will be and yes, Jaimy, please hold me and touch me and...*

...there's that old knock again. *Wham! Wham! Wham!* Just like before.

*Damn!*

"Miss!" comes the call from outside the door. "I know what you're going to do in there and I'm going to be in so much trouble if you do what you're planning to do. I'll be demoted and flogged and..." I think Private Rodgers is out there actually crying and pleading on his knees.

"All right, Jeffrey," I say with a sigh. I look into Jaimy's gray eyes right in front of mine. "Lift me up, Jaimy."

He gets up and gives me his hand and I get up.

"Fill your eyes with me, Jaimy, and then kiss me, and kiss me hard and long, for it may be the last time."

He does, *oh yes, he does.*

"Now go, Jaimy."

And with one last feverish kiss, he does.

After I calm myself, I put on my old faithful blue dress, the one I made back on the *Dolphin,* which I had my Marine pull from my seabag. Then I go back to my cell and wait to be called. When Private Rodgers, relieved to have me safely back in my cell, has his back turned, I slip the fork under the thin mattress on my bench.

I put my ring back in my ear and squeeze it shut.

Both Corporal Martin and Private Rodgers come to collect me to take me to the Captain's cabin for dinner. Along the short way on deck I am able to wave to some of my old friends. I see Drake and Harkness and I hold Jared's gaze longer than I do the others. Then I am in the cabin.

All rise and I am taken and seated to the right of Captain Trumbull, with Jaimy to my left. There's Tom and Ned looking all gallant in their uniforms and looking to have each grown a foot since last I saw them. *My bold Knights Errant* I call them again, and they flush and look down, but I know they are pleased. And Georgie is there, too, all pink and stuffed into his uniform, which is growing too small for him, as well.

Lieutenant Beasley, the other officer Captain Trumbull brought to the *Wolverine* with him, has the watch, so it's all old friends here. Except for the Captain, of course, and he seems to be mellowing a bit, too.

"A glass of wine with you, Miss," he says. Higgins comes over and fills my glass. I give him a smile and a pat on his arm. He nods, in his solemn way, and goes on to pour for the others.

"Thank you, Sir," says I with a friendly, open Look upon my face. Sort of a half-Look, appropriate for such an occasion. "It was very kind of you to invite me, considering my...status as your prisoner."

"Well, there's never an excuse for bad manners, is there?" he replies, knocking back his wine. I take a sip of mine and it is very good. I look up at Higgins and wink. He has plainly been into the stores of Tonda-lay-o, Former Queen of the Ocean Sea. That's fine, for they are certainly doing me no good now, and if it's helped Higgins in his new post, all the better.

"I assume all these fine things you had in stores were plunder from the ships you took?"

"No, Sir, these were all bought properlike. It is now you who have done the plundering." I put a little twist on that.

"Well, I'll have it either way," says Captain Trumbull, "with my compliments and my thanks." He says this with a slight bow in my direction.

*Well should you be thankful, Captain,* I'm thinkin', *a fine feast, fine drink, excellent service, and seated next to you, a neat 250 pounds sterling.* On the hoof, as it were. Would that the old Cheapside gang could know what I am now worth—more than double my weight in silver. I've come a long way, it seems.

I look about this familiar space and let myself drift back. How well I remember when, not so long ago, this cabin was mine and I would sit at this very table with my booted feet upon it, leaning back in my chair and gloating with my officers over our latest prize. Now I sit here a captive and I see that my Jolly Roger has been festooned across a trunk over there, as a trophy, I suppose. As I, too, am now a trophy, a prize. Ah, well.

"I have read the book of your experiences on the *Dolphin*, Miss Faber. Mr. Piggott there lent it to me," the Captain goes on. "Very interesting. It is too bad your adventuring must come to an end." He sounds genuinely a little bit sorry.

"Let us put thoughts of the future aside, Sir," I say. "Let us delight in the present, in good food, good wine, and good friends. All about me here are my friends, and, as you have been so gracious as to invite me to your table, permit me to count you also as my friend, as well as my captor."

I lift my glass to him. *Sparkle, Jacky, sparkle.*

"Well said, Miss," says the Captain and *hear, hear!* is heard all around. "I did not make the Fletcher connection when first I read the book," he says, when all are quiet again. He pointedly looks at Jaimy and me, who both have our hands under the table, those same hands being clasped together in my lap. "But now I do."

We sheepishly bring our hands back onto the tabletop.

Higgins brings in the mighty roast beef to great acclaim and we fall to and all are stuffing themselves to the point of stupefaction when there is a knock on the door and Mr. Beasley comes in and bows to the Captain.

"Your pardon, Sir, but a signal from the Flag. Lord Nelson has brought the combined French and Spanish fleets to bay off the Spanish coast. All British warships are to make speed for Cape Trafalgar to join the fight."

# Chapter 51

The dinner was over right quick after that. The Captain got up and roared out orders to bring the ship about and head her south and I was sent back into my cage, protesting all the way. *Please, Captain, don't put me down there for the fight! I don't wanna drown like a rat in a trap! Let me help!* All to no avail. Back down in the cell I went.

The ship is in high uproar, clearing decks for action, bending on all possible sail to get to Trafalgar as quickly as possible—*Not a moment to lose!* is the cry. Men are sanding cannonballs to make them rounder, the Marines are putting extra rifles and powder horns into the maintop and foretop, where they will stand during the battle, shooting down onto the decks of the enemy. Men are making wills and signing them and making their peace with whatever God they worship.

Me, I'm down in my cage, twisting a fork. My Marines are distracted with the excitement of the coming fight, but they still keep an eye on me and I can't talk any sense into 'em. *Please, Jeffrey, if it comes to a fight, say you'll let me out, say you will!* This gets me *I'm sorry, Miss, but you'll be safer down here.* Right, and if the ship goes down, I go down, too. *Please, please, I'd rather die out in the open air!*

I find out from Jaimy during the few times I get to talk to him that it's gonna take us a good three or four days to get there, sailing in convoy with the rest of our squadron, Trafalgar being down by the Strait of Gibraltar, but we're making good time, about eight knots average, so maybe we'll be there in time for the fight. *Great.*

We're out in the open ocean now, in the Bay of Biscay, so any notion of me jumping overboard and swimming for freedom is out. I decide to shut up, escape notice, and work on making a key.

I work the same scam. I tell the Marine I've got to use the pot and when he goes out, I try my fork. I had studied the key hanging there and twisted down the tine of the fork in imitation of the tab at the end of the key.

"Corporal, if you would. Nature calls," I say, and he goes outside. It ain't hard for him to do that, what with all the excitement out there, I know he doesn't want to come back in.

I put the fork in and try it. Nothing. I rattle it some more. Sideways, this time. No. Somehow I've got to make the other tab.

"Corporal Martin. I'm done."

It's been two days of this and I'm getting scared. I still don't have it and I ain't got a lot of time. Jaimy comes down to see me more now, since we're in a certain routine in our dash for Trafalgar, and I can't do anything when he's visiting, so it's getting tight.

I know I can't ask Jaimy to do anything in the way of the key, 'cause of his word of honor and all, and 'cause he'd probably agree that I'd be safer down here during a battle. I don't agree, and I ain't forgot about that noose that's probably waiting for me in London should I survive this.

I've found a place, a joint between a bar and a cross brace, where I can put a tine of the fork and have a good deal of control over how it bends. I have bent one of the three tines back out of the way so it doesn't get in the way of the others, and I've taken the second one and forced it out sideways to look like the second tab on the key.

"Oh, Private Rodgers..."

I jam it in as soon as he leaves and wiggle it around. Nothing. I lift up the handle of the fork and try again. *Third time's the charm*, I pray and twist it in the lock.

*Clack!*

I suck in my breath. The lock is open! The door swings open an inch. Great! Now to get it closed before Jeffrey comes back.

I twist the fork the other way. *Click!* It locks again.

I put my key fork away and call Jeffrey back in again.

I resolve to practice the drill till I can do it under tension and so under fire, as well.

*Try to hold Jacky Faber, will you?*

# Chapter 52

**October 21, 1805**
**5:50 A.M.**
**Signal from HMS *Achilles* to Lord Nelson**
**on board HMS *Victory*:**
**"Have Discovered a Strange Fleet"**

The signal is passed down to me by Private Rodgers. I know from a very excited Jaimy that we have formed up with the main body of Nelson's fleet. *You should see it, Jacky! There're over thirty-two of our Ships of the Line out there! And that's just the First-Raters, not counting frigates or little brigs like us!* He darts back up to the deck.

So I guess some lookout has spotted the enemy fleet. I guess right.

**6:10 A.M.**
**Signal from Nelson on board**
**HMS *Victory* to Fleet:**
**"Form Order of Sailing in Two Columns"**

Again Rodgers repeats the signal. I make myself be calm. I make no more demands to be let out. I pretend to be a good girl sitting here with my hands folded in my lap, letting the big, bold men take care of me.

## 6:22 A.M.
### Signal from Nelson to Fleet:
### *"Prepare for Battle"*

Then more orders from Lord Nelson: *Bear up and sail large on Course E* and many orders to Admiral Collingwood who, Jaimy tells me, is the commander of the Lee Column of our ships, while Nelson commands the Weather Column, which is what we are in. *Lee* and *Weather* have to do with the direction of the wind, which is off our port quarter and almost dead astern. That would be good, except that the winds are very, very light. It looks like Nelson intends to drive two columns of our ships straight into the flank of the enemy lying off the coast, and, since the winds are so light, we will be punished going in. I shiver a bit. It's going to be bloody.

We wait. More signals back and forth between Nelson and his commanders and his big ships as we draw closer to the enemy fleet. More signals. We wait and get closer.

At 10:45 I'm pleased to see Higgins enter the hold with a tray of food and drink. He snaps open a portable tray holder and places it outside the bars. He also has a small chair hooked over his arm.

"This might be more to your liking, Miss, than what has been served to you in the past week or so," he says.

I smile and say, "Thank you, Higgins. It is so good to see you."

I pick up a hot biscuit, butter it, and bite down. It is wondrous good. The thought that one might die very shortly makes the senses very acute. "You will not get in trouble for this?"

"No, Miss, I will not get in trouble. I have found the Captain to be a fair man, and he is very, very busy today."

There is plenty of food and two glasses and I invite him to have some of it with me, as that would give me great comfort and pleasure.

"No, Miss, I thought maybe your young man might share this with you on this auspicious day. I mentioned it to him on my way down."

*Ah. Good, good Higgins, what a jewel you are.* I make a quick decision and I stand and pull up my skirt and stick my finger in one of the pouches of my money belt and pull out my emerald. I let the skirt fall back down and hand the stone to Higgins.

"Take this," I say. "Of all of us, you're the one most likely to get back to London, alive and free. Sell it and take enough for you to maintain yourself till you find a new post. Then give the rest to the Home, so it can run a while longer. All I have left in the bank shall go there, too. Tell Grandfather and Mairead what has happened, but not to worry about me."

He takes the jewel and slips it in the pocket of his jacket in such a way that Private Rodgers doesn't see. "I will do that, Miss."

"Don't you worry about me, either, Higgins. I have a way of popping back up, so don't count me out yet."

He smiles and says, "I would not be so foolish as to do that, Miss. Ah, here is Mr. Fletcher now. Good-bye, Miss. May I tell you that it has been the joy of my life to serve you?"

I stand up and face him, the tears beginning to flow. "Good-bye, Higgins," I sob and reach through the bars to grasp the lapels of his jacket so as to pull him to me and kiss him on his broad forehead. "You are the finest gentleman and the absolute best of men."

Higgins blinks and nods and places the chair so Jaimy can sit next to the bars, close to me. He bows to me one last time and then turns and leaves. I watch his straight, white-coated back disappear through the hatchway. *Good-bye, Higgins.*

"This was very considerate of your man," says Jaimy.

"Yes. I will miss him very, very much," I say, sniffling and wiping my eyes. "But here, have something to eat. You will need your strength. A glass of wine with you?" I pour it and we lift our glasses and drink to each other.

It is a most pleasant meal. We might almost be sitting on a grassy hillside at Dovecote, having a nice picnic, instead of where we are, here at the edge of a battle.

"Another signal, Lieutenant." Both of our heads turn around and I have to smile and shake my head.

"You shouldn't smile at that, Jacky," says Jaimy, kindly. "After all, you made lieutenant before I did."

## 11:48 A.M.
## Signal from Nelson to the Fleet:
### *"England Expects Every Man Will Do His Duty"*

We both stand up.

In a moment there's another signal from Nelson to the Fleet: *Make all sail possible with safety to the masts.* That means we're going in.

"Good-bye, Jacky. I'll see you again in this life or the next."

"Jaimy, I…" But I can say no more. I look at his face and the tears pour from my eyes as I press against the bars and we come together for maybe the last time and *Oh, Jaimy…* and then he's gone.

At the ringing of the noon bell, a faraway boom is heard. The firing has started. Private Rodgers pokes his head out for a moment. "Lord, Miss, there must be fifty or sixty enemy ships out there, lined up against us," he says when he comes back. Right after that, he is called away to take his battle station as a sharpshooter.

"I'm leaving the key hanging here, just in case…so that you could be let out if the ship is sinking," he says. "It…it has been an honor…guarding you, Miss."

"Thank you, Jeffrey. I have enjoyed your company. May God be with you."

"And you, Miss."

I watch his red-coated back with its two crossed white belts disappear up the gangway. Then I wait.

I cannot break out too soon, or I will be caught and put back in here. No, it has to be in the real heat of battle. There are more distant booms but nothing from our ship yet.

One Bell. It's 12:30. Many more shots. I know from the feel of the ship that we are sailing in very light winds, so we must coast into the enemy's range taking their full broadside fire while we can only fire our bow guns, so it's going to be very hot work and…*there!* I feel the *Wolverine* shake. We have fired!

*Not yet, though. Sit, girl. Don't even open the cage yet—someone might still come down.* We fire again, then again. Then I feel us turn and I feel the port guns fire and from outside I hear the cry *Were-wolves! Were-wolves! Were-wolves!*

Then there's a terrible crash as we take a hit up forward. *Now!*

I leap up and take the fork and jam it in the lock and twist. *Damn! Calm down, easy now. There!* The door swings open and I run for my seabag, but before I get there, I'm knocked off my feet by another blast. I hear screaming now and the crash of our full starboard broadside. We're firing on both sides—the enemy must be all around us.

I reach my bag and pull out my uniform. I whip off my dress and wriggle into my shirt and pants—I had not put on anything under my dress this morning 'cause I figured it would come to this. On boots, on jacket, on sword. I stick my shiv in my jacket. I gotta get this all on right or the plan won't work. Put on hat, close up bag, pick it up, and head up the hatchway and into the battle, my hat crammed down low over my face.

I blink in the sudden bright sunlight and for a moment I stand astounded. There is wreckage everywhere. There are men down, there is blood on the deck, there is constant pandemonium of shouted orders, blasts of cannon, and screams of agony.

I look out over the sea. There are dozens and dozens of ship-to-ship fights going on. There is smoke everywhere—a cloud of it hits me in the face and makes me choke, but it blackens my face, too, which is good, so maybe I won't be recognized. But I don't think anyone cares right now 'cause when the smoke clears, there's a great shout as we see the huge bulk of Nelson's Flagship, the hundred-gun *Victory*, heave up on our right side, all three decks of cannon pointed over us at the *Redoubtable*, a French ship of the same monstrous size, that is bearing down on our port side. We're going to be pinned and crushed between them, with eighty thirty-two-pound cannons pointed over us.

The mighty ships come together against us and the *Wolverine* groans as her timbers are bent and broken. There is a tremendous roar as the two big ships fire their broadsides point-blank into each other, with us poor souls in the middle.

The first salvo takes down all of our masts and spars. There are more terrible cries of pain as men are pinned by the falling rigging. I look up, almost as if in a dream, to see the mainsail come floating almost softly down on me.

It doesn't feel soft when it actually hits me and forces me to the deck, though. *Don't panic!* I tell myself, even though I'm smellin' smoke and the sail presses down hard and I can't get up. I pull out my shiv and poke it through the rough, thick canvas and rip myself a hole big enough to wriggle through. I pull my seabag out after me.

I stand up and look about. I can't hear anything anymore but the crash of the cannons overhead. The *Victory* and the *Redoubtable* continue to pound round after round into each other's sides. There are men falling from their decks to ours, dead men, headless men, armless and legless men, parts and pieces and showers of blood.

I stagger over the wreckage to my old station, my old Division One, to the port guns, some of which are still firing. *Oh, Lord, there's Harkness lying over there facedown in his own blood.* I look over at the *Redoubtable* and I could reach out and touch her sides, she's that close.

Numb, I go over to take Harkness's place.

"Swab! Powder!" I see a blackened Tucker give up his load of powder and head down for another. "Wad! Ball! Wad! Clear behind! Fire!"

*Crrrrash!*

I don't have to aim. I just pull the lanyard and the gun bucks and another ball crashes into the side of the *Redoubtable.* "Swab!" I shout again.

Through the smoke I see another huge ship pulling up on the other side of the *Redoubtable.* I can see the ship's name writ on her side. It is the ninety-eight gun *Temeraire* and now the *Redoubtable* is taking it from both sides.

"Powder! Wad!" *The* Temeraire…*that's the ship that Willy's on,* my dazed mind remembers. *Willy from the Brotherhood. Where's Davy in all this? And Tink? I know Robin's over there on the* Revenge, *but where…* "Ball! Wad! Clear behind! Fire!"

*Crrrash!*

Our charge spits fire and flame and iron into the enemy's side, not two feet away. Splinters fly everywhere and men cry out, but still they reload and fire and reload again.

Through the smoke I see that one of the *Redoubtable's* gunports most near us, which had been closed, now opens and instead of a gun pointed at us, it is a crowd of Frenchmen who are trying to board us. They're crowding right through the port and coming at us with pikes and muskets and cutlasses and the battle is now hand to hand and as nasty as it gets. Their muskets *pop* and a man by my side cries out and falls and I see that it is Shaughnessy and I pull out my sword and I strike at an arm that holds a pike and feel the point of my sword ripping through skin and muscle and hitting bone. I am sickened when I feel that horrible ripping of flesh and hear the scream that follows it, but still I thrust and thrust and thrust again at the men coming through the portal and I'm screaming, too. *Come on, boys! Pikes! Swabs! Axes! Anything to keep them away! Push 'em back! Oh, lads, we've got to push 'em back!* and my men are at my side hacking and flailing away at the would-be boarders until they retreat into the darkness of their hold to lick their wounds and we pause to lick ours.

I kneel down and lift Shaughnessy's head, but I see that he is gone and so I gently lay him back down and stand up and go back to the guns and *Swab! Powder! Wad! Ball! Wad! Clear behind! Fire!* Don't think about nothing, just do it, over and over and over again. Don't think about nothing...

*Crrrash!*

The pounding of the great guns from the *Victory* goes on and on and on and my ears are now numb with the sound so I can't hardly hear anything anymore. The *Redoubtable* reels from the pounding it's taking. It can't take much more of this, it just can't, getting it from both sides, I'm thinking, and I am right. With a great wrenching, snapping crackle, her main comes down and then her mizzen and the mortally wounded *Redoubtable* lurches away from us and begins to sink.

It will not take long. She will go under and hundreds and hundreds of French officers, men, and, yes, boys, too, will go down with her and I helped put them there and *may God have mercy on my soul…*

The *Victory,* herself wounded, pulls away from our starboard side. The *Wolverine* is shattered and, for sure, her battle, our battle, is over.

I have lost all sense of time. I don't know whether it's been minutes or hours since this all began. I stand exhausted, weak in the knees as men swarm around me, swinging axes to cut away the fallen rigging. *No, no, girl… you must move.* I shake myself out of my daze and I sheath my sword and I dash up to look at the quarterdeck. *Thank God!* Jaimy's there and still standing on both his legs.

I take up my seabag again and hurry across the deck to one of the two lifeboats, the one right now not buried under the wreckage. I spy a man nearby and order, in my deepest voice, "You there! Lower that boat! I have an urgent message for the Flag!" I am covered with powder dust, but it doesn't matter, for the man turns and it is Jared and he knows me right off. *Am I now undone, after all this?*

No, I am not. He goes over to the boat davit and says, "Aye, Lieutenant." He keeps up the pretense and the boat goes down into the water and the sail is raised. I throw my seabag over the rail into the boat and then ready myself to jump in alongside it. I go to Jared and put my hand on his arm and look into his eyes. "Good-bye and thank you, Joseph Jared. Thank you for saving my life one more time."

He puts his fingers to his brow and salutes, smiling his cocky grin in spite of everything lying in ruins about us. "Good-bye, Lieutenant. I'll collect my thanks from you when next we meet."

I jump down, put the tiller over, and pull away from the *Wolverine* to freedom.

As I thread my way out, I look at all the devastation around me and I am sickened. So much death, so much waste.

I twist around to take a last look at the *Wolverine*, hoping maybe to see Jaimy again and...

*Uh-oh.*

The *Wolverine* is sinking. She's already lost two feet of freeboard and she's going down by the stern. They are abandoning ship. They are passing the wounded down into their one remaining lifeboat. There will not be enough room for all of them because I have taken the other lifeboat. I, the one to whom they have been most loyal and true. I have taken their lifeboat, that I might save my own life.

Captain Trumbull comes to the rail and looks out at me. He might try to pry up boards from his deck to make a raft to carry his wounded, but I know he will not have enough time.

*Damn!*

I put the tiller to the boom and, turning the boat around, I head back to the *Wolverine* and, probably, to my doom.

I pull up alongside and men climb down into the boat. There's Tucker and Eli, and Drake, too. Then Tom comes down, his face ashen. "Tom," I say, "is Ned..." A quick shake of his head is all he says in reply. It is enough. *Oh, God, Ned...*

More men come down into the boat, then I hear "Wounded coming down," and I look up and I see George Piggott all limp, cradled in Higgins's arms, Higgins's once-white steward's coat spattered with blood...Georgie's blood. Higgins gently hands him down. *Aw, Georgie, no...*Blood from a wound on his left side splatters onto my upturned face as he's lowered into my lap.

His eyes flutter open as he looks up at me. "I stood up, Jacky. I did. I... I stood up." His eyes close again.

"I know you did, Georgie," I blubber, my tears falling on his bloody face. "I know you did." I hold him and rock him and keen, "I know you did," over and over and over.

All the survivors are on the boats now and next to us the *Wolverine* sighs, turns over, and slips quietly under the sea. The boats make for a ship that is taking on wounded from other ships. There is a floating platform tied alongside and a gangway leading from it to the deck, so that the wounded can be brought more easily aboard.

The other boat gets there first and takes off its wounded. Jaimy's on that boat and I see him going up. The rest of that boat's men go aboard and now it's our turn. Captain Trumbull is in my boat.

I hand Georgie up to men who take him and go up the ladder. I give Tom's shoulder a squeeze as he goes over. The other men file out, and then it's just me in the boat with the Captain. He gets out and stands on the platform and looks back at me sitting there in my grief and sorrow.

"Please don't put me back in a cage, Sir," I say wearily. "Please let me help take care of my friends. I promise not to escape again. You can take me back to London."

He reaches down and unties the bowline of the lifeboat from the cleat. He puts his foot on the front of the boat. "We take care of our own, Miss," he says, and he shoves off the lifeboat, sending it, me, and 250 pounds sterling drifting backward.

"The prisoner escaped during the heat of battle. Good-bye...Lieutenant Faber," and with that, he turns and he goes up the ladder.

In wonder and with thanks, I again take the tiller and pull in the mainsheet. The sail fills and I'm off.

*Where shall I go?* I wonder. I can't go over there to Spain. I can't go back to England as there's a price on my head. Then I know.

I set my course westward and am under way when I look back and see Jaimy standing at the rail of that ship looking out at me. It's too far to say or shout anything, so I stand up in the stern of the boat and put my arms out to my sides and make the semaphore signals.

Jaimy reads them and nods and puts his own arms to his sides and starts to signal and he manages to signal the letter *I* before a burning hulk of a ship comes between us and I see Jaimy no more.

I sit back down and steer for the west. Oh yes, and the letters I signaled to him were:

**B O S T O N**